DEPTH OF DECEIT

OTHER BOOKS BY BETTY BRIGGS

Quality Concealed

Image of Deception

Challenge of Choice

A Tuff-to-Beat Christmas

DEPTH OF DECEIT

a novel by

BETTY BRIGGS

Sunrise Selections

Cover Image: *Cure for the Troubled Mind*; Against a Montana Sunset, Kelli Brown and Major, Ancient Pine Looks on

Cover design and photography by Scott and Betty Briggs

Published by Sunrise Selections, Provo, Utah

Additional copies are available from Sunrise Selections, P.O. Box 51602, Provo, Utah 84605-1602, or at Amazon.com.

ISBN 10: 0-9656307-5-7
ISBN 13: 978-0-9656307-5-7

To my grandchildren—McKenzie (and husband, Shawn), Heather, Ethan,
MaKenna and Kyson.
Writing this book made me realize even more
the importance of love and family.

ACKNOWLEDGMENTS

As always, I am grateful to my husband for his love and support and for his willingness to share his phenomenal computer and photographic talents. I am thankful for my two children, their spouses, my five grandchildren and so far one spouse, who are sources of continual joy and pride.

I appreciate the friendships of two wonderful groups of people—my kindred spirits from the stable and my legal buddies from work. They have brought a special richness to my life and, I think, my stories.

And then there are my writing pals, especially those in my critique group of fourteen years—Linda Orvis, Rebecca Crandell, Judy Anderson, Lisa Peck, John Thornton, Linda Huntzinger, Norma Mitchell, Karen Pool, Estel & Rena Murdock, and Phyllis Gunderson. Thank you for your patience, knowledge, creativity and camaraderie in helping me bring *Depth of Deceit* to life.

CHAPTER 1

She perceived her error in judgment too late. Stephanie Saunders screamed as the sorrel gelding she rode stumbled across the solid log jump and fell. Kingston sprawled onto the snow-dusted ground, throwing her off. The parka, breeches, leather boots and gloves failed to keep Stephanie from shaking, though not only from the cold. She struggled to her feet and dragged her aching body toward the gelding. He lay still.

Stupid, stupid, stupid! How could she have endangered Kingston by jumping on ground less than safe? She didn't even own him, but loved him as if she did. And she called herself a horsewoman. "Kingston," she cried and reached out to touch his neck.

He raised his head, braced his front feet and pulled himself to a standing position. She was beside him in a moment, rubbing her hands over his legs, checking for injuries. Grasping his reins, she led him forward a step, then another, scrutinizing every move. He seemed fine, and her knees nearly buckled with relief. "Oh, thank you," she whispered, staring heavenward.

A sharp pain stabbed her hip and she almost fell. She grabbed onto Kingston's mane to steady herself. She shook her head. Just her luck. Charles, her boss, would be furious if she failed to make it to court today to defend clients who were probably guilty. Charles, who hated indigent defense work, made sure it was her specialty. She frowned. Charles and her other boss, Paul, never assigned her any good cases. She'd struggled through law school for this? It was a whole lot more glamorous on TV.

Her hip ached more by the minute. Somehow she needed to get back in the saddle if she were to make it to the barn. Her teeth chattered. Even though it was about forty degrees this March morning and warmer than usual, she shouldn't have ridden. She led Kingston to the log jump they'd fallen over.

"It's okay, boy," she told the horse. She knew she should take him over something small, or ride him in the arena so the fall wouldn't be what they'd remember later, but she just couldn't do it—another demerit on her horsewoman report card.

In addition to her injured hip, she felt sick to her stomach. She had for several weeks. Probably the flu. It had been going around lately.

She attempted to climb up on the jump, but stumbled back, crying out in pain. She tried again, this time using Kingston's stirrup to pull herself along. Luckily, the gelding seemed to sense her distress and stood still. She swung her sore hip up and over, easing into the saddle. At twenty-five, she'd have thought she'd outgrown horses, but they were still as much a part of her life as breathing. As long as she had them, she could put up with a job she wasn't crazy about and a boyfriend who sometimes confused her.

On their way to the barn Stephanie held Kingston at a slow walk, riding lop-sided to keep weight off her sore hip. Tears stung her eyes. Some horsewoman she was. She'd thought she possessed a special talent. Her understanding and skill with horses had seemed unrivaled, as a room full of ribbons and trophies attested. But after this morning, it all seemed a lie; she'd been fooling herself and everyone else. She had better shape up and concentrate on being a good attorney. She had no business calling herself a trainer.

At her condo later that morning, she hurriedly showered and dressed for work, but couldn't shake the sadness that hung over her like a threatening gale. As if to add to her turmoil, her hip hurt like blazes and she couldn't settle her stomach. Court today was going to be a very long ordeal.

Surprisingly on time, Stephanie leaned back in her chair and surveyed the day's new crop of lawbreakers. Hollow-eyed, malnourished, pierced and tattooed, they looked as if drugs, alcohol, or whatever other abuses to which they submitted their bodies, had completely polluted their systems. Dressed in bright orange jumpsuits, wrists shackled in handcuffs since they'd probably failed to appear for previous court dates, any of the five men and three women could have answered a casting call for "criminal" in a Hollywood movie; not exactly entertainment law's "pretty people" Stephanie had once dreamed of representing.

A scholar of Perry Mason TV reruns, Stephanie, too, had vowed to protect the innocent. The only problem, Perry's clients were always innocent. Hers were, well like Carlos Ortega, whose wife, the poor woman, now stood at the lectern.

"But you see, Your Honor, I don't need a restraining order against my husband," Mrs. Ortega said. Behind her on the right sat the prosecuting attorney, counsel for the State of Utah. To her left sat Stephanie, in her role today as indigent defense attorney, representing those who couldn't afford a lawyer.

The first thing Stephanie noticed about the young Hispanic woman was her long dark ponytail, so thick and frizzy it covered her entire back, cascading to her waist. It wasn't until the woman turned her head that Stephanie saw the split lip, bulging black eye, and stitched forehead. No doubt the young woman would tell the judge she'd fallen down the stairs, that or some other dubious explanation. This happened all the time—women protecting husbands who beat them, men Stephanie would be called upon to defend.

"I was depressed . . . um . . . and locked myself in the bathroom, and my husband . . . ." The injured woman glanced over her shoulder at the greasy-haired, bearded man who sat in custody on one of the jury chairs. "He was worried about me." She stole another look at him, "um . . . and when he broke the door down . . ." she paused, "it hit my face."

"Do you think I'm stupid?" Judge Anderson appeared very stern in his black robe. From his elevated desk, separated from the rest of the courtroom by an oak barrier, he peered down at the woman.

Zoning out on the rest of their conversation, Stephanie asked herself, for the millionth time, why she had accepted this job at Connelly and Foster. Charles Connelly and Paul Foster were the ones who had bid for the indigent defense contract, not her. Yet here she sat in court every day doing what they had pledged to do. Fresh out of law school with her whole career in front of her, she asked herself once again, why? Why indeed? Money. Pure and simple. She needed the money. She had school loans to pay off, not to mention she needed a place to stay and something to eat once in a while.

Connelly and Foster was not the first law firm to whom she'd presented her resumé. Small though it was, Connelly and Foster was the sole firm to offer her a job. If only her grades in law school had been better. She sighed. They would have been if . . . if. If was such a big word. If only her parents had not taken that fatal plane ride. If only the pilot had been more seasoned. If only it hadn't stormed that night. And then there was that matter of no life insurance and her father's debts.

She guessed she should count herself lucky. Yes, lucky. Lucky she'd been able to finish law school at all—lucky Connelly and Foster had offered her a job, any job. She'd hoped to live in California after law school graduation and represent some famous writer or sports figure, even a movie star. She sighed. Her shoulders slumped. She'd learn what she could at Connelly and Foster and then move on. That plan had kept her this side of desperate, at least on some days.

"How do you plead, Mr. Ortega, guilty or not guilty?" Judge Anderson asked.

"Mr.?" Carlos Ortega was about as far from being a "Mr." as Stephanie was from being an Olympic show-jumping rider. She grimaced and shifted in her seat to a more comfortable position, pulling the navy blue skirt of her fitted pin-striped suit to rest at the top of her knees. The pain in her hip from this morning's fall made her a little dizzy. The over-the-counter medicine she'd taken earlier proved unsuccessful.

"Not guilty, Your Honor." Ortega stood on one leg, then the other.

"Do you have an attorney?" Judge Anderson asked.

Ortega looked as if he needed a good bath. Stephanie caught his rancid scent and her stomach lurched.

"No, Your Honor," the man replied. "Can't afford one."

"Okay. Trial is set for . . ." The judge glanced at his clerk seated behind her desk just in front of him.

"April 22nd at 9:00 a.m.," said the middle-aged woman in the lavender skirt and sweater with earrings and lipstick to match.

"April 22nd at 9:00 a.m.," Judge Anderson repeated. "You'll be provided with indigent defense counsel." He glanced up from the papers on his desk. "Miss Saunders?"

"H . . . her?" Mr. Ortega stammered, brow wrinkled.

Judge Anderson frowned. "Yes, her."

"Can't I have a real attorney?" He glanced at Stephanie, then back at the judge.

"What do you mean real attorney?" The judge narrowed his eyes. "Miss Saunders is a member of the Bar."

"I don't care if she drinks, but—" Mr. Ortega stopped talking when one of the female defendants giggled.

The judge peeked down his nose at her and she immediately sobered. Then he leveled his gaze at Mr. Ortega. "Do you have a legitimate reason for not wanting Miss Saunders?"

"Well she looks like a—"

Stephanie found herself leaning forward in her chair.

"What is it, Mr. Ortega?" Judge Anderson grumbled, clearly out of patience.

"Well, she looks like a—well, I don't know. A skinny Brittany Spears or somethin'. Can't I have a smart attorney?"

Stephanie's mouth fell open. Smart! She was smart. Well, probably smarter than Mr. Ortega. Why was it that people, mostly men, actually, failed to take her seriously? Sure, she was young and inexperienced, but couldn't they just give her a chance? She thought about Charles and Paul and the clients they represented.

Once they'd asked her to answer phones in the front office because their secretary was ill, and the client who'd called said something about raising the $50,000 they'd needed. Stephanie wanted a client capable of raising that kind of money. It was as if the other attorneys felt that a woman who was halfway decent to look at, and okay, blonde, had no brain. They had even started referring to her as "prom queen." Stephanie wanted to strangle her boyfriend, Todd, for calling her that in front of them once and setting off the whole thing. And having actually been a "prom queen" twice in high school hadn't soothed her a bit. One of these first free days, Stephanie swore, she would dye her hair black.

Now it was "Brittany Spears," a "skinny" Brittany Spears. At least he'd said "skinny." She was thin, but she'd put on a couple of pounds lately that caused her concern.

Ortega's comment about a "smart attorney" had drawn chuckles from all the defendants and a male observer with a ponytail and a turquoise necklace laughed loudly from the back row of the courtroom.

The judge pounded his gavel. "Order! I want order."

Besides the judge and his support people, two uniformed police officers, the prosecutor, Mrs. Ortega, the defendants, Stephanie, and the laughing ponytailed man from the back, the courtroom held only two other people—an observant young man, probably a college student, whose fingers flew across the keyboard of his laptop, and a more casually dressed older man who had been dozing, but now straightened in his seat.

Everyone quieted. The judge surveyed the room, then with measured words stated, "You may obtain counsel at your own expense, Mr. Ortega, represent yourself, or Miss Saunders will be your attorney. Those are your choices."

Mr. Ortega stared at the steel blue tweed carpet which lent a slight reflection of color to the stark light gray walls. A clock, the sole adornment except for a large white dry erase board, ticked away the minutes. "Well, I guess she's better than nothing," he said finally.

Better than nothing? From somewhere deep down Stephanie found the strength to maintain a calm exterior.

Judge Anderson sighed. "We all have our opinions."

What? Sometimes Stephanie felt as if she were merely a cardboard figure used to meet the requirement of providing legal counsel. But no, darn it. That wasn't right. She was a defense attorney, an integral part of the legal system. Defense attorneys were important. She was important.

As guilty as these defendants may have appeared right now, the law stated they were innocent until proven guilty. Her job was to ensure that the prosecutor met the burden of proof, beyond any reasonable doubt, of each and every element of the defendant's crime. If not, there would be no conviction. She would see to that. She believed, as her law professors had said, that it was better to have ten guilty people go free than one innocent person lose his or her liberty.

Stephanie had come to court to represent as many "innocent" people as the judge determined were not only too poor to hire their own attorney, but whose crimes would more than likely send them to jail, which would qualify them to receive indigent defense. The city did have other indigent defense attorneys to whom the judge could assign defendants, but Stephanie's firm held the main contract.

She could do this, she told herself as the parade of deviants continued. Interestingly enough, regardless of the coarse and uncouth language they spoke on the outside, in the courtroom the defendants always addressed the judge with respect, knowing he had complete control over their lives.

Barely coherent enough to form a sentence, a tall blonde, with hair sprayed blue on top, managed to plead "not guilty" to drug abuse. A mother accused of beating her child voiced concern for her son's welfare should the judge sentence her to do time. One underweight, leathery man pleaded guilty to public intoxication, promising to pay a little each month toward the fine.

Forming what really was a "jury box," an oak partition paneled off the jury seats from the rest of the courtroom. There the occupants could be segregated from anyone who might hand them a gun, a note, or approach them inappropriately. Stephanie thought it odd that the defendants now sat in the hallowed chairs of the jurors who might later decide one or more of these defendants' fates. During a trial, when the jurors entered or left the courtroom, all were required to stand. There would be no such respect shown today for the occupants of the seats.

The final defendant somehow seemed different from the rest. If only he'd shave off that mountain man beard, cut his thick, curly hair and lose the gold loop earring, Stephanie suspected he might look fairly respectable. Of course he did have one of those barbed wire tattoos around his bicep. Stephanie felt her eyes grow wider. His bicep was really big.

"Number eight, Joshua Durrant—assault, domestic violence, class A misdemeanor." The judge flipped through the papers on his desk, or "bench" as it was referred to in lawyer land. "How do you plead, guilty or not guilty?" Judge Anderson asked.

Stephanie found herself staring at the defendant, waiting for his answer. His handcuffs clicked as he rubbed his wrist. What a waste. Probably another wife beater—a bully.

How Stephanie hated bullies, so like those who had pushed her around. From the next-door neighbor boy who took her lunch money when she was a kid to a boyfriend in high school who treated her like a prize poodle to be trotted around on a leash.

Again she wondered about her job choice, where she was called upon to defend bullies. Maybe if things didn't work out for her at Connelly and Foster, she could get her old job back at the stable. She hadn't mucked out stalls for months. Before this morning she'd thought she was a better horsewoman than she was attorney. She rubbed her hip. Not likely. These days she wondered if she were good at anything.

Okay. This had to stop. She was a defense attorney and she'd defend these criminals to the best of her ability. It was their constitutional right. She believed in the Constitution. She'd show everybody that she could hold her own with the big boys in spite of, as Todd called them, her long Barbie legs. She drummed her peach-colored nails on the oak table.

"Not guilty, Your Honor." Durrant held himself much straighter than the other defendants had.

"Can you afford an attorney, Mr. Durrant?"

There it was, the "Mr." again. Actually, the judge always addressed the defendants Mr., Mrs., Ms. or Miss.

"No, Your Honor." Durrant's jaw flinched like he was unaccustomed to taking charity.

"Miss Saunders?"

"What?" popped out of her mouth. Josh Durrant had drawn too much of her attention. "Uh, I'm sorry. Yes, Your Honor." Stephanie turned her gaze to the judge and somehow kept it steady. His white hair added to his aura of authority.

"I'm assigning Mr. Durrant to you." Judge Anderson perched loftily in his big black leather chair, the dark blue Utah State flag stood sedately behind him on one side, the U.S. flag on the other.

Of course he was assigning Josh Durrant to her. She could hardly wait to hear this defendant's story, emphasis on the "story."

Behave, she told herself. Remember, "defense attorney," emphasis on "defense."

All of a sudden she felt like she'd eaten rotten meat or something. She put a hand to her queasy stomach and choked down a gag. Then, if only to take her mind off her predicament, she glanced at Josh Durrant again. Could he be that truly innocent person that a defense attorney always looks for? He did have beautiful, liquid green eyes staring out from all that hair.

She cocked her head. Wait one cotton-pickin' minute! Had he just winked at her?

CHAPTER 2

Stephanie lifted the receiver and spoke the words that came automatically to her whenever a ringing phone interrupted what she was doing: "Good afternoon, law office." Several times last week she'd found herself answering her home phone with that same phrase. It was Deidre's fault, of course. The girl, who they laughingly referred to as their secretary, routinely came down with diseases unknown to the public at large.

"This is Matthew Dawson," a voice barked so harshly that Stephanie yanked the receiver from her ear. "Put me through to Connelly. I hear he's back."

Even though her face went hot, Stephanie managed to keep her voice calm. "I'm sorry, sir, but Mr. Connelly is in depositions and cannot be disturbed." Matthew Dawson was one of the firm's most influential clients. In fact, he was the man who had been discussing the fifty thousand dollars with her boss.

"He hasn't checked in with me for weeks. Are the depositions there in the office?" The tone of the man's voice did not lighten. He expected a lot if he thought Charles was going to keep him informed of his comings and goings. Half the time, Stephanie didn't even know where Charles was.

"They are, but as I said before, Mr. Connelly cannot come to the phone." She felt perspiration bead on her forehead. "Could someone else help you?" Actually there was no one else, Paul, Charles's partner, was out of the state on business.

"Young woman, are you deaf? I need to speak to Connelly." He said the words slowly, distinctly, as if talking to a child.

After her morning in court, Stephanie's patience was meager at best. "No. I'm not deaf, at least I wasn't before you screamed in my ear." The heat in her face had gone from hot to boiling. Her voice rose until she nearly shouted the last four words. At that moment she didn't care who he was. "You need to calm down," she said, not believing those words had sprung from her mouth.

"Don't tell me what I need to do. You need to put me through to Connelly. Oh, forget it, I'm coming down there. And he'll speak to me if he knows what's good for him."

"But, Mr. Dawson—" She glanced at the caller ID and jotted down the number before it disappeared. Her heart beat so fast it made her light-headed.

The phone rang again. She grabbed the receiver. "Mr. Dawson?"

"Hi, Babe. No, it's only me. Answering phones again?"

It took her a second to recognize Todd, her too-handsome-for-his-own-good boyfriend of four months.

"Yes, I am, and remember I told you not to call me Babe." No one respected her these days. She rested her water bottle against her cheek.

He chuckled. "If memory serves me, you told me not to call you Prom Queen." His voice was warm and tempting, like melted chocolate, as were his eyes, she reflected—dark brown and also tempting.

"Well . . . don't call me Babe either. Babe is a big blue ox."

He laughed.

Returning the water bottle to the desk, she pulled the name Matthew Dawson up on the computer under clients' addresses.

"You may call me Counselor, Miss Saunders, or . . . how about Stephanie, Your Majesty."

"How about Stephanie, My Love?"

"Just Stephanie."

"Okay, Just Stephanie. So where's Deirdre today?"

Since Todd nearly always won their verbal sparring, Stephanie mentally declared a truce. "She's sick again, or should I say, as usual?" She studied the computer screen, matched the number Mr. Dawson had called from with his home address and decided he'd be arriving in about twenty minutes. Her heart pounded as she pondered the man's arrival. "What's worse," she continued to Todd, "I think I'm getting Deirdre's flu."

"You're sick? Really?" His voice sounded overly concerned, but then he continued in a more normal tone, "They say it's a nasty flu this year. I wish you'd take better care of yourself."

"I'm sure I'll be okay." She pressed her fingers to her forehead, hoping to clear the dizziness.

"And you did take a nasty fall."

"My hip does hurt, but my stomach bothers me most." And now she was dizzy. She'd better not mention that to him. "I'm so glad Kingston wasn't hurt."

"You've got to be more careful." His voice was serious again. Of course he didn't mention the welfare of the horse.

"Yes, Daaaddy." She hated it when he was right, but with her job and the horses she trained, she had a lot of responsibilities and sometimes she did put her health at risk. She hoped she really did have the flu, that her symptoms weren't caused by the fall. She'd try to limit her out-of-the-office, barn time to giving lessons and schooling the more seasoned horses.

"I'm serious, Stephanie. I'm concerned about your riding."

"Oh, come on. I was riding when you met me." Her temper control gauge, which Matthew had severely taxed, moved slightly, then hovered around "just slightly ticked" when she remembered that day four months ago. Todd had been standing outside the arena watching her work Territory Kid, one of the stable's thoroughbreds. There he'd remained during the entire workout, gratifying her glances with his chiseled good looks on each canter-by. Later he'd told her that he'd been interested in buying the gelding as an investment. But since he had still not made the purchase, Stephanie figured he'd probably decided what she already knew—that few horses make their owners money. "Did you call for a reason, or are you simply trying to harass me?

"Me harass you? Why, Prom . . . uh, Babe . . . uh, Just Stephanie . . . ."

"You're impossible." She glanced at her watch.

"Me impossible? Me? You can't be serious. I merely called about tonight."

She studied the calendar Deirdre kept on her desk—March 14th. No clue there. "Did we make plans?"

"No," he said, and Stephanie knew he'd be grinning. "But do you want to make some?"

Stephanie looked at her watch again. Matthew Dawson would be arriving soon. "Todd, may I call you back in a few minutes? I've got sort of an emergency here." Her heart seemed to be pounding in her throat.

"Anything I can do?"

"I wish." Stephanie gazed through the see-through doors in the oak and glass panel that separated the secretarial desk from the conference room. Once both of these areas had formed the front parlor of the old house her bosses had converted into office space.

"Are you sure you'll be okay?"

"Probably." Although Stephanie could hear nothing from inside the conference room, she saw that her bearded boss, Charles Connelly, was talking to the clean-cut opposing attorney, who sat across from him at the large oak table. Once Stephanie had thought the beard made Charles look distinguished, but now she'd decided it made him look shifty. The court reporter, a stout woman in a serious dark suit, tapped out everyone's dialogue on her portable machine.

"Probably you'll be okay?" Todd asked.

"Yeah." Telephone still in hand, Stephanie stood, grimacing at the pain in her hip. She knew now she had no choice. She had to interrupt Charles to tell him about Matthew Dawson.

"I'll see you tonight then?" Todd asked.

"Okay," she said, without thinking. "Oh, what? Tonight? Probably."

"Stephanie—"

"Todd, sorry, but I've got to go." She hung up the receiver and, limping the first few steps, moved to the conference room door.

Crinkles showed around narrowed blue eyes as Charles watched her enter the room. Leaning down she whispered, "I'm sorry to interrupt, but Matthew Dawson is on his way to see you, even though I told him you couldn't be disturbed. He's upset about something."

Charles blinked and cleared his throat. "Gentlemen, and lady," he nodded toward the court reporter. "Will you give me a moment? Something extremely urgent has come to my attention. I won't be long. Stephanie will get drinks for you while you wait."

Stephanie will get drinks? She was a waitress now? She sighed and inwardly seethed. Smile, Stephanie, she told herself. "We have all kinds of sodas, bottled water and juices. What would you like?" she asked each of the five people. Wow. One mention of

Matthew Dawson and Charles bolted out the door like a scalded dog. She followed him back to Deirdre's desk.

Charles grabbed her arm. "When will he be here?"

"I think any minute. Is everything all right?" She'd never seen Charles act like this.

"Of course," he said too quickly. "Just fetch the drinks, okay?"

Fetch, what an appropriate word. Now she was a golden retriever. Her head spun—a queasy golden retriever.

Stephanie had her face in the refrigerator when she heard the front door open with such force that it slammed against the inside wall.

"Why Matthew, what a nice surprise. What brings you here today?" Charles put his arm around the shoulder of an impeccably dressed, very handsome man. Charles guided Mr. Dawson up the stairs to the attorney's newly remodeled office, once the old home's master bedroom and adjoining suite.

Carrying a drink-filled tray, Stephanie leaned back against the wall next to the stairs and strained her ears to hear.

"You know why I'm here," Mr. Dawson hissed before the door to Charles's office closed.

How Stephanie wished she could have made herself invisible and sat in on that meeting, but by the time she had performed her role as waitress, Charles and Mr. Dawson came down the stairs, chatting amiably like old buddies. Charles was good. No doubt about it. What had he done to appease Mr. Dawson so quickly? Stephanie wished she had his talent with people.

Until Mr. Dawson left, though, she decided she'd retreat to her own office, the once formal dining room, which adjoined the conference room on its far end. Yet, since her office and the conference room formed a large rectangle with a wall in between and the only door out of her office led through the conference room, she'd have to disturb the deposition again if she didn't want to be trapped in there. Her office did sport a window to the outside, but she knew Charles would frown on her climbing out of it, especially wearing a skirt. Besides, her hip hurt. She decided, however, to avoid Mr. Dawson at any cost and slipped into her room.

She collapsed into her chair feeling giddy with relief. She wondered how long she'd be able to stay before she was missed. Her phone buzzed immediately. Shaking her head, she snatched it up.

"Stephanie, please come out here. I want you to meet Mr. Dawson," a now calm Charles said.

"We've met—on the telephone." Her back straightened in her cloth-covered chair. She didn't want to meet Mr. Dawson—the reason she was now hiding. Of course, Charles didn't know that.

"Stephanie," he repeated over the phone.

"I'll be right there." She slammed down the receiver, took a couple of deep breaths and silently invented new cuss words on her way through the conference room. She nodded to clients, the opposing attorney, the reporter and others, reminding herself that she was a professional and had better act like one, even though no one treated her as such.

The owner of the gruff telephone voice beamed at her as she entered the room. She checked to see if maybe her blouse was unbuttoned. It wasn't, but he kept staring anyway.

Probably around fifty, Matthew was far more handsome than his voice had indicated. He was tall and athletic, with thick wavy hair tipped with grey. Stephanie wondered if his hairstyle was natural or if he regularly visited the corner beauty shop. Maybe his "crowning glory" wasn't even real.

"This is our new associate, Stephanie Saunders," Charles said, pale blue eyes twinkling.

New associate? Stephanie hadn't expected this. For a moment she forgot her aching hip.

Mr. Dawson stretched out a manicured hand. The man was definitely a beauty shop regular, right along with his wife, Stephanie supposed. She'd heard from Deirdre during one of the girl's gossip tirades that Matthew's much-younger wife was really beautiful and extremely rich, the heir to some diamond fortune or such, and that the wife—what was her name, oh yeah, Jessica—was "a real nut job." According to Deirdre, Jessica kept Matthew on a "pretty short leash" and he granted her every wish, or else. Right now, Stephanie would have paid good money to see Jessica work her magic on Matthew.

"I'm so pleased to meet you. Charles tells me you're a real asset to the firm," Mr. Dawson said, smiling like a used car salesman. His teeth were probably capped, too.

"Really?" Maybe her hard work was finally paying off. She vowed to try even harder. Perhaps Charles would let her help him with Mr. Dawson's cases.

"Oh, yes. Charles said you've really helped him out of a bind." The men exchanged glances. For a second Charles's eyes dulled, but then he smiled.

"She's a pureblood. That's for sure." Charles had even picked up on some of her horse language. Maybe she was more important to the firm than she'd ever imagined.

"Well, it's nice to meet you too, Mr. Dawson." Stephanie felt the back of her neck prickle. "I'm sorry about my behavior on the phone earlier."

"Call me Matthew. I wasn't my normal pleasant self either. Well, good-bye. Stephanie. May I call you Stephanie?"

"Of course," she said weakly, as a new wave of nausea struck. She swayed and both men reached to steady her. "Whew. Too much excitement, I guess. I'd better sit down." She slumped into her chair—uh, Deirdre's chair.

"Are you still hurting from that fall from the horse?" Charles asked.

"Fall from a horse!" Mr. Dawson glared at Charles as if he could have prevented the accident.

Enough about the fall, thought Stephanie. "How did you know about that?"

"I have my sources," Charles said, his face smug.

Stephanie cocked her head.

"Deirdre keeps me informed."

Stephanie just bet Deirdre kept everyone informed about everything. "Maybe I'm just getting her flu." Stephanie lifted her chin, daring either man to contradict her.

"I hope not. Maybe you'd better see a doctor. I can recommend one." Matthew opened his fancy suit jacket, reaching for the gold pen in his shirt pocket.

Feeling like she'd soon smother, Stephanie gulped in a deep breath. "I'll be fine," she said and leaned away.

The phone rang again, and Stephanie grabbed it, relieved for an excuse to cease communication with these overly attentive men.

Charles walked Matthew to the front door and disappeared outside with him. Before the door closed completely, Stephanie heard Matthew mention her name. How she wished she could hear why they were still discussing her, especially when everyone in the conference room was waiting for Charles's return.

"I need to speak to that lady attorney," said the voice on the phone, polite compared to that of Mr. Dawson's earlier.

"This is Stephanie Saunders." She sighed.

"You answer phones, too?"

"Who's calling please?" She intentionally ignored his question.

"Josh Durrant. I'm the guy the judge assigned to you this morning."

"I remember." He was the cute one, if criminals could be cute.

"I guess I need an appointment. And just so you know, I didn't do it."

Of course he didn't do it. Wasn't that the case with most of her clients? "Do you have facts that prove you're innocent?" Stephanie asked.

"No."

"That makes my job harder then, doesn't it?" She knew she shouldn't be catty with defendants but she'd about had it with men today, and besides she felt crummy.

"But you'll still be my lawyer, won't you?"

"According to Judge Anderson, I already am." She glanced at the appointment book Deirdre kept for the attorneys. "I have an opening at 10:00 a.m. on Friday? You can tell me your version of what happened then."

"My version? I'll tell you what really happened."

"Great. If you think of anything that would make the judge believe you over what your wife is saying . . . ."

"She's not my wife."

"She's not?"

"Not really."

"Well, is she or isn't she?"

"I married her, but she's not my wife."

"If you married her, there's a good possibility she is your wife."

"But we've never . . ."

"Okaaay. Let's talk Friday." Stephanie's stomach did a flip-flop. She really didn't feel very good.

Placing the receiver in its cradle, Stephanie eased the phone book from the desk drawer. She ran her finger down the columns under "physicians," until she found the name: Andrews, Jennifer, MD. At least she could select a female doctor and maybe get some pain medication for her hip. But why did she feel icky so much of the time, and why was Charles discussing her with Matthew, and why did she have to get stuck with Josh Durrant?

CHAPTER 3

"Miss Saunders you may get dressed now, but I'd like to visit with you in my office before you leave." Dr. Jennifer Andrews peered through narrow grandma glasses at the papers she held in her hands. Undoubtedly those documents revealed the results of the multitude of tests to which Stephanie had been subjected since her arrival at the clinic, what seemed an eternity ago. She searched the doctor's face, but no clue surfaced.

"Is everything okay?" Stephanie forced out the words. Was this the end of her life as she knew it? Had her luck run out?

"I don't believe your hip is broken, but you've no doubt pulled some ligaments," Dr. Andrews said, her eyes still glued to the papers. "If you're not eighty percent better in two weeks, come back and we'll get you into physical therapy."

"Aren't you going to X-ray it?" Stephanie didn't know much about medicine, but thought an X-ray would have been one of the first things they'd do. Maybe she should have selected another doctor farther down the list in the phone book.

"Not at this time." Dr. Andrews made a few notes, then clicked her pen shut. "Open the door when you're ready and the nurse will show you into my office."

Stephanie didn't like the sound of that, but before Dr. Andrews stepped out, she turned and smiled, making Stephanie feel a little better. Perhaps the news wasn't as bad as Stephanie feared, but she wouldn't let herself hope.

Atop the examining table, she shivered in the flimsy cotton gown. What was wrong with her? Had she injured some vital organ in her body during the fall? Was she going to experience problems for the rest of her life? Was the doctor going to tell her she had to give up riding? She'd die first. Oh, no. Was she going to die?

She pulled on jeans and a sweater with shaking hands. Thank heavens it was Saturday and she didn't have to go to work. Whatever the doctor told her, she'd have some time to digest it before facing her associates' inquiring minds. She had a date with Todd tonight, but could always cancel. If it was bad news, she'd want some time alone, maybe just with the horses; they never asked questions or judged her. One hour with her equine friends and she could face the world again. She opened the door to the hall.

A nurse showed Stephanie to Dr. Andrews's office, which was, not surprisingly, much nicer than her own. Maybe she should have been a doctor. No, on second thought, she'd probably inspire even less confidence in that profession than she already did in hers. Dr. Andrews, on the other hand, appeared capable of handling most anything from treating accident victims to hunting bear with a stick.

The sturdy, solemn-faced doctor had shed her white coat, replacing it with a charcoal jacket that matched her long, straight skirt. She probably thought the lack of a white coat put patients more at ease. It didn't. Stephanie had never before been so nervous, not even while waiting for a jury to come back with a verdict. Of course, that verdict had never sealed her fate. This one would. The doctor again flipped through the deplorable test result papers, then took off her glasses and laid them on her mahogany desk. She stared at Stephanie as if she didn't know where to begin.

"You might as well come out with it. What's wrong with me? I'm not going to die, am I?" Stephanie hated that her voice shook.

Dr. Andrews chuckled.

How dare she?

"No you're not going to die, at least not right away," she said. "You're young and healthy."

Healthy? What a wonderful word, Stephanie thought. "I'm healthy?"

"You're very healthy."

For an instant Stephanie felt better than when she and Kingston had won at their first horse show. "Then what's wrong with me?"

The doctor' eyes narrowed. "You have no idea?"

"Not really, unless it has something to do with the fall, or the flu."

"Miss Saunders . . ." The doctor shifted in her seat. "When was your last period?"

"What?"

"Your last menstrual period. When was it?"

What kind of question was that? "I don't remember. It comes when it comes. I guess I've been so busy I haven't kept track. What difference does it make?" Stephanie had always felt uncomfortable discussing female problems.

"I see that you checked 'no' on this questionnaire where it asked if you were pregnant."

"That's right. I'm not pregnant." It was one thing she was positive about.

"Actually, you are, could be around six weeks." The doctor placed her hands, palms down, on the desk as if to say "end of story."

All the air left Stephanie's lungs as her mind struggled to make sense of what the doctor had said. Then she laughed. "Oh, come on. That's not funny."

"I'm not trying to be funny. Your test was positive." The doctor tapped her pen on the desk.

"Then my test is wrong."

Dr. Andrews shook her head. "You're welcome to take your own test which you can buy at any drugstore, but I think it will show the same result. The tests we give are 99% conclusive."

Stephanie felt her face flush. "But there's no way I could be pregnant."

"Why's that?" The doctor leaned back in her chair and raised her brows.

"It takes two, you know, and I haven't been with anyone."

"Never?" The doctor stared at her like Stephanie was sure she'd stared at her clients when she knew they were lying.

"Well, it's been a long time. I slipped up once in high school, and that was such a disaster that I vowed sex was something I'd save for marriage. Anyway, I don't believe in premarital sex." Stephanie squared her jaw.

"Good for you." The doctor put her glasses back on and studied the test results once more. "You're free to get a second opinion, of course. I can recommend another doctor.

"So there's a one percent chance your test could be incorrect?" Now Stephanie wished she'd never come to the doctor. She should have waited longer for the symptoms to go away. She probably just had the flu. At least now she knew that there was nothing internally wrong from the fall.

"There's always a chance, but I've never known one to be inaccurate."

"Ah-ha. In this case, it is." Stephanie stood to leave.

"So you're not with someone now?" The doctor closed Stephanie's file, laying her pen across it.

"I am, but like I said before we haven't been together." This was something she and Todd had discussed and, once he knew where she stood, both decided they would wait. It was one of the things Stephanie liked most about Todd. She never felt at risk with him. He may kid her and call her Prom Queen, but he was always the perfect gentleman with her.

"Well, Miss Saunders, feel free to come see me again if the need arises." The doctor stood. "You shouldn't go too long before seeing an OBGYN." That unbelieving look again. The doctor really should work on her camouflaging technique. Actually, so should she. Now Stephanie realized how it felt when her clients knew she doubted their innocence.

Turning toward the door, Stephanie grimaced. "What about pain medication?"

"Try Tylenol."

"You're not going to give me anything stronger?" Surely she would, wouldn't she?

"Afraid not."

Great. The appointment had been a total waste. "Tell you what," Stephanie said. "I'll come back to say hello in six months just to show you your tests are wrong." She smiled and offered her hand. She didn't want to make an enemy here. "I'm afraid you're going to feel pretty silly."

Dr. Andrews smiled, too, and took Stephanie's hand. "One of us will."

* * *

How embarrassing. Dr. Andrews thought she was pregnant. The mere thought of such a thing sent tremors of dread through her soul. Stephanie guessed that's why people called it the practice of medicine. Luckily she hadn't slept with anyone or she could have almost believed the doctor's diagnosis. She had some of the symptoms, but the exhaustion, upset stomach and tinges of dizziness could also be attributed to the flu, couldn't they? Sure they could.

As she drove the ten miles to the stable where she rode Kingston, she tried to decide whether or not to tell Todd about the appointment. The trouble was, he'd probably ask. She might as well tell him. He'd get a chuckle out of the doctor thinking she was pregnant. Of course, there was always the possibility he'd wonder who else she'd been with since he couldn't be the father of any child of hers. No, he wouldn't doubt her. He really would be entertained by the whole ordeal and would kid her mercilessly.

It was a beautiful day, even for March. With a big sigh, she decided to postpone worrying about the doctor's appointment, work, and even Todd for a while, and glory in the freedom of these stolen hours with the horses. How she loved the change of seasons in Utah. The landscape now slept under winter's pale palette, but soon, she knew, the pastures, trees and bushes along the winding rode on which Stephanie traveled would come alive with spring's green brilliance.

Unable to pass on the narrow, snow-lined, winding road, an old white pickup truck followed behind. Stephanie had been poking along as her thoughts wandered. She sped up a little, and the pickup dropped back. Pulling into the parking lot at the Mountain Green Stable, she watched as the white truck passed by, its driver probably relieved to have her out of his way.

Kingston whinnied when Stephanie climbed out of her car, her boots crunching on the snow. She trained the big sorrel gelding for the Frandsens, the wealthy owners of this stable. A warm feeling glowed inside her each time Kingston whinnied upon her arrival, even though she realized it was probably the carrots she brought rather than her company that earned the greeting.

Thoughts of Todd also stirred warm feelings, and she didn't even have to offer him carrots. In her fondest dreams, both man and horse would be a part of her future life. She shrugged. The horse was too expensive and the man too independent. She guessed she'd have to settle for the way things were, at least for now. She opened the trunk of her car, changed into her boots and slipped into her barn parka. The zipper stuck halfway up. Her coat had been loose the last time she'd worn it. She shuddered, remembering the doctor's possible explanation. Shaking her head, she unzipped the parka and left it open. She'd gained a little weight. That was all.

Stephanie waved at Kathleen, the forty-something manager of the barn, who stood in the center of the covered arena where five little girls trotted their stylish ponies around and around. What Stephanie would have given to have owned her own pony at that age. Probably something similar to what she'd now give to own Kingston. With all her "big girl" expenses, she never seemed to get any closer to coming up with enough money. Maybe by the time she had a daughter she'd be able to help that child share a friendship with, not only her own pony, but with other girls who loved horses. Maybe someday; emphasis on the someday. Stephanie kicked a chunk of piled snow with the toe of her boot. She was not pregnant. No matter what the doctor thought. Stephanie didn't even want to consider how much of a disaster that would be. She grabbed a halter out of her locker and forced the notion from her mind. She was with the horses now where no unpleasant thoughts were allowed to intrude.

Kingston's paddock was in a row of four enclosures, across from the twelve stalls under the roof overhang of the arena. In one of the stalls Stephanie noticed a new sorrel. At least she thought it was a horse. It could have been a hat rack with skin stretched over it. The mare stood with her head drooped in the corner of the stall, her long mane and tail tangled in dreadlocks. Bite marks scarred her dull coat, and a swelled belly sagged below protruding hipbones and ribs. Although hay lay on the sawdust at her feet, the mare seemed uninterested in eating.

Tears of anger and grief sprung to Stephanie's eyes. She wanted to scream and clobber whoever was responsible for this atrocity. She grabbed the stall railing for support.

Stephanie knew all the horses at the stable by name, their breeding and age. Sometimes she forgot the owners' names, but never the horses'. This time, however, she would not rest until she learned the owner's name and turned him over to the authorities for cruelty to animals. Just let a judge try to assign her to defend the creep. A person who treated an animal like this should be starved for a month, then forced to watch others eat Thanksgiving dinner. Slivers under fingernails also came to mind.

"Pathetic, isn't it?" Apparently leaving the girls to cool out their ponies, Kathleen now stood beside Stephanie.

Kathleen was a no-nonsense type woman. Although twenty-five years had passed since a modeling career, her attractive looks had once fooled Stephanie into thinking Kathleen would be a pushover. That couldn't have been further from the truth. Stephanie had never seen a better hand with a horse or a more shrewd businesswoman. If you obeyed the rules, you were her friend. If not, watch out.

All Kathleen's horses were champions. They had to be, and all of the horses stabled here were of the same high quality. So why was this horse here? Stephanie was certain its owner had already received sharp words on the appearance of the animal. Although Kathleen was a master at dispensing discipline, Stephanie ached for a chance to add some of her own.

"It's criminal. Who would treat a poor defenseless animal like this?" Stephanie's fist clenched. "Who owns her?"

"I do. At least for now." Kathleen grabbed a nearby pitchfork and scooped up a pile of manure. Everyone was supposed to clean up after their own horse, so someone would be in her bad graces.

"You do?" Stephanie released the stall railing and relaxed out of her fighting stance. "Okay, I know you didn't let her get into this shape. What's her story?"

"Durrell had her."

"The slaughter guy?"

"Not anymore. He used to buy a lot of horses at auctions. He'd find homes for the good horses and only send the lame ones to slaughter. Now since slaughterhouses and auctions are outmoded, people still call him to help them deal with unwanted horses. He does what he can."

Kathleen grabbed a broom and began sweeping blown snow from the walkway. "I guess Durrell went to visit his nephew who works on a big ranch in Wyoming," she continued. "Apparently the ranch owner runs his brood mares out on government leased ground. This mare and another one somehow got shut up in a corral for a couple of months. The other horse didn't make it. Fortunately there was a stream and a little hay left in the feeder, but this mare had started to eat the bark off the cedar posts in the fence before they found her."

Stephanie shivered. "That just makes me sick." Actually, upon saying that, she realized for the first time in quite a while, she felt pretty good. The horse was a different matter. "How terrible it must have been for her and the other horse. What a horrible way to die."

"I know."

"So how did you get her?"

"Since she's nearly twenty and in such bad shape, the nephew was going to put her out of her misery. Durrell stopped him."

"I like Durrell better already."

Kathleen nodded. "I knew you'd say that. Well, anyway, she's a purebred Thoroughbred in foal to a champion Quarter Horse stallion, and, just my luck, Durrell thought I'd be interested in her or at least the foal—like I don't have enough horses to worry about." She rolled her eyes.

"She's in foal?" Stephanie unlatched the gate to the stall and stepped in. It occurred to her that according to the doctor, she and the mare had the same problem. "The poor thing. She can barely keep herself alive." No. There was absolutely no similarity. Stephanie felt much better and, unlike the mare, there was no way she could be pregnant.

The mare turned her head to sniff Stephanie's palm.

"I know. She's worse off than I figured, and I don't know how long I'll be able to keep her around. With all the horses I'm supporting I can't afford to put much money into her when she might just die." Kathleen picked up a bucket. "If she starts eating, I'll put her out in that front pasture where I free feed the hay and see what happens. Hopefully she'll live to raise her colt."

"Hi, sweetheart." Stephanie said to the mare. "Will you let me look in your mouth?" She stroked the horse's head, her hands resting on either side of the soft nose. The mare didn't object when Stephanie lifted the long, narrow head, pulled down on the slack jaw and peeked into the yellowed mouth. "Ouch. Will you look at this? Her teeth are horrible. There are sharp points everywhere and sores on her cheek and tongue. No wonder she doesn't feel like eating. When's that equine dentist coming?"

"Next week, but I'll be honest with you. I just don't have money to put into a horse like this." Lifting the lever on the nearby water standpipe, Kathleen filled her bucket, then poured it into the mare's water pail, which hung on the metal railing.

"I'll pay for it." The words escaped from Stephanie's mouth before she could stop them. Inwardly chiding herself, she decided that she could take the money from her meager Kingston account. She'd probably never save enough to purchase the gelding anyway and the mare truly needed a friend.

"Really? You'd do that?" Kathleen returned the bucket to its place by the water standpipe.

"Yeah." Stephanie knew she was thinking with her heart and not her brain, but the mare had no one else. "Have you tried her on beet pulp? It's soft and maybe she could get some of that down."

"Good idea. I've been soaking a couple of buckets full for several of the other horses. I'll give her some after I finish my lessons."

"I'll do it, then I'll work Kingston."

"That would be great."

"What's her name?" Stephanie asked.

"The mare's? Don't know. If you and I name her, it's more likely we'll get attached."

And that's a bad thing? Stephanie thought, but said, "You're probably right. She should still have a name." Stephanie rubbed the mare's neck.

"You give her one then."

"Okay." Stephanie leaned back to take in the full view of the skinny horse. Kathleen was all business when it came to horses. Durrell had thought the colt might be worth Kathleen's time. Saving the mare to raise an unseen colt could be costly and risky. "How about Risky Business? We can call her Risky, or Riskie, spelled with an 'ie' because she's a girl."

"She is risky. That's a good name for her." Kathleen started back toward the arena. "Have a good ride on Kingston."

Before Stephanie worked the gelding, she left a bucket of beet pulp in Riskie's stall. By the time she'd groomed and put Kingston back in his paddock, the mare had completely finished her softer food.

Stephanie smiled as she retrieved the bucket from Riskie's stall. "Good girl. I'll see you tomorrow." Stephanie trudged through the snow easier now than when she'd first come. Her hip felt better with the exercise, both on and off the horse, and her stomach had settled. She must be recovering from the flu. She couldn't believe how much better she felt out in the fresh, cold air with mostly good thoughts to occupy her mind.

After putting all her gear into the trunk of her Honda, Stephanie climbed in and headed onto the road. She glanced in her rearview mirror and noticed an old white pickup following her. Was that the same one that had been behind her when she'd arrived? The truck had gone past when she'd pulled into the stable's parking lot and now it was back again. Maybe it was a different white truck. She squinted into the setting sun. No. It really looked like the same one.

She blinked her eyes and squinted again. Shoot. She'd left her sunglasses at the stable. She'd better go get them. She'd need them in the morning. She pulled into a driveway, then reversed and headed back. The white truck continued on. Stephanie blew out a deep breath.

At the barn, it took only a minute to retrieve her glasses from the locker. She climbed into her car again and pulled onto the road, her tires slipping a little. She stared as the white truck headed down the road toward her. She glanced at the driver. He had long hair and a shaggy beard. Kind of reminded her of her new client. What was his name? Oh yeah, Josh Durrant. Boy, how paranoid could she be? Maybe Durrant lived in this area. Stop it! It was not him. Stephanie pressed on the gas pedal, all the time watching in her rearview mirror. The white truck continued down the road in the opposite direction.

Stephanie's throat went dry and her knuckles turned white on the steering wheel. She well remembered the conversation she and one of her cop friends had several weeks ago about a client who attacked his attorney with a knife because he didn't like the way his court case turned out. The attorney ended up in the hospital with multiple stab wounds and the client with another attorney to defend him on the new charges. But that was an isolated incident. Most clients respected their attorneys, didn't they? Still, the driver of the white truck did look a lot like her new client, and maybe, just maybe, he had been following her. But why? She'd done nothing he could be unhappy about. She'd barely even talked to him. The whole thing made her jittery. Some of the attorneys she knew actually obtained concealed weapon permits. Maybe she should get a gun. Of course, she'd have to find someone to give her instruction, she realized, or she'd more than likely shoot herself.

Pulse racing, all the way home she visualized cars following her, and she probably drove faster than she should have. At least it had taken her mind off what the doctor had said. Why couldn't she just dismiss the diagnosis as a mistake? Surely it was as much of a fallacy as clients in white trucks following her.

CHAPTER 4

The doorbell to Stephanie's rented condo rang at precisely eight p.m., a Todd trademark. Although she'd been behind schedule returning from the stable, she'd hurried through her household chores to find time to give extra care to her appearance that evening. A turtleneck sweater, beige jacket and tweed slacks replaced her riding boots and breeches, and her blonde hair, earlier pulled into a tight bun beneath her riding cap, now fell soft and full around her shoulders.

She peered though the peephole in the door and smiled, slipping the chain from its holder carefully so he couldn't hear that she'd used it. The door glided open to reveal Todd, handsome as ever—dark hair, slightly long the way she liked it; brown, almost black eyes twinkling now as he watched her. No matter how many times she saw him, his good looks always made her stare. Tonight he'd dressed in jeans, cowboy boots, a white shirt and a brown leather jacket. Even though she rode English style, she loved a man in jeans and cowboy boots. She loved Todd in jeans and boots—or suits, or sweats. She guessed she just plain loved Todd these days.

"Hi Babe . . . or I mean, Just Stephanie." He grinned, showing off an impressive set of dimples.

Taking his hand, she pulled him into the room and slipping her arms around his waist, laid her head against his solid chest.

He smelled wonderful, clean, freshly ironed and spicy. His arms encircled her shoulders, and for the first time that evening she felt protected. She knew Todd would battle demons for her. She guessed now it really had bothered her when she'd imagined that truck was following her. She dealt with criminals every day and even though in court she was on their side, maybe she really did need to be more alert. But she wouldn't worry about that right now. This evening, she was safe with Todd and they were headed to his cabin where he'd promised to cook dinner for her.

"You look beautiful," he said, studying her from his six-foot-one-inch height. "Of course, you always look beautiful."

She giggled and tipped her head back to gaze at him. "That's what I was thinking about you. I love the boots."

A lock of his dark wavy hair fell across his forehead. He took his hand from her back long enough to guide the lock into place. "Oh, and I thought you were going to say you love me."

Deep in mock thought, Stephanie rubbed her chin. "Hmm. I guess I could say that."

He bent to kiss her and she kissed him back. Arms around her, he held her so tight against his strong body she felt almost crushed. "I love you too, you know," he said, his dark eyes luminous, like lake water at midnight. "No matter what happens, always remember I love you."

She grinned and expected his easy smile, but he stared away into nothingness. It was almost as if he were going away. Oh no, was he breaking up with her? "Why so serious?" she asked.

Cradling her face in his hands, he said, "I'm always serious where you're concerned."

That was a much better reaction than she'd expected. They'd never talked about love before, and Stephanie felt like she'd been touched by the sun. "Good answer."

As she stood there in his arms, she decided that if circumstances were different she could almost see having a child with Todd, even though a baby was the lowest thing on her want list right now. Actually, the more she thought about her doctor appointment, the more she was convinced she never wanted to be a mother.

"You ready?" He took her hand and headed for the door.

"Almost." She led him to a chair where she grabbed her purse, flipped off the light, locked the door, thought about bolting it, but didn't.

"How was your day?" Todd asked, as they began the forty-five minute drive up Hobble Creek Canyon in his black Toyota Camry.

"Good and bad," she said. "There's a new, really skinny horse at the stable . . ." she paused, and earlier I went to the doctor . . . She completed the answer in her head.

"Wow, a skinny horse. Is that the good part of your day or bad?"

She playfully punched him on the arm.

They discussed the mare and Kingston for the rest of the drive. Stephanie noticed that while there was a little snow at her place, here an inch or two covered the road and piled up to about two feet alongside.

"You've got a lot of snow," she said.

"We do. That's why I came to get you. I didn't want you driving up here at night by yourself." He reached for her hand.

She gave it to him and squeezed his. "And I appreciate your concern."

Unlike the other times he'd brought her here, he'd left on the lights of the cabin's huge chandelier, which hung from the exposed beam ceiling. When Todd had first mentioned his "cabin" she'd pictured a little Hansel and Gretel house. This place, however, was a four-story A-frame. The front part of the house was mostly windows, which revealed the large, open front room, complete with a three-story lava rock fireplace.

"Work must still be going well," she said

"What's that?" He turned his head, brows raised.

"In order to afford this modest little cabin."

He chuckled. "I guess you could say I got a really good deal on it." He pulled the car under the overhanging deck and into the garage.

Stephanie slid out and followed Todd into the basement family room. She noticed a new leather couch and matching chair near the wood-burning stove. They climbed the stairs leading to the large front room a floor above.

For some reason she paid more attention to cabin's interior this time than she had on earlier visits. She admired the front room's paneled walls and structural dark stained beams that extended up two more floors and the beautiful oak railing and banister that matched the huge chandelier. Near the two overstuffed sofas, logs rested in the giant fireplace, ready to add ambience to the already rustic, yet classic scene.

A wonderful scent drew them into the kitchen, where a chicken casserole baked in the modern double oven, and the large oak table, tonight adorned with multicolored stoneware dishes, rested on a tile floor.

Stephanie and Todd joked and giggled through dinner. Afterwards, with their stomachs full and the dishes done, they cuddled on the sofa next to a crackling fire.

"You must have gotten over your flu," Todd said, toying with a lock of her long, blonde hair. "Did you go to the doctor?"

Stephanie sucked in a deep breath at the sudden reminder of the topic she'd tried to ignore. Why was she nervous? The doctor was wrong. She had to be. "I did."

"What did he say?"

"She," Stephanie corrected.

"Of course." Todd nodded as if he should have known she'd select a woman. "What did she say?"

Stephanie struggled to organize her thoughts, trying to decide how to begin. "I don't think she's a very good doctor." Stephanie's heart thumped in her chest.

"Why? What happened?"

"Well, she took a bunch of stupid tests and came back and told me I'm—" Stephanie felt dizzy.

Todd sat up straight, looking directly at her. "You're what?"

His face turned pale, which did nothing for Stephanie's self-confidence. Just tell him, she thought. When she'd rehearsed this scene in her mind earlier, it had actually seemed a little humorous. Maybe she should say it was believed she was "with foal."

"The doctor said . . . ." She cleared her throat. "Of all things, the doctor said that I'm . . . I'm pregnant." There, the secret was out. "Can you imagine?"

Todd's mouth fell open and he just stared at her.

"Well, say something." Stephanie playfully nudged him. "You and I both know that can't be true, and Todd, believe me, I've not been with anyone else."

His eyes lowered. He couldn't seem to look at her. "I know you haven't." He was even paler than before, if possible. "Stephanie," he took hold of both of her hands and dragged his gaze up to meet hers. "I'm afraid you really could be . . . pregnant." It seemed difficult for him to even say the word.

"What?" Stephanie felt like all the air had been squished from her lungs. "What are you saying?" Tears sprung to her eyes.

He looked away again. "I was hoping you'd never have to know." The hands holding hers tightened. "I'm going to kill Brad."

"Brad?" She couldn't make sense of what he'd said and frantically tried to clear her head. "Who the hell is Brad?" Stephanie never swore but if there was ever occasion for it, the time had arrived. She pulled her hands away from his vice-like grip.

"That SOB." Todd's lip curled. "He's a friend, a former friend, a very former friend."

"But we've never . . . ." Her voice broke.

"I think we did," Todd whispered.

"You think?" She pressed her fingertips to her temples, trying to block out his words. "Isn't that something we'd remember?" She slid away from him, suddenly cold.

The firelight reflected in Todd's eyes, making them appear red. "Unless someone made it so we couldn't."

"What are you talking about?"

He looked scary with red eyes. Suddenly Stephanie remembered her dream the night before. As the sun had set in the distance, a white truck came toward her in the opposite direction. She couldn't remember what the driver had looked like as he passed, only that his eyes had shone red when he looked at her. A white truck? Todd didn't drive a white truck.

"Do you remember that night toward the end of January?" he asked. "It was the last time I cooked for you here. I picked you up, like I did tonight, because it was snowing. We ate dinner and drank cold duck. Then we decided that you should stay here because it was still snowing and we were both so tired."

Stephanie willed herself to stay motionless instead of leaping up and scurrying from the room. She didn't want to hear this.

"All I recall was waking up the next morning in your extra bedroom, and you were upstairs asleep in your room."

He chewed his lip, then stammered, "Have you ever heard of rohypnol?" His eyes no longer appeared fire red.

"The date rape drug?" Her voice shook. "Wait a minute. You gave me a roofie?"

"I wouldn't do that." His hands reached out and again claimed hers.

"But you said . . . ." Her voice broke. She couldn't face this. For a moment panic overtook her. She wanted to run. Here she was in this lonely cabin, far away from the safety of anyone she knew, with only snow-covered trees and mountains to hear her scream. Wait. What scream? This was Todd. She wouldn't need to scream.

"I think Brad gave you a roofie, probably me one too." He pulled her into his arms like he'd sensed her earlier thoughts. "I'm so sorry."

Her head spun, and she gasped for air. "Why would he do that?"

Todd stroked her hair. "I'm afraid it was to get even with me."

Thoughts bombarded Stephanie's brain. The words—Why would he want to get even? formed in her mind, but tears of anger and hurt flooded her eyes and what came out was, "Is having sex with me so bad? I'm only asking because, you see . . . I don't remember."

"I don't remember either." His arms loosened around her, but he still held her by the shoulders. "In addition to everything else, I think I was drunk and so were you."

The fire in the lava rock fireplace flickered. She couldn't bear it if it made his eyes appear red again. She looked away. "But we didn't drink anything."

"Except for the cold duck . . . spiked with—I'll bet it was vodka."

Stephanie sniffed and looked for something on which to wipe her nose. "This can't be happening. I don't drink. I don't take drugs. I don't sleep around." She pulled away from him, grabbing a discarded napkin from the coffee table. "And I don't like babies. I can't be pregnant. I'm an attorney."

Blinking at her outburst, he opened his mouth to say something, then closed it and shrugged.

"So what happened?" She blew her nose. "How come you know everything and I don't? You better tell me."

"I don't know everything. I'll tell you what I've kind of figured out and then we can decide what probably happened."

"Let's get on with it then." Discovery was her favorite part of any case, but this wasn't just any case, it was her life. She moved to the matching sofa across from Todd. She felt like she needed a shower.

He leaned forward, elbows on knees, firelight now making his jaw look even more chiseled. She wouldn't let herself think about his looks just now.

Taking a deep breath, he began. "I woke up with a fuzzy head at about three that morning and let's just say I wasn't in my bedroom."

"You were with me?" She grimaced.

He nodded.

"In the guest bedroom?" Her voice squeaked.

He nodded.

"In a compromising position?"

"I don't know how compromising it was. Actually it was pretty nice." He flashed a mischievous grin.

She glared at him before burying her face in her hands. "Why didn't you tell me?" The one and only other time that she'd been compromised she'd been in high school, young and stupid. She had vowed then that the next time would be with her husband. She guessed she was still stupid.

Todd stood to pace in front of the fireplace. "I couldn't tell you. I knew your stand on . . . on what we'd probably done and I figured if I didn't say anything, no one would need to know. It never entered my mind that you could get pregnant. It was only one night."

"You still should have told me." She pushed her fingers back into her hair, pulling it away from her face. "What am I going to do?"

"Not you. Us." He sat on the hearth, close to her sofa. "Do you think I'd let you go through this alone? I know you'd never have an abortion, would you?"

Wrapping her arms around her middle, she shivered. "How can you ask me that?"

He placed his hand on the edge of her couch. "I said I know you wouldn't consider it. I didn't mean that I wanted you to." His brow crinkled and he leaned closer.

Although he seemed to need to be near her, she wished he'd keep his distance.

"Well, good. You better not have . . . ." She made a shooing motion with her hand. "Well, go on with your story."

"It's not a story. It's what happened." His eyes were soft and moist.

"If you say so." She brought her knees up under her chin and wrapped her arms around her legs. "Tell me about Brad. You're a little shaky on those details. Who is he and why would he do this to us? I could probably bring him up on criminal charges."

Apparently getting her message that she didn't desire him near right then, he moved from the hearth to the sofa across from her.

"You probably could, if you could find him. He left town. I don't know where he is now."

Stephanie sighed and rolled her eyes. "Why am I not surprised? They've never found the murderer in the O.J. case either. It seems the guilty always mysteriously disappear."

"This isn't like the O.J. case."

"Promise?"

He moved to the opposite end of her sofa. "I promise." Again the firelight reflected in his eyes, but this time they weren't scary.

"So tell me again why he'd do this."

"To get even with me. He knows how much I care about you—as much as he wished I would have cared about his sister. He wants you to dump me like I did her. You're not going to, are you?" He slid toward her.

"I don't know what I'm going to do." She felt trapped and moved as far away from him as the arm of the couch would allow. "What sister? I'm in one heck of a mess because he wanted to get even with you? I don't get it." She slumped back onto the sofa.

He slid a little closer, like a snake inching up on its prey. "Brad and I have a history. It started out good and ended very badly. He and I were once friends and then I got involved with his sister. She liked me a whole lot more than I liked her. To make a long story short, I tried to break it off with her and she went ballistic. She stalked me for weeks and I finally had to turn her in. Brad and I fought, literally. I ended up with a black eye, but I gave him a broken jaw. We didn't talk for months. He couldn't and I wouldn't." Todd didn't look at her. He peered into the fire.

"Then I saw him again around Christmas and he acted like all was forgiven," Todd continued. "I invited him up to the cabin several times and it seemed as if I was talking to my old buddy again. In the course of our conversations, he mentioned that Colleen had found someone else and asked if I had." He turned to Stephanie and reached for her hand. Reluctantly, she let him take it.

"I told him all about you," Todd went on. "I find myself doing that too much lately. I told him how happy I was and what a great person you are. It was like old times again, before Colleen. Then as talk does sometimes between guys, Brad asked me how the sex was."

Pulling her hand away, Stephanie rolled her eyes.

Todd held up a finger. "I told him we weren't into that right now, that we'd decided to wait. He could hardly believe it."

Stephanie said nothing, merely staring at Todd as he told her what had happened.

"He was with me that afternoon in January, when I was getting everything ready for my date with you. He told me to go ahead and pick you up and he'd finish here. As it turned out, he did finish here. He put vodka in the cold duck and he added a little something extra in your glass, maybe even mine." He put his hand on her arm. "I remember now it bothered me that the goblets were full when we arrived, but then I didn't think about it again."

"That's just crazy. How do you know all this?" She felt tears forming in her eyes and fought to hold them in check.

"He told me. The next day, after our night together . . . ."

"Don't say that." A tear escaped and rolled down her face.

He wiped it away with the tip of his finger. "Sorry. Well, the next day, he came here to ask how my date was, and I asked him if he'd put something in our drinks. He just laughed and wanted to know how the sex was. I couldn't believe he'd actually show up after what he'd done. Maybe he thought I'd be okay with it, but of course, I wasn't."

She stared at him and bit her lip to keep from saying anything and interrupting his story.

"We fought, again. I think he had more bruises than I did. Before I tossed him out, he told me that Colleen had not found someone else, that she'd experienced a mental breakdown and left college to return home, wherever that was. I haven't seen him since. I never did know where he was staying. He always came to my place. I've checked around and he's just disappeared."

"How lucky for him." She mentally went over all the charges she'd have liked to file against him. "If you hear from him again, you'll let me know, won't you?"

"Of course. I think he just determined that since we don't sleep around, something bad would happen when we woke up in the same bed the next morning. He didn't figure I'd wake up earlier and set everything straight and, of course, he didn't think there'd be a baby."

"So I'm really pregnant." She started to sob. "I didn't want to believe it. What am I going to do?"

"We could get married." He pulled her into his arms.

Her mind raced. Get married? Did she love Todd enough to marry him? She didn't want to get married just because she had to. How embarrassing. How would she ever face Charles and Paul, and what about Deirdre? What would her clients think? What would this do to her career? She felt like a corralled bronco and again fought the urge to just run and run until she woke up from this nightmare. But she wasn't going to wake up. This was her life now. She had to do what she had to do. How could she not marry Todd? "Is this a proposal?"

"It is if you want it to be."

Wow! How romantic. The most important choice of her life influenced by a man with a grudge against someone else. In all of her daydreams, it had never been like this. "May I think about it?"

"Of course."

"Will you take me home now?"

"If that's what you want."

"It's too late for what I want, but you can take me home." She saw the hurt flash in his eyes, and it bothered her a little but she was hurting too, and her distress was far more disabling. Would her life ever be good again?

CHAPTER 5

On her way in that morning, Stephanie pulled a file she needed from a shelf next to Deirdre's desk. Heading to her own office, she spun around and nearly collided with a person who burst in through the front door.

"Oh! I'm sorry," she said, looking up to see who she'd nearly run down. Her mouth fell open and still staring, she stammered, "May I help you?"

The woman looked enough like Stephanie to be her sister. Similar long blonde hair fell in soft curls around the woman's shoulders, and curious brown eyes bored into Stephanie's of the same color. Their figures were comparable, at least for now, and their faces, identical enough to be creepy.

"I'm Jessica Dawson, Matthew's wife," the woman said, her head tilting to the side as she studied Stephanie. "I'm here to see Charles. Is he in?"

"He's not," Stephanie managed. "In fact, I think he went to breakfast with your husband." She guessed Matthew and his wife didn't discuss everyday matters.

"Oh, how silly of me. I remember now." Mrs. Dawson chuckled, placing a manicured hand across her mouth. The diamond on her finger looked large enough to ransom a small country. Stephanie wondered that the woman could lift her hand at all, to say nothing of the long red nails. "You must be

Stephanie Saunders," she continued, reaching out to push up on Stephanie's chin, closing her gaping mouth. "My husband told me all about you."

"He did?" Stephanie stammered, trying desperately to regain her composure. "What did he say?"

"Oh, he mentioned that you look a lot like me." She stroked her flawless hair, then touched a lock of Stephanie's and rolled her eyes. "Do you think we look alike?"

"A little, maybe," Stephanie replied. She wouldn't give Matthew or his snooty wife the satisfaction of agreeing with them. And, she wished Mrs. Dawson would keep her hands to herself.

"I'd say we look a lot alike, or could." She gave Stephanie a critical once-over and sighed. "I wonder if we could be related. What was your mother's maiden name?"

So this was why Matthew had appeared so interested in her. Stephanie thought maybe Charles had told his client that she was an excellent attorney. She should have known. Being continually distinguished by her looks made Stephanie crazy. "Dinsdale," she said quickly, then wondered why she'd even answered. Her mother's maiden name was none of this woman's business. Trying to ignore Mrs. Dawson, Stephanie opened the file and began reading silently.

Mrs. Dawson cleared her throat daintily. "There are no Dinsdales in my pedigree. What was your grandmother's maiden name?"

"I don't remember." Stephanie closed the file and tried to hold Mrs. Dawson's stare.

"You don't remember?" the woman's tone conveyed the impression that she was unaccustomed to being ignored.

"I really don't," Stephanie said, dropping her gaze. "It was nice to meet you Mrs. Dawson. If you'll excuse me, I have a lot of work to do."

Thankfully, Deirdre reappeared, probably on her way back from an early bathroom break. She carried a novel. "Oh, here's Deirdre. She can set you an appointment with Charles if you'd like."

"No, no, that won't be necessary." Mrs. Dawson reached into her purse and brought out her keys. "I'll speak to Matthew and Charles about it."

Stephanie tipped her head in a good-bye and continued to her office, wondering as she walked what Mrs. Dawson was going to speak to Matthew and Charles about. Was it the question that had initially brought her into the office, or would it be Stephanie's behavior? Actually, Stephanie really didn't care.

She felt Mrs. Dawson's stare boring into her back. A quick glance over her shoulder revealed that the woman was, indeed, watching her departure. Stephanie stepped into her office and closed the door, leaning against it to prevent further invasion of her privacy.

Her phone buzzed as she sprawled into her chair.

"Well, how weird was that?" Deirdre asked. "Did you know that you and Mrs. Dawson look so much alike?"

"We don't look that much alike."

"Hello! You two could be twins—well, sisters." Deirdre smacked her chewing gum.

"I've heard it said that each of us has a look-alike out there somewhere," Stephanie said.

"Well, you've found yours. I'm reading this book about two sisters who trade places and one of them gets murdered."

Stephanie's head began to ache. "Thank you for that, Deirdre. I think we both need to get to work now."

The phone went dead. Clearly, she'd upset the girl again, but Deirdre loved to talk and Stephanie wasn't in the mood. Wouldn't Deirdre be delighted to know Stephanie's secret? Deirdre would earn big points with Charles for such information.

Stephanie placed the file she'd retrieved onto the pile of court files from the day before, which was right next to stacks from weeks earlier. She folded her arms on the desk and rested her forehead on them. She'd dreaded coming to work this morning and that was even before she'd met Mrs. Dawson. She groaned. What a train wreck that had been. Stephanie didn't even want to ride Kingston later that afternoon. She felt as if all the enthusiasm had leaked from her body like a hole in a bucket. An unwanted pregnancy could do that to a woman, and she couldn't even discuss it with anyone. No one could know she was pregnant, at least not until she'd decided what she would do.

She'd merely brushed her hair this morning and left it long and straight, but she'd managed to dress in a charcoal skirt and light gray sweater. A little mascara and some pale lipstick and she'd crawled into her car for the solemn drive to the office. Breakfast had been out of the question. No wonder Mrs. Dawson had beheld her with such distain, especially when the woman's husband had suggested they looked so much alike.

What a colossal mess! Darn Todd. Darn his olive-skinned hide. It was all his fault. Wasn't it? He had asked her to marry him, and if she did, he'd be just as stuck as she was—almost. It was her flat belly that would be stretched way out of shape. It was her body that would feel the effects of a stranger growing inside, and after the baby was born it would be a constant reminder of . . . of what? Had Todd told her the truth about how this child had come into being, or had the whole thing been a lie? Would this baby be a constant reminder of something that had happened to her that she didn't even remember? She sat up straight in her chair. No. She couldn't face the possibility that Todd would lie to her. Even though, as an indigent defense attorney, she was constantly surrounded by clients who told half-truths, and she'd probably conditioned herself to believe no one. But, she just had to believe Todd. It would be too horrific not to. And she cared deeply for him, didn't she?

Lifting her chin, she combed the hair from her face with her fingertips. This was ridiculous. She needed to pull herself together. What had happened to the girl who freely dispatched advice to others in tough situations? Sure, it was easier to give advice when she was not the one needing it, but she was better than this wallowing, tearful female that last Saturday night had produced. Although Todd had called every day, she hadn't seen him for nearly a week. She'd asked for time to consider his proposal. She'd figure something out, maybe even today.

Her phone buzzed and she lifted the receiver.

"Mr. Durrant is here to see you," Deirdre chirped in a sing-song voice far too deceptively sweet for Stephanie's upset stomach. Deirdre would be dishing out payback for the rest of the day, Stephanie was sure.

Oh boy. The last thing she needed this morning was Mr. Durrant. Maybe if she could have called him "Criminal Suspect Durrant," or "Loser Durrant," it would have set with her better, but she doubted she'd be able to get away with that. She supposed "Mr." would have to do. Stephanie wondered what type of story he'd come up with. At least Deirdre was back from her extended illness. She guessed that was a plus.

"Send Mr. Durrant in," Stephanie said emphasizing the "Mr.". A chill raced down her spine as she remembered that the other night she'd surmised that Josh Durrant had been following her. She frowned. And she'd thought she had problems then.

"Yes, madam," Deirdre said. "Will there be anything else?"

"No thank you," Stephanie returned and sighed.

"Is it dark in here, or am I going blind?" Josh Durrant asked upon entering.

Stephanie squinted, noting for the first time that she'd neglected to turn on the lights when she'd come in.

"Sorry," she said, trying to keep her face from reddening. "The light switch is there on your right. Would you mind?"

Turning, he flipped it on. Today, dressed in jeans, a flannel shirt and wool-lined Levi jacket, his beard and long hair gave him more the look of an Alaskan mountain man than that of a convict. "Do you like being in the dark?"

What did he mean by that? Basically she'd been drugged, raped and impregnated and she remembered nothing. But, of course, Mr. Durrant wasn't referring to that. Maybe he thought she was in the dark about him, which surely could be the case, or perhaps he'd just meant what he'd said—that she liked having the lights off, which right now was correct. Get a grip. Stephanie told herself. "I'm not feeling well." She blinked at her own response. Could she be any less professional?

Durrant dropped into a chair opposite her desk, bringing the ankle of one leg up to rest on the knee of the other. Leaning back nonchalantly, he leveled a stare at her as if he had not one care in the world. Like many of her seasoned clients who appeared unconcerned about their criminal charges, he was the picture of calm. And she was like a hurricane about to hit land. What was it she'd said about pulling herself together? She'd better get on with it before she burst into tears.

"I'm sorry, Mr. Durrant." She plucked his file from atop one of the piles on her desk.

"Josh." He grinned, showing perfect white teeth.

Papers slipped out of his file and scattered onto the floor around her feet. She flew out of her chair to retrieve them.

"Need any help?" He leaned forward in his chair.

"No," she blurted, holding up a hand. "I'm fine."

Papers gathered, she eased herself back into her executive chair and smoothed her skirt. She tapped the ends of the papers on her desk to straighten them. "Now then," she said, holding her voice steady. "You were charged with domestic violence. You beat your wife?"

"Live-in girlfriend."

Stephanie's brow lifted in surprise. "Okay. You beat your girlfriend."

"No. I didn't do that, either."

She studied his face. At least she tried to. It was difficult with his thick beard. "Okay. Why don't you tell me your story."

Positioning both feet on the floor, he squared his body. "It's not a story. It's . . . what happened."

That's just what Todd had said the Saturday night when she'd told him to go on with his story. She definitely needed to revise her wording. "Okay. So what do you think happened?"

He stared at her with narrowed green eyes—beautiful green eyes, so green she wondered if they were real or if he wore tinted contact lenses. "I don't think it happened. I know it."

"Go on then," she said. "What happened?" She got the feeling that Durrant had won Round One of the questioning.

"I tried to break up with her."

Stephanie's hands came down noisily on her desk. This also sounded like what Todd had said. Couldn't these men come up with something more original than how hard it was for big, strong masculine males to break up with pitiful, clinging, helpless females? "Sorry," she said, placing her wayward hands in her lap. "Please go on."

"We were driving, talking about us. I told her I wanted to move on. She started hitting me." Durrant studied the edge of Stephanie's desk.

"Oh! You poor thing." She sounded sarcastic even to herself. Was her attack really directed at Todd? To keep from saying more, she chewed her bottom lip.

He shook his head. "Do you want to hear this or not?"

"Sorry." Round Two to the defendant.

He glanced at Stephanie briefly before settling his gaze once again on the edge of her desk. "I held her wrists together so she'd quit hitting me, opened the car door, pushed her out, and drove on."

"Was the car moving?"

He sighed like Stephanie was perhaps the dumbest person he'd ever met. "No. I stopped first. She said I didn't, but I did. Do you think I'd push any female out of a moving vehicle?"

He made her feel like a little girl in a my-daddy's-bigger-than-your-daddy contest. "Well, you do have a domestic violence charge filed against you."

"What happened to innocent until proven guilty?"

"Are you guilty?" she shot back.

"No, I'm not. And, aren't you supposed to defend me?"

"Well . . . yes." He did have a point. It was her job to defend the defenseless. She noted the width of his shoulders and felt her eyes widen. He was hardly defenseless. She wrinkled her nose. But, of course defenseless in this sense meant attorneyless. It was her job, like it or not, to defend those unable to provide legal counsel for themselves. Why did she have to constantly remind herself of that fact? "I need to have something to work with," she said. "Do you expect me to create a defense out of what you've told me so far?" Holding up her hand, she ticked off her next questions on her fingers. "What time of day was it? Did you consider that something bad could have happened to her? Do you know how she got home?"

Shifting in his chair, he appeared uneasy for the first time, but only for a moment. "Oh, come on. It was early afternoon and right in the middle of town."

"Oh. I see. You pushed her out of the car, and since it was in the middle of town and in the afternoon, it was okay. You're quite a gentleman, you know." She was taunting him despite her better sense. As a rule, she was never rude to her clients, even the scummy ones.

"I didn't say I was proud of what I did. Haven't you ever done anything you regret?"

Boy, had she ever. She wondered for an instant if he could read her mind and dropped her gaze to study the file. "You don't seem to have a prior record," she said, looking up.

"You act surprised." He favored her with a lopsided grin.

"Well, hauling you off to jail on a first offense seems a little extreme."

"That's what I thought, but there's something else I should probably mention."

"What else?" She wondered if she really wanted to know.

"Carly's father is the judge."

"What? Judge Anderson is your girlfriend Carly's father?" Stephanie couldn't believe her ears.

"Yeah, she probably went straight to daddy's office after I dumped her off."

"You've got to be kidding?" Stephanie tried to stifle a giggle, but failed.

Josh frowned. "Ex-girlfriend, remember? No, I'm not kidding. And, it's not funny."

On second thought, it really wasn't funny. No wonder Judge Anderson had been so set on her defending Josh. The judge figured she'd lose. In fact he must have been counting on it. He was letting the legal system take out his daughter's vengeance on Josh. Stephanie's face went hot. She couldn't decide if she were more angry at the judge for doubting her legal ability or for trying to unfairly punish her client, and wasn't this whole thing a conflict of interest? She'd put that in the pleadings if the case went that far.

"One more thing." Stephanie studied the pages of the police report. "It says here that Carly had bruises on her legs and a scrape on her elbow."

"Well, she did fall a little when I pushed her out of the car."

"A little? How does one fall a little?" Stephanie asked, not liking the fact that she'd fallen at all.

Josh peered out from beneath his honey colored mane and shrugged.

All at once Stephanie felt as if she'd pass out. Her eyes blurred and her heart raced. "Is it hot in here?" she asked. "I've got to open that window."

Standing, Josh reached out his hand. It seemed for a moment that he wanted to come to her and offer comfort. "You sit," he said. "I'll do it."

This man was supposed to be the bad guy. Maybe he'd even been following her earlier that week, but he seemed truly concerned.

The cool air from the window cleared Stephanie's head, and she began to feel better. "Do you drive a white truck?" she asked, removing the lid from her red pen and nervously fiddling with it.

"I do. Why?" He returned to his chair.

"I was at a stable near Salem the other night and I thought I saw you." The ink leaked onto her fingers.

"Really? You could have, I guess. I go to see my friend quite often. He lives near Salem." He placed his forearms on the arms of the chair.

For some strange reason the ink on her fingers looked like blood—perhaps her blood if something bad happened to her. She held her hand as far away as she could, staring at it.

Rising, Josh handed her a clean, white handkerchief. He didn't seem like the kind of a guy who'd carry a handkerchief, especially one that was clean.

"No thanks. I don't want to get blood . . . uh, ink on it." The skin prickled at the back of her neck.

Josh lifted a brow.

She grabbed a tissue from a box on her desk and cleaned her hand the best she could.

"Well, okay." Walking to her desk, Josh retrieved the pen and tossed it into the trash can. "So do you think you can get these charges dropped?"

Was he trying to take her mind off of her seeing him near the stable? "That's what I'm here for." That *was* what she was here for. At least that was supposed to be why she was here, and the appointment with Josh had made her think about something besides her own problem—if only for a moment. And Todd hadn't pushed *her* out of the car.

What was she doing? Comparing Todd to Josh—putting Todd in the same category as Josh? Two men, two stories. Who was lying? Both? Neither? Maybe both men were telling the truth.

"Should I be worried?" he asked.

"What?"

"I said, should I be worried?" he repeated.

"When a crime is committed, one should always be worried. And then you've got that judge problem," she finished under her breath.

"But I didn't mean for her to fall," Josh continued. "Carly was the one hitting me. Wouldn't it be like self defense?"

"If we can convince the judge to see it that way. Of course, I'll have to request a different judge, and it is hard to believe that you would be defenseless . . . ."—that word again as applied to Josh—"against a woman who is—" She ran a finger down the police report. "Who is five-feet-six and weighs one hundred twenty-five pounds."

"More like five-feet-four and one hundred fifteen pounds. The cop over-estimated her size."

"And you're six two, one hundred eighty-five pounds?"

"Six three, one hundred ninety-five pounds."

"I rest my case."

"But you'll defend me, won't you?

"You want me to?"

"Sure, unless I can have that Charles Connelly guy."

"No. You can't have him. He doesn't do indigent defense work." The harshness of her words surprised even her. Deciding she'd better lighten up, she continued, "I guess you want a real attorney?" She quoted the words of Carlos Ortega in his court appearance.

He grinned. "Oh, I think you're pretty real. I just thought that since Mr. Connelly is your boss, he'd be the best."

Barely holding her anger in check, she narrowed her eyes at him. "Where indigent defense is concerned, I'm the best."

"I guess I want you then." The tone of his voice made his statement sound like a come-on.

Now it was Stephanie who shifted in her seat.

"Well, okay, I'll have Deirdre set you another appointment in a week or so. I'll do some discovery, maybe talk to the police and your girlfriend and see if I can't put together a defense."

"Ex-girlfriend."

"Okay, ex-girlfriend. Let's see, your court date is April 23rd, right?" Inwardly grimacing, she wondered how long it would be before she'd be showing. She glanced at the red ink stain on her fingers. Boy, her emotions must really be on edge if ink reminded her of blood.

"You're going to talk to Carly?" Josh asked.

"Is there any reason I shouldn't?" She tried to read his mood.

Again his bearded face betrayed no clue. "No, but you know she'll make me look like the bad guy."

"You are the bad guy." Only half joking, Stephanie grinned. She did hope he wasn't too bad. After all, if he really had been following her . . . .

Josh shook his head. "Are you going to be a good little defense attorney or not?"

Stephanie gave him a narrowed-eye glare. He really was stretching the limits of her good nature. "There are always two sides to any story and good little defense attorneys always check out both."

"Well, just remember, while hers is a story, mine is the truth."

"I'll try to remember." She stood. "I'll walk you out, Josh, uh, Mr. Durrant."

"Josh."

"Follow me, Mr. Durrant."

His mouth twisted. "I'll do that, Miss Saunders."

Miss Saunders. How long would she be able to pass for a miss? "This way." She gestured with her hand. It shook. Quickly she dropped it to her side. "Let's get that appointment set with Deirdre."

"Okay. If you say so." He strode out through the conference room to the reception area. Stephanie followed with quick steps.

"Mr. Durrant needs another appointment. Set it in about a week," she told Deirdre.

The girl's frizzy blonde head bent over the appointment book. "Okey, dokey. How about April 8th at 10:00 a.m.?"

"Will you write that down for me on the back of one of Miss Saunders's cards?"

"I'd be glad to." Deirdre beamed up at him.

The sound of loud voices coming from Charles's upstairs office drew Stephanie's attention. She strained her ears to decipher what was being said, but Deirdre's loud chatter with Josh kept Stephanie wondering. The sharp pitch of both upstairs voices sounded angry and momentarily she wondered if Mr. Dawson had returned with Charles after breakfast.

If Mr. Dawson were indeed here, Stephanie had no desire to face him again. She nodded her good-bye to Josh and retreated to her office. Never in her life had she been this uncomfortable in her surroundings. Shoot. She'd never been so uncomfortable in her skin. She glanced at the pile of files on her desk and then turned to stare out the window. A sparrow perched on a branch of the tree outside. As Stephanie watched, the bird took flight, gliding effortlessly into the air. How Stephanie envied its freedom. She paced her office for several minutes.

She just had to get away, that was all there was to it; if in fact Mr. Dawson had returned and there was even the slightest chance he'd want to visit with her again, she knew she wouldn't be able to stand it. She looked out the window once more. Pretty nice day—just a little snow here and there—and her hip was feeling better. It would be a simple matter to just climb out and be gone. Deirdre wouldn't even know she was missing for a while. She'd leave a message on her phone for her clients to call back.

With her purse slung over her shoulder, she slid the window up, leaned out the open frame to check for passersby, and climbed through. Too bad she hadn't worn pants today.

Out on the sidewalk she eased her skirt back down.

"If you don't mind me saying, you have very nice legs," a voice behind her said.

Stephanie whirled around to behold a beaming Josh Durrant. Why was he still here? He'd had plenty of time to clear out. He'd probably been flirting with Deirdre. Well, of course, he had. What a ladies man. Stephanie would have to warn her secretary about him. "Actually, I do mind," she said.

Josh grinned. "Do you have something against doors?"

She knew her cheeks were blushing. "No. I just . . . just, oh, never mind. It's really none of your business."

"I guess you're right about that, but you can't blame me for admiring the view." He grinned again. Actually he leered again. She wanted to slap his handsome face, or the face she figured would be handsome under the beard.

"Don't you have somewhere you have to be?"

He scratched his head. "Really, no, not right now." He certainly did have beautiful hair, long though it was.

"Well, I do." Holding her head high, she marched to the curb and opened the door to her car.

"Oh, Miss Saunders," Josh called.

"What?" Stephanie shouted.

"You might want to check yourself in the mirror before you go any place important. Your slip's hanging down several inches in the back."

All the air seemed to escape from Stephanie's body. She felt faint and almost wished she could pass out to avoid further embarrassment, but she held her voice steady. "Thank you, Mr. Durrant. I'll try to be more conscious of my appearance in the future so you won't have to add that to your growing list of concerns."

"What a relief." He tipped an imaginary hat.

Shaking her head for Josh's benefit, Stephanie crawled in behind the wheel of her silver Honda, but she bit back the smile that tugged at the edges of her lips. Josh had said she had nice legs. Well, she did, of course, sort of, especially when they were lotioned and tanned. She gripped the steering wheel with knuckles that turned white. Stop it. She told herself. Josh was a criminal, well sort of, and she was pregnant. Her smile faded. But she was pregnant by a man she couldn't help but love—yes, love. Things could be a lot worse, she decided.

Wait a minute. Stephanie turned in her seat. Was that Todd's black Toyota Camry parked two spaces in front of where her car had been? She slowed her Honda and peered back through the rearview mirror. It was Todd's car. She recognized the "ToddCat" license plate. Where was he? Why was he here? Was he in the office waiting for her?

Suddenly a troublesome thought invaded her mind, forcing her to pull off the road and park alongside. Had it been Todd upstairs arguing with Charles?

CHAPTER 6

By the time Stephanie arrived at her condo, it was nearly noon. She'd wasted practically the entire morning. She had encountered Jessica Dawson—what an experience that had been—and she'd met Josh Durrant, another curious individual. Stephanie would have to start working on his case as soon as she got her head together. Well . . . probably sooner than that. It was going to take more time than Josh had before his trial for her to accomplish that task.

She guessed the judge would soon disqualify himself from Josh's case because of the obvious conflict of interest. She wondered why he hadn't done so immediately, but decided he had wanted to stay at least long enough to make sure she was assigned as Josh's counsel. The judge was counting on her inexperience to help him ensure that Josh got what he deserved. She'd just have to show the arrogant old grouch. Pondering why a judge's daughter had become involved with someone who couldn't even afford to pay his own legal expenses, she'd decided that parents seldom have control over their children's choices.

Strange how she could almost forget her own problems when she started thinking about the law. She guessed she really did enjoy competing in the cat and mouse games attorneys played for their clients. How would having a baby affect that?

She found the condo key in her purse and pushed the door open a crack. A flowery aroma met her senses, and for a moment she wondered if someone wearing strong perfume had been in her home. She gasped, thinking of the person in the white truck who may or may not have been following her. Would that person wear perfume that smelled like flowers? She dug in her purse again. Her fingers found the pepper spray a police buddy had acquired for her. Armed and ready to run at any moment, she pushed the door wider and stared.

Resting on her coffee table, both end tables, her television set and kitchen table were several dozen innocent looking arrangements of long-stemmed red roses. She dropped the pepper spray back into her purse.

A card protruded from one of the bouquets. Stephanie plucked it from its plastic holder. "Marry me?" it said. "I love you. Dinner tonight? Todd."

Stephanie flopped onto her sofa. How easy it would be to marry Todd. What girl wouldn't want to? He was handsome, rich, and most of all, kind. And she loved him. But, could she trust him? What was he doing talking to her boss, no, actually arguing with her boss? Maybe it wasn't Todd. After all, she'd just heard voices. Todd could have come to see her, and since she'd climbed out the window, maybe she'd missed him.

Leaning forward to sniff one of the roses, Stephanie thought of another night Todd had given her roses. It was on their first date, the night after he'd watched her ride Kingston. He'd told her that, like herself, he was an orphan. They'd have to stick together because then they'd never be alone. She and Todd had been inseparable ever since.

She leaned back against the soft cushions on her couch. Of course he hadn't lied to her—about anything—and it probably hadn't even been him arguing in Charles's office. She glanced around the room at all the flowers. He must really want to marry her. She walked to her phone and dialed his cell. It went straight to voice mail. Was Todd still with Charles? No, that couldn't have been him.

She called her office to tell Deirdre that she'd be back after an extended lunch.

"I didn't even see you leave," Deirdre said.

"You were on the phone," Stephanie fibbed. "Is there still someone with Charles?"

Stephanie held her breath.

"I had to run some papers to court so I asked Paul to answer the phone. Of course, he wondered where you were." She sounded smug. "Since I've been back it's been pretty quiet. Do you want me to ring you through to Charles?"

"No!" Stephanie blurted.

"A little cranky today, are we?" While Deirdre was always respectful of Charles and Paul, the girl never gave Stephanie the same consideration.

"Sorry," Stephanie returned. She really wasn't and wished she could come up with a smart comeback to put Deirdre in her place. But Stephanie was just too tired to think of anything right then. Actually she doubted she'd have done it anyway.

In her bedroom in front of her full-length mirror Stephanie shed her sweater and skirt and noted that Josh had in fact been correct. She had torn her slip when she'd climbed out of the window. Her face went hot when she thought of how insufferable he'd been when he'd pointed it out. She tossed the ruined slip into the trash can. All at once an overwhelming desire came over her to go see Kingston. She could think straight around the horses. Hurriedly she dressed in breeches, boots, a turtleneck sweater, and parka, and headed for her car, happy that her hip injury hadn't held her back any longer than it had.

She'd selected one of the roses from her bouquets and placed it on the seat of her Honda as she drove to the stable. She smiled when she glanced at it and allowed herself to luxuriate in thoughts of a happy marriage to Todd. She still couldn't envision a baby in the picture, but contemplation of Todd and her together did give her comfort—at least the man she hoped was Todd. Stop it, she told herself. She knew the real Todd.

Halter over her shoulder, she headed for the pasture to bring Kingston in. He raised his head from the dried winter grass when he saw her and started walking forward. What a fine horse he was—tall and strong. He was the Todd of the horse herd. How handsome he was, how much fun. He seemed to understand her every need. She could talk to him for hours and he'd always make her see the bright side. She realized that although she'd started thinking about Kingson, she'd ended up focusing on Todd. That happened a lot. She chuckled to herself.

So what if Todd had lied to her about what had happened at his cabin? Maybe he'd slipped up and was afraid to tell her because he didn't want to lose her. Could she accept a lie if he'd lied for a good reason? But Todd wasn't lying.

She cross-tied Kingston in the saddling area and gave him a good brushing. Then she stretched up to place the saddle on his high back. He pinned his ears when she pulled the girth tight. She laughed and rubbed his shoulder to coax him from his bad mood. A lot of horses were cinchy.

Stephanie warmed Kingston up in the covered arena at a walk, trot and canter. Then took him over a series of jumps. He seemed to fly over the obstacles, free like the sparrow she'd noticed earlier that day. She took him around again. If only she could stay astride Kingston forever and never have to face what lay ahead. Maybe if she missed a jump and fell, there'd be no baby. Allowing that thought to formulate for only a moment, Stephanie grimaced. She could never allow herself to ponder something so evil. No way could she murder the innocent child she now carried.

All too soon, Kingston's labored breathing signaled that her ride must come to an end. She reined the gelding toward the front of the arena where she'd first seen Todd. She could visualize him standing there as he had nearly five months before. Wait. There was someone there. Her heart leaped as she realized it really was Todd.

She and her horse approached at a canter and she raised her hand in greeting as she pulled Kingston to a stop.

"I love watching you ride," he said. "It's like you and Kingston are one. I wish you and I were. Have I given you enough time to decide to marry me?"

She slid off the horse and rushed into Todd's outstretched arms. She did love this man and was going to believe him because she wanted to. For once in her life she would be impulsive—just let her heart rule. Go with the flow, as Deirdre would say. Was she quoting Deirdre now? That was unsettling.

Todd drew Stephanie close and bent to kiss her. Tingles crept through her body. She loved him despite what he might have done. His eyes shone with love. They wouldn't lie to her.

"I have something for you," he said and dropped to one knee.

"You mean besides all those beautiful flowers?" She could barely catch her breath.

He pulled a small velvet-covered box from his pocket and held it up. "I love you, Stephanie. Will you do me the honor of becoming my wife?"

Now this was how Stephanie had pictured the moment. The man she loved on one knee, offering his love to her forever, her favorite horse close by.

Kingston nickered and tossed his head as if nodding approval.

Stephanie and Todd laughed.

"Well, at least he has the right answer. How about you? Say yes. Don't think. Just say yes."

Stephanie glanced from horse to man—two awesome specimens in their own right.

"Yes," she whispered.

"Was that really a yes?" Todd stood and threw his arms around Stephanie. "It was a yes, wasn't it? Let's get married right away. I don't want to wait. I'll move in with you."

Under the circumstances, she guessed a quick wedding was the way to go, probably why Todd had suggested it. She let disappointment creep into her mind, but only for a moment.

Like most girls she wanted to be queen for a day. She wanted the white dress, flowers, photographs, the beautiful reception where all her friends would come to fawn over her. Wait. She didn't have any friends, only those people she worked with. Somehow she couldn't picture Deirdre as her Maid of Honor.

Actually a quick, no fuss wedding would be better. "You'd give up your beautiful cabin and move into my cramped condo?" she asked Todd, instead of hinting at what she'd been thinking.

"You bet. I don't want you driving those winding mountain roads every morning, and I'll be happy just being with you." He gave her a hug. "I know someone who wants to rent the cabin. You say the word and I'll give him a call."

"Well, I've always wanted a roommate." Stephanie snuggled against his solid chest and sighed. She hadn't been this happy in weeks. She felt comfortable with her decision to marry Todd.

"A roommate?" He leaned back to stare at her.

"A husband might even be better." She grinned. Actually, after what had happened in the cabin, she didn't know if she ever wanted to go back, let alone live there. Todd was right, he should move in with her after they were married.

Todd still held the velvet-covered box in his hand. "So, do you want this ring, or shall I take it back to Wal-Mart?"

She punched him playfully in the belly. "Give it to me tonight at dinner when my hands are clean, okay?"

"That's a deal."

"But don't lose it."

"Never," he said and returned the box to his pocket.

They led Kingston into a wash stall and unsaddled him. Stephanie groomed one side of the horse while Todd took care of the other. Then they switched sides to critique each other's work.

"So when shall we get married? Tomorrow?" Todd peeked under Kingston's neck.

"Tomorrow? What's the hurry?" Stephanie asked, as she would have under normal conditions. Of course, she knew they had a time deadline but didn't think they had to get married super fast.

"I don't want a child of mine born to someone who isn't my wife." Todd moved around the horse to stand by Stephanie.

Glancing down at her still-flat belly, she said, "I think we have a little time."

He placed his hands on her shoulders. "Come on, let's get married soon."

Stephanie had seen a classy white suit at Dillards the other day, and she guessed she could put up with Deirdre and Charles for a quick ceremony, maybe even at the courthouse. They could all go to dinner afterwards and have a little celebration. Paul would probably be out of town, like always.

Touching Todd's hand, Stephanie said. "Give me a week, okay? A girl likes to dream about her wedding for a while, and I'd like to do some planning. Who should we invite and where should we hold it?"

"Let's elope. Let's drive to Vegas and not inform anyone. It will be our special day. We could tell everyone that we secretly married back in January and then no one will be counting on their fingers when we enlighten them about the baby. I know it's old fashioned, but this is my baby and you're going to be my wife. I want it all legal." He pulled her into an embrace and held her tightly. It was almost as if he were afraid he was going to lose her, or the baby. It was kind of sweet—a little out of character for Todd—but sweet.

"I'm not going anywhere, you know, and neither is the baby." She leaned back in his arms.

"I know," he said. "I just love you so much, and you shouldn't blame me for being anxious. In addition to everything else you are, have you looked in the mirror lately?"

How sweet was that? As a matter of fact she had looked in the mirror just hours ago and the thought of it now made her think of her embarrassing encounter with Josh. It really would be a comfort to have Todd around all the time. She'd never have to worry about entering a lonely apartment again. He'd always be there to protect her. "Okay. Let's get married in a week. I'm anxious, too." She snuggled against him.

"And let's just keep it to ourselves. There'll be plenty of time to tell everyone after we're married and then we won't tell the exact date." With a finger under her chin he tipped her head to kiss her lips.

She kissed him back before saying, "Okay, but I feel like I just have to tell someone."

He gave her a quick squeeze. "You can tell Kingston."

Giggling, Stephanie drew away, and walking to the horse's head, she unsnapped his cross-ties. "I think he already knows. I believe he's been eavesdropping." She bent the gelding's ear and whispered into it. "Don't tell anyone, okay?"

Part of the fun of being engaged was sharing your happiness with loved ones. Besides Todd, Stephanie had no loved ones. So yes, she'd probably come back later and discuss everything with Kingston.

"That's the spirit." Todd clipped the lead rope to the gelding's halter. "I'll bet our secret's safe with him. Someday I'm going to buy you this horse."

She nudged Todd with her shoulder. "You'll never have enough money, especially now that we're getting married. By the way, how much did you spend on that gorgeous ring?" As much as she wanted Kingston, she knew she had to face reality. Her chances of ever owning him were fading by the month. She touched her stomach.

"The cost of the ring is none of your business, and haven't you heard that two can live as cheaply as one?" He led the horse forward.

"How about three? Can they live as cheaply as one?" She followed.

"Three's only one more than two." He looked back at her and winked. "I've done the math."

She sighed. "It appears that's not all you did. And at pretty remarkable odds, too."

Todd slapped his hand over his heart and staggered a few steps like he was having a heart attack. "You sure know how to hurt a guy."

Stephanie grinned.

"And speaking of guys," Todd nodded toward Kingston, "where does this fellow go?"

"Let's put him in here." She opened the gate to a stall. "He stays in the pasture in the day and his stall at night."

She removed the horse's halter and stroked his neck for a moment. "Good night, Kingston, my love," she said upon leaving.

"Should I be jealous?" Todd asked.

"You bet."

He breathed an exaggerated sigh. "I guess I'll have to learn to handle it."

After leaving Kingston, Stephanie and Todd strolled hand in hand along the walkway in front of the stalls.

"That's got to be the saddest looking horse I've ever seen." Todd stopped short, staring at the abandoned mare Stephanie had visited earlier in the month.

"I know. She's had a tough time." In spite of all the good feed, Riskie didn't look much better than she had the last time Stephanie saw her.

"What happened to her?" Todd placed his arms across the top rails of the mare's stall and stared.

"It's a long story. I'll tell you what I know about her later, but, among other things, she's pregnant."

"She's pregnant?"

"Yep. She's pregnant like me." She felt Todd's arm wrap around her shoulder. "I'm so sorry, Stephanie. Can you ever forgive me?"

She leaned into him. "From what you've said, neither of us is to blame and as long as we're together . . . ." She trailed off, hoping he'd pick up where she'd left off.

"We're in this together, Stephanie, and you have my word. I will never do anything to hurt you ever again." His warm hand moved from her shoulder to her neck. It tingled where he touched her. He did have a way with words.

"I'm not hurt, I'm pregnant." She flashed him a grin. "And look here, the mare's not complaining. I guess if she can do it all by herself, I can do it with you at my side."

"And you'll have me there the whole way." He chuckled. "You never can tell, maybe we'll like being parents."

She scratched her head. "I wouldn't go that far." She still couldn't get excited about being a mother.

Dark eyes twinkling, Todd said, "You're going to be a great mom, and I'll try like crazy to be the best husband and dad ever."

"Then what more can I ask." She spoke with greater confidence than she felt.

"Nothing. I'm hoping."

"I wonder if they've scheduled the horse dentist to come do her teeth?" Stephanie unlatched the gate and stepped into the mare's stall.

"Whose teeth?" Todd followed.

"The mare's."

"There's a dentist for horses?"

"Of course. I told Kathleen I'd pay for it because no one else will stand the expense and her teeth are horrible." She rubbed the mare's neck.

Todd placed a tentative hand on the mare's back. "How do you know?"

"I looked."

"You looked in her mouth?" Todd sounded as if that were the strangest thing he'd ever heard, and for a split second Stephanie wondered why he didn't know about horses' teeth since horses were why she'd met him in the first place.

"Yes. That's where her teeth are." She'd play along. Surely he was joking.

"Do they do fillings and crowns on horses?"

"Of course not, silly. They just grind off the teeths' sharp edges so horses can eat better. I'm guessing that's one of the reasons this mare's so thin. But you know all this stuff, don't you? Aren't you the guy who wanted to buy a horse that first day we met?"

"Yeah, sure, but that doesn't mean I know all about them, and you're thin, too." Todd grinned. "Do you need your teeth done?"

"My teeth are fine. See." She opened her mouth so he could take a look. She guessed there were a lot of people who bought horses on a whim.

He gathered her into his arms and kissed her.

She wasn't sure she was used to this new hovering Todd, but figured it would be fun growing accustomed.

Noting that he stared over her head at the mare, Stephanie asked, "What's wrong?"

"How far along do you think she is?" he asked.

"Probably about eight months." Stephanie peered back over her shoulder. "It's hard to tell, though. I'm guessing she was last with the stallion in about August, but it's all guesswork—nothing that would stand up in court." She babbled on while Todd continued to stare at the mare.

"You're not going to look like that when you're eight months pregnant, are you?"

She pulled a pouty face. "Probably much worse. Will you still love me?"

"You bet." He hugged her again.

"Well, goodbye Miss Risky Business," Stephanie told the mare as she and Todd left her stall.

"You call her Risky Business?" Todd asked.

"Yes, or just Riskie—probably best spelled with an 'ie' since she's a girl."

"Good name."

Todd and Stephanie continued walking to the parking lot where Todd's Camry waited next to her Honda.

"You go first," Todd told her. "I'll follow you home. Then let's get some dinner to celebrate, and, of course, there's something I have to give you." He patted his pocket.

"You're on."

She was still smiling as she backed out of the parking lot. She caught a glimpse of something white in her rearview mirror and jerked her head around in time to see a white pickup disappear down the road.

Oh come on, she told herself. White pickups were about as common as maggots on a corpse. Maggots on a corpse? Why had she come up with that? She shivered and watched in her mirror to make sure it was Todd's black Toyota that followed and not a pickup the color of bleached bones in the sand. No, darn it—white sails in the sunset, billowing clouds over mountaintops, whipped cream on a banana split. She shook her head, but all she could picture in her mind's eye were the bleached bones—and she'd forgotten to ask Todd about his visit to her office.

CHAPTER 7

"Deirdre tells me you'd like next Monday off." Charles templed his fingers on his mahogany desk and leveled a stare at Stephanie. If she had ever wondered why her boss was so successful in court, cross-examining witnesses, she knew now. She felt as if he could see into her very soul where she kept the secret she and Todd shared.

Stephanie felt sweat form on her brow. "Yes. I'll work late on Friday, and I've called the court to make sure I don't have any cases scheduled, and I've contacted our conflict indigent defense counsel . . ." Stop it, she told herself. She had every right to ask for a day off. She deserved it. "Yes," she finished simply and straightened. She placed her hands on the arms of the leather chair on the opposite side of the desk and faced the matching, larger executive chair from which Stephanie's boss reigned.

Charles smiled, sort of. Actually, in his case it was probably the best he could do. "Of course you may take a vacation day on Monday. You've been working hard, and everyone deserves a day off every once in a while."

She took in a quick breath. Deserves a day off . . . He really could see into her soul. Her hand rose to cover the diamond ring hanging from the silver chain beneath her sweater. "I'll be back first thing Tuesday morning. Thanks, Charles, uh . . . Mr. Connelly."

"Oh, call me Charles. You're one of us now—a member of the firm, that is." Another hint of a smile. "I hope you're not traveling far away. I hear there's a huge storm blowing in this afternoon—strange for the first part of April. With luck it will have passed over by the weekend."

Stephanie set her jaw. Was Charles fishing for information? She'd watched him use this same tactic in court. Well, two could play this game, especially when one of them had so much to hide. "Not too far away," she said, intentionally offering no new information. Why did he even care what she did while away from the office? It was none of his business.

"So you'll have someone driving with you?" Charles smoothed his silk tie.

"I will."

"Good. Then I won't have to worry about you." He leaned back in his chair. The leather squeaked.

Worry about her? Would he really? It was a nice thought anyway. Maybe Charles was sincere in his concern about her welfare. She wished she could tell him where she was going and share her happiness with him as well as the others in the office.

When Charles had hired her last summer, she'd sensed that he liked her, but she'd never felt fully accepted in the office. She missed that and wondered how everyone would treat her when they found out about her marriage. Worse still, how would they act when it became evident why she'd rushed off and eloped? Maybe she and Todd could pull off the deception that they'd married in January if no one found out about this trip. But she wouldn't think about that now. She'd accomplished what she'd come for. She had Monday off, and she'd have to be satisfied with that. If she'd wanted a father figure in her life, she'd blown any possibility. Charles wouldn't like it if he found out she'd lied to him. She lowered her eyes. The expression on her face must have betrayed this disappointment.

"Is everything okay?" Charles's steely expression softened. "If you ever need someone to talk to . . . I hope you know you can always come to me."

Stephanie blinked. Had she heard correctly? Her voice almost broke when she said, "I'll remember that." What was wrong with her? Someone who is normally harsh suddenly treats her nice and she dissolves into tears? It must be hormones. Whatever was she going to do for the next seven months? Taking a deep breath, she mentally counted to ten. She had Todd. He was all she needed. Smiling now, she rose from the chair. "Since I'll be gone Monday, I better get back to work. But thank you."

Charles stood, too. "I mean it, Stephanie. I can be a good listener." He looked very distinguished and wise in his expensive dark suit and crisp white shirt.

"Well, with all your clients, I'm sure you've had lots of practice." She raised her chin. After a slight break in her facade of strength, the shield was back in place. She'd not weaken again.

At her desk a while later, she spent the rest of the morning reviewing files, answering phone calls and dictating pleadings, including a motion and order requesting that Judge Anderson be removed from Josh Durrant's case. She'd become so engrossed in her work that lunch time slipped by unnoticed. By four o'clock she wondered why her stomach kept growling.

A glance at her watch told her she had only three hours before Todd would pick her up for dinner at seven—just enough time to visit Kingston and squeeze in a ride, if weather permitted. Since she'd worked through lunch, she felt okay about leaving early. To quiet her stomach on the way to the barn, she devoured a stale breakfast bar she'd previously discarded in her car.

Stephanie studied the gray sky and wondered how much longer the storm would be held at bay. She figured her ride would be brief, but well worth the effort.

Still wearing the same brown sweater she'd selected that morning, she changed into breeches in the barn's cramped bathroom, noticing for the first time the snug waistband. With a frown, she pulled her hair into a low ponytail and shrugged into her parka.

For the first of April, it was unseasonably cold. Fortunately it was three full days before she and Todd would be leaving for Vegas. The weather would probably be better by then. Everything would. She'd be a bride, and even though a baby had never been on her list of priorities, its existence would be easier to face after she and its father were married.

As she walked toward Kingston's stall, she heard a voice, "I understand you'll be paying my bill."

"Excuse me?"

"The mare."

Stephanie had been so obsessed with her own problems that her mind had blocked out anything else. What was this stocky woman dressed in men's overalls talking about? "The mare?"

"Yeah. Kathleen told me you'd be paying for work on her teeth. I'm the horse dentist." She gestured with a tipped head down the row of stalls where she'd apparently just come from.

A light bulb finally flashed in Stephanie's tired brain. "Oh. I'm sorry. Of course. I'll get my checkbook. How much?"

"One hundred and twenty dollars. Make it out to Clara Little."

The "little" woman charged a big fee, but Stephanie had made a promise and she would keep it. After all she had Todd to stand by her. The mare had no one. She'd be the mare's Todd. "I'll be right back," she told Clara. One hundred twenty dollars from her account right now was quite a bit. Stephanie bet Clara wished the day had been warmer and her fee had perhaps reflected the fact that it had not. Oh well, it was only money.

"She might pick up some weight now," Clara said as Stephanie handed her the check. "The mare had an infected tooth which I pulled and sharp edges on several others," the horse dentist continued. "Poor old girl. Where did you get her?"

"Oh, she's not mine," Stephanie said quickly. Then squirmed like a traitor, but she was a better judge of horseflesh than to buy a horse like her. "I just felt sorry for her. She needs a break."

Clara placed her dental instruments in the back of her pickup. "Well, you're a good person. There's gotta be a place in Heaven for folks like you."

Yeah, sure. If only the woman knew. Stephanie was just this short of being an unwed mother. She couldn't help feeling some responsibility. She wondered how she'd acted that night. In her drugged state, had she contributed to what had happened? She shook her head. She didn't really want to know.

"I doubt that, but thanks for the thought." Stephanie raised her hand in parting and continued on to locate Kingston. She glanced toward his stall to determine if he were there, or out in the pasture. Her eyes fell on the sorrel mare who stood in one corner of her stall with her head down, her belly hanging even lower, if possible, than before. She looked pretty miserable. Clara had probably sedated her for the dental work and it was probably wearing off.

Stephanie opened the stall gate and stepped in. "How you doing, Riskie girl?"

The mare lifted her head and nickered.

A warm feeling flowed through Stephanie, as tears came to her eyes. "You're kind of a sweetheart, aren't you?" She drew Riskie's head into her arms and stroked her long nose. All at once she felt a closeness—actually more of a kinship—with this mother-to-be. Somehow she'd try to protect Riskie, as Todd would protect her.

She spent several more minutes with the mare before spotting Kingston standing by the gate to his pasture. "Hey, guy," she called and he whinnied, just as the mare had done. Stephanie vowed she'd continue to bring healthy treats in order to remain popular with the horse crowd. She felt for the alfalfa cubes in her parka pocket. Concerned that Riskie would choke until all of the sedation had worn off, she reluctantly decided against giving one to the mare.

"I'll see you, girl," she told Riskie as she headed off to fetch Kingston.

After tacking him up, Stephanie climbed on and they headed off at a brisk walk to the cross-country course. The footing on the course was still unsafe for jumping, but would be fine if she kept Kingston at a walk.

Head high, the gelding strutted around the snow-sprinkled field like the thoroughbred he was. During these precious moments on horseback Stephanie knew her problems would all but disappear, like the soon-setting sun. She reined Kingston back toward the covered arena where lights already shone. Drawing in a deep breath, she felt an excitement for life she hadn't experienced lately. Maybe everything would be all right after all.

Her heart raced when she noticed someone standing at the railing. That sweet Todd had come to pick her up. She waved and trotted Kingston forward to meet her intended.

She dropped from the saddle and led the horse toward the man at the rail, fully intending to leap into his arms, but when he turned around to face her, Stephanie stopped so abruptly that Kingston bumped into her.

"Oh," she stammered and drew away. The horse, apparently sensing he'd done wrong by entering her space, threw himself back into a rear.

"Whoa, boy. It's okay. Easy," she told Kingston. He lowered his head and let her pet him. With the gelding calmed, she turned to face the man who'd walked forward to assist her.

"What are you doing here?" she hissed.

"Apparently you were expecting someone else," Josh Durrant said, then reached forward to let Kingston sniff his hand.

"Apparently I was," Stephanie grumbled. "I repeat. Why are you here?" The better question was, why was she acting like this? He couldn't help it if she'd thought he was someone else. Could it be she was a little afraid of him? Maybe. She stepped closer to Kingston as if he could protect her.

"I'm sorry. I told you I had a friend who lives near here. I saw you riding and stopped to watch. I'm sorry if I upset you."

Looking directly into Josh's hypnotic green eyes, Stephanie straightened. "You didn't upset me."

His brow raised. "Good. Contrary to popular belief, I'm not all that bad."

Right now, standing here alone with him, she really wished she could believe his statement. "Tell that to Judge Anderson's daughter."

A slight smile touched his lips. "Guess I'm guilty until proven innocent, right?"

"Time will tell." She placed her foot in the stirrup and swung up onto Kingston where she felt much safer. The horse could run like an antelope. "I did request that a new judge be assigned."

"Good. I don't think I'd like jail much." He stuffed his hands into the pockets of his wool-lined Levi jacket.

"I really doubt they'd send you to jail for this particular offense, even if Judge Anderson remains on the case." She much preferred gazing down on Josh from Kingston's lofty back. The guy actually made her jumpy and she wasn't really sure it was his status as an accused criminal that accounted for all of her nervousness. "But you're right, it would be better to have another judge."

"Glad to hear you think I'm right about something." He grinned a fabulous smile, showing beautiful, straight teeth. Most of her clients had yellow, tobacco-stained teeth.

She knew he was trying to bring her guard down. If only he wasn't so good-looking, in his dangerous sort of way. She glanced at her watch. "Oh. I've got to go."

"Do you need help with the horse, putting him away or anything? We could discuss my case." Hands out of his pockets now, he took a step forward.

"No. I'm okay," she said a little too quickly, then gained control of her nerves and continued, "We'll discuss your case when you come into the office again. Too bad you already made your appointment. I know how you like visiting with Deirdre." She just couldn't help but egg him on.

He favored her with a sidelong glance. "Deirdre is cute. Not jealous, are you?"

Okay. Enough was enough. "Me jealous? Are you kidding? I have a really cute, intelligent boyfriend, who treats me like a queen." At least lately anyway, she thought. "I'm actually meeting him at seven tonight. That's why I have to hurry." If Josh knew she was pregnant he wouldn't be able to run away fast enough, she guessed. But he shouldn't be flirting with his attorney, anyway, and she shouldn't allow him to hang around her outside of the office . . . as if she'd had any choice.

"A boyfriend, huh? Darn." He walked by the side of her horse as they headed out of the arena.

"Yes, and if you don't mind me asking, don't you have enough trouble with women without upsetting your attorney? Besides, I don't date clients."

"I didn't ask you." His lips thinned.

He was exactly right. Stephanie felt her face go hot. Maybe his flirting was all in her head. How embarrassing. Her mind raced, searching for a safer subject. "I bet you don't know a thing about horses, so how could you help me with this one?"

"Don't bet. You'd lose. I've actually been around horses all my life."

"No you haven't."

"Yes, I have. Do you want me to prove it?"

"How?"

"I can ride this horse."

As much as Stephanie would have liked to see Kingston wipe that arrogant smile off Josh's face, Kingston wasn't hers to let others ride without his owner's permission, and she really didn't want to lose her position of power on the back of this big animal. "I've got to go," she repeated, nudging Kingston with her heel.

"You don't think I can do it, do you?"

Actually, she was afraid he could. Being able to ride a horse, especially this one, made him even more interesting. Interesting? He shouldn't have been anything to her, for more reasons than she could begin to count. "I really have got to go. As I said before, I'll see you in my office if you want to come in and talk about your case. Otherwise, I'll see you in court," she said in a tone that should have left no question in his mind that she was serious. Safely astride Kingston, she waited for Josh to leave.

He nodded a farewell. "Okay. I'll see you on the eighth." He started walking away, but turned back around. "Does your boyfriend know how lucky he is?"

Oh, brother. "Goodbye, Josh."

Looking one way, then the other, he said, "I really don't feel good about leaving you here alone. It will be getting dark soon and I'll bet it's going to snow. Can you leave the arena lights on as you leave, or do you have to turn them off?"

Many nights during the winter she finished riding after dark. She'd never been afraid. Maybe she'd been wrong. "The lights go on and off automatically. I imagine there'll be other people coming to ride soon in order to beat the storm. I'm surprised I've had the arena to myself this long."

"I really can help you with the horse." Josh sounded very sincere.

If he'd meant to hurt her, wouldn't he have hidden in the shadows and grabbed her when she wasn't aware? Now he had her thinking that if he left her alone, something bad just might happen here in the dark.

"Okay." She climbed off the horse. "You can stand watch if it makes you feel better. But don't get in the way. You'll just slow me down. And don't think that if you're nice to me I'll reduce my fee. The office does all of my billing."

Josh slid the stirrup irons up the leathers on the saddle.

Maybe he really did know what he was doing.

"I'm indigent, remember?" he said flatly.

"I keep forgetting." With a quick glance, she gave him the once-over—jeans, jacket, boots. With his beard and western clothing, all he needed was a Stetson to look like the Marlboro man. "You sure don't dress like you're poor, or act like it either."

"Attorneys are expensive." He loosened the saddle's girth. Then walked behind the horse and unhooked the girth from the other side and laid it across the saddle.

He was doing more work with the horse than she was. "Not that expensive. What is your story, anyway?" she asked.

"I'll come in for my appointment and then we can talk."

"You're not going to tell me, are you?" Maybe he was embarrassed.

She reached for the saddle, but he beat her to it and pulled it from Kingston's back. "Not unless I need to for my defense." He eased the saddle into the open tack closet, then took a brush from the top shelf.

"You don't talk like you're poor either."

"How does a poor person talk?" He handed her the brush.

"Like they haven't had an education." She stood like a statue.

"I never said I ain't had no schoolin'. I'm just short on dough." He nodded toward the brush while pointing at the horse.

"Why don't I believe you?" She began brushing Kingston.

"I take it as a bad sign when my attorney doesn't believe me." He replaced the horse's bridle with a halter.

"It probably is. Maybe you should remedy that?" She groomed Kingston so hard that he swung his head around, ears flattened.

"Sorry, boy," she whispered.

"You already told me I can't have that Charles guy," Josh said.

Stephanie glared at him, but he seemed not to notice.

"I think Deirdre likes it when I call, unlike some people I know." Josh reached for the brush. "You done?"

She shoved it at him.

He took it and, with a smile, nodded as if she'd done him a favor.

"Deirdre likes anything male," Stephanie continued, upset that she couldn't ruffle Josh. "The girl's in constant flirt mode," Stephanie said, retrieving Kingston's blanket from the locker.

Josh took it from her and put it on the horse. "Maybe you could learn something from Deirdre." He led Kingston from the saddling area. "Where does this horse go?"

Stephanie hurried to stay ahead as she led the way. "I know how to flirt, but I told you I have a boyfriend, and I don't date clients, especially ones who beat up their girlfriends." She held up a hand. "I know. I know. You didn't ask me."

He smiled. "Right. And I didn't beat her up. I told you what happened." Once inside the stall, Josh took the gelding's halter off, patting the big horse as he found hay in the corner.

"Yes. You told me what happened." She backed out of the way while Josh secured the chain on the gate.

"You don't believe me?" Josh put the halter in the closet along with the saddle and grooming tools.

Stephanie looked on. "I want to. I have to defend you."

"What's this boyfriend of yours like? He's perfect, I suppose. He's always treated you with love and respect?"

"What? That's none of your business." Whoa. She was pregnant because of Todd. The law might say he'd actually raped her—something much worse than Josh had done to his girlfriend. "I didn't say that."

"Yeah. See. I may not be that bad of a guy. Now if that boyfriend of yours were out of the way . . . ." He put the lock on the closet door and dropped the key into Stephanie's hand.

"Don't even think that. You wouldn't do anything to . . . ." She started off toward the parking lot.

He grabbed her arm. ". . . to what? Hurt him? What kind of a man do you think I am?"

She twisted away. "I don't know. That's the problem. I guess we'll find out in court." She walked faster, careful not to step in any mud puddles.

At the car, her hands shook so violently that she dropped the keys when she tried to unlock the door.

Josh picked them up and completed the task. "You don't need to be afraid of me, you know. I'd never hurt you."

She wished she could be sure. There was something so unsettling about him and she didn't think it was his broad shoulders or his total masculinity. "You better not," she said and slid into the safety of her Honda. She locked the door and opened the window a crack. "I'll meet with you in the office for appointments, but I don't want to see you around here anymore."

"Oh, you won't see me." His lip curled.

"That's not funny, Josh. I mean it. Don't come here anymore, okay?"

He stroked his beard. "You know I have a friend who lives nearby."

"Nearby, not here." Stephanie sounded stern, but she meant to.

"Well, okay, I can take a hint." He lifted his chin.

"I believe it was more than a hint."

He placed a hand on the roof of her car. "Are you sure this boyfriend of yours is a good guy?"

Stephanie drew a deep breath. "Why would you ask that?"

"Just making conversation."

"Well, don't."

"Be careful, okay? I'd probably feel bad if something happened to you. Good attorneys are hard to find."

CHAPTER 8

Snowflakes rested on the windshield of Stephanie's Honda, then quickly disappeared as she drove home from the stable. This must have been the storm Charles had mentioned earlier. Talk about a change in the weather.

Despite her need to watch the road ahead, her eyes were continually drawn to the rearview mirror. Was that Josh following her? She had no way of telling on a night like this.

Safely at home, she had only thirty minutes to prepare for her date with Todd. They had planned to drive to Salt Lake City for dinner, but she wondered if they still would, now that it was snowing. She dressed rapidly in black slacks, boots and a red sweater, and tried on her form-fitting black parka to see if it would still fit. Although it zipped easily, Stephanie knew that this particular parka's days were numbered.

In spite of the upset in her life right now, a smile crept onto her face. She had to admit that she was excited about the night and especially anxious to see Todd.

The doorbell rang at seven o'clock precisely. No one was more prompt than Todd—just one of the many things she appreciated about him.

She raced to the door and opened it to meet his broad grin. "I'm a lucky man," he said upon entering. "You look absolutely beautiful." He reached for her left hand and held it up for inspection.

Counting on their dinner being out-of-town, Stephanie had worn the engagement ring on her finger like a real bride. She gave Todd a warm smile.

"Perfect," Todd brought her hand to his lips. Then he pulled her into an embrace. They stood in each other's arms for several minutes, as if taking strength from their togetherness.

After conquering the snowy roads out of the canyon, Todd declared that freeway driving to Salt Lake City would be easy. Besides, they'd be at the restaurant in less than an hour.

"Let's take my car," Stephanie said, slipping out of Todd's embrace. "I haven't removed my snow tires yet, and remember, you did. Not one of your best decisions." She playfully nudged him.

"Don't rub it in. I had that flat, remember, and since my snow tires were shot, I decided to get new regular tires because I thought summer was coming." He put his arm on her shoulder. "Okay, let's take your car. When you're right, you're right."

Glad for her Honda's front-wheel drive and snow tires, Stephanie watched the snow fall and couldn't believe that just three hours ago she'd been riding Kingston. She turned to study Todd's handsome profile. She had never before noticed how long his dark lashes were.

"What," he said, apparently feeling her gaze.

"Oh, nothing. I was just thinking that you're kinda handsome."

He chuckled and took her hand. "I guess I'd have to be tolerably attractive to keep company with you."

She glanced out the window again. There were plenty of other cars on the highway, but they were going slower now as visibility lessened. "Do you think this weather will keep us from going to Las Vegas on Saturday?"

"Nothing could keep me from that." He winked at her. "Actually I think we'll be okay. This storm should pass over before we leave and I don't think there's another one due until next week. Can you believe it? It's April. Oh well, by that time we'll be happily married." He squeezed her hand.

Her heart raced. She really would be a married woman by next week at this time. She wiggled in her seat to relieve the pressure caused by the tight waistband. Thank goodness. Then another thought occurred to her.

"Will you be able to make it back up the canyon?" She almost suggested he stay at her condo that night, but then thought better of it. Silly as it sounded in her condition, she didn't want things to get out of hand.

"Oh sure. I've driven in worse. I was just thinking, though, in a few days I won't ever have to leave you again."

Stephanie tingled all over. Todd said all the right things. He loved her and he respected her. She knew now for a certainty that he was as much of a victim of the drug-enhanced night as she was. He would have never done anything knowingly to hurt her. She basked in that knowledge for the rest of the drive.

They pulled into the parking lot at the Market Street Grill. Tonight they would take advantage of the valet. Todd came around and took her arm as a young man from the restaurant slid into the driver's seat.

Inside they stomped snow off their feet. Todd's dark hair was flecked with snow, as she was sure hers was. She shook her head.

Although they would sacrifice the intimacy that a table would have provided, they elected to sit at the food bar. Not only would they avoid the hour wait, but they could catch the action of the waiters behind the scene of this wonderful restaurant.

Hand in hand Stephanie and Todd sat upon high stools and watched across the bar. Waiters and waitresses dressed in black slacks and vests balanced heavily loaded trays above their heads and dodged one another as they headed out to wait on tables.

"I've booked a suite at the Bellagio," Todd said.

"The Bellagio? Wow! Isn't that kind of expensive? Not that I'm complaining." She watched as a tiny waitress loaded a tray with five entrees and hefted it up over her head. Stephanie was glad she'd gone to law school. She knew that if she were in the waitress's position, the entrees would have been splattered all over the customers. She grinned at Todd.

"No. This will be our honeymoon. Nothing's too expensive for that." He too watched the tiny waitress negotiate the turn and head off with her entrees to parts unknown.

"You're sweet." Stephanie touched his arm.

They stared into each other's eyes, neither seemingly willing to turn away.

"Hello. Welcome to Market Street Grill. Oh I'm sorry." A dark haired young man, probably a college student, stood at the front of the counter, pencil and small notepad in hand. "Are you ready to order?"

Stephanie pulled her hand from Todd's arm and sat straight. "I'd like the halibut, boiled potatoes, garden salad with the house dressing on the side and a diet coke."

The waiter's big brown eyes opened wide. "Oh. You've been here before."

Todd chuckled and, putting his arm around Stephanie's shoulder, pulled her close. "She's a quick study."

"Yes she is," the waiter smiled. "And for you, sir."

"I'll have prime rib, hmm, I think, medium."

The waiter noted Todd's choice on the pad. "Boiled potatoes, rice or fries?"

"I think I'll have rice—no, fries." Todd winked at Stephanie. "No. I'll have boiled potatoes."

"Garden salad or clam chowder?"

Todd thought for a moment. The waiter glanced at Stephanie and smiled.

"He's not a quick study."

Todd squeezed her even closer. "Say, that's enough out of you." He grinned at Stephanie, then looked back at the waiter. "I believe I'll have the chowder."

"And what to drink?"

"What do you have?"

The waiter and Stephanie glanced at each other, and Stephanie started to giggle. The young man tried to keep from laughing, but ended up covering his smile with his notepad.

"I'll have a regular coke with lime," Todd said as he playfully poked Stephanie in the ribs with his free hand.

The waiter nodded. "I'll be right back with your drinks." He escaped quickly, probably before he erupted into full-blown laughter, or maybe he was embarrassed by their actions, which made heat flow to Stephanie's cheeks.

"Did I mention we'll be on the Bellagio's thirty-sixth floor, that's the very top, overlooking the fountains?" Todd said.

"I love you." Stephanie lay her head against his shoulder. She didn't care what the waiter, or anyone else, thought, although for a minute she considered how much this weekend really would cost them. Oh, well, it wouldn't be as much as a formal reception and would require so much less work and planning.

"I love you, too," Todd said in a low voice that made Stephanie know he really meant it.

Stephanie watched another waitress tear parsley off a large stock and place the small pieces on the artistic-looking entrees, then the girl filled up little containers with salad dressing, tarter sauce, etc. "I can hardly wait for the weekend," Stephanie said, momentarily wishing she could cook.

Todd drank some of the coke the waiter had silently brought. "Then you'll be mine and no one can steal you from me."

Briefly remembering Josh's words, if something happened to Todd, Stephanie was silent for a moment.

"Then you'll be mine," Todd repeated and nudged her shoulder.

She smiled at him. "It'll be great. Then we'll be together forever." Nothing was going to happen to either of them. She wouldn't allow it.

The waiter brought Stephanie's salad and Todd's chowder. He tasted some of her salad and she tasted his chowder. Soon they'd be sharing everything, including a baby.

Her heart pounded when she thought of a baby. She was not ready to be a mother. She wasn't sure she ever wanted to be one. At least she and Todd would be married soon and then their secret could come out. What would Charles say? Who would take over for her when she went on pregnancy leave? Who would care for the infant when she went back to work, and how would she keep her wits about her after a sleepless night up with a newborn? What a fine mess she'd gotten herself into. Well, that wasn't exactly right, but she was in a mess anyway.

Todd offered her another spoonful of chowder and she took it, although the delicious soup almost caught in her throat. She'd try not to let thoughts of the baby spoil this night, or especially this weekend. What would it be like to share a bed with Todd when she wasn't doped?

She glanced at him—that jaw, his straight aristocratic nose, the dark hair that fell across his brow. It probably wouldn't be too bad, not bad at all, she decided.

The waiter brought their entrees, which they shared, visiting back and forth. They discussed how early they'd leave on Saturday, when they'd actually get married, what live shows they might attend afterward, and how much they looked forward to just being together.

Dinner was so perfect that they temporarily forgot about the weather. It wasn't until they walked outside to wait for the valet that Stephanie expressed her concern.

"It's really snowing hard, isn't it? Maybe we should have stayed closer to home tonight."

Todd put her arm through his and walked her to the car that had been brought around for them. "We'll be okay. Hondas are good on slick roads, and I'm a great driver."

Hurriedly she jumped in the car and watched as he scurried around through the snow to climb in beside her. "I know you're a good driver. It's the other drivers who worry me."

"I won't let anything happen to you, I promise." He put the car in gear.

The tires spun a little as they climbed a slight incline out of the parking lot, but then finally grabbed hold.

At times, especially recently, Stephanie dozed during their drives, but not tonight. She kept her eyes glued to the road, and once she noticed the slippery surface she clung onto the armrest until her hand ached.

"So how was your day today?" Todd asked, as if trying to keep her mind off the treacherous road.

"It was really busy but I skipped lunch so I was able to leave early and go riding." Thinking back, it was hard to imagine that it hadn't been snowing then.

Todd adjusted the windshield wipers to a faster speed. "How much longer do you think you should be riding?"

Stephanie felt anger heat the back of her neck. That darn baby again. Why was it always her that had to sacrifice for a child she didn't even want? The words as long as I darn well please formed in her mind but she said, "For a while longer. I've known women who've ridden right up to their delivery date, but I'll stop before that."

"Good," Todd said.

Stephanie glared at him but knew he couldn't see her in the dark.

There were far more cars on the highway than Stephanie figured possible on such a night. It seemed that she and Todd weren't the only people who ignored storm warnings.

"If I'd known you were going to ride today, I'd have come to see you." Todd kept his eyes on the highway, which relieved Stephanie. He really was a good driver.

"That would have been nice, but guess who showed up?" Somehow Stephanie knew she'd feel better if she told Todd about Josh.

"Who?"

"My client, Josh Durrant."

The car swerved and Stephanie gasped.

Todd quickly regained control. "What was he doing there?"

Stephanie stared at him unable to believe his uncharacteristic reaction. "He said he has a friend who lives in the area."

"And you believe him? Give me a break." Todd grasped the steering wheel tighter.

Apparently telling Todd about Josh had been a mistake. But why should it have been? She'd always figured he would respect her judgment. "Josh could have a friend nearby," she said. "He was very nice, actually very protective."

"I'll bet he was. Use your head, Stephanie. He's a suspected criminal."

She always used her head and she didn't appreciate his inference that she wouldn't. She felt anger bubble inside her. "You don't get to tell me what to do."

Todd blinked. "I'm sorry, Steph. I just worry about you." He glanced at her tentatively as if testing to see if she were going to remain upset.

As sweet as Todd was most of the time, it was hard to stay mad at him for long. "I'm sorry, too, but don't worry about me. I won't let myself get into something I can't control." The words were barely out of her mouth when she realized that hadn't always been the case.

"Think about what you're saying, Stephanie," he said. "Neither of us could have predicted what happened that night at my house."

"When you're right, you're right." Stephanie repeated his words of surrender. She felt guilty about growling at Todd, and wondered why she'd been so ready to do it. Her concern about Todd's reaction to Josh's visit also resurfaced. She could blame hormones for her outburst, but he had no such excuse.

It was ten o'clock before they got back to Stephanie's condo. Todd pulled her Honda into an extra, uncovered parking stall next to her carport where they'd left his Toyota. Many of the other cars in the lot were blanketed with snow, but his had escaped the onslaught. The wind had apparently cleared away the snow on his car that had been there earlier.

Placing her hand on Todd's arm, Stephanie turned in her seat to address him. "Are you absolutely certain you can make it up the canyon tonight?"

Todd shut the car off and said in a western drawl, "My dear, you're looking at a guy who's driven miles on slippery roads and who owns one heck of a car capable of coming out of that canyon pushing snow with its bumper."

"Wow," Stephanie said in an awed voice. "I'm impressed. Maybe we should have taken your car tonight."

"Yours was probably better on the icy highways, but I'll be fine."

"We could trade cars for tonight, if you want."

He took her hand and squeezed it. "I'll be fine." He was silent for a moment and then continued, "And just think, if I'm all packed by Saturday, I won't have to drive up there for a while."

"That will be great." She grinned. "Because, like I said earlier, I've never had a roommate before." She always enjoyed teasing him about being her roommate. Of course he'd be much more than that, and she found herself looking forward to it.

"Hmm," was all he said, and she felt a little slighted.

Leaving the warmth of the car, he jumped out and backed his Toyota from Stephanie's space. He left his car sitting behind other parked cars beneath the carport while he returned to her Honda and pulled it into the appropriate space.

"I'll walk you up." He climbed back out of the Honda, shuffling around through the snow to help her out.

He locked her car and dropped the keys into his pocket. He always unlocked the door to her condo for her.

At the top of the stairway, just outside her door, he drew her into his arms and playfully hugged her. "Roommate, huh? Well, this roommate will be expecting lots of kisses."

She giggled and kissed him, not feeling slighted anymore. "And you'll get them." She peeked around his shoulder to make sure they didn't have an audience. She stiffened.

A white truck had pulled to the curb across the street.

"What's wrong?" Todd leaned away from her. "Are you out of kisses already?"

"The white truck. It's over there." She pointed.

"What?"

"Look over there. Do you see it? Isn't that a white truck under the sycamore tree?"

Todd's jaw tightened and his eyes narrowed. "I've had just about enough." He started down the stairs. "You stay here. I'm going to get to the bottom of this. I don't want him following you anymore."

"No, Todd. Leave it alone. I'll tell someone at the police department tomorrow."

"And have this guy deny everything. I'm putting an end to it right now." He was at the bottom of the stairs.

"I wish you wouldn't . . . ." Her eyes flew to the white truck which was pulling away from where it had parked.

"The coward." Todd raced to his car.

Stephanie ran down the stairs after Todd.

The white truck swerved onto the road.

"Todd, don't. Please stop."

"I love you," he mouthed as he drove his car out of the parking lot just ahead of her.

"I love you too, Todd. Please don't leave."

But he was gone, following the white truck as it gained speed down the road.

Stephanie watched in horror as both vehicles slid around the corner and disappeared in the distance.

She realized she was shaking and headed for her car. She'd follow them. She reached for the latch on the door. It was locked. She fumbled through her purse, spilling its contents into the snow. Her heart sinking, she remembered her keys were in Todd's pocket.

Scooping up her damp belongings, she dashed to the curb, peering down the road on which the vehicles had disappeared. Shivering, she climbed the stairs to her condo and choked back a sob.

For Todd's benefit, she'd earlier hidden a spare key to her condo behind a loose brick beneath the windowsill. Glancing around, she retrieved it and opened the door.

The warmth of her home greeted her as she threw herself onto the couch, drawing a wool throw around her. Still shaking, she grabbed the phone from the end table and quickly dialed Todd's cell phone.

It rang seven times before switching to voice mail. She heard Todd's recorded voice and tears flooded her eyes. Where was he? She drew the blanket tighter around her.

She grabbed the remote and watched Leno for a few moments before dialing Todd again. No Todd, again only his recorded message. She leaped from the couch and began pacing.

What was that? Her blood seemed to freeze in her veins. Off in the distance she heard sirens—one, then another, then it seemed like hundreds.

She dashed to her study and dumped the desk drawer onto a chair, searching for where she'd left the extra key to her car. No luck. Where had she put it? Oh, yes. She remembered now. The cookie jar—she'd put it in the cookie jar—inappropriately named in her case since the jar never contained cookies. She hurried back into the kitchen, grabbing the phone as she ran. She pressed the quick dial button and listened for Todd to answer. Please God. She counted the rings. One, two, three, four, five. "Hello," Todd said.

Her knees buckled and she collapsed onto the couch. Thank Heavens. He was okay. "Todd. Todd. Where are you?" Her voice broke.

"This is Officer Christopherson. Who's calling please?" His voice sounded solemn.

Stephanie knew Officer Kent Christopherson. "Kent, this is Stephanie Saunders. What's wrong? Where's Todd?"

The officer cleared his throat. "Stephanie. Uh . . . I'm , I'm so sorry. I'm afraid there's been an accident."

CHAPTER 9

Stephanie's knees wobbled like those of a newborn foal. She steadied herself against the doorjamb. "It's bad, isn't it?" Officer Christofferson had sent Kelly Frances, the City's Victims' Advocate, to pick up Stephanie.

Kelly wore a long, black wool coat and a serious face. Stephanie knew the older woman from work but she was more of an acquaintance than a friend. Stephanie very much needed a friend right now. Todd was her best, if not only, friend. At least Kelly could get her to him.

"I don't know how bad it is, Stephanie. I'm sorry. Christofferson just told me to get you to the hospital." The expression on her face, beneath the short, boy-cut hair, softened. "Are you ready?"

An over powering feeling that she'd need to be strong tonight nearly suffocated Stephanie. "I guess so." She grabbed her parka from the sofa.

"Let's go then." Kelly put her arm around Stephanie and led her to the car.

Fighting back tears, Stephanie said little during the short drive. She shivered and wrapped her coat more securely around her shoulders.

At the hospital she and Kelly were ushered into a private, plain looking area near the emergency room.

"Have a seat," Kelly said, shedding her black coat and scarf to reveal a dark sweater and slacks beneath. She probably hadn't planned on dressing like an undertaker tonight. "I'll see if I can find out what's going on."

Stephanie didn't take a seat on the faded, overstuffed couch, but paced like a tiger in a small cage. She needed to see Todd. He'd want her with him.

Tears leaked from her eyes, and she grabbed a tissue from a box on an end table. Why did they have tissues and a Bible in this room? She coughed and blew her nose. This was a holding room for desperate loved ones waiting for bad news. She had to get out of there. Todd was okay. He had to be. She opened the door and dashed out, running directly into the steadfast Kelly.

She stumbled and Kelly grabbed her, guiding her back into the room that Stephanie feared would soon be permeated with grief. She collapsed onto the couch and gathering her courage, brought her eyes up to meet Kelly's.

The woman was silent for a moment, as if she could find no words. Then she began slowly, "They're doing everything they can, but it doesn't look good. I'm so sorry. I assume you and he are close."

Hugging her arms around her middle, Stephanie whispered, "We were going to be married on Saturday." Their secret was out. It didn't matter. The only thing she cared about was that Todd lived.

"Is there anyone else we should call?" Kelly sat next to Stephanie and placed her hand on her arm.

"There's no one. His parents are dead." As were hers. She wished there were someone to call. Neither of them had anyone, just each other. She drew in a deep breath.

"Are you okay?" Kelly asked.

Okay? How could she ever be okay without Todd? He was her life, the father of the child she could only endure because of him, the single bright spot in her existence, except for a horse she didn't even own. Of course she wasn't okay. "Yes," she lied.

"How about calling a friend or someone from your church?" Always the trained professional, Kelly kept her voice steady.

There was no one from church. Stephanie had stopped going after finding out about the baby. She almost suggested Kathleen from the barn, but knew the horsewoman was out of town for the night. Charles. Maybe she could call her boss. He'd seemed almost friendly earlier. She really wished she could seek solace with Kingston. Strangely, thinking about the horse offered her the most comfort.

The door opened and Stephanie jolted. She dragged her stare from the floor to wander up blue scrubs to a face that looked too young to be there. She stood slowly.

"I'm Dr. Bradford," he said, "the attending physician in the ER tonight."

She didn't care who he was. She didn't care about anything, but Todd. Why wouldn't he tell her about him? She didn't want to hear.

"Maybe you better sit down," the young doctor said.

"Just tell me what you came to say."

He cleared his throat, once, then again. "I'm really sorry. We did everything we could, but Mr. Saxton's injuries were too severe and Todd . . . ."

"No. Don't say it." Stephanie put her hands over her ears. "He's not dead. He can't be."

"I'm so sorry."

Stephanie staggered forward, collapsing into the doctor's arms. He picked her up and settled her on the sofa.

Tears streaming down her face, she struggled to sit up.

"You might want to stay still for a moment. Maybe you should put your head down between your knees if you feel faint."

"I'm okay," Stephanie whimpered, knowing full well that she would never be okay again. "May I see him?"

"Give us a few minutes, okay?"

"What difference will that make?" Her voice broke.

Kelly sat next to Stephanie and rubbed her back. "I'm so sorry. I wish there was something I could do."

Staring at a worn spot in the carpet, Stephanie mumbled, "There's nothing anyone can do. It's too late." She began to cry. She couldn't help it. Big, loud sobs shook her shoulders. She jumped when the door opened again.

"You can see him now." Dr. Bradford reached for Stephanie's hand, pulling her up from the sofa. He steadied her against him as he led her down the hall.

She stood in the doorway, rooted to the floor. She could see a sheet-draped body lying on a roll-away bed. Various life-giving and monitoring machines stood silent next to the bed, like defeated soldiers, guns lowered, the battle lost.

"Would you like to be alone?" The doctor let go of her arm.

Not knowing if she could bear to look at Todd, Stephanie remained silent for a moment.

"Miss Saunders?"

"Yes, I would."

"Take all the time you need." Dr. Bradford started down the hall.

Swallowing hard, Stephanie nodded her good-bye. "I will. Thank you."

Moving forward with small, halting steps, Stephanie drew closer. She gasped when she saw his face.

Since he died in a crash, she thought he'd look terribly injured, but other than an unstitched gash across his forehead from which blood had ceased to drain, Todd could have been sleeping. "Oh, Todd," she sobbed. "What am I going to do without you?" She touched his cheek, already growing cold.

She pulled a nearby chair closer and sat, reaching beneath the sheet for Todd's hand. She nearly dropped it when she felt the shredded flesh. His knuckles showed scraped, bloodied, white bone, and the end of one finger had been crushed. She placed the hand back under the sheet, tears blurring her eyes. She vowed she'd not peek beneath the sheet again. The doctor had said that Todd died of massive internal injuries. Hadn't the airbag deployed? Maybe Todd had been hit from the side. She pulled the sheet up more securely under his chin. She'd remember his perfect body as it had once been.

Never had she felt so alone and vulnerable, not even when her parents had died. The presence of the baby might have comforted some women, but she felt even more helpless knowing this little alien was growing inside her, sapping her strength.

She lay her head on Todd's silent chest and cried and cried. She cried for Todd's short life and for the happiness he'd miss, and she cried for herself and the hardships she'd have to face without him.

When she could cry no more, she pulled away, shaking her head. She had to get a grip on herself. Although at the moment it might be easier just to lie here and die alongside Todd, it wasn't going to happen. She'd have to toughen up. She had things to live for. Right now she couldn't think of any, but there had to be some. Life for her would go on, darn it.

She leaned down and kissed Todd's cold and, for the first time ever, unresponsive lips. "Good-bye, my love. I will never forget you." With a final look, she stumbled from the room and stood in the hall, wondering what to do.

Thinking she'd find Kelly and ask to be taken home, she whirled around and ran directly into a big, cement wall of a man. "Oh, I'm sorry," she said, looking up to see if her apology had been accepted.

"Stephanie?" the man asked. "What are you doing here?"

If she had looked Satan straight in the eyes, she wouldn't have been more horrified. "You!" she screamed, pounding Josh Durrant on the chest with her fists. "You killed him."

Josh pulled her against him so she could no longer strike. "Killed who? What are you talking about?"

"Let go of me, you murderer." Stephanie struggled against the vice grip of his arms.

"Not until you settle down and tell me what's going on." He squeezed harder, then loosened his grip. "Okay. Is it safe to let go?"

Glaring up at him, Stephanie snarled, "You better let me go or I'll have you arrested."

He released her so fast that she stumbled back. He grabbed her before she fell.

She jerked away.

He held up his hands like he was about to be shot and circled around her. "Okay. Okay. Tell me what happened."

"What do you mean what happened. You know very well that Todd's dead."

"Who's dead? Todd? Is he your boyfriend?"

"You know who he is, or was." Her voice broke.

Josh stepped forward as if to take her in his arms, but one look from her stopped him cold. "Why do you think I had anything to do with his . . . . Did you say he's dead?"

"Don't act so innocent. I saw you."

"You saw me? When? I've been here at the hospital all evening."

Stephanie snorted. "Sure you have. I saw your white truck tonight. Todd was chasing you when he had his accident. It's all your fault." She burst into tears.

This time Josh stayed his distance. "Was Todd chasing someone in a white truck? It wasn't me. Like I said I've been here all evening."

"Do you expect me to believe you? I know what I saw."

"Well, you didn't see me. Here, look." He pointed at a man being pushed by a nurse down the hall toward them in a wheel chair. "That's Jim Drake. He lives by your stable. He had an unfortunate encounter with a tractor tonight."

Sure enough, there sat a young man with his arm in a cast from hand to shoulder, propped out from his body at an odd angle. He looked very pale, except for the dark circles under his sunken eyes. At least he was alive unlike poor Todd. Stephanie blinked back tears.

"You can take him home now, Mr. Durrant, but he shouldn't be alone tonight," the nurse said.

"I'll stay with him." Josh leveled an accusing stare at Stephanie.

She glared at him, glad for an opportunity to be angry instead of sad.

The nurse stopped the wheelchair next to Josh and Stephanie, apparently to relay more instructions.

The man turned pain-filled eyes up at her. "Hello."

"Stephanie, this is John Drake, the friend I've been telling you about," Josh said.

Forcing a smile, Stephanie nodded.

"He can take one of these every four hours," the nurse said as they continued down the hall.

Turning back around, Josh called over his shoulder, "I'm sorry for your loss, Stephanie."

Something Josh had said refused to settle in Stephanie's mind.

When she didn't answer, Josh returned to face her. "I mean it, Stephanie. If there is anything I can do to help you, just let me know."

At last she knew what it was that bothered her. "So, is your friend's name Jim Drake or John Drake?"

Without so much as a pause, Josh answered, "His name is Jonathan James Drake. He answers to either."

She studied Josh for a moment. His face remained expressionless. He was either the best liar she'd ever met or he was telling the truth. But right now she didn't have the strength to decide.

Avoiding her stare, he touched her cheek. "I'd like to help if you'll let me."

Stephanie opened her mouth to answer, but nothing came out. She really didn't know what to say. She knew she should run from this man, this criminal, as fast as she could, but somehow she felt strangely drawn. Now, without Todd she had no one. That must have been it, she needed someone to lean on, anyone would do.

"Your friend's waiting," she said.

A door at the end of the hall flew open and Charles came running toward Stephanie.

Josh patted her shoulder and made a quick exit, nodding at her boss as they passed. For a fleeting moment, Stephanie wondered if they knew each other, but then decided they were just being polite.

"Stephanie, my dear," Charles said, drawing her into his arms. "Kelly called me. I'm so very, very sorry. I'll be taking you home with me."

"But . . ." Stephanie started to object.

"No. No. Don't worry about a thing. I have a very large house. You'll have all the privacy you want. Come along now. My housekeeper has everything ready."

CHAPTER 10

During the twenty-minute ride to Charles's house, Stephanie tried to talk herself into believing that staying with her boss and his housekeeper was a good thing. She wasn't succeeding. Charles, of all people. Hadn't he always kind of frightened her? She glanced at him. It was a stretch to think that interacting with this man might help take her mind off losing Todd. Actually, she couldn't bear the thought of being alone, and there was no one else. She doubted she'd even find comfort with Kingston right now.

Charles's home, more correctly described as a mansion, was probably beautiful in the daytime, but tonight as they pulled in through the rock pillars and rail fence the gray stone structure with multiple gables looked spooky. Dark and foreboding, it was exactly the type of house she would have imagined for Charles, except not quite this large. Apparently the practice of law had been good to him.

Reaching up, he touched a button above the rearview mirror of his black Lexus. One of the doors of his three-car garage opened. The headlights illuminated the huge space, spotlessly clean, and painted a pale green.

"You said your housekeeper lives here with you?" Stephanie waited nervously for his answer. She never would have agreed to coming home with Charles had it not been for the housekeeper. Of course, she'd only stay one night.

"Yes, she does, but there's plenty of room. Janeen has been with me since before my wife died." Charles switched off the ignition. "I'm sorry about your boyfriend. It appears we've both lost people who were dear to us."

Blinking back tears, Stephanie turned to Charles. "I don't know what I would have done without you tonight. I bet you didn't bargain on me being so much trouble when you hired me."

"Nonsense. You've been a huge asset to our firm." He handed her a handkerchief from his pocket. "I'm looking forward to great things from you. I know you don't think so right now, but you have a fine career ahead."

Yeah, sure she did. Her brilliant career included an illegitimate baby. What would Charles think about that? She felt so alone and vulnerable. Fresh tears flooded her eyes. She'd thought she was about out of tears, but there seemed to be an endless supply. "I'm sorry. I keep thinking about Todd. I don't know what to do without him."

He patted her hand. "Don't worry about a thing. I'll be there to help. That's what friends are for."

Stephanie raised her brows. Friend? She didn't know they were friends. "Thank you, Charles. I just can't face it all right now."

"Of course you can't. You shouldn't have to encounter such things at your young age."

She thumped her forehead with the heel of her hand. "Oh no. I still don't have the keys to my car and I'll need to drive it to work tomorrow, unless I can ride in with you." Another sob escaped her lips. "The keys were in Todd's pocket."

"Don't even think about going to work." He gave her a sly smile. "I have some influence with your boss, and you're not to worry about work tomorrow or for the rest of the week, not until you're feeling stronger."

The thought occurred to her that she would never feel stronger if she weren't allowed to be strong, but she'd worry about that another day. "You're being so kind. How will I ever repay you?"

"I have a pretty full desk and calendar. I'll think of something." He drew out the "I'll." It occurred to Stephanie that he really would think of something, but that was okay. She'd need to keep busy.

The overhead lights flashed on in the garage and a door from the inside opened. Out strode a large woman in a navy blue uniform similar to what police officers wore, but without badges and patches, and Stephanie couldn't see a gun. She checked again. No. No gun. Any imagined romantic connection between Charles and his housekeeper ceased to exist.

The housekeeper, Janeen—Stephanie kept thinking that her name should have been Bertha—stood in the doorway as if awaiting orders. She probably was. Did she sleep in her uniform? It was nearly two in the morning.

"Janeen," Charles opened the car door and slid out. "Will you show Miss Saunders to the main guest room. She'll be staying for a while."

A while, Stephanie thought. A very short while. She offered the woman a tentative smile.

"Of course, Mr. Connelly." Janeen came around to the passenger side of the car and opened Stephanie's door. "Is there luggage?"

"No. Miss Saunders didn't know she'd be staying. She suffered a great loss tonight. No doubt you can find her something to sleep in, and there's an extra toothbrush in the guest bathroom."

"Of course, Sir. Come along, Miss." She offered their visitor a hand. Stephanie allowed herself to be helped from the car. As she began to walk, her head spun and she tried to steady herself. Blinking her eyes to clear them, she focused on Charles.

He came around and assisted her into the house while Janeen went ahead to open doors and pull the red quilted spread down on the king-size bed. Stephanie sank into its softness.

She became aware of Charles standing nearby, holding out a glass of something almost clear. "Here, take this," he said.

"What is it?" Stephanie mumbled, rubbing her eyes.

"Something herbal to help you get through the night. Don't worry. It's completely safe, for everyone." His face testified to the truth of his statement.

With an unsteady hand, Stephanie took the offered glass and held it to her lips. Her mind threatened to explode from overload. Right now she wished she could go to sleep and never wake up. She tipped her head and drained the glass. It tasted like tea.

Sleep was good. Stephanie welcomed a deep, comforting slumber.

* * *

Stephanie sat up in bed, placing a hand to her temple. Her head throbbed as she struggled to organize her thoughts. Where was she? What time was it? Why did she have this terrible sinking feeling of doom that tried to smother her?

Groaning, she lay back down as memories of the night before flooded over her. She cried again until tears dampened her pillow. She tossed back and forth, wondering how she could put an end to this pain of loss. Strangely, a vision of the old mare standing bravely in her stall materialized. She thought of Kingston and how she enjoyed her time with him and all the animals at the barn. Despite how horrible her life was now, she had to get hold of herself. She could be sad for Todd, worried about her condition, but she couldn't let it get the best of her. She was better than this. Todd would want her to be brave.

She sat up again, dropping her legs over the side of the bed. She was still dressed in her sweater and slacks, the ones she'd selected the night before because Todd had said he liked them. Come on, she told herself. Inch by inch she needed to move forward, start small and work up to something bigger, harder. She needed to find her keys, get someone to take her home, and begin to think about arrangements for Todd. She'd start there. She glanced at her wrist. No watch. What time was it? She studied the room in the dim light. It was big. Making her way across the plush, gold carpet in her stocking feet, she pulled the heavy, brocade drapes aside.

Sunlight flooded the room, revealing an overstuffed chair, a spindly-legged divan and end table, a potted tree and fern—things not normally encountered in any bedroom she'd ever been in. Outside, a frozen wonderland, complete with stone fence, snow-laden pines and iced-over pond, reminded Stephanie that she was the guest of a very influential man. She didn't belong here. She'd better get back to the life she knew as soon as she could, despite the fact that it was far less than perfect right now.

Feeling rested, she guessed by the light outside that it was about nine or ten, Wednesday morning. Good, she hadn't slept too long, even though she'd been exhausted last night.

In front of the beveled mirror above the mahogany dresser, Stephanie smoothed her long blonde hair. Taking a deep breath, she eased open the bedroom door and peered into the hall. To the right she saw an oak table and chairs arranged on a hardwood floor. A wonderful scent of bread baking drew her to the kitchen. Her stomach growled.

"Hello, Miss." Janeen stirred a pot resting on the stove. The woman looked different this morning—more approachable. The stiff uniform had been replaced by a white blouse, a dark straight skirt, support hose and sensible shoes. She looked to be around sixty. Stephanie hoped she wouldn't still have to be working at sixty, but now with Todd gone and a baby on the way, she would probably always have to work. There'd be no other man for her.

"Are you hungry?" the housekeeper asked.

"Starving." Stephanie had thought earlier that she'd never eat again. "Do you know what time it is?"

Janeen glanced up at a clock on the wall that Stephanie had just noticed. "Eleven thirty."

Stephanie nodded. "I see it now. At least I didn't sleep the whole day away, but I can't believe I slept nine and a half hours. I haven't done that in years."

"Well, actually you slept more like thirty-three and a half hours."

"What?"

"It's eleven-thirty on Friday morning.

"Oh, no. Friday? What happened to Thursday? You should have awakened me. I've got so much to do." Had Charles given her something to calm her, or had she dreamed it? She guessed if he had, it was too late to worry about it. She had more pressing problems at the moment. "Where have they taken Todd? Do you know if he's still in the hospital? Do you even know who Todd is?"

The housekeeper wiped her hands on her apron and came to stand beside Stephanie. "Yes, Miss. Mr. Charles told me about him. Mr. Charles had me check on you all day yesterday, but he didn't want you disturbed. He's very protective of you. We're both so sorry for your loss."

"Thank you." Stephanie stared at the floor for a moment, thinking about Todd and a protective Charles—a protective Charles was a stretch. "And work. I've missed work."

"Mr. Charles told me to tell you that he's taken care of everything." Janeen pulled a chair out from the table and motioned for Stephanie to sit.

"What does he mean everything? What about Todd? Where is he? He doesn't have anyone but me. And what about his funeral? I don't know who would come, but he needs something. I don't even know where to bury him. Bury him?" Stephanie's voice broke. "This can't be happening."

Janeen lay a comforting hand on Stephanie's back. "Don't worry. Mr. Charles will help you. He'll be home soon for lunch. You can talk to him then."

Stephanie's head shot up. She hadn't planned on having to encounter him before evening. "Do I have time to splash water on my face and brush my teeth? I've got to get home. I need to change these clothes." She resisted the temptation to again think about dressing for her date with Todd in this outfit.

"I don't believe Mr. Charles wants you to leave just yet. He's afraid you'll be too lonely. He can be very kind, you know. He'd like you to stay here with us for a while so we can look after you."

Stomach tightening, Stephanie answered quickly, "That's sweet, but I really do have to get home. Did Charles say anything about the keys to my car?"

"No. I'm sorry he didn't."

"They were in my fiancé's pocket during the . . ." She couldn't continue.

Janeen took a seat at the table and reached out to squeeze Stephanie's hand. "I'm sure Mr. Charles will help. You've got to quit worrying. You've had a terrible shock."

"Charles said he would, but he's so busy. I don't want to be a problem."

"Well," Janeen patted Stephanie's hand, "let's get you some food." She scooted her chair back, stood and stepped to the stove.

"I feel guilty sitting while you're working. Why don't you eat with me and I'll help clean up later." It would seem good to do something—anything.

"Oh, no. You're the guest. I'm the housekeeper. That wouldn't be right." Janeen placed a bowl of beef stew in front of Stephanie.

"That's silly. You need to eat too." Stephanie tasted her food tentatively, not sure how her stomach would react.

"I'll eat later after Mr. Charles leaves. He's my employer, after all." Janeen returned to the counter area, opening the oven and several cabinets.

"He's mine too." The first bite went down okay, so Stephanie tried another, this time savoring the hearty taste on her tongue.

Back at the table, Janeen offered Stephanie a slice of bread from a napkin-lined basket. "That's different. You're an attorney like Mr. Charles. I'm nothing special."

"Anyone who can cook and keep house like this," Stephanie gestured with her hand, "is very special. I didn't think I'd be able to eat anything, but this is delicious."

"Thank you, dear." The housekeeper brought butter and jam to the table.

"Well, look who's finally up." Charles strode into the room. Stephanie hadn't heard him coming and jumped at the sound of his voice. As usual, he looked pressed and starched in his dark suit. With raw emotions threatening to surface, she felt grubby and insignificant in her slept-in clothes.

"Good afternoon, Stephanie, Janeen. Lunch smells wonderful. I'll take mine now. I've got to get right back to work."

Stephanie stood, brushing a butter knife onto the floor with her sleeve. She stooped to retrieve it. "I should get back too. You've probably spent time you don't have on work I should be doing. I need to find my keys and get my car so I won't be such a bother." Not exactly sure where she was heading, she turned to leave.

Charles caught her by the arm. "Deirdre's rescheduled most of your clients. I saw a couple of them who couldn't wait. She's also called the hospital and she'll go pick up your keys later. I'll bring them home this afternoon, then drop you at your condo so when you come back later, you can drive your own car."

Deirdre was actually working, making phone calls and everything? Impressive. "Oh, I won't be back." Stephanie said. "Although it will be hard, I'll stay at my own place tonight." She eased her arm from Charles's grasp. "I appreciate all you've done for me, but I've got to get going." She paused for a moment and then in a quivering voice asked, "Do you know where Todd is? I should get started on some kind of memorial."

Placing an arm around her shoulder, Charles led her back to the table and pulled out her chair. "I hope I haven't been too presumptuous, but when they called from the hospital I went ahead and made a few arrangements. I didn't want to disturb you. Sleep can be very important at a time like this."

"You made a few arrangements? What do you mean?" She collapsed onto the chair. "Where's Todd now?"

Charles walked around the table, seating himself across from Stephanie. "He's at the mortuary."

"The mortuary?" Her voice squeaked. "Which one? I need to start planning his funeral."

Interlacing his fingers, Charles placed his hands on the table in front of him. He stared at them for a moment and then peered up at Stephanie. "I wondered if you really wanted a funeral for

Todd since you'd mentioned he had no family living and knew no one from around here." Charles cleared his throat. "Funerals can be so draining for the people left behind, especially if there are no loved ones from whom to draw strength. Of course, those of us from the office would come, but maybe not a lot of others. I thought that perhaps a graveside service would be more appropriate."

Stephanie blinked. "Really?" She'd never thought about anything but a funeral. Perhaps Charles was right. It would be so sad for Todd to have a funeral that was poorly attended.

"Graveside services can be so beautiful," Charles continued. "We'll order a lot of flowers, and we'll get someone, maybe from your church, to say a few words. You might also want to participate."

"Well, maybe." Stephanie chewed her lip. Would a graveside service do justice to Todd's memory? Her eyes burned. She couldn't let herself cry again. "But if I decide I want a funeral for Todd, is it too late to change the arrangements?"

Lowering his head, Charles swallowed hard. "I think it might be. They've already set everything up. I guess I should have awakened you when they needed a decision, but you'd been so upset and you were finally sleeping—out of pain for a while."

"But Charles, I really think it was something—" Her voice broke, but blocking her emotions, she continued in a tone harsher than she'd planned. "I should have been consulted about what I wanted for Todd." She thought about asking Charles if he'd really given her something more potent the other night, but when she noted his expression, she decided that now was not the time.

Moisture crept into Charles's eyes. "I'm so sorry, Stephanie. I thought I was helping." Face drawn and sad, he looked so repentant Stephanie decided not to be overly critical.

As if not wanting to interfere in the serious conversation, Janeen moved slowly to the table to replace Stephanie's empty bowl with a full one and to serve Charles his first. Stephanie wondered what the housekeeper thought of the situation, but the woman hid her sentiment well.

Stephanie turned back to Charles. He quickly glanced away as if he were afraid she'd continue to vent her feelings. He seemed truly shaken, and Stephanie felt a little sorry for him. Was he getting old and losing his edge? He had been extremely caring since Todd's death. "I want to see Todd, though, before the . . . the burial." She could barely get out the word.

"Of course. We can go there later today." He blotted his mouth with his napkin.

We? Would Stephanie never be able to shed her new protector?

"Todd won't be buried until tomorrow." Charles finished quietly.

"Tomorrow?" Stephanie blurted. "What's the hurry?" Tomorrow was the day she and Todd were to have been married. How could she bury him on their wedding day? She glanced at her finger. The diamond glistened under the glow of the hanging light fixture. She turned the ring around, so the jewel wouldn't show. For some reason she didn't want Charles to know about her engagement. He seemed to know everything else.

Charles took a deep breath and whispered, "I didn't see any reason to delay."

Heat spread up the back of Stephanie's neck. "You. You didn't see any reason to delay? What about me?" This time she didn't even care that her voice was harsh.

"I was thinking of you, and Todd." Charles shifted in his chair.

"Todd?" She barely held her anger in check.

"I don't know if you believe in an afterlife." He left his spoon untouched in his bowl.

"Of course I do." Stephanie had also stopped eating.

"When my wife, Cynthia, died I got the feeling that her spirit stuck around until after her burial. As hard as it was for me to say goodbye, I wanted her to get on with her life, and I knew I had to get on with mine. I had to begin to heal so I wouldn't go crazy with the pain." Leaning back, he steepled his fingers under his chin, giving Stephanie the fleeting impression of an angel.

She had never heard Charles talk like this previously. The man truly did have feelings, something she'd doubted earlier. Wow! Did she feel like a jerk. What good would it have done to wait? Todd was dead. Waiting would not bring him back. She narrowed her eyes as her thoughts changed direction. She never remembered talking to Charles about Todd's background. Hmm. She'd probably forgotten. "Okay. Maybe you're right. I guess there's really no reason to delay, but when you come back, will you take me straight to my condo? I'll go see Todd myself."

Charles cleared his throat. "Do you think you're up to going alone? It will be very draining. I know." He sipped from a glass of lemonade. "I thought we'd go see Todd as soon as I get back from work. I'll come home early and bring your keys. We'll stop by the mortuary on the way to your condo, before it gets too late. I'd hate for you to miss seeing Todd." He reached across the table and patted her hand. "I'll wait for you at your place and you can follow me back. Believe me, you don't want to go either place alone. It is just too sad." Charles smiled at Janeen who offered him some homemade bread.

Was this how the President of the United States felt with secret service agents forever near, Stephanie wondered? Charles did seem to be concerned for her welfare. "So you really will be home early?" Stephanie asked.

"I have an important three o'clock appointment, but I'll be home right after that. This is an all right place to stay, isn't it? Janeen and I have tried to make it comfortable for you." Charles's eyes were soft and reassuring.

"It's beautiful, and you've both been very kind." They really had and they actually seemed to want her to stay. Even though she wasn't entirely at ease with them, she had a feeling she wouldn't like being alone either.

"We'll take really good care of you, won't we, Janeen?"

"What was that, Sir?" Janeen drew her head out of the refrigerator where she'd been reaching for something at the back.

"You'd like to have Stephanie stay a little longer, wouldn't you?"

"Oh yes. I like having Miss Stephanie around."

Stephanie smiled at the woman, and decided there were worse things than staying in a magnificent home, being treated like a princess. Why not pamper herself a while longer? There'd be plenty of time to face things at her condo later, after she'd healed a little. Healed a little? Oh yeah, sure. She would never heal. Avoiding problems was not going to make them go away. Like she'd decided earlier that morning, she needed to face some of them right now, starting easy and working up. "Was Todd's car totaled?"

"I'm afraid it was." Charles spread a thick layer of jam on his bread.

"So I guess I won't have to worry about that. I suppose it was insured. I'll have to call his insurance company. I believe it was State Farm." Stephanie ate her bread plain. It was delicious.

Charles swallowed his food. "Now I hope you won't be upset with me again. I just wanted to save you further suffering." He peered up at her through his stubby lashes, like a repentant child. "I had Deirdre call. His vehicle was only insured for liability."

Well, maybe avoiding her problems would work, especially since Stephanie seemed to have acquired a fairy godfather. "Really? What about the cabin and all his belongings?" Not that she really cared about any of his stuff, short of taking care of what was dear to him. She'd not be entitled to anything anyway. Although, in her predicament, a little cash might have come in handy.

"Stephanie." Charles steadied an intense gaze on her. "There's something you should know about Todd."

Her head began to whirl. Briefly, she thought of Todd's car parked in front of the law office. Had he really been there to see Charles that day? Was that why Charles seemed to know so much about her fiancé? Her voice shook when she said, "What is it?"

"Todd had nothing left." Charles straightened in his chair. "I was handling his bankruptcy."

CHAPTER 11

Stephanie drew her coat tighter around her shoulders as the cold breeze threatened to freeze her solid. Although snow still covered the ground, someone at the cemetery had cleared a swath from the road to Todd's burial site. Two tall cedars rested near the head of his grave, like giants standing guard, and several headstones peeked out from under the snow as if anxious to see who their new neighbor would be. Stephanie took some comfort from those stately trees and in the beauty of the quiet little cemetery where Todd would soon be laid to rest. She shivered. It might be warmer beneath the ground.

"Are you okay?" Charles asked, touching her arm.

She forced a smile, but couldn't keep the tears from flowing.

Only four darkly clad mourners came to bid Todd farewell—Stephanie, Charles, Janeen and Deirdre. Paul Foster, Charles's partner, had planned to be there, but he was in the middle of a lengthy trial in Salt Lake City. Six strangers from the cemetery awaited instructions, as it was their job to attend. Stephanie sniffed. Had there been no mix-up in the newspaper and more time, surely Todd's obituary would have solicited more attention. Some of her acquaintances from the barn might have come had they known earlier. Of course, her best friends lived in stalls.

The funeral director stepped closer to Stephanie. "Would you like to wait for a few minutes in case more people . . ."

Although she doubted that anyone else would show up, Stephanie nodded.

A dozen padded folding chairs rested near the coffin, which was suspended above the freshly excavated grave. Janeen and Deidra dropped onto two of the chairs.

"The flowers are beautiful," Stephanie said. A spray of yellow roses lay on top of Todd's casket, and two large stands of similar flowers stood on either side, complementing the bronze coffin. The yellow roses were Stephanie's idea. Todd had loved those flowers and brought them to her on numerous occasions. Now Stephanie wished she'd ordered more, regardless of the expense. Even though Charles had told her not to worry about the cost of the burial, which Stephanie knew would be considerable, she didn't want to take any more advantage than she already had. Her boss had spared no expense on Todd and had actually chosen more expensive items than she would have selected.

"Yellow was a good choice." Charles reached out to finger one of the roses.

A gust of wind blew snow out of a nearby tree, plopping a pile of white on top of the casket. Stephanie brushed it away. "Why are you doing all this?" she asked Charles.

"What do you mean?" He buttoned his topcoat.

"Why are you so kind to me—paying for the funeral, asking me to stay at your home?"

He shrugged. "You have no one else, and you're in a bind. You've been a great addition to our firm, and why shouldn't I do something nice for someone? I have plenty of money. I'm glad to help."

Eyes burning, she stared at Charles. He not only had feelings as she'd discovered the other night, but he had a heart too, a big one. It just proved that first impressions weren't always correct.

Look at Todd. She thought she knew everything about him, but apparently she'd been wrong.

"You're very kind." She smiled at Charles, then stammered, "May I have a look at Todd's bankruptcy file when I get back to the office?"

"Of course." Charles gave her a sidelong glance that seemed to say *you don't trust me to handle this?* "Are you sure you want to put yourself through that?"

Motioning to Charles, Stephanie stepped away from Todd's coffin as if her fiancé could hear what she was about to say. "I need to find out everything I can about him. I feel bad he had secrets from me."

"You should put it behind you." Charles lowered his voice. "Remember only the good things."

"I'm trying to. Were there more bad things I should know?"

"He's gone now. It doesn't matter," Charles said.

"It matters to me."

"This is his funeral, Stephanie."

"I don't care." Her voice rose, causing Deirdre and Janeen to stop visiting and stare at her. Stephanie ignored them. "Please tell me," she whispered to her boss.

A muscle flinched in Charles's jaw. "He didn't want you to know about the bankruptcy. He said he'd tell you later." Charles squared his shoulders. "It's just my opinion, and I don't want to speak ill of the dead. . ." He turned his back on the coffin. "but I think he figured you and the money you make could help him out of his financial troubles. That's just my opinion, mind you. I wonder if he had a gambling problem or some such thing."

The thought flashed through Stephanie's mind that Todd had suggested they go to Las Vegas, the gambling capitol of the world, to get married.

"I think he loved you, though. He talked about you all the time . . ." Charles's voice trailed off.

"Now what is it?" Stephanie asked.

"Nothing."

"It's something. Tell me." She pulled the collar of her coat up around her neck.

Charles took a deep breath, then let it out slowly. "Come to think of it, he talked about how much money you could make at a different firm. He hinted that I should give you a raise."

That didn't sound like Todd, Stephanie thought, but why would Charles tell her something that wasn't true?

"I'm going to give you a raise, by the way," Charles said. "You have a wonderful future with us. I've talked to Paul and we're going to offer you more responsibility. It might mean some late nights and travel, but you're ready. The sky's the limit, as they say."

If it was possible for Stephanie to be excited right now even after what Charles had told her, she was on the verge. More responsibilities. That was just what she needed. Wait! What about the baby? How would a baby fit into this exciting new career Charles planned for her?

She felt dizzy and stepped closer to Todd's casket, placing both hands on it. If Todd could lie to her about money, perhaps he'd lied about wanting to get married and about keeping the baby. Maybe he'd even lied about that night the baby had come into being. But how could she think about that now when her whole being ached to be with him again?

"I think we should proceed," the funeral director said, as his workers climbed out of their van.

Just then, everyone turned to stare as a white limousine pulled up. To Stephanie's dismay, Matthew and Jessica Dawson stepped out and paraded to the graveside, like show poodles in center ring. Well, almost. They seemed to be arguing about something. Mrs. Dawson glared at Mr. Dawson until she noticed everyone watching them. Then she took her husband's arm and instantly plastered on a fake smile.

"I don't believe it," Charles said under his breath. He seemed as unhappy to see them as Stephanie was, which surprised her.

Matthew walked straight to her, shook free of Jessica, and gave Stephanie a huge hug. "I'm so sorry for your loss."

Jessica studied Stephanie as if assessing her choice of wardrobe. Stephanie's dark blue suit, beneath her cloth trench coat, could not compete with Mrs. Dawson's black sheath, diamonded studded ears, and long black, cashmere coat with the fur of some unfortunate animal sewn to the collar and cuffs. "Yes, it's such a tragedy," Jessica stated in a tone as sincere as that of a losing politician.

How did they learn about Todd's graveside service? Surely they weren't readers of the local obituaries, and why would they suspect that Todd was special to her? Someone was doing a lot of talking behind her back. Stephanie suspected Deirdre.

"Thank you for coming," Stephanie said as politely as her fury would allow.

Charles respectfully acknowledged Mr. and Mrs. Dawson and they said hello to him, at least Matthew did.

"We were about to begin," the funeral director announced. "Won't you take a seat?"

"Of course," Matthew said.

With a shooing hand gesture, Mrs. Dawson scooted Deirdre and Janeen down a couple of chairs so she and her husband could sit next to Stephanie and Charles.

Deirdre shared the blanket she'd brought from her car with Janeen but didn't offer it to the late arrivals.

How different this was from another sad day in Stephanie's life. Remembering her parents' funeral and the many who attended, she dabbed her eyes. Held in a church, all the local members of her faith had attended. She wished now she'd not procrastinated when she'd first arrived here to work, nor later allowed the guilt of the pregnancy to keep her from pursuing friendships. She mused sorrowfully that if she died tomorrow, there'd probably just be the same five mourners standing over her grave. Actually, maybe there'd be only two, since Deirdre probably wouldn't attend and the Dawsons had already accomplished their showy entrance and garnered the attention they no doubt felt they deserved.

After a moment, Charles stood and moved to stand beside Todd's coffin. "We've come together this day to honor Todd Saxton and to find a way to say goodbye."

Stephanie didn't hear what else Charles said. Her thoughts drifted back to the night before at the mortuary, when she'd first seen Todd lying in his coffin. Dressed in a charcoal suit, white shirt and striped tie, he looked incredibly handsome even in death. The mortician had done an exemplary job covering up Todd's injuries. Had it not been for the gash across his forehead, which makeup had failed to completely conceal, Todd might have been sleeping.

His right hand shielded the severely injured left—the one she'd touched at the hospital that had made her cringe. Last night she'd covered those stone cold hands with hers, trying to lend them warmth if only for a moment. She remembered how those gentle hands had caressed her cheek, guided her over icy pathways and disappeared into soapy dishwater at her condo. She'd sat alone with him for almost an hour, longing to remember only the good times, yet she couldn't help but search his lifeless face for answers to the questions that plagued her. In addition to the bankruptcy, what else had he kept from her?

"Stephanie . . . Stephanie," Charles said, bringing her back to the present.

She felt everyone's eyes upon her and looked to her boss for direction.

When he had regained her attention, Charles went on, "In closing, shall we all take a minute and share what made Todd special to us?"

Stephanie glanced from side to side as if to grasp what those comments could possibly be. "That would be nice," she said. Nice or impossible. No one except her really knew him. Did she even really know him?

Everyone nodded and Deirdre began—going on and on about how good-looking he was. Charles spoke of potential wasted. Janeen remained silent as did the Dawsons, who had never met him. Since none of these comments were the heartfelt sentiments Stephanie would have wished for, she shared more of her feelings than she would have otherwise.

She told of places they'd gone, the good times they'd shared and how wonderful he'd been to her. She singled out one special night in early December after a wonderful dinner and concert. Since they were both dressed warmly, they decided to take a walk in the lightly falling snow. Hand in hand, they kidded and laughed as they strolled along streets, beautifully decorated for Christmas. They had chatted for over an hour, with Stephanie doing most of the talking. With full love and acceptance Todd had listened, really listened, as she rattled on about her past, her present and of future goals and dreams. That night she'd felt she could tell him anything and he would always be there to add support. Breaking down in tears, she couldn't continue. How she wished he hadn't kept secrets from her.

The mortician took pity and concluded the service by reading from the Bible.

Her curiosity apparently satisfied, Jessica stood to leave. "Well that was short and shorter," she said. "Hardly worth getting dressed up for."

"You're the one who wanted to come," Matthew said.

"Well, now I want to leave." Jessica brushed off the back of her coat and held onto her husband's arm as they made their way back to their waiting limousine. The chauffeur opened the door and they slid in.

Glances were exchanged among those left behind.

"Well, I feel honored, don't you?" Stephanie heard Deirdre say. "What a pain in the asteroid."

"I'm sorry, Stephanie," Charles said. "Matthew sometimes has trouble controlling Her Royal Highness."

"Why doesn't he rein her in?" Stephanie asked.

"Oh, how I wish he would," Charles said almost wistfully. Then, as if not realizing that he'd said his last statement out loud, continued, "I think he really loves her and wants to make her happy, and . . . she's the one with most of the money."

"That'd do it for me," Deirdre said.

The legitimate mourners started back to their cars. Janeen and Deirdre had come together, as had Charles and Stephanie. Even the men from the mortuary headed toward their van, since the cemetery people would take care of lowering the coffin and filling in the grave.

Looking back over her shoulder at Todd's bronze coffin, bold and shiny against the white of the snowy landscape, Stephanie held onto Charles's arm as they walked to the car.

She stumbled and would have fallen had Charles not caught her. Wait. It wasn't Charles. It was someone else much taller and stronger.

"What are you doing here?" she snarled, recognizing the man who'd taken hold of her waist. She tried to pull away from him and slid in the snow. "How dare you show up here after what you did?"

Josh Durrant settled her on her feet, straightened the flowers he carried, and stepped away. "I thought we'd been over that. I was at the hospital with my friend the night Todd was killed, remember?" He spoke to her as if she were a child.

"That's your story," Stephanie shot back. She had met his friend at the hospital, but somehow she still didn't believe Josh. Why did he keep popping up? Why was he alive and Todd dead?

"Stephanie, be nice." Charles stepped between them as if he thought he'd need to keep the peace. "I'm sorry, Josh."

"Josh? How do you know Mr. Durrant? He's my client." Charles was actually siding with this criminal against her?

"Josh and I met yesterday. I was able to get his case dismissed."

"You got it dismissed without even discussing it with me?" Why had Charles gone out of his way to help Josh? The Durrant case was one that could easily have waited for her return. Had Josh gone behind her back to retain Charles, the attorney he really wanted? Now she truly felt inferior and unimportant. "That was fast." Her voice sounded venomous, but they both deserved her wrath.

"I had a little talk with Judge Anderson. He knew he'd have to take himself off the case. I just persuaded him to dismiss it."

"You've got to be kidding."

"I never kid."

"When you're right, you're right," Stephanie whispered. Their ignoring her professional contribution was almost as bad as Matthew and his snooty wife showing up at Todd's funeral uninvited. Stephanie started for the car. She wanted to get away from there. Maybe she'd come back later when she could be by herself to say her final goodbye.

"See, I'm not the hardened criminal you thought I was," Josh called after her.

Just because he'd gotten away with it didn't mean he didn't do it. For some reason Charles had worked his magic. Stephanie peered over her shoulder at Josh. Dressed in a dark sweater and slacks, beard trimmed and hair combed, he looked pretty good, actually very good. She let out a deep breath. What was she thinking? Her fiancé not yet buried and here she was admiring another man, and not a particularly admirable man. She wouldn't let Josh's good looks change her mind about him. "Be that as it may, Mr. Durrant, I doubt we'll ever have occasion to run into each other again."

Josh smiled.

Stephanie seethed.

Charles came up from behind her to open the car door. "On the contrary. Josh is going to be doing a little work for us." He stopped suddenly, putting a hand over his mouth. "Oh, I'm sorry, we shouldn't be discussing this now. We'll talk about it after . . . ." He made a sweeping gesture with his hand. "After all this."

Even though talking business over Todd's grave probably wasn't respectful, Stephanie couldn't keep herself from asking, "What do you mean, us?"

"The firm. He's a pilot." Charles motioned for Stephanie to climb into the car, but she remained standing.

"I guess you're stuck with me." Josh grinned, looking silly, big man that he was, rooted there holding flowers—yellow and white carnations for Todd. They should have been red, like blood, since Josh brought them.

Stephanie really needed to leave, go someplace where she could be alone with her memories. "I rarely fly," she said. "Now I'll make certain I never do—at least not with you, and how is it that a pilot had no money to pay for an attorney?"

"I was between jobs." He shifted the flowers from one arm to the other. "And then dating Judge Anderson's daughter got expensive."

"I'll bet it did." She wanted to scream. Josh's surly attitude would have been difficult to handle on a good day. "Just go put your posies on Todd's grave and leave." She turned her attention to Charles. "And why do we need a pilot?" She started to climb into the car.

"We have a plane."

"We, who?" One leg in the car, Stephanie stopped, backed out and stared at Charles.

"The firm," he answered.

Stephanie realized how little she'd been a part of things at work. "Why didn't I know about it?"

"There was no reason before, but now that you're going to be taking on more responsibilities, you'll be using it." Charles actually puffed out his chest.

"Oh, no. Not me. Airplanes are dangerous." Stephanie dropped onto the car seat.

"So are cars . . ." Josh's voice trailed off, and for once he looked embarrassed. Stephanie didn't need to be reminded that was how Todd had died.

She glared up at Josh. Somehow, being mean to him helped take her mind off Todd, if only for a moment.

"So where is this plane?" She asked no one in particular. Josh probably knew more about it than she did. He and Charles seemed real chummy all of a sudden. What was going on? It wasn't like Charles to pick up strays. Well, actually he'd picked her up.

"It's in our hangar," Charles answered. "I used to fly, but I've gotten a little rusty with age and was considering selling the plane, but now that we have a pilot I think we'll keep it for a while. At least as long as Josh sticks around."

"I'm not going anywhere." His eyes locked with Stephanie's and a twitch of a smile crossed his lips.

Heat prickled the back of her neck. "Do you think we can leave, Charles? I have a bad headache." She didn't, but might if they stayed.

"Of course. I'm sorry." He closed her door and hurried around to the driver's seat and started the car.

Josh tapped on the window. In spite of herself, Stephanie rolled it down.

"I just came to pay my respects." He held up the flowers.

"You didn't know Todd."

"I came because of you. I wanted to tell you how sorry I am. It didn't go the way I'd planned, but know that I am truly sorry."

Tears threatened, but Stephanie fought them back. "If that's true, thank you for coming."

He nodded and headed toward Todd's grave.

Stephanie turned to Charles. "Are you completely certain about hiring Josh? I'm not sure we can trust him."

Patting her hand, Charles said, "He'll be fine. It doesn't hurt to give someone down on their luck a chance."

He'd given her a chance, hadn't he? Charles hadn't reminded her of that fact, but she knew his meaning. She guessed she was stuck with their new employee.

As they left, Stephanie glanced out the rear window at Josh. After placing the flowers on Todd's coffin, he hurried to his white truck. She drew a deep breath. Josh's truck really was just like the one Todd had followed the night of his death, but she guessed there were more than one similar white truck in the area. Yet . . .

The road out of the cemetery circled back around and passed Todd's gravesite. Josh followed in his truck. Janeen and Deirdre had gone on ahead. As had the men from the mortuary, leaving Todd alone. The workers at the cemetery would wait a respectable time until all mourners had left before lowering the coffin into the ground. Stephanie took another look. She couldn't hold the tears back any longer. She blinked to clear her eyes. Wait. Todd wasn't alone. A young woman, holding flowers, stood beside the coffin.

"Stop, go back," Stephanie cried.

"What?"

"There's someone with Todd."

Charles turned around. "I don't see anyone."

"She's right beside his coffin." Stephanie pointed to where the young woman had been standing, but no one was there. She blinked. "I must be losing it."

"You've had a hard day." Charles steered the Lexus onto the highway.

"I really have," Stephanie mumbled, as she stole one last glance at Todd's lonely coffin.

CHAPTER 12

"Stephanie, this is Officer Christopherson." The last time he'd called was to notify her of Todd's accident. His voice carried that same no-nonsense tone.

"Hi, Officer. Uh, . . . how did you find me here?" Even though five weeks had passed since Todd's funeral, Stephanie still lived out of a suitcase at her boss's mansion. There were days she asked herself why. The only answer she'd been able to come up with was that living at Charles's was kind of like being on vacation. When she went home, real life would happen. Was Officer Christopherson about to give her a dose of "real life" now?

"I asked around. It's my job," the police officer returned. "Actually the girl at your office told me."

Of course, Stephanie thought, the mouthy Deirdre strikes again. "I haven't been able to convince myself to move home yet." Why did she feel she had to explain? Could it be that she was unmarried, pregnant and living with a single man? But no one knew about the pregnancy—yet. Obviously that would soon change.

"It's nice you have someone to be with, but—" Officer Christopherson began.

"His housekeeper lives here too." That's enough, Stephanie told herself. After all, she wasn't at the house all the time. She'd been back to work several busy afternoons, and she'd visited the horses, even ridden a couple of times.

"Okaaay. I'm sure you'll stay where you feel the most comfortable right now."

"It's not that I feel . . ." she caught herself. "I'm sorry. I keep interrupting. I'm sure you had a reason for calling."

"I do," Officer Christopherson said hesitantly. "We've been looking at your friend, Todd . . . ."

"Fiancé." During the course of her stay at Charles's, she'd felt secure enough to tell him that she and Todd were to be married. Charles hadn't seemed surprised.

"He was your fiancé? I didn't know. I'm really sorry."

"No. I'm sorry. I keep interrupting. Please go on." She just wanted this whole nightmare over, even though in her present condition she knew it never would be.

"As I was saying, we've been searching through Todd Saxton's car to see if there was anything other than the weather that contributed to the accident."

Stephanie's heart raced. "And was there?"

"It hasn't been ruled out, but that's not why I'm calling. There was something in his car that I thought you might be able to help us with."

She took a deep breath and held it. "What was it?"

"There was a notebook stuck between the driver's seat and the console that he'd made some notations in . . . ." Officer Christopherson's voice was muffled for a moment as if he'd secured the phone between his chin and shoulder to free his hands, "you know, things to remember, grocery lists and such. Then there was the beginning of a letter he was trying to write to you."

"To me?" Her knees began to wobble. She leaned against the wall in Charles's guest bedroom. "Why would he write me a letter? He saw me practically every day."

"I don't know, but a lot of words were crossed out as if he wanted to tell you something, but it was better to write it down. You know, like it was important to choose the right words."

Tears welled in her eyes. "What did it say?"

"I actually called to see when I could meet with you so you can go over it."

"Have you read it?" She didn't want to wait for him to come over and she certainly didn't want him coming to Charles's.

"It's part of the investigation, Stephanie, I'm sorry."

"I understand. You might as well just read it to me then."

"You sure?"

"Yes. Go on." Fresh hurt threatened to smother the progress she'd made toward recovery.

Officer Christopherson cleared his throat, then began to read in a quiet, almost reverent voice. "My Dearest Stephanie, I want you to know how much I truly love you. Please remember that no matter what happens . . . . He crossed out 'no matter what happens' and wrote, 'in spite of what I'm going to tell you . . .' He skipped a few lines and wrote, 'Before I go on, I must ask you to destroy this letter as soon as you read it.' He crossed out 'destroy' and put 'burn.' Then he wrote, 'I haven't been completely honest with you.' He crossed out 'completely,' so it now reads, 'I haven't been honest with you.'"

She felt light headed. He loved her and he was going to tell her everything.

"Then it appears he didn't know what to say," Officer Christopherson went on, "because he tried several other sentences: 'I've been involved . . . . You need to be aware . . . . I need to warn you . . . . What I'm about to say will . . . .' He crossed them all out and started again. 'When I came to town a "year ago, I became acquainted—"' Officer Christopherson stopped.

"What? What?" Stephanie shouted into the phone, gasping for breath.

"That's all he wrote."

"No. Look again. Look on the back. You said it was a notebook. Look later in the book." Helplessly, she collapsed onto the bed.

"We've done all that, Stephanie. Do you have any idea what he was talking about?"

"No. None at all."

"It sounded like he was trying to warn you about something, or someone. Is there anyone you think might be a threat?"

"No," she said quickly, but then thought. Of course there was someone, but did Todd even know Josh? Or what about Todd's friend, Brad, who had drugged them both? Or had he? At least she'd been drugged. She still couldn't remember what happened that fateful night. And then there was Brad's sister, Colleen, who Todd said experienced a mental breakdown. Was she the girl Stephanie saw at the cemetery? Had she seen a girl at the cemetery? Of course. There was no doubt left in Stephanie's mind. She raked her fingers through her hair, pulling it away from her face.

"Are you sure there's no one?" Officer Christopherson asked.

Although Stephanie knew Kent Christopherson fairly well, he was not someone with whom she felt comfortable sharing her deepest secrets, or pointing a finger at "only maybe" guilty people. "Yes. I'm sure." She grabbed a tissue from a box on the lamp table and wiped her eyes. Straightening her blouse, she squared her shoulders. She'd do some investigating on her own, then perhaps get back to Officer Christopherson if she came up with something solid. "May I have Todd's notebook when you're through with it? And I hope you'll keep me informed on anything you discover about Todd's car."

"Of course, but I'm sure you know we'll have to keep the notebook in evidence until our investigation into Todd's death is completed. We'll keep his cell phone too, although there's nothing of interest on it."

"Okay. Sure. Thank you for calling, Officer." She couldn't wait to get him off the phone. It was as if Todd's message had given her new strength. What was he trying to tell her? Who was she was supposed to fear? A bigger question surfaced. Was there anyone she could trust? The answer came as a jolt. There was no one. Not only would she have to be more mindful of her own safety, but she'd have to figure out what Todd was trying to tell her. She had a new direction, something important to do. She needed to get out there and find answers. But where to begin?

Well, she'd not learn a thing sitting here in Charles's house doing nothing. She was dressed and heading out the back door, when Janeen, the housekeeper, stopped her.

"Where are you going in such a hurry?" she asked, dust cloth in hand.

"Nuts if I don't get out and do something. Maybe I'll visit the barn." No one would question her desire to be with the horses, and although an afternoon with them would have relieved some tension, after backing her Honda out of Charles's driveway, that was not where she headed.

Since it was almost the middle of May, there remained few traces of the storm that had caused Todd to slide into an oncoming truck. At least that's what the initial accident report had affirmed. Stephanie had her own theory. Now as she traveled up this winding canyon road, she switched radio stations several times, seeking tunes that might draw her mind from thoughts of the destination she had hoped she'd never have to revisit.

Staring out the car window, she pondered her surroundings. These were the sights Todd would have viewed had he still been alive. Would her pain never end?

Big puffy clouds in an otherwise blue sky rested atop peaks where patches of snow still lingered. On the lower slopes, a tapestry of trees in shades of tender green and yellow poured out from mountain gorges. Dandelions poked yellow heads up through fields of lush grass, and pinecones relinquished from ancient ponderosas rested alongside the winding road. Only the leaves of the rough barked oaks still slumbered, suggesting to Stephanie that she too should awake from her self-imposed hibernation.

When she pulled into the driveway of Todd's former home, her mouth was so dry her lips felt stiff. What had Todd been trying to tell her? If only he'd finished the letter. If only he were still alive and felt no need for correspondence.

She climbed out of her Honda, hesitated for a moment, gathering strength, then made her way to the front door. She wasn't sure why she'd come here, only that she didn't know where else to start. Maybe it would spur some feeling or lend a clue to what Todd had wanted to tell her, or perhaps being where Todd had last lived would offer a little comfort to the ache that impaled her heart.

Beside the path on which she now walked, red tulips stood at attention. She wondered if Todd had planted them last fall. She frowned. Now they were here and he was not.

At the front door, she knocked, not really expecting anyone to answer. Reaching for the doorknob, she tried to turn it. The knob stayed solid in her hand.

Stepping out onto the deck that ran along the front of the cabin, she brought her hands to either side of her face and leaned in to stare through the front room window.

"May I help you?" a male voice asked.

Shocked and embarrassed, Stephanie jumped back and turned to face the lawn below. "Oh. You scared me. I was just . . . . My fiancé . . . . Are you the new tenant?" she stammered.

"I was about to ask you the same question," the man said.

Stephanie blinked. Up here in the canyon she expected to see a macho-looking man dressed in jeans and boots and maybe carrying an axe to cut wood. No, she wouldn't have wanted him to be carrying an axe, maybe a bucket to haul water. But that was not the case. The man who stood before her, actually the man who leaned on a cane before her, was anything but macho. He was old, quite old. Actually for an old guy, he was quite macho.

She put a hand to her chest as if to keep her heart from leaping out. "My fiancé, my late fiancé lives here, uh, lived . . . used to live here."

"Sorry. Didn't mean to scare you." His thick white brows formed a ledge over narrowed eyes. "Late? You say late? He's dead then. I wondered what happened to him."

"Todd died about five weeks ago." She couldn't keep the tremor from her voice. "He was in a car accident."

"I'm sorry." Standing beneath her on the unkempt lawn, the old man placed his cane in front of him and rested both hands upon it. "Actually I didn't know him well. He kept pretty much to himself, but he seemed like a nice enough fellow."

"He was nice." Stephanie's eyes stung. She changed the subject. "You live around here?"

He took one hand from the cane and pointed to a small cabin nearly hidden amidst tall oaks and pines. "Over there. My wife and I used to come up from town once or twice a month, but now I spend every weekend here. I lost her last fall. We'd been sweethearts for nearly sixty-seven years, but now she's gone. I don't suppose I'll last much longer. I hope not."

Stephanie knew how he felt. Many times she'd wanted to join Todd. "I'm so sorry. So you've lost someone dear to you, too. It's hard, isn't it?"

"It sucks."

"You're right. It does suck." She swallowed a giggle at his response. "I'm Stephanie Saunders." From the short deck she reached out her hand, then realizing he was several feet beneath her on the lawn she said, "Oh, sorry."

He stuck up his cane for her to shake. "Joseph Jacobsen, at your service. My, but you're a beauty."

"Thank you." For the first time in weeks, Stephanie felt like smiling. She figured Mr. Joseph Jacobsen would have that effect on many people. How lucky Mrs. Jacobsen must have been.

"It's nice to meet you." She looked from him to the house and then back at him again. He shifted from one foot to the other. He must have been getting tired standing on his wobbly legs. "Well, I don't want to keep you, Mr. Jacobsen. I thought it might help me to hang around here where Todd spent his last days, but it looks like it's all locked up."

Mr. Jacobsen hobbled toward to stairs. Stephanie hurried over to offer assistance. "May I?" she said.

"Let's just sit here on the stairs. I'll be fine if you'll help me up."

"That's a deal."

He plopped down on the second stair. She sat beside him. For some reason she felt as if they were dear friends, not new acquaintances.

"I think his stuff's gone," Mr. Jacobsen said. "If anything's left, I'd be surprised."

"Really?" Charles had told her they'd disposed of all of Todd's belongings to keep her from having to do it, so this was not new information.

"Yep. Several weeks ago a truck came pulling a covered trailer, backed right up into here. A few hours later, they were gone. Poof. Just like they'd never been here. Didn't anyone tell you? Being his fiancé, I'd have figured they would have checked with you first."

Even a stranger could see how things should have gone. "One would think so, wouldn't they? I guess my friends thought it would be too hard on me." She really wished Charles would have included her.

"Maybe that was the case. My daughter, Silvia, and I started going through my sweet Martha's things. Silvia had to finish because I couldn't do it. I was able to keep a few special things that reminded me of Martha, though—her purse, the clips she wore in her hair, her favorite sweater, even her pill holder—silly things really, but I still take them out of the dresser drawer once in a while and reminisce. It seems to bring me closer to my sweetheart. I wish you would have had a chance to keep a few things like that. I guess your friends weren't thinking, or maybe they haven't lost someone dear to them so they just didn't consider."

Charles should have known. He had lost his wife.

"So did your fellow's parents have a chance to save anything of his?"

"His parents are dead."

"You were all he had then."

"I was." Her voice shook. When would she ever be able to talk about Todd without crying? How she wished she had something to remember him by. She thought about the baby. Maybe the child would be a gift after all. She frowned. How could something that was going to cause her so much trouble be a gift? No, she still wished she'd had some say over where Todd's things ended up. Of course, when she'd asked Charles about it, he had told her that there hadn't been much, that most everything had been repossessed.

Mr. Jacobsen patted her knee. "Martha would have liked you."

"I bet I'd have liked her too."

They sat silent for a moment and then Stephanie said, "Did you recognize anyone who came to get Todd's stuff?"

"What? Recognize? No," Mr. Jacobsen said. "Like I mentioned before, I didn't know your gentleman friend very well."

"But did you see what they looked like?" Finally maybe someone could tell her something, anything.

Mr. Jacobsen turned to gaze at her with light blue eyes. She could imagine Mrs. Jacobsen getting lost in them. "Just men," he said. "Four of them, all young and strong looking. Oh, then there was that older guy—not older than me, few people are, but older than them—who drove up in that fancy car."

Stephanie's senses peaked even though this wasn't new information either. "You don't look that old." She bumped her shoulder against his. He really didn't look that old. "Was it a black Lexus?"

"Could have been. It was black, anyway."

Of course it was a black Lexus. Of course it was Charles, but he'd told her that there hadn't been much stuff, unless he was overseeing the bankruptcy crew.

"And then there was that other guy."

Stephanie felt her jaw drop. "What other guy?"

"He was younger than the guy in the fancy car, actually pretty young. He stayed hidden in the trees over on the Washburn property. I wouldn't have seen him at all but I was walking over to see if Clyde wanted to play a game of cribbage, then I remembered that Clyde and Grace had gone to visit their son in Oklahoma, so there'd be no cards that day. Well, I noticed this young guy watching all the activity and asked him what he was doing on Clyde's lot. He said he'd heard about some property that was for sale and was trying to find out about it. I mentioned I didn't know of any, but that maybe the property they were moving from would be available. He must have been really interested because he never left, just kept watching the move."

"What did he look like?"

Mr. Jacobsen shifted a couple of times on the hard stair. "Well he was young, like I said, and he really needed a shave and a haircut. I remember telling Martha, before she died, that young people these days don't pay much attention to good grooming and this young fellow proved it. She wouldn't have liked the looks of him."

So Josh had been here too. The guy showed up everywhere. He'd probably parked his white truck down the lane. "Did he watch the whole time?"

"I don't know. I didn't go back over to Clyde's because he was gone, you remember, but after a while the other guys in the truck and the older fellow in the fancy car left, so I imagine the young man left too."

"So they moved everything out?"

"I couldn't see what they took. The men backed the truck right up into the driveway and loaded stuff directly into the covered trailer. It seemed like they were there for a while, but maybe they were just relaxing or having a smoke." He straightened one leg, then the other as if relieving stress on his knees. "Hard to tell."

She'd questioned the poor old guy enough. "Well, thank you for the information. If you're ready, I'll help you up, but maybe

I'll stay here awhile, sit on the porch and watch the birds." It really was beautiful there and strangely calming.

"Mind if I stick around a bit, too? This is the most fun I've had since I trapped Clyde's marble in Chinese checkers." Mr. Jacobsen chuckled. "Clyde said it was like the man who was running for the outhouse in the middle of the night and encountered the clothesline. He wouldn't have made it anyway."

Stephanie and Mr. Jacobsen shared a good laugh, and although Stephanie would have preferred to be alone, she didn't have the heart to send her new friend away. "Sure, if you want," she said, "but I'm liable to be pretty boring. I really wish I could go inside."

"At your age you have no idea what boring is. Boring is trying to guess which way an ant on the floor will turn, or reminiscing about the good times when getting out of a chair wasn't a major undertaking."

Somehow she knew what he was feeling. Years ago she'd spent a lot of time with her grandfather before he'd died. So many people had left her in her life. "Okay, let's get acquainted for a while. I suppose if someone comes, they won't be too upset with us just sitting here minding our own business."

"We don't care if they are, do we? Might be exciting."

"I do believe there's a bit of a rogue in you."

He laughed. "That's what my sweet Martha used to say. You remind me a little of her—when she was younger, of course."

"Of course. I'll take that as a compliment."

"It was meant as one."

"Thank you." She smiled and changed the subject. "The tulips sure are pretty. Do you know who planted them?" Maybe she'd been correct in her thinking earlier that Todd had. It really didn't matter, but somehow it made her feel closer to him.

"Wait a minute. Wait one solitary minute," Mr. Jacobsen said, drawing her out of her thoughts. "You just reminded me of something." He held out his hand. "Give me a pull, will you."

She stood and reached out to him.

Several groans and a grunt later, he made it to his feet. He steadied himself on his cane and picked his way down the stone pathway that curved in front of a flower garden. Lava rock, probably from the same supply as that of the cabin's fireplace and chimney, outlined the garden.

He tapped his cane on one of the jagged rocks. "See what's under here," he said. "I watched your young man once. He walked down here, glanced around, stooped and then went back to the front door. It didn't occur to me until now, but maybe he hid an extra key under one of these rocks."

Stooping, Stephanie turned over the designated rock. "Oooh," she said and grimaced.

Several sow bugs crawled away to hide beneath a nearby stone and, stretching its slender form, an angleworm also sought refuge. Stephanie glanced at Mr. Jacobsen.

"He tapped another rock with his cane. "Try this one."

Hesitant to see what creature she might disturb, Stephanie nonetheless turned over the second rock. She took in a quick breath.

Nestled in an army of ants, a silver key glistened in the sunlight.

"You are a super sleuth," she told the old man. She grabbed a twig off the ground and threaded it through the hole at the top of the key. Most of the ants fell off when she picked the key up, but she dragged it across the grass for good measure. At last she claimed her prize and held it up for her friend's inspection.

He gave her a thumbs-up. "Are you going in? I won't tell if you don't."

"I think so." She headed up the stairs to the front door.

"Will you be okay or do you want me to come along?" He stood ready with his cane.

Stephanie smiled to herself. Although old and feeble, Mr. Jacobsen wanted to protect her. They didn't make men like him anymore. Mrs. Jacobsen had been a lucky woman. She tried the key. A perfect fit. She pushed the door ajar. "I'll be fine. If I'm picked up for trespassing, I don't want you involved."

He started toward her. "Oh. I'd hope it wouldn't come to that."

"I'll be fine." She held up her hand.

"You're sure?"

"I'm sure."

"Well, okay. I can tell that you prefer to go in by yourself."

"I kinda do. You understand, don't you?"

"I most certainly do. Martha would have wanted to be alone under the same circumstances."

Stephanie blinked back a tear. "I'll put the key back when I'm through, even though I may encounter those horrible ants." She tried to lighten the tone of the conversation.

Mr. Jacobsen smiled. "Just remember . . ." He paused, and she thought he would say something profound. "You're bigger than they are," he finished.

She giggled. "Good point." Standing on the porch, she stared at him for a moment, not knowing how to say good-bye. "You've been great." She couldn't help herself, and turned and ran back down the stairs. Reaching out, she gave Mr. Jacobsen a big hug. "Thanks for your help. You're awesome."

"Well, thank you." He put his arms around her. "I wish Clyde were here to see this. He'll never believe it. Maybe you can give me another hug some time soon when he's around."

"That's a deal, and again, thank you." She bounded back up the stairs.

"Don't be a stranger," he said and plodded across the road to his own cabin.

"I won't," she yelled and watched as he disappeared inside.

Like in a horror movie, the door squeaked when she opened it. At least it wasn't raining. She tried to calm her breathing as she came through the front hall into the living room. Just as Mr. Jacobsen had surmised, absolutely nothing remained. Nothing. The room had been stripped clean. She wandered into the kitchen and opened cupboards. Everything was gone. The bathroom and downstairs bedrooms were completely empty as well. She found her way back to the front room and realized now that she couldn't have seen in through the window even if Mr. Jacobsen hadn't interrupted her. The shutters were closed and drapes drawn. She flipped on the lights to the huge chandelier.

Sweet and bitter memories blended together in her troubled brain. Standing by the now cold and forbidding fireplace, she remembered other times when she and Todd had curled up next to it on the couch.

She turned and began to wander. Peeking into the bedroom where Todd had awakened her that fateful morning, her stomach lurched. She shook her head. This was not the feeling she sought. She'd hoped for comfort or at least closure that up until now had been denied. If only she could shed the sorrow that smothered her. She'd thought that seeing his house again might offer some sign, some answer, some message from him that all would be well and she could go on with her life. She climbed the stairs and leaned over the balcony to peer at the living room below. She called his name and pretended that he would answer. Sighing, she walked into his bedroom.

Maybe if the room had been how Todd had left it, she might have felt comforted. It was as if he had never existed. She walked into his closet and looked around. Glancing up onto the top shelf, she noticed a tiny speck of white. Frantic for any memory of Todd she stood on tiptoes and reached up. Her fingers touched something that slipped beneath them. She stretched up as far as she could and slid the paper forward. It glided to the floor. A picture of a younger Todd grinned up at her. His hair was longer and his skin darkly tanned, but it was Todd, no mistaking that.

A warm feeling came over her and tears clouded her eyes. This was the sign she'd been looking for. This was Todd's way of telling her that he was okay and that everything would work out. It truly was, wasn't it? Wasn't it? What about his letter to her that he never finished? Who had he been trying to warn her about? She couldn't think of that now.

She shoved the picture into her shirt pocket and made a final walk through the house, letting her mind dwell only on the good times. She would never return. She didn't need to. It was as if he'd come back from the grave to tell her good-bye and let her know that he'd be watching over her. It was all she needed. She could go on and face what lay ahead.

After placing the key back under the rock, she returned to her car and climbed in, feeling happier than she had in a long time. She'd been right to come. At this moment, only good memories remained.

Turning up the radio, she hummed along with a familiar tune. Before she realized it, she was cruising down the winding road faster than she should have. A deer darted across the pavement. She slammed on the brakes and skidded onto the gravel shoulder. Missing the deer, she stopped just short of a twenty-foot drop. She switched off the ignition and rested her forehead against the steering wheel, trying to force air back into her lungs. Shaking her head she scolded herself. What was she trying to do? Join Todd? Kill this baby she carried? True, she didn't want it, but she didn't want to kill it. So many people desired babies these days—people who were part of a family, people who were parent material. She was not parent material. Actually, what kind of material was she? Was she any good to anyone?

She reached into her pocket for Todd's picture. It had given her strength earlier. She held it up between thumb and forefinger. She sneezed and the picture flipped out of her hand and fell down between the passenger seat and console. Searching for it, she couldn't believe how frantic she became. At last her fingers found it and she drew it up. She started to turn it over so she could see Todd's face, but then noticed that something was written on the back in pencil, lightened by time. She moved the photo into the direct sunlight and read. "Thanks Chris."

"Thanks Chris," what did that mean? Who was Chris? Was Todd thanking someone named Chris by giving them his picture? She chewed on her bottom lip. Was Chris a boy or a girl?

Had there been a comma and the writing had read, "Thanks, Chris," it would stand to reason that Todd had given someone the picture and signed it "Thanks, Chris," but it should have been "Thanks, Todd." A thought kept nibbling at the edge of Stephanie's mind and when she brought it to the forefront, her pulse quickened. Todd never used punctuation. She'd kidded him about it many times. Maybe Todd's name was Chris Todd Saxton, or even Christopher Todd Saxton.

A chill ran down her spine. Maybe Todd's name wasn't Saxton at all. Maybe it wasn't even Todd. An awful thought hit her like a mule's kick. What if she didn't even know the real name of her baby's father?

CHAPTER 13

A week later the words on the back of Todd's picture still bothered Stephanie, but she kept her concerns to herself. She hadn't found time to do any research and wondered if she hadn't because she really didn't want to. Like it or not, Todd was the father of her child and she'd loved him.

She was still thinking about Todd when Deirdre came into her office and said that Charles wanted to see her.

Good, Stephanie thought. It was not only past time to tell Charles she was moving back to her condo but it provided an opportunity to confess her life-changing secret.

Feeling as if she were one of her clients waiting for sentencing, Stephanie sat across the desk from Charles in his spacious, newly decorated office. She'd put off this confrontation long enough. It probably would have been easier earlier. She raised her chin. "Charles, I'll be moving out of your house this weekend." She'd tell him the easiest thing first, then move on to the zinger.

The leather chair creaked as her boss leaned back, steepling his fingers. "Haven't Janeen and I made it comfortable enough for you?"

It had been six weeks since Todd's death and Charles had always come up with reasons for her to stay. Surely he wasn't that lonesome. He had Janeen. Well, maybe he was that lonesome.

"It's too comfortable," Stephanie said. "If I'm ever going to be able to move on, I need to get back to real life." After she told him about the baby, he'd probably be glad to get her out of his house. She hoped he wouldn't want her out of the office, too. It was enough to give her hives. She hadn't figured on that before—pregnant and jobless.

"Really. I was hoping you'd consider going to Montana for me this weekend." Charles smoothed his beard, which had been recently trimmed. Stephanie decided she liked this new beard. Slightly graying, it made Charles look very distinguished.

"Montana? Why Montana?" He was doing it again. Another delaying tactic. Still, if he really meant it, the trip sounded interesting. She'd always wanted to go to Montana.

While he talked, Charles put on his reading glasses, scanning documents in a file on his desk. "It's a property dispute between brothers. They own a ranch together. Thought they had it sold so they all bought new property. Ranch deal fell through. One of the brothers, Andrew—he's my friend—wants to give up some of his shares in the ranch so he can keep the new property. Other brothers want the ranch corporation to own Andrew's property. It's a mess. They're having a meeting this weekend. The attorney who has historically represented the ranch will be there. My friend wants me to come up and watch out for his interests."

"You should go then. He wouldn't want me." So much for Montana.

"I told Andrew I can't go." Charles closed the file. "I have that big Sanderson trial starting Monday. Paul may be able to fly up if the case he's been working on continues, but we thought you might want the experience and Andrew sounded okay with the idea. We think you're ready to take on more responsibility."

Stephanie couldn't help smiling to herself. Charles had begun to trust in her abilities. His approval was something she'd long sought. How would he feel when he learned she had been stupid enough to get herself pregnant? It wouldn't matter that she and Todd had both been drugged. Would Charles believe that? Did she? Wait a minute. Had Charles said fly?

"Did you say that Paul might fly to Montana?"

"Yes, fly. That's why I hired a pilot."

"Josh Durrant?"

"Yes. I told you about him, remember?"

"I remember." Stephanie rolled her eyes. "But Josh Durrant. I don't think I want to be in a plane with him. I barely know the guy and I have a hard time thinking of him as anything other than a defendant. Did you say Paul's case might continue?"

"It might and then he could go, but I don't think you need to worry about Josh. He's not a defendant anymore. The charges have been dropped, remember."

Easy for him to say. Charles didn't have a white truck, probably belonging to Josh Durrant, following him around. "Yes. I know you're a good attorney," Stephanie said, "but it just seemed too easy."

Charles raised a brow as if she should know better than to question him. "I talked it over with the judge and in addition to there being a conflict of interest, I guess his daughter decided to drop the charges."

Stephanie shook her head. "It still sounds fishy."

"Fishy?"

"Yes, fishy."

"That would be right after fiduciary in the Black's Law Dictionary."

"Correct." She smiled.

Charles shook his head. "From what Josh tells me, he wasn't guilty of the charges anyway."

"From what most defendants say, none of them are guilty." Why couldn't she believe Josh was innocent?

"I know, but I really think Josh is telling the truth."

Stephanie wagged her finger at Charles. "I think you just like him because he can fly an airplane. Do you know anything else about him?"

"No, not much. He seems like a nice enough fellow, though, just down on his luck."

"And now he works for you."

"Now he works for us, the firm. He's a good pilot. I flew with him yesterday."

It was all happening too fast. One day Josh was a client, the next an employee. "I don't know . . . ." Maybe she didn't trust Josh because she should have been more wary of Todd.

"Give him a chance, Stephanie. I think you'll like him." She kinda had liked Josh. That's what worried her. But what did she know about him? What had she known about Todd, or Chris, or whatever his name was?

"If Paul can't go, will you consider it?"

Wasn't this what she'd been hoping for—Charles's trust? Now this little parasite she carried was going to ruin it for her. An unmarried pregnant woman wouldn't speak well for the firm. Charles was going to have a fit, but she had to tell him. One of these first days he'd be able to see for himself and he'd be furious with her for trying to keep it from him. Now she wished she'd told him sooner. Why hadn't she?

"I'm flattered. I really am. I can't believe you'd trust me to handle things for your friend. You've been so kind. You've treated me like a daughter, not just an employee. I will never be able to repay you, but now . . . now I have to tell you something that might change your opinion of me." She felt her heart speed up.

"I doubt there is anything that would change my opinion of you. You are not only a gifted attorney, but a wonderful, caring person. I think you have a marvelous career ahead of you. I only hope it will be with this firm."

"I'm pregnant," she burst out. She'd held it in as long as she could. It was almost a relief, even though she knew her disclosure might mean disaster.

"Excuse me? I thought you said you're pregnant." Charles grinned.

"It is what I said." Her voice shook.

Charles peered over the top of his reading glasses. "My goodness, Stephanie. In this day and age. Don't you know what causes pregnancy and how to prevent it?"

She narrowed her eyes. "Of course I do. I didn't know I was getting pregnant." This was so embarrassing.

"You really should pay more attention."

Stephanie shifted in her chair and blurted. "I was drugged." She hadn't meant to go into the whole nightmare, but Charles acted like it was all a joke.

"What? By whom? Do you know who the father is?" Now it wasn't so funny.

"Of course I know. It was Todd." Her face went hot.

"Did he drug you?" Charles stiffened.

"No, his friend did. Both of us. It's a long story that I don't want— His friend is gone. We couldn't find him. And now Todd's gone, too."

"His friend is dead?"

"No, just gone."

"No wonder you were in such a hurry to get married."

"Well, now you see my problem."

Charles was silent while Stephanie tried to read his expression, but being a practiced litigator his face told her nothing. "I don't suppose you'd consider an abortion?" he asked.

She glared at him. Of course that would be his first suggestion.

"That's what I thought. So are you going to keep it? You know it would complicate your career."

Stephanie shook her head slowly, not so much in answer to his question, but to suggest her frustration. "It wouldn't want me for a mother."

Charles stared at her as if trying to come up with something nice to say . . . . Apparently unable to do so, he kept quiet.

"No. I don't want it," she continued, a little hurt. "I'm going to give it away. Do you know anything about unwanted babies and adoption?" Would he continue to help or abandon her to her own resources? She held her breath.

"I might," he said, finally.

All of a sudden Stephanie burst into tears. This was all so humiliating. Never in her worse nightmares had she ever thought this could happen to her. She had always maintained control over her life. "You do?" Maybe Charles would stick by her after all.

"I might know someone. They may even be willing to pay your expenses." He shuffled through some files on his desk, but didn't find the one he sought. "They've been wanting another baby for a year or so. They were thinking of a foreign adoption, but this would be even better. Have you been to the doctor?"

Wow. He was so matter of fact. No emotion—just get on with the problem solving. He'd been an attorney too long. "Yes. I've been to a doctor and I really am pregnant. Denying it hasn't made me any less so." She whisked away her tears with the tips of her fingers.

"Well, now I hope you'll forget this nonsense of moving back into your condo and stay with Janeen and me. You shouldn't be alone with the baby coming." He stroked his beard. "You know, we could send you to Montana to work as the time gets closer. I have a beautiful condo there."

Stephanie felt her mouth drop open. Where did he get all his money? Someone, probably Deirdre, said once that his late wife had been rich. That was probably it. The practice certainly didn't seem that lucrative. If it was, they hadn't been sharing much with her, yet now they wanted to make her more a part of it all and she and this baby might have blown it.

She stood and began to pace. "Why are you being so nice to me? I've just told you that all your plans for me have been jeopardized."

"Why wouldn't I be? Didn't I tell you I lost a daughter to cancer? If she were in your predicament, I'd want to be there for her." His head turned to follow her as she paced back and forth.

"I feel like such a failure," she said, her stomach knotting. Apparently Charles continued to care about her even after all she'd told him, and she'd been ready to accuse him of something bad in connection with Todd and his belongings. She was in no position to judge. She had just better accept his help and his conditions.

"You're not a failure. Don't talk like that," Charles said, removing his glasses and laying them on the desk. "This is just a little set-back. Five and a half, six months from now, you'll forget any of this happened and be back in court."

How did he know she was three and one-half months along? She didn't feel like she showed much yet. The waistband on her slacks was tight, that was all.

She stopped pacing. "You're a good guesser."

"What do you mean?" For a moment his face turned red.

"How did you know I'm three and one-half months along?" She really wanted to trust him. Who else did she have? Yet—

"Did I say you were three and a half months along?"

"You said in five and one-half, six months, everything would be over."

"Just a guess. Women usually find out when they're about two months along and Todd has been gone six weeks."

Okay. She could understand his reasoning, but why had he blushed? Maybe he just didn't like talking about things like pregnancy with his associates. She knew how he felt. Her face was probably cherry red, too.

She took a deep breath and asked what she knew she must. "So do you want me to quit?"

"Quit what?" He picked up a ballpoint pen and clicked it.

"Working at the firm?"

"While you're pregnant, I assume you'll have to slow down some." He clicked the pen over and over.

"No. I mean permanently. I know it wouldn't look very good for the firm, me being pregnant and unmarried. I know many people have babies these days who aren't married, but an unmarried, pregnant attorney doesn't look too professional." She began pacing again.

"You're probably right. We'll send you to Montana, create a story about your husband dying in Iraq. Then after you have the baby you can come back here and no one will be the wiser." The clicking stopped.

She plopped back down in her chair. "Why would you do this for me?"

"I told you. You need a break and I would hope someone would have done it for my daughter had she lived and I had not." He clicked the pen again.

She placed her hands on the edge of his desk. "Do we have to tell Paul and Deirdre about all this?"

"No. It'll be our secret." He put the pen down.

"Really?" For the first time in months, she felt as if her life could go on. Now she had to tell Charles the rest.

"No one needs to know." He gave her a reassuring smile.

She took a deep breath. "I drove up to Todd's cabin yesterday."

"Really."

"I thought it would make me feel better."

"Did it?"

"Not really. It was like he'd never been there. I should have listened. You told me all his stuff was gone."

He leaned forward. "I'm sorry I didn't let you help. I thought it would be too hard for you. Janeen cleared everything out after my wife died."

That's why he hadn't thought to include her. How different he'd been from her new friend Mr. Jacobsen. "So there wasn't much left."

"No. The bankruptcy court took the majority of it."

"I met someone who said there'd been a truck."

He stared at her for a moment as if trying to read her mind. "I told you the bankruptcy court took most everything."

"So you weren't there."

"No."

But Joseph Jacobsen had said he had been. Perhaps Charles didn't want to admit his part in the loss of Todd's possessions.

"I wonder what will become of the house now that Todd is gone? It's really nice."

"I arranged to have it purchased," he stated, placing both hands on his desk.

"You what?"

"I bought it."

"Why didn't you tell me?" Here again, he hadn't included her. "What are you going to do with it?"

"Rent it. Since the bankruptcy court was involved, it was a great investment."

Stephanie didn't know if she was relieved or furious. It had been Todd's house. Had they been married, it could have been hers had she been able to save it from the bankruptcy court. Now, without even telling her, Charles had bought it, or as he explained "had it purchased." She wondered if that was even legal, him being the attorney on the bankruptcy and all. She supposed he had finessed it.

"Can I rent it?" she asked before she had time to think.

"I'm sorry. It's already taken."

"You're kidding. Who did you rent it to?" Then all of a sudden she knew. As if one could take the other's place, Charles had substituted one good-looking mysterious man for another. "Tell me you didn't rent it to Josh Durrant."

Charles leaned back in his leather chair and once more steepled his fingers. "I didn't think you'd mind."

CHAPTER 14

Josh Durrant had the most annoying habit of showing up when Stephanie least expected it. Thanks to the continuation of Paul's court case, however, she had escaped the misery of flying to Montana with her former client. The fact that he was living where Todd should have been, made her anxious to avoid Josh. All during the following month, whenever he'd come in to see Charles she'd close the door to her office. She feared he might turn up at the barn one day, the way he had earlier. As it turned out, he arrived just in time.

Cantering Kingston over various obstacles in the back pasture had filled Stephanie with so much joy that she'd had to sing out loud and release some of the long-absent happiness before it bubbled over into hysteria. Night threatened and she and Kingston were running short of breath when they began their return to the arena and nearby stalls. It appeared she'd outlasted the few riders who had been there when she'd first arrived.

Her glance settled on the spot at the end of the arena where she'd once seen Todd waiting for her. She longed for a repeat of that special moment. Frowning, she remembered that Josh, too, had stood in that same place. She found herself scanning the landscape, planning a hasty retreat if he did so again. Satisfied that he was nowhere around, she clucked to Kingston. He blew and tossed his head. A bath and a clean bed were beginning to sound good to her, too.

She had Kingston groomed and settled in his stall when she heard it—a wild whinny—no, more of a frantic scream, then another from a different source. Dashing out of Kingston's stall, she secured the gate and headed in the direction of the commotion. She took a quick detour to turn on the overhead lights and saw one of the horses at the end of the line of stalls lunge against the rails at another horse. Strange behavior since these animals were normally accustomed to their stall mates. It occurred to her as she hurried toward the horse that it was Belle, a quarter horse mare in foal to a champion barrel racer, causing all the noise. Stephanie hoped nothing had happened to her.

When she arrived in front of Belle's stall, she noticed that a large dark object lay beneath the railed panel halfway between the two stalls. Her heart leaped when Stephanie saw it move and realized it was a newborn foal—Belle's foal, still partially covered in afterbirth, stuck beneath the stall panel. Wait. Belle still had a belly as big as a barrel. It wasn't her baby. Stephanie glanced into the next stall. Oh no. It was Riskie's foal. Riskie, probably a first-time mother, stood back wanting to get to her offspring but afraid of the more dominant mare. Belle must have thought the colt was hers. From what Stephanie could remember, Riskie's foal wasn't due for another two weeks, probably why she hadn't been moved to another, larger stall.

Unhooking the halter that hung on the gate, Stephanie hurried into the stall to catch Belle. The mare lunged at her, knocking her to the ground. Determination and fear for the colt made Stephanie bold. Picking herself up out of the sawdust, she tried once more. Belle reared and with teeth bared came at Stephanie again. The next thing Stephanie knew someone grabbed her by the shoulders and pulled her back out of the stall.

"Stay here," Josh Durrant ordered. Then with a long buggy whip in one hand and a halter in the other, he headed into the stall. Within seconds he had the mare pinned in the opposite corner of the enclosure. Belle waited for his approach with ears flattened against her neck. She lunged at him once, but he brought the whip down hard on her shoulder. She backed up, reared once and stood shaking as Josh haltered her. Battle won, Josh rubbed Belle's neck and led her, nickering, out of the stall, tying her securely to a nearby fence post.

Stephanie didn't wait for Josh's return. Unafraid, she unlocked Riskie's stall and was immediately beside the foal. Hesitant to approach, Riskie hung back while Stephanie dragged the foal into its mother's stall. Taking off her sweater, Stephanie cleaned the afterbirth from the foal, paying particular attention to its nose and mouth. It still made no attempt to get up and Stephanie fought back a sob.

Josh kneeled beside her. Taking the foal's nose in his hands, he gently blew into its mouth. Immediately it drew back, then lifted its head. Taking Stephanie's hand, they stepped away to allow the mare to welcome her baby, but she didn't move. Stephanie had the fleeting thought that Riskie didn't want her baby any more than she wanted hers. Josh put his belt around the mare's neck and led her over to the foal. She stood quietly but didn't drop her head to greet the new arrival. Maybe they should've let Belle keep the baby. Silly thought. Stephanie knew that Belle would have nothing to do with this foal as soon as her own arrived.

"Hold her," Josh told Stephanie. "The foal needs something to eat right now or it will die. First milk is the most important." Josh was telling Stephanie things she already knew, but how did he know them?

With strong arms, Josh lifted the foal and placed it on wobbly legs. It struggled to remain standing and would have fallen had

Josh not held onto it. "A filly," he said upon closer examination. "Bay with a pretty little star on her face."

A little girl, Stephanie pondered; she would have liked a little girl. What was she thinking? She didn't want a girl or a boy. She didn't want a baby, period. Babies brought countless problems, as witnessed by the scene before her.

Once again Josh lifted the filly, supporting her with his knee as he guided her head up to the mare's bag. Having never experienced an uninterested mother before, the foal didn't know how to nurse. Josh reached up under the mare, collecting some milk on his fingers. He then stuck them into the filly's mouth. Her little ears pricked and she licked her lips. Josh chuckled. He was enjoying this. Stephanie caught the spirit. She rubbed Riskie's neck and stepped over to help Josh hold the filly with one hand while she held onto the mare with the other. Again and again Josh brought milk to the filly's waiting lips. At last, as he guided the little nose up under the mare, the foal grabbed on. Josh smiled at the vigorous sucking sounds. Stephanie smiled too.

"I think they'll be fine now." Josh removed his belt from around Riskie's neck. "But what will we do with the would-be mother over there?" He nodded at Belle, who pawed the ground.

"Why don't we switch stalls with Kingston. He'll be interested in the filly, but I bet he won't challenge Riskie." Stephanie retrieved her sweater, shaking off the sawdust. "Wait a minute." She narrowed her eyes at Josh.

"What?" he asked.

"Where did you come from? Are you following me? And how do you know about horses?" She put her hands on her hips.

"Which do you want to know first?"

"Your choice."

"Okay. Someone I was close to once raised horses."

"A girl?" Why did she say that? Why did she care? She didn't. "Maybe."

"Okay, it was a girl. No doubt about it. I bet you have lots of girls in your past. It wasn't Judge Anderson's daughter, was it? No, I'd know if the judge had horses." Stop it, she told herself. She was answering her own questions. Clearly Josh made her nervous. Well, why not? Once again she found herself alone in the dark with a criminal suspect. Well, Charles didn't think Josh was a criminal, but how did he know for sure? Josh may not have been found guilty of this past charge, but Stephanie had a feeling he'd been in trouble before. He had trouble written all over his face, what she could see of it behind the beard. She wished he'd shave. Why wouldn't he? Was he hiding something? Wait. She was letting her mind run wild again. Charles had a beard, after all.

"It wasn't a girl," Josh said.

"Yeah. Sure, it wasn't." Not really believing what he said, she followed her former client over to where Belle stood.

"Do you want to get Kingston now and put him in this mare's stall?" Josh untied Belle.

"Okay." She hurried toward the gelding's stall, then stopped short. "Wait a minute. You didn't answer my questions."

He tugged on Belle. "I told you how I know about horses."

Clearly Belle wanted to stay near the filly. Even though she hadn't given birth to the foal, she seemed to think it was hers, kind of like an adoptive mother. Adoptive mother. The words resonated in Stephanie's mind. She shook her head to clear it. "Are you following me?" she blurted.

"Yes."

Reaching for Kingston's halter, Stephanie's hand stopped in mid-air. "Well, at last. You admit you've been following me then."

"Guess so." He nodded toward Kingston's stall and gestured for her to hurry.

She slipped the halter onto the gelding's head and led him out. "Not that I'm sad you showed up this time. I don't know what I'd have done."

"I think it's pretty clear . . ." He turned the mare into the stall. "Probably got your butt kicked."

"Doubt that."

"If I'm not mistaken, I believe I just witnessed a pretty good butt kickin'."

Smart aleck. "She caught me off guard, that's all." Stephanie led Kingston toward Belle's stall.

"Clearly."

She turned back and glared at him over her shoulder. "Why are you following me?"

"Well, I'm heading in the same direction as you."

The guy was impossible. "I don't mean now. Why have you been following me? Why are you here right now?" She turned Kingston into Belle's stall.

The gelding pricked his ears and studied the sleeping foal for a minute, then he walked to the opposite end of the stall and stuck his nose into a pile of hay.

She tilted her head toward Josh and tried to control her emotions. Just what those emotions were, she couldn't be sure. "I'm waiting." She stood by the gate to Belle's stall.

Josh hurried to the gate and opened it for her. "After you."

"Oh, for Pete's sake. I can open a gate myself." She forbid herself to laugh at his antics. "I'm waiting to hear why you've been following me."

"Oh. That." He grinned at her, his deep green eyes twinkling.

"Yes that." Deep breaths, she told herself.

"Well, remember my friend? You met him in the hospital." Josh repeated his former explanation.

"Don't give me that." She wanted to slap him, but darn he was attractive.

He sighed. "Well, okay. This time Charles was worried about you and sent me to check on you."

"You've got to be kidding." Now she had two men looking out for her. How she wished Todd was still around to fend them off. "So now you're my babysitter?" What an inappropriate choice of words, considering her condition.

"I wouldn't say babysitter. Bodyguard, maybe." He looked her up and down. "Pretty nice body, actually, even though you've got sawdust all over your backside." He chuckled. "Like I said . . . a butt-kickin'."

She swung at him, but really didn't aim. As ridiculous and dangerous as it sounded, somehow she was pleased that he'd noticed her in that way. What would he think in a month or so when she started to look like Riskie had?

He caught her arm and pulled her into him. "You're a little wildcat, aren't you? If I can gentle Belle, you should be no problem."

"You might be surprised." For some reason her words came out in a flirty manner. He was just so good-looking tonight. Masculine and dangerous.

He drew her closer and bent his head toward her until his face was only inches from hers.

She met the gaze of his vivid green eyes. She would not look away until he did, she vowed.

One brow raised and the side of his mouth lifted. His hand brushed her face. "Don't tempt me," he said and released her.

Don't tempt me, Stephanie thought. She wanted to grab the water bucket attached to Belle's stall and dump it over her own head to restore her senses. Even if she were seeking a new relationship, Josh was strictly off limits. Just because Charles seemed to trust him, she didn't. She knew little about him and what she did know was bad, except that he had just helped her out of a very precarious situation. "I won't," she said.

Belle whinnied from Kingston's stall.

"Do you think we better help the foal nurse again before we leave?" Stephanie asked, returning their discussion to safer territory.

"We? So you want my help?"

"Don't you want to?"

"Say please."

"I should give Kathleen a call. She's the manager." Stephanie started toward her car and her cell phone. It would soon be pitch dark and the wind had started to blow, threatening a storm. She hoped the foal would be okay. Maybe Kathleen would move the mare and her baby to a warmer enclosure.

Josh stepped in front of Stephanie. "Say, Please, Josh. Won't you help me with the foal? You're so talented and handsome and know so much about horses."

Stephanie rolled her eyes. "Please, Josh. Won't you help me with the foal?"

"What else?" He made a circling motion with his hand. "Talented, handsome, know so much . . ."

"I said please, didn't I?" She stepped around him.

He chuckled. "Yes you did, and that's a lot coming from you."

"What's that supposed to mean?" She stopped walking.

"It means you haven't been very nice to me." He caught up to her.

"You're a client, a crim . . ."

"A criminal, you were going to say? Thanks to Charles that's all been taken care of."

"Don't remind me." That still bothered her, too.

"I suppose you've never made a mistake. How does it feel to be Little Miss Perfect all the time?"

She could tell from the tone of his voice that she'd made him angry. "I'm not perfect, far from it."

"When have you ever done anything wrong? I'll bet you never even leave your bed unmade. You probably feed all the stray cats. I'll wager you've never even kissed a guy on the first date."

"Oh, yeah. I'm perfect. If only you knew." For some reason, she'd almost let her secret slip. She was an imposter putting on the airs of a pure woman. Since he worked for Charles now, surely Josh would soon discover what she'd been hiding and then what would he think? Surprisingly, it had been a big relief to inform Charles about the pregnancy. It seemed that secrets shared lessened the burden.

"If only I knew what? Now you have to tell me." As they walked, he playfully tapped the top part of her arm.

"No I don't." She returned the tap with a slug. Actually, guilt nibbled at the edges of her conscience for calling him a criminal. She was in no position to judge. Besides, he'd been a huge help with Belle, and so sweet and gentle with the foal.

"Sure you have to tell me. So you're not Little Miss Perfect. You must have kissed a guy on the first date, or maybe you just beat him to death." He rubbed his shoulder as if she'd injured him.

Feigning annoyance, she shook her head. "Oh, poor little you. One would have thought you could take a punch better than that."

"One would have thought you couldn't deliver one that deadly." He lifted his arm, as if to test its strength.

"I'm sorry," she said, touching his hand. "Did I hurt you?"

"No." He chuckled, "but I had you going, didn't I?"

"You . . ." She drew back ready to really wallop him.

He grabbed her arm and pulled her up against him. "So I guess you have kissed a guy on the first date. "

She didn't know if she was more upset with him or with herself. She didn't mind being close to him, but she pushed away regardless. "Actually, I haven't, but I could tell you something that will shut you up permanently, and maybe then you'll quit following me around." Nothing like telling a guy you're pregnant to douse any romantic flames.

"Remember, I'm doing this on Charles's orders." He put his hands in the pockets of his jeans.

"Sure you are."

"Well, I am now. Actually I've had worse duty." He grinned at her.

"So you admit you were following me before Charles told you to." She started walking again.

"I didn't say that, but what if I were? I wouldn't be the first guy to try and cross paths with a beautiful woman. I figured you might not hate me as much if you got to know me." He caught up to her.

"I don't hate you." These days her pulse started to race whenever he came near.

"You could have fooled me." He flashed her that little boy look he was so good at. "Remember, I'm good with horses. Couldn't you use another friend?"

Could she ever. She guessed she'd see what kind of friend he'd make. He'd probably run at the first sign of trouble.

"I'm pregnant, all right?" Without warning, she burst into tears.

The wide-eyed expression on his face went from shocked, to thoughtful, to apologetic, and back to shocked again. "Well, that explains it."

"Explains what?" She sniffed.

"Why you're so grumpy."

"I'm not grumpy," she yelled and choked on a sob.

Drawing her into his arms again, he held her tightly.

She started to shake, whether from emotions or cold she didn't know, but his warmth felt good.

"You're freezing. Here." He took off his jacket and placed it around her shoulders. She put her arms through the sleeves, and he helped zip it up. With his arm still around her he asked, "Do you still want to check the filly or just go home?"

"We'd better go see her." Stephanie blotted her tears on the sleeve of his jacket.

He smiled and returned with her to see the filly.

Riskie had decided to be a mother after all. The mare stood quietly while the little filly nursed with loud slurping sounds.

Back leg cocked, Kingston dozed in the corner of Belle's stall, and when they checked on the now silent Belle, it appeared that she had given up her plight to be mother to Riskie's foal and drowned her sorrow in the consumption of a quarter bale of hay.

After turning off the lights, Josh walked Stephanie to her car. The full moon peeked through the clouds, making their trek to the parking lot much easier than it might have been.

"I'm sorry, Josh," Stephanie said.

"For what?"

"For being mean to you."

"That's okay. I'm tough." He opened the door to her car and she slid in.

"Thanks for tonight and thanks for not asking about my . . . my problem."

"What problem?" He winked. "I'm a pretty handy guy to have around in a bind, and if you ever need anything, anything at all, I'm your man."

How nice it would be if she really could rely on him. "Thanks, Josh. I'll remember that. Oh, here." She unzipped his jacket and handed it to him.

"Are you sure you don't need it?"

"I'm fine." She turned the key to start her car, but nothing happened. "Maybe I'm not fine."

"Do you have a flashlight in your car?"

"I think I do, in the trunk."

"Open it, will you, and I'll take a look."

She hit the button and the trunk popped open.

Josh reappeared at her window. "You do have a flashlight. Now hit the hood button."

It only took a few minutes before Josh said, "Try it again."

The motor started right up.

"The cable had come loose on the battery. I tightened it the best I could. I'll follow you home to make sure you get there, and if Charles has a screwdriver I'll tighten it again." He tapped on the roof of the car. "Off you go. I'll be right behind you."

Just like old times, she thought. "Thanks again, Josh. I'm going to have to take back all the bad things I've said about you."

"What bad things?"

"Only kidding." She smiled at him. The mountain man with a heart and probably an extremely handsome face behind the beard. Actually, she was getting used to all the hair. It suited him. A lot of things about Josh were beginning to appeal to her, which she hoped wasn't an error in judgment. Her car was just fine when she'd left it earlier that day. Josh had arrived after she had. Since she'd left the car unlocked, he would have had plenty of time to fiddle with it. But why would he? Now here he was following her again, this time with full permission. Was she becoming reckless? Her thoughts kept her on edge all the way to Charles's.

CHAPTER 15

It was the middle of July before Stephanie saw Josh again. She wondered if Charles had sent him to Montana, or on some other assignment in her behalf. Although she was dying to find out, she knew she'd never ask either of them. She disliked bringing up the subject of her pregnancy with Charles, and she didn't want either Josh or him to suspect that the former had been missed.

When her unpredictable ex-client finally did stop by the office after a month's absence, she realized how much she really had wanted to see him. Her heart raced despite how many deep breaths she took. Instead of hiding behind a closed door as she had several times before, Stephanie beckoned him in. Besides Charles, he was the one person who knew she was pregnant. She still couldn't fathom why she'd told him. A vulnerable moment, she supposed, or maybe it was in preparation for future weeks. She wouldn't be able to hide her pregnancy much longer, and then she guessed she'd be off to Montana. She figured since Charles would be unable to leave the practice for any extended time, it would probably be Josh, her newly appointed bodyguard, who would accompany her, at least initially.

She was five and one-half months along now and even her most roomy clothes were beginning to bind. She suspected that many of her associates thought she was just getting fat. Deirdre had made a comment recently that they had better keep the office donuts away from Stephanie. Charles had winked at her and released some of the tension, but Stephanie practically had to sit on her hands to keep from slapping the secretary. For some reason, she was glad Josh knew the real reason she didn't look her best.

"How's the baby?" he asked upon entering her office.

"I'd rather we not talk about it here," Stephanie stammered as she glanced around, wondering if anyone else had heard.

Josh leveled a perplexed stare at her before a light seemed to go off in his brain. "The filly," he said.

Stephanie's face felt flushed. "Oh. She's fine. Turns out Riskie is a great mom." For sure better than she herself would be. "Kathleen, at the barn, really likes her. She thinks the filly may even have jumping potential—lots of bone and all."

"No ill effects from the birth then?"

"None at all. She's great," Stephanie said and motioned to the chair across from her desk.

"And the mom?" Josh dropped into the chair.

"The mare's great, too—still thin—but doing better. I don't know if Kathleen is going to keep her after she weans the filly. I hope so. I don't know what will become of her if she doesn't."

"That hardly seems fair. The mare gives Kathleen a nice filly and then gets sent down the road when she's no longer useful."

Strange reasoning for a man, Stephanie thought. "That's the horse business. Kathleen barely keeps all the horses fed as it is. She can't be picking up strays."

"It just doesn't seem right."

More and more Stephanie had a difficult time remembering where she'd first met Josh. Statements like this made her wonder how he could have ever been accused of anything violent.

And today—wow. Today he was dressed in form-fitting jeans and a plaid button-down, long sleeve shirt, thankfully covering the barbed-wire tattoo. Minus the beard and collar-length hair, Stephanie felt he could have masqueraded as a college boy—a senior or graduate student. He'd ditched the gold post earring and his hair was clean and combed back behind his ears. Working for Charles had done wonders for his appearance . . . wonders and then some. Now he was head-turningly handsome—tall, about six-three, Stephanie guessed, with trim hips and broad, broad shoulders. She stopped herself. A woman in her condition and situation should not be assessing the attributes of a handsome young man, especially a man with a questionable past.

"Do you know anything about computers?" The sentence popped out before Stephanie realized the words had actually come from her mouth.

"Don't tell me you don't know how to type." Josh's green eyes twinkled.

"I can type okay. I'm just a little Internet challenged."

"Aren't we all?" Josh leaned back and crossed his legs at the ankles.

"So you don't know anything about the Internet?" Shoot. She was going to have to figure it out herself.

"Depends. What are you looking for?"

Standing, Stephanie moved to the door and closed it. Out of the corner of her eye, she watched as Josh's head turned to follow her every move. What was going through his mind? He probably thought she looked fat, too. She wished she were back to her former figure. She'd cried this morning when she couldn't button her slacks. Some days she had a hard time not blaming Todd for all her problems, but he'd been a victim too, hadn't he? "I want to do a search on someone—see if I can turn up anything on the Internet about him."

Sitting up straight, Josh squirmed in his seat, almost as if he were afraid she wanted to search his past. "Who do you want to find out about?"

She stared at him for a moment. Was she crazy? Why on earth would she put her trust in this man she barely knew? "Oh, no one, forget it." She sat back down in her chair across the desk from him.

He leaned forward, reaching across the desk until he touched her hand. "I asked you not long ago if you needed a friend."

"I remember."

"I may not be a lot of things; but, contrary to public opinion of late, I am trustworthy, and if I like someone, I'm loyal."

Stephanie squared her shoulders. "Well, I guess the big question is, do I fall into that category?"

He rubbed his beard as if he were deep in thought. "Actually . . . even though you've made it hard sometimes, I'll have to admit that you do."

She stared at him again, testing the water, remembering that he had kept quiet and held his opinion after she'd told him she was pregnant.

He stared back a moment, then crossed his eyes and pulled a face.

She laughed.

"Sorry. I couldn't help myself. So you were saying?"

"I'm wondering about . . ." How could she say it? What kind of girl had doubts about the father of her baby?

"Just spit it out. As you know, we've all had problems in our past," he said. "Look at me."

"That's what worries me."

"But I was innocent, right?"

"You were found not guilty. I don't think you've been innocent since you were in diapers." She found she enjoyed bantering with him, if only it were on a different subject.

"I was very hard to train." He winked at her.

"I need to look into the background of my baby's father." There she'd said it. She felt breathless.

"Okaaay, but weren't you going to marry him?"

"Yes."

"And did you still not know him very well?"

"Okay. Okay," she said. "It sounds stupid."

"I didn't say that."

"But you were thinking it."

"So what was his name? Todd, wasn't it?" Josh stood and walked behind the desk to stand beside Stephanie.

"Yes. Todd."

"So what's your concern?" He leaned over her shoulder bringing the keyboard closer. He smelled wonderful—fresh and spicy—not at all like she'd supposed he would.

"Lots of things." She didn't move away from his closeness. "I don't want to go into them right now."

He put his hand on her shoulder. "I bet Charles could help you with this. He probably has connections with private investigators and others like that."

"I don't want to involve Charles anymore," she blurted. "That's why I'm asking you, a strange . . ."

"A strange what?"

"A stranger. Someone who doesn't know me very well, or care about me."

"Who said I don't care about you?"

"It's pretty evident sometimes."

"Well, it's not intentional. I mean, I care about you." He brought his mouth close to her ear and she felt her pulse race. "Do you know how to turn the computer on?" he whispered.

She leaned closer. "Don't you just press the button?"

"Well, do it then."

Shaking her head, she complied.

"Now go to Google and type in your name," Josh said.

"My name?"

"Humor me. Let's just see what we get."

Stephanie watched as a page materialized on the screen. She leaned forward, surprised to find her name listed on several lines. In addition to showing her as a defense attorney with the law firm Connelly and Foster, she also appeared under the heading of Admittees to the Utah State Bar. Several of the papers she'd worked on in law school had also made it to the Internet. Also there was a listing that highlighted her win of the Jumper Stake astride Kingston the summer before.

"See. You're famous." Josh leaned over the back of her chair and pointed at the screen.

"Now let's see. His name was Todd. Todd what?"

"Saxton. Todd Saxton." She whispered. She would have been Mrs. Todd Saxton had things gone as planned. She experienced a moment of longing before she refortified herself and typed in the words Todd Saxton.

Ten pages of listings showed up. After all, Todd worked from his home on the computer. Sure there would be lots of listing for him. Why hadn't she thought of this before?

She searched through the first page. Josh still leaned over the back of her chair, dangerously close, but somehow she didn't mind.

There was a Todd Saxton, MD, Internal Medicine, and a Player Bio for a Todd Saxton—Football. There was even a

Should Todd forgive Blair for sleeping with Saxton listing. She searched through the entire ten pages looking for her Todd Saxton. But none of the Todds, Saxtons or Todd Saxtons appeared to be her Todd Saxton.

"Hmm," Josh said. "What do you think about that?"

Unfortunately she didn't know what to think.

Remembering the name on the back of Todd's picture she typed in Chris, for Christopher, and a Todd Saxton, putting all the names in parenthesis as Josh told her to do. There were twelve pages for a Christopher Todd Saxton and nine for Todd Christopher Saxton. Quickly she scanned all the pages, racing Josh to the end of each page. He always finished first which surprised her. And she thought she could read fast.

There were five pages of listings for T.C. Saxton and fifteen for C.T. Saxton. There were six pages for Christopher Saxton, one of which even listed him as a jockey. None of the listings were for the Todd Saxton Stephanie had known and loved.

After their search, Stephanie sat silently, staring at the computer screen.

"I thought you said his name was Todd. Why did you type in Christopher, TC and CT?" Josh reached around her to click off the computer.

Temporarily defeated, Stephanie leaned her head against his arm. "It's a long story. I'll have to—"

Just then Deirdre burst in through the door to Stephanie's office. "Oh, excuse me." Her eyes narrowed as she noticed how close Josh stood to Stephanie. "I just told Charles that you were gone. Usually you are gone, and then your door was closed."

Josh placed his hands on Stephanie's shoulders. "We wanted to be alone," he teased.

Deirdre's eyes flashed as she glared at Stephanie. It was clearly evident in her expression that Deirdre thought of Josh as hers. She didn't want Stephanie interfering.

"Hmm. Well if you like—" Deirdre didn't continue. If she would have said "if you like fat girls," Stephanie might really have slapped her.

Stephanie wiggled under Josh's touch. If she'd been in fighting form, she would have teased along with Josh if only to make Deirdre mad, but as it was, she merely said, "Josh was helping me with my computer. That's all. I guess I didn't realize the door was still shut." As hard as it was, she bit back more comment. Deirdre had no right to question whatever she wanted to do. Stephanie was Deirdre's boss, after all, and an adult who didn't need supervision.

"Well, sorry to interrupt," Deirdre said, in her sassy voice reserved mainly for Stephanie. "I was just bringing you these papers. You don't need to make a federal case out of being disturbed. It was only Josh after all."

"Hey," he said. "Only. Only?"

"It might not have been only Josh." She smiled at him.

"What's going on in here?" Charles asked, stepping to the door. "Oh, Stephanie, Deirdre said you were gone."

"No, I'm here as you can see. Deirdre was mistaken." She might have added as usual, but she held back. "Do you need something, Charles?"

"When you're finished here will you come to my office?" He redirected his gaze at Josh. "Hello, Josh. Did you come in to see me?"

"I just wanted to drop off the bill for those airplane supplies, but I put it on Deirdre's desk." He glanced at the frizzy-haired blonde and winked.

Stephanie felt her face go hot. How she hated flirts.

"Well, Deirdre and I will leave you two alone." He gave the secretary a look of dismissal and she scurried from the room.

It seemed as if Charles was happy to have Josh stay as long as he wished. Why was Charles so taken with Josh? What if everything she shared with Josh went straight to Charles? Maybe she'd been wrong to trust him, or anyone with her questions about Todd.

All at once she was done with Josh. He was nothing but a flirt anyway. She was anxious for him to leave so she could get on with her search without his curious gaze, and she did wonder what Charles had on his mind.

She stood. "Thanks for your help, Josh."

"You're dismissing me, huh?" He feigned hurt. "You pick my brain and then you're done with me. I feel like a trained seal, one who performed his trick but never got his fish reward. I feel compromised."

She rolled her eyes. "I really shouldn't keep Charles waiting."

"No, I can see that."

"He is my boss."

"He sure is. He calls; you come. Good girl. Of course, you do live at his house and let him meet your every need."

"It's not as bad as all that, is it?" Was her reliance on Charles that evident? No wonder Deirdre had been snippy with her. "Okay. I'll let him wait." She walked around the corner of her desk to direct Josh away from the chair she was going to sit in.

He took the bait and settled into the chair he'd been sitting in before. "Do you want me to ask around and see if I can find out anything more on Todd?"

Stephanie hated to think who he would ask. "No. I want you to forget I even talked to you about it." She'd been wrong to take him into her confidence.

"So now you've decided that you can't trust me." He placed both hands on his knees. "You can, you know." His eyes were soft and sincere.

She wanted to believe him. It would be nice to have someone to trust.

"I'm serious," he repeated.

"Okay. I might have to call on you someday." Her reply was noncommittal and meant to move the conversation in another direction.

"I hope you know you can." His green eyes caught hers and held.

"Thank you, Josh," she said, but didn't know if she meant it.

He stood. "I'll let you go see Charles now."

"I have your permission, then?"

"I didn't think you needed it, but yes, you have my permission." He'd managed to turn her snide remark around. She'd have to remember not to leave herself open like that in the future.

He sauntered to the door, brought his hand to his brow as if tipping his hat and walked out, closing the door behind him.

She put a palm to her burning cheeks. He always managed to knock her off center. Why did he have that effect on her?

Charles was hovering over his computer when Stephanie walked into his office. He only did his own typing when he was working on something he wanted kept in strictest confidence. She'd consulted with him on one such case before, but she'd done the typing. This case must be something really important. Like a bloodhound on the trail, her heart raced at the possibility that he would want her help. He finished at the computer and as the printer hummed into action, he turned to face Stephanie.

"How are you feeling? You look pale. How are things going for you?"

Since he knew most everything she accomplished in her mundane life, he must have meant how was the baby.

"Fine." She didn't want to talk about the baby with him any more than she did with Josh, but somehow talking about it with Josh seemed easier.

"So is the pregnancy progressing normally?" He removed papers from the printer and, holding them on either side, tapped them on his desk to straighten them. He placed the papers neatly in a file with no label on it.

"As far as I know," Stephanie said. "Of course I've never done this before, so how should I know?" Maybe he wasn't going to discuss the secretive case with her after all. If not, she was out of here.

"You haven't been back to the doctor then?" He picked up a pen and clicked it several times, as was his habit when discussing a subject that made him uncomfortable.

"I'll find one in Montana. No need to get anyone else involved, is there?" She tried to suck in her belly, but it was not the kind of belly that would suck in.

More pen clicking. "You really should go regularly. I'll have Janeen schedule an appointment for you."

"I'm perfectly capable of scheduling my own." Stephanie's chin lifted and set. So Janeen was in on the secret, too.

"Very well. I really wish you'd do it soon, though."

"I'll think about it."

He opened the secret file. "Along those lines, I've taken the liberty of preparing some custody documents saying you are willing to give the baby up. We may as well get started on the arrangements."

Stephanie had known she'd eventually be required to have this conversation, but different emotions bombarded her brain. Even though she didn't want this baby, papers testifying to the fact seemed heartless and cold. Was she ready to have everything so final? She swallowed once, then again. She really wasn't. How she wished she could run away and ignore this whole nightmare she'd found herself starring in. "Do we have to do this right now?"

Charles steepled his fingers over the offending documents. "I thought this was all settled. You said you wanted to give the baby to a deserving couple who could offer it a wonderful home. Besides, the firm's got so many plans for you. A baby will seriously impact your career."

"I know that," Stephanie barked. "I just wish all of this were over. I wonder what Todd would think of me giving his child away? He was excited about the baby, you know. Maybe I should give this more thought."

Charles sighed deeply and looked everywhere but at Stephanie.

"What?" Stephanie asked, daring Charles to look at her.

"Nothing," he said, still staring away.

Stephanie pounded her fist on his desk. "Nothing, my foot. Tell me. Do you know something about Todd you haven't mentioned?"

He studied his hands then dragged his eyes up to face Stephanie. "I didn't want you to know. I hoped you could feel positive about your last days with Todd so it would be easier to move on with your life, but now . . ."

"Now what? Charles, you better tell me." Somehow she'd always felt he knew more about Todd than he was letting on.

"I've been keeping this from you because it will make you sad. Now, however, facing this important decision, you need to know all the facts." He sat forward in his chair. Its leather squeaked. The sound wore on Stephanie's frazzled nerves.

"Tell me," she said through clenched teeth.

Charles cleared his throat, opened his mouth, then closed it again. His face appeared drawn and sober. Stephanie knew the news would be bad. "Todd was not the man you thought he was," he said finally, "so if you're worrying about being loyal to him, forget it."

"Tell me," she repeated. "I need to know everything." She felt sweat forming on her brow.

Shaking his head, Charles drew a deep breath. "I knew you were pregnant long before you told me. I even knew about the night the baby came into being."

"The night we were drugged?" she choked out.

"The night you were drugged. I don't believe Todd was. Of course he didn't tell me about the drugs. You did. I also doubt there was a former best friend or a sister who'd been in love with Todd. I believe it was all a lie so he could be with you." Charles rested back against his chair as if relieved to finally get this out.

No sister? Then who was the girl at the cemetery? Stephanie blinked. Why worry about that now? There were bigger issues to be faced—huge issues. "No," she sobbed. "Todd wouldn't do that. He loved me."

Charles picked up his pen and clicked it twice. "I think he did love you toward the end. Who wouldn't? You're a beautiful woman, and he loved the money he knew you were going to make."

"He had plenty of money." She couldn't keep from defending him, or was it herself she was defending?

"Stephanie, Todd had a gambling problem. He was taking out bankruptcy, remember. I was his attorney. He knew that anything he told me in our client/attorney relationship would have to be kept in confidence." He kept clicking his pen until Stephanie wanted to grab it from him.

"Excuse me for saying this, but I don't have money," she exclaimed. How could her wages be a temptation? Charles was wrong about Todd.

"You will, Stephanie. He knew how proud I am of you and the plans I have for your future." Now he tapped the end of his pen on the desk.

"How did he know about your plans? You just barely told me." Like a person drowning in a river, she had to keep grabbing for low hanging branches.

Charles looked down. "I blame myself for that. I guess I was bragging about you, and I'm afraid things got out of hand. He told me he was going to marry you. It was the way he said it, his smirk, the toss of his head. He was challenging me. I told him you'd never have someone like him. He said you already had. I asked what he meant by that. He told me to guess." Charles paused for a moment as if to access Stephanie's reaction before pressing on. "I told him I didn't believe him, that you would never sleep with a man before marriage. He bragged that he already had slept with you and that it was great. Of course he didn't say anything about the drugs. I got that from you."

Stephanie tried so hard not to cry that she felt light-headed. "He was bragging about sleeping with me—to you, my boss?"

Charles nodded solemnly.

Her hands formed into fists. "Wasn't he afraid if I married him that you'd fire me just to get even, and then there'd be no money?"

"Oh, he had that covered. He said that since you were such a good attorney, if I didn't cooperate he'd just take you away to a big city where you could make even more money."

"Why . . . why didn't you tell me? You say you care about me, forget the client/attorney privilege. Even I could have gotten around that."

"I was going to, but then he told me you were pregnant, and that he was going to marry you and he hoped for your sake we could all just get along."

"So he was happy about the baby?" Couldn't Charles at least throw her a little life line?

Charles pressed his lips together and Stephanie feared he'd inflict more misery.

"Charles, tell me!" She felt as if she'd been beaten with a bat and another swing wouldn't matter. "Tell me!"

"Only that the pregnancy had forced you into saying yes. He made the comment that maybe he could talk you into getting rid of it later. I'm sorry, Stephanie. He didn't want it. I think he may have cared for you some, but you were a meal ticket and he was in dire need of any help he could get. I think he'd been threatened by the people he'd borrowed money from. I'm not entirely sure his death was an accident."

Tears of betrayal and shame burned Stephanie's eyes. How could Todd have done this to her? She had loved and trusted him. He'd taken everything from her and left her with . . . . "Where are those papers?" Stephanie grabbed them from Charles's outstretched fingers, and without so much as a quick scan, signed them with a shaking hand.

Not wanting Charles to see how much his news had devastated her, she tossed the papers on his desk and fled the office. She felt dirty, and used, and wished she could go home and take a shower. Fighting back tears all the way to her office, she silently passed Deirdre in the hall.

Even though she felt a slight prick of guilt somewhere in the back of her subconscious, she knew she'd done the right thing. She wanted no reminder of Todd and his deeds. She wished it were months from now when the baby would have been born and given away. She would have her body back, and Todd would be nothing but a horrible memory that she'd fight to erase.

She plopped into her chair and tried to focus on something, anything, to take her mind off what she'd just heard. She pictured Josh sitting as he had earlier in the chair across from her desk. He'd said she could trust him. How she needed someone to trust. What a sad state of affairs she found herself in when her best opportunity for a friend was someone with a dubious past. But how dubious had it been? Charles had experienced no trouble getting him off on the battery charge, and Josh did say he really hadn't pushed the girl? He was even working now and trying to be an exemplary member of the community.

If only to take her mind off Todd, Stephanie turned on her computer and brought up Google. Absently she typed in the words "Josh Durrant." There were three pages of Josh Durrants, most referring to a professional golfer. And at the end of the list, just the name, "Durrant." She clicked on that and a people portal opened up another three pages of Durrants. She clicked on the name Josh Durrant and the computer took her to a page that asked for the birthday and home state of the person she sought. She didn't know Josh's birth date, but she typed in Utah. A page popped up showing six Josh Durrants along with their ages and city residences. There was a Josh Durrant who lived in Spanish Fork and was 28 years old. She clicked there and the computer brought up a page offering background reports for a fee. One of the reports told of a statewide criminal check. She clicked on that selection and wondered if she should spend forty-nine dollars and ninety-five cents to satisfy her curiosity about this Josh Durrant since she could get criminal information, if any existed on Josh, from the police department.

While she considered her options, she plugged in the name "Todd Saxton" into the same search engine. Although fifteen

"Todd Saxtons" showed up, none appeared to be her Todd Saxton. She frowned. She would no longer refer to him as her Todd Saxton.

She typed in Josh Durrant again and scrolled through the options until it came time to order the report. She retrieved her purse and took out her Master charge card. The expenditure of forty-nine dollars and ninety-five cents seemed a small enough price to pay to keep her background check of Josh Durrant secret and timely. Several minutes passed before her computer pinged, telling her she had an email.

Opening the email, she scanned its contents. Her eyes soon riveted on the section that listed criminal offenses. There were six offenses covering a period of three years—a Driving While Under the Influence, an Open or Consume Liquor in Public, a Landlord Tenant suit and three Batteries, not even including the one with the judge's daughter that had been dismissed. Even though the site only listed the charges and not the circumstances, it seemed Josh preferred to settle his differences with his fists. Was he even safe to be around? Sick to her stomach, Stephanie stared at the computer screen. Clearly Josh was not as innocent as he'd tried to persuade her to believe. As much as she wanted to, she couldn't trust him. Now there was no one. She grabbed her purse and headed out. Her day just had to get better, didn't it?

CHAPTER 16

Covered with sweat and blood, Riskie stood in the corner of her stall, head down, eyes nearly closed. A gaping wound lay open on her shoulder near her withers, another ugly mark on her belly. Her front legs looked as if they'd been caught in a thrashing machine. Flaps of skin hung loosely in multiple places except where globs of flesh had been torn away exposing angry red holes. Whenever Riskie stepped onto one of her front legs, blood gushed from beneath the fetlock. She looked like a slight nudge would topple her over. The foal, caked with sweat but no blood, hugged close to her side with white-rimmed, bulging eyes.

Kathleen, the stable manager, stooped near the mare's mangled front leg. She slipped her cell phone into her jacket pocket as she straightened.

Stephanie gasped. "What happened?"

Pale beneath her weathered dark skin, Kathleen shook her head, and made a gesture of helplessness with her hand. "It's those dogs—a whole pack of them. I warned Harold to keep them away from here, but he wouldn't listen. He said they were gentle and wouldn't hurt a flea." She shook her finger. "Well, he hasn't heard the end of this."

"She needs a vet." Stephanie struggled with the lock on the gate and was finally able to let herself in. "Did you call him?" She crept toward the mare, careful not to upset her further.

Kathleen grabbed Stephanie by the arm. "It's too late. She's barely standing. The vet's on his way to put her down."

Tears sprung to Stephanie's eyes. "No," she cried and pulled from Kathleen's grip. "We can save her. She deserves a chance."

Kathleen shook her head.

"What about the foal?" Stephanie pleaded as a last resort.

"We'll have to bottle feed her, I guess." Kathleen stared at the foal, so brave by her mother's side. Kathleen's eyes misted and she looked away. "Maybe she'll be able to nurse the foal one last time and give us a chance to find something else to feed her."

So the mom was expendable. Stephanie's lip curled. The mare had given Kathleen a beautiful baby and now Riskie was no longer needed. "We've got to at least try. Look at her. She's waiting for us to help." Stephanie's head spun and bile rose in her throat when she glanced down at Riskie's mangled front legs.

"Think for a minute," Kathleen said, her face drawn. "The mare's worthless. I can't afford to spend another dime on her. She'll probably need transfusions and antibiotics, heaven only knows what else. It's kinder to put her down."

"You mean cheaper." Stephanie felt the tears coming but couldn't stop them. "And you say you love horses." She was out of line, but Stephanie didn't care.

"I do love horses." Kathleen massaged her temples with the tips of her fingers. "But I don't have the luxury of letting my heart rule my head like you do. I have to think of all the other horses under my care. Horses are expensive, and what I spend on her I can't use on the others."

"Oh for Heaven's sake. You're worried about the money? I'll pay the stupid vet bill, if that will make you happy." This wasn't like Stephanie. The words shot from her lips without ever touching her brain.

"You don't have any money either," Kathleen mumbled. "What about Kingston? I thought you were saving to buy him."

"I don't care. We've got to give Riskie a chance." Stephanie was sobbing now.

Kathleen shook her head. "I don't believe this. I was so hoping you wouldn't show up today."

"So we can try?" Stephanie wiped her eyes with the back of her hand.

"You can try, but you'll have to pay for it." Kathleen emphasized the last part of the sentence.

Just then a silver truck with a covered bed drove through the parking lot toward the gate that led into the barn area.

"There's the vet now," Kathleen said, clearly relieved. "But Stephanie, look at me. If he says it's better to put her down, you have to listen to him. Understand?"

Even as Stephanie said, "I understand," she knew if it took her last cent, she would see that the mare got what she needed, and she would not let the vet off easy. She straightened, mentally preparing for battle.

Dr. Lee climbed out of the truck, waved, then walked to the bed of the truck to retrieve his medical supplies. Stephanie had always liked Dr. Lee and was glad he was the vet who had answered Kathleen's call. Although Stephanie had no horse of her own, she'd been around when he'd come to see other people's horses. Peeking out from under thick blond hair hanging over his forehead, he had always reminded Stephanie of a big kid. Both the animals and their owners seemed to love him. She took a deep breath. Maybe she'd have an ally in Dr. Lee. Anyway, she knew he'd do what was best for Riskie.

"Ladies." Dr. Lee opened the gate to the stall. "Let's see what we have here before we do anything final. Oh my. Dogs, you say." He smacked his lips. "Hmm. I hope they won't be coming back. Have you reported them? Dogs like that running in a pack can be dangerous. Imagine what they could have done to a child."

They shuddered in unison.

"I did call animal control and told them who probably owns the dogs. They're handling it," Kathleen said. "I don't know what will happen to the beasts. At this point, I don't really care."

Stephanie stared at her. Even though she hated what they'd done, she didn't want the dogs killed. She was glad she didn't have to be the judge.

With gentle fingers, Dr. Lee examined Riskie's wounds.

The little mare stood bravely on three legs. Her pain-filled eyes mirrored the trust she seemed to feel in Dr. Lee.

"I'm most concerned about this leg," he said, noting the gash out of which blood spurted. "There are two arteries in a horse's ankle. If both are gone, she'll lose her foot. Also there are three tendons. If the dogs got one tendon, we might be okay. If they got two, she has about fifty percent chance of recovery, if all three, then less than ten percent. By the way she's standing, with her fetlock almost touching the ground, I'm afraid two of her tendons are gone."

"So we should put her down?" Kathleen asked.

"No." Stephanie cried, even though she knew Kathleen was not addressing her.

Dr. Lee looked from Stephanie to Kathleen, then back again. "Oh. I thought Kathleen owned this horse."

"I do," Kathleen said, narrowing her eyes at Stephanie.

"I told you I'd pay her bill," Stephanie challenged. Why was she acting like this? If it was better for Riskie to be put down, maybe they should. But strangely, at this exact moment, it seemed to Stephanie that giving up on Riskie was like giving up on her own life.

"She might have a chance," Dr. Lee said and smiled at Stephanie. "Let's get her cleaned up, stitched and see what we've got, especially in view of the foal. The longer she can feed that baby, the better it is and maybe, just maybe she'll make it."

Kathleen sighed and shook her head. "I give up. I should have known I'd lose out to both of you."

Stephanie put up her hand to high-five Dr. Lee. "Thank you." She turned to Kathleen. "And thank you. You won't be sorry."

"That remains to be seen," Kathleen said, looking upward to the heavens and wrinkling her brow. "Just remember, Stephanie. She's your responsibility now. In fact, since you'll be paying her bill, if she lives, she's your horse. I don't have time for her. Actually, hear all those whinnies? I've got to go feed right now. Thanks for coming, Dr. Lee." She sighed. "I guess."

"Always a pleasure, Kathleen," he said and grinned.

For over two hours Dr. Lee worked on Riskie with Stephanie helping in any way she could. Even though Stephanie could tell from her eyes that Riskie was in tremendous pain, she seemed to know that they were helping her and made no move to hinder them. The foal stayed close and several times Dr. Lee had to move her aside.

The doctor checked Riskie's pastern, injecting sterile saline solution directly into the joint to flush out contamination. He clipped away mutilated flesh and shaved hair for a closer look. "The dogs severed one of the arteries. See here. That's where all the blood's coming from. I'll tie it off. I think the other artery is intact, though. We'll know soon enough if it isn't." He returned to his truck to fetch more supplies.

Stephanie rubbed the mare's nose and stared into her pain-filled eyes, wondering if she'd been selfish to put her through all this.

Dr. Lee returned with a stainless steel bucket filled with little boxes and packets. He stitched the tears on Riskie's shoulder and belly and applied disinfectant cream. Then he returned his focus to her legs.

"Like I said before, I'm most concerned about this front leg." He dropped to his knees in front of the mare. "One artery and I'm afraid two tendons have been affected. I'm going to stitch what I can, bandage what I can't, and then go ahead and cast this leg up to the knee. That will give her support and keep the leg clean and safe. Of course I'll have to change the cast and dressings numerous times during her recovery. That is, if she does well. I wish I had a more positive prognosis for her, but all I can say is that we've given her a chance. Now everything is up to her." He smiled up at Stephanie. "But she's a game little mare. I'm glad you decided to help her. I'm afraid you'll have a pretty big bill."

"I don't care about the bill."

"Oh, don't say that," Dr. Lee warned. "But perhaps the owner of the dogs can be 'persuaded' to pay."

Stephanie shrugged. "So you can cast her right here. You won't need to take her to the clinic?"

"I can do it here, but I'll need your assistance."

It was another half hour before Dr. Lee had stitched and bandaged the less injured front leg. He finished that one off with blue duct tape to keep the bandages secure. Then he stitched, bandaged, and padded the more injured leg, and with Stephanie's help, applied layer after layer of fiberglass strips, dipped into water. The strips hardened into a cast within minutes. He gave Riskie a shot for pain and another one for infection.

As they cleaned up empty boxes, bags and paper from the stall, Dr. Lee said, "Well, that's a good sign."

"She's actually standing on it." Stephanie couldn't help but hug Dr. Lee. "Thank you so much."

Chuckling, Dr. Lee hugged her back. "I'll have to admit. Things went better than I thought they would when I first arrived. Look, little miss there is even getting dinner. At least she'll have a mother for a while yet." He put his hand on Stephanie's shoulder. "Now listen to me. The mare's not out of the woods yet. Watch her really close. Sometimes with puncture wounds, and she has lots of them, it takes six or seven days for a problem to show up. I think we treated everything, but sometimes there's dead tissue down deep where we can't see it and infection starts brewing."

"I'll watch her. I'm going to stay the night."

"I don't think you need to do that. I'll be back in the morning to check on her and give her more shots."

"But I want to stay."

Dr. Lee smacked his lips. "Well, she's lucky to have you. Take care now." He waved as he climbed into his truck and drove off.

Taking special note of the pitchfork as a tool of defense, should she need any, Stephanie was in the process of cleaning out the empty stall next to Riskie when Kathleen returned. "Wow," she said. "She looks like she's been through the war."

"She has. Do you know what will happen to the dogs?"

Kathleen chuckled. "You're still worried about the dogs? Have you ever heard the term 'bleeding heart'?"

"I've been called worse."

"If it will make you feel any better, animal control just contacted me and said that Harold is sending several of his dogs off to his brother's farm and is only keeping two. He promises he won't allow them to run at large. He has offered to pay the vet bill, so maybe you're off the hook. I don't think he has any idea how much it's going to be, however, and he'll have fines to pay."

"Whatever." Stephanie rested both hands on the top of the pitchfork handle.

"Who are you cleaning out the stall for?"

"Me."

Kathleen blew out a deep breath. "Don't tell me. You're not planning on spending the night."

"Yep."

"I'm sure you don't have to," Kathleen said.

"What if the dogs come back?"

"Well then, maybe they'll attack you. Did you consider that?"

Stephanie frowned. "They won't be back, but Riskie might need something?"

"She won't and you're going to freeze."

"I'll borrow Kingston's blanket. I'll clean all these stalls, though. It will give me something to do before I call it a day." Stephanie plopped a big pile of manure into the wheelbarrow.

"You don't have to do that."

"I know. I want to."

"You're impossible." Kathleen shook her head.

"I know."

Kathleen was still shaking her head as she disappeared around the corner, heading in the direction of her house. She was back in about fifteen minutes with a sleeping bag, blankets and a pillow. She sat them down by the clean stall. "I can't talk you out of this, I guess."

"Nope."

"Well, thanks. You would have made me feel guilty enough to stay with you tonight, except my husband and I have a big fund-raiser that I can't miss. We'll be home late. I'll come check on you then."

"I'll be fine."

Pausing for a moment, Kathleen studied Riskie and her foal. "I hope she makes it. She's such a good mom."

"Yes she is," Stephanie had to agree.

The words "such a good mom" reverberated in Stephanie's mind. Riskie had almost given her life to protect her baby. The least Stephanie could do was give up a night of sleep to protect this mare.

All at once it hit her like a snowball in the face and she had to stop shoveling manure. What was she willing to do for her baby? The question gave her pause and she wasn't sure she liked the answer she came up with. What a selfish self-centered brat she was. Her own baby deserved her protection. Her baby deserved her love—a mother's love. But wasn't that what she'd wanted to give it—a home with two loving parents. She wasn't mother material. Was she? Why not? To the untrained eye, Riskie wouldn't have been thought of as mother material either, yet look at what a wonderful mother she was.

Standing on wobbly legs, Riskie encouraged the foal to nurse. Her nose lovingly touched her baby's rump.

Sweat formed on Stephanie's brow as she thought back to earlier in the week when she'd signed Charles's papers. What had she done? She hadn't even read them. She'd been so upset about Todd's betrayal that she hadn't stopped to think. It wasn't this baby's fault that its father had been dishonest and its mother stupid. Stephanie chewed her lip. But wouldn't someone else give her child a better home than she could? Well, maybe. Or, maybe not.

She'd heard horror stories of adopted children who were never loved as much as someone's own child. Sometimes adopted children were even abused.

Why should she risk something bad happening to her baby? Did she have a choice? Was it wrong for her to put so much emphasis on her career? Of course, Charles would say no. But what did she think? What did she really think?

She didn't know what to think. That was the problem. She was too chicken-livered to really consider it right now. One thing was for sure, though. She didn't want to be a mother. She had never wanted to. She frowned. Riskie had probably not been given the choice either. But Riskie was a horse. Stephanie was a person with a future, with the power to reason. She did have the power to reason, but had she used it? Had she made the decision to give away her baby, or had she been talked into it? Had Charles influenced her because according to him a career was everything in life? He couldn't comprehend any other way. Millions of people, in worse circumstances than she, supported a child, even many children. After all, she was an attorney. Why couldn't she support a child? Maybe she wouldn't even have a job if she didn't do what Charles wanted and wasn't able to answer his every whim.

Riskie circled and lay down. Stephanie immediately came to attention. Holding her breath, she watched until Riskie settled comfortably into the sawdust and bent her neck around toward her body. She seemed perfectly at ease under the circumstances. The foal immediately lay down and cuddled beside her.

Suddenly tired, Stephanie switched off the overhead stall light, removed her boots and slipped into the sleeping bag in the adjoining stall. The pile of shavings she'd dumped there gave off a pleasing aroma and the moon acted as a perfect night light. Her eyes closed and she drifted into a deep sleep with the trusty pitchfork lying protectively at her side.

Some time later, her eyes flew open. Someone was walking toward them on the gravel pathway. In the moonlight, Stephanie could see that Riskie and the foal were now standing, ears pricked, their heads turned in the direction of the sound.

Of course—Kathleen had said she would check on them later. Stephanie relaxed, then realized that these were not the footsteps she heard almost daily. She pulled on her boots.

A tall form came into view and Stephanie gasped. At least it wasn't the pack of dogs she'd been prepared to fight, but right now she might have preferred them. She grabbed the pitchfork.

"Stephanie?" a male voice asked.

When she recognized who it was, she couldn't decide if she'd need the pitchfork or not. "Is that you, Josh?" she whispered.

"The one and only."

"What are you doing here?" Her hands relaxed on the pitchfork.

"I think the better question is, what are you doing here?"

She put the pitchfork aside and made her way out of the stall, over to the light switch.

Both Riskie and her colt blinked at the unwelcome light.

"Riskie was hurt. See," Stephanie said. "Now it's your turn. What are you doing here?"

"Looking for you." He studied the mare for a moment.

"How did you know I was missing?"

"Charles, of course. He worries—you didn't come home tonight." Josh emphasized the last sentence. "Didn't you think he'd notice?"

"I've got to move out of there." She walked passed him, back to the safety of her own stall.

"I wasn't going to say anything, but yes, you should."

"Don't tell me what to do." Stephanie straightened, ready for debate.

"I'm just saying—"

"Well, now you can see I'm fine. You can go."

"Do you know what Charles would do to me if I let you stay here all alone?" He joined her in front of her stall.

"I'm fine."

"Let me take you home." He reached for her arm.

"No. I'm staying." She slid out of his reach.

"Then so am I."

"No you're not."

"Yes I am." He folded his arms.

"I'm not sharing my sleeping bag." She opened the gate to the stall, bringing it between Josh and her.

"No one asked you to." He stepped around the gate.

She squeezed through the separating bars into Riskie's stall and ran her hand along the mare's neck. Riskie seemed okay, maybe a little more stiff on her leg but that was probably to be expected.

"What happened to her?" Josh asked, still standing in the adjoining stall since he'd have been unable to fit through the bars. Stephanie had been surprised that she still could.

"She fought a pack of dogs, and lost," Stephanie said.

"The filly looks fine," Josh observed.

"Riskie protected her."

"What a good mother." There was almost an insinuation in the tone of Josh's voice, but how could there be? He didn't know she'd signed away her baby. Maybe she just felt guilty.

"Yes she is," Stephanie said, wondering what Josh would think when he knew about her. "Are you sure you won't leave?" Even as she asked, a part of her hoped he would indeed stay.

"I'm not leaving."

"Okay for you." She exited Riskie's stall, moved to the light and switched it off. The moon provided enough illumination for her to stomp back to her sleeping bag, pull off her boots and crawl in.

"May I at least share your stall?"

He'd actually said may. "If you must. It's a big stall."

"I might freeze."

"Well, that's your own fault. You said you wanted to stay."

"Are you using the extra blanket I saw when the lights were on?"

He failed to duck when the blanket flew across the stall, hitting him in the chest.

"Oops. Sorry," Stephanie said, clearly unrepentant.

"You are so kind," Josh said, as if he really meant it. "Is there only one pillow?"

Stephanie let out an exaggerated sigh. "Only one."

"I was just curious."

"I guess you can share, if you won't hog it." Stephanie couldn't help but chuckle at how meek Josh was acting.

"Well, I most certainly won't hog it. See, I knew you were happy to see me."

"Okay, I'm not sharing."

Josh curled up in the blanket and snuggled next to Stephanie's sleeping bag. He lay on his back, scooting his head over onto her pillow. "It's actually pretty out here, isn't it? You can see the moon over the top of that small shed. Reminds me of home."

"Where's home to you?" Stephanie asked.

"Mont . . ., uh, Montpelier."

"Vermont?"

"No, Utah, up by Logan."

"I thought that was in Idaho." She yawned.

"No, it's Utah. I bet you're tired, aren't you?"

"I really am. I'm not usually this tired."

"Not usually?"

"No, I think it's the . . . the, my job. It's stressful."

"That's probably it."

"Probably." She yawned again, her mind shutting down. She couldn't seem to think anymore. She drifted off into sleep.

"Stephanie. Stephanie." The voice wouldn't leave her alone.

"Yeah," she mumbled through the fog in her brain.

"Even if things don't completely add up all the time, one thing's a constant. I hope you know you can always trust me, no matter what."

She snuggled up against him. "I know I can, Todd," she said, her voice tapering off. "I'm sorry I gave our . . ." she yawned and whispered. "I'm sorry I had to give our baby away."

CHAPTER 17

Squinting against morning sunlight, Stephanie pried her eyes open and tried to decipher where she was. The scent of hay, sawdust and manure met her nose and left absolutely no doubt. She hurriedly sat up in the sleeping bag and searched for Riskie and her foal.

Although still standing primarily on three legs, the mare appeared to be favoring the more injured leg less than she had the night before. The foal nursed noisily by her side as if afraid she'd soon be separated from her source of nutrition. Stephanie hoped that wouldn't be the case.

The breath caught in her throat as she remembered. She'd had the most wonderful dream. Todd had been here with her—the man she'd thought he was before Charles had set her straight. No. No, it hadn't been Todd. Now that sleep no longer dulled her brain, she realized it had been Josh resting next to her, and it hadn't been a dream.

Josh's blanket lay neatly folded in the corner of the stall, but he had disappeared. Sighing, she admitted that last night it had been comforting to feel his strong body through the sleeping bag next to her, even if it had been due to Charles's instructions.

She crawled out of the sleeping bag and tossed it over the stall rails. She'd roll it up later, somewhere cleaner where it wouldn't gather sawdust and straw.

"Good morning, Riskie and little junior miss." She'd have to find out what Kathleen was going to call the filly. Maybe the barn manager didn't want to name the foal until sure it would survive. If Riskie had to be put down, the filly might also die. Stephanie lifted her chin. She just wouldn't let that happen.

She was studying Riskie's leg when the vet drove up.

"How's our patient?" Dr. Lee climbed out of his truck.

"I think she's doing better. Here, have a look." Stephanie stepped out of the way. "You start early."

"Actually, it's not that early," Dr. Lee chuckled and plucked a stock of hay from Stephanie's hair.

"It's not?" She glanced around. The horses were all eating. Kathleen must have come, fed, and gone. "What time is it?"

The vet looked at his watch. "A little after ten."

"Ten o'clock? Oh no! How did it get to be ten o'clock?" She'd be really late for work. Charles would be ticked.

"Time passes quickly when you're having fun." Dr. Lee grinned at her, then stooped to have a look at Riskie's legs. He didn't say anything for several minutes while he completed his examination. Stephanie held her breath.

"The mare does look better than I expected. You're a good nurse," the vet said.

Stephanie grimaced. "Not really. I'm afraid if she'd have needed me, I'd have slept right through it." Why was she so exhausted all the time? Oh yeah. The baby. She stared at Riskie's water bucket while she pondered something brewing in the back of her mind.

Now she remembered. She'd been exhausted last night and when Josh had disturbed her as she drifted into slumber, she'd called him Todd. Ouch. But that wasn't all that bothered her. She thought harder. She'd said something about the baby—about giving up the baby. Well, shoot. She guessed her secret was out.

She sighed. It probably wasn't too bad of a slip. Since Charles had apparently assigned Josh to look out for her, she assumed that sooner or later the guy would be privy to the full plan. Unless . . . unless what? Unless she kept the baby? Oh sure, she was certainly in a position to do that. No, she couldn't even think of such a fool thing. A baby just didn't fit into her plans.

"What a good mother," Dr. Lee said.

"Uh, what?" It was as if he'd heard her thoughts and was taunting her.

"The mare surely is a good mother," the vet said again.

"Oh. She sure is."

"She might have been able to keep away from the dogs if she hadn't been trying to protect her foal." He smoothed Riskie's mane.

Okay. Okay. Did everyone have to say it? Riskie got the Mother of the Year award. She herself was the anti-mother. "She is a good mother," Stephanie repeated and felt a prickle of guilt heat the back of her neck.

"Well, I'll have to say I'm encouraged about her progress, but time will tell the whole story." Dr. Lee retrieved two syringes from his pocket, removed their protective covers and injected the mare with pain medicine and an antibiotic. "I'll come by again tomorrow. She's doing well enough today, so you should go home."

Stephanie nodded. "I probably will. I should show up for work sometime today. My boss is probably ready to fire me. I've been gone so much lately."

"If he does, come work for me." Dr. Lee touched her shoulder. "I could use a good assistant who knows horses."

"I'll keep that in mind." Suddenly, Stephanie stopped short and placed a hand on her belly. It had moved all on its own. She'd felt stirrings like this before, but not as strong, and she'd tried to pass them off as something else. She sucked in a quick breath. Today she realized without doubt this was her baby. The whole nightmare was real. She could no longer ignore it. Stephanie shivered. Sure, she could work for Dr. Lee. Picture it now. She'd be out wrangling broncs with the vet, her big belly hanging over her belt.

"Are you okay?" Dr. Lee asked, concern showing on his face.

"Probably something I ate," she said.

"Or didn't," Dr. Lee countered. "Go home, okay?"

"Okay." She didn't move.

"I'm waiting here until you go."

"I have to take care of the sleeping bag."

"I'll roll it up. It will be okay."

"Are you sure?" Stephanie started toward her car. She glanced over her shoulder.

"Keep walking," Dr. Lee called.

"Okay, okay." She was smiling when she climbed into the Honda. Too bad Dr. Lee was married and had several kids of his own.

As Stephanie drove, she told herself she should go to her condo instead of Charles's house. Every time she told him she was leaving, he had an excuse why she should stick around longer. When had she lost control of her life? Once she had been a free, independent woman. She would be again, when she wasn't so vulnerable. After the baby.

As if it had heard her speak, the baby kicked again. What a strange feeling, sort of like butterflies flapping around in her stomach. It wasn't so bad really, kind of . . . well, comforting. At least, for a while, she wouldn't be alone. She put her hand across her belly. Like Riskie, for a while she'd have a buddy.

Unexpectedly tears welled in her eyes. Did it really have to be for only a while? A lot of women had careers and children. Yeah, but a lot of women were married and had really wanted a baby. If she lived in a perfect world and things were exactly how she would have planned them, would she have wanted a baby? No, not a baby, but maybe this baby. She let herself daydream for a moment. If Todd had lived and they'd married and there was no cloud on his character, as Charles suggested, would she want this baby? Maybe, maybe not, but maybe. She thought of Riskie and her baby and what the mare had done to protect her foal and for the first time Stephanie felt a tenderness toward this child she carried.

She swallowed hard. Charles would understand how she felt, wouldn't he? He'd been like a father to her through this entire mess. Surely he'd support her if she had a change of heart.

But what if he didn't? What if he fired her? What would she do then? Sighing, she grit her teeth. She could find another job. Big belly or not, maybe she would work for Dr. Lee. Warmth flowed through her body as she pondered holding her child in her arms, watching it smile up at her . . . hearing it cry all night when she had court the next day, wondering who would tend it when her regular babysitter unexpectedly took a day off.

What had she been thinking? She couldn't keep this baby. She didn't even want to. She'd been feeling motherly because of Riskie. But Riskie didn't have a career, a reputation to keep, or bills to pay. Stephanie shook her head. How could she have paralleled her life with that of Riskie's? She'd better just give this baby to someone who would love it and provide it with everything it deserved, including a mother who didn't take instruction from a horse. Besides, although she hadn't allowed time to read it, she had signed a contract, and there'd been a reason she'd signed it without deliberation. If what Charles told her was true about Todd, this baby was a product of a violent act.

As she pulled into Charles's driveway, the baby kicked again and Stephanie fought the vision of Riskie and her foal that bombarded her brain. It was no use. This was her baby, hers and Todd's. There would never be another child like this again. She was its mother. It would be looking to her for protection and love. Maybe she'd just talk to Charles about going back on the contract and see how he reacted. She'd hurry and get ready for work and if he were in a good mood today, maybe she'd find some time to talk to him alone. Laying a hand on her belly, she nodded. She'd at least see what Charles would say. That decision made, determination strengthened her body.

She walked into work straight and tall, but when she saw Charles coming down the stairs talking with Matthew Dawson, the client who had become inexplicably friendly toward her, she turned and darted into the safety of her office. At her desk she reached for the morning mail, her hand shaking. Her phone buzzed and she knocked the receiver off its cradle. She grabbed it and held it to her ear. "Yes?" she said, fighting to keep her voice normal.

"Oh, good you're here now," Deirdre said. "Josh wants to see you."

Stephanie was wondering how Josh would react to the secrets she'd disclosed the night before, when he knocked and peered around the door.

"Good morning." He glanced at his watch. "Or shall I say good afternoon?"

"Very funny. Come in and close the door." Stephanie sat back in her chair, undecided as to what to say next.

Josh helped her out. "How's the mare?" Forever the mountain man, he looked great in jeans and a flannel shirt, well, as great as he ever looked with his beard and long hair. No one would have guessed he'd spent a sleepless night in a stall.

Stephanie could hardly wait to convey the good news. "The vet came again this morning, and she's doing better than expected."

"And the baby?"

"She's fine too, eating like a little pig."

"I mean your baby. So you've decided not to keep it?"

Heat flowed up the back of Stephanie's neck, as it did whenever her child was discussed. "I guess I told you that last night?"

Josh's brow wrinkled. "You told Todd last night."

"I was afraid of that." She slumped in her seat.

Josh perched on the chair across the desk from Stephanie and leaned forward. "So the plan is that you go to Montana, have the baby, give it away and no one's the wiser?"

"That's the plan." It sounded so heartless. What must Josh think of her?

"So it looks like I'll be flying you there in a couple of months," Josh informed her. "Charles said he needs you here until then, and since you're still pretty skinny, it should be okay."

Pretty skinny? They should try to fit into her jeans. Fortunately, she had a long torso and strong stomach muscles from riding. "He told you that, but not me?" Again Stephanie felt that her life was being torn from her. Why had she allowed Charles so much say in her life? Probably because he was her boss and had complete control over her future, or maybe it was that deep down she wanted the same things he did.

"Why are you hiding?" Josh gestured with outstretched hands. "These days women have babies all the time without being married. Of course, if you're going to give it away—"

"Not if they work for Charles."

"Charles is making you do this?" Josh's hands came down, and he gripped the arms of the chair.

"He's helping me."

"So you want to give the baby away?"

"I didn't say that. I just can't take care of it."

"What do you mean you can't take care of it?" Josh stood. "You have a job and a condo. At least you had a condo. Did Charles make you give that up too?" He walked around the desk to stand by her.

"Charles doesn't make me do anything." She swirled her chair around to face Josh.

"Oh, I can see that. How long has Todd been dead now?"

"Don't be mean." She turned away from him.

He grabbed the back of the chair and swirled her around. "Don't you think it's time you moved back to your own place?"

"What's it to you? Are you jealous?" Why had she said that? This conversation wasn't going at all like she wished. She really needed someone to confide in. After last night, she thought maybe it could have been Josh, but he was proving her wrong.

"What if I am?" His gaze held on her.

Josh jealous? How could he be? That would mean he actually cared for her some. "No you're not."

"Okay. I'm not. You know everything, don't you? You're the attorney. I'm just some dumb defendant."

"Nobody said you were dumb." But he had been a defendant. She'd better remember that.

"It's just what you think of me. You never will forget how we met, will you?" Anger darkened Josh's face and he shoved a pile of files from Stephanie's desk onto the floor.

"How can I? You keep reminding me with your actions." She nodded toward the files.

Josh stooped to pick them up, placing them in a neat pile on Stephanie's desk. Then he turned to leave. "I'm sorry, Stephanie.

Maybe you shouldn't trust me." He stared back at her over his shoulder.

Tears sprung to Stephanie's eyes. "I'm sorry, too." She stood, walking toward him. He held out his arms, and she melted against him. He wrapped her in an embrace.

"I'm so scared," Stephanie said into his shoulder. "I've been thinking today that maybe I would keep the baby, but I already signed papers giving it away."

"You signed papers? What did they say?" Josh tipped his head back to look at her.

"I didn't read them."

"You didn't read them? Attorneys read everything."

"I was upset."

"Then you shouldn't have signed them."

"It's what Charles told me about Todd."

"What did he say?"

"Basically, that Todd forced me."

"What?" Josh scratched his head. "I don't know much about . . . about that. I guess I've never been charged with . . ." he pulled a face, "but didn't you know?"

"I was drugged."

"Todd drugged you and you were still going to marry him?"

"I didn't know what Todd did until Charles gave me the papers to sign." Still standing close to Josh, Stephanie jumped when someone knocked on her door. "Yes," she said in an unsteady voice.

"Charles wants to see you right now," Deirdre said, uncharacteristically through the closed door. Normally she would have barged right in. Maybe she was actually honoring Stephanie's requests.

"We need to continue this later." Josh touched her arm gently, but his jaw clenched.

"Maybe." She wondered if Josh were upset with her, Todd or Charles, but she headed for the door.

Josh took her by the shoulders. "I'm here to help you, any way I can. You've got to trust me."

Stephanie had never seen this side of Josh before. His whole countenance seemed to change. It was as if he were another, gentler man. "I so want to be able to," she said.

"I swear to you on . . . on Riskie's life—no, on your child's life—that you can."

Stephanie stared into his deep green eyes for a moment. "I might have to hold you to that someday soon," she said and opened the door.

When Stephanie walked into Charles's office he was sitting at attention, hands on his desk, fingers intertwined. "Nice that you could join us, My Dear," he said in a tone that manifested anything but that she was his dear. "Have a seat."

Feeling like a rebellious teen summoned to the principal's office, Stephanie said, "I'm sorry, Charles. A pack of dogs chewed up a mare's leg at the barn."

"And that involves you how?"

"She's the horse I've been looking out for." What business was it of his? She felt her face redden as her anger flared. She counted to ten.

"Doesn't your cell phone work?"

"I wasn't aware I had to report to you after working hours." Perhaps she should have counted to twenty.

"I was worried about you." His mask of authority softened a little.

"And why was that?"

"Why was what?"

"Why do you worry about me? You don't worry about anyone else at the office. You don't worry about Deirdre."

Charles arched a brow. "Deirdre?" He chuckled. "No one worries about Deirdre. She can take care of herself."

Stephanie shifted in her chair. "I can take care of myself."

"It's just that you don't have a very good track record lately," he said.

She seethed. Did he have to continually rub it in? She was about to say something catty when he continued, his voice calm and comforting. "You have no family. You need someone to watch over you, at least while you're pregnant. Maybe after the baby comes . . . We'll find a nice family for it, and then you can continue with your life as if nothing happened."

Stephanie's heart raced. "So you haven't found a family yet?"

His eyes widened and Stephanie thought she saw fear flash across his face. "Why do you ask?"

"I was just thinking . . ." She wiped sweaty palms on her slacks.

"You're not going back on your agreement. You signed a contract, remember?"

"Of course I remember, but—"

"But what?"

"It was under . . . under duress." She wasn't even sure if duress would apply in this instance.

"Duress?"

"You'd just told me about Todd."

"Yes, that he more or less took you by force and bragged about it. That he was about to take out bankruptcy and planned on making you his meal ticket."

"That's what I said. You'd just told me all that, and I was under duress."

"You can't call that duress—more like stupidity."

She bristled. "I surely wouldn't want to take you to court on this."

A vein stood out on his forehead. "Oh, feel free. You and I both know that you could never beat me in court." His eyes flashed and the tips of his ears turned red. For a moment she thought he was going to come out of his chair. She pictured Riskie's pack of dogs.

Rage flowed through her body. She thought back to Todd's funeral, the sale of his home, and how Charles constantly discouraged her return to her own condo. She hadn't realized it before, but he'd kept her in a constant state of upset ever since Todd's death. "I can't believe this. I thought I could trust you." Her voice shook. "You've always said you wanted what was best for me. I'm afraid you're not the man I thought you were." Maybe she'd finally seen him for what he truly was.

It was as if someone had jerked his head around, or held up a mirror revealing his cruel expression. His face paled. "I do want what is best for you. Oh, Stephanie, I'm sorry. It's just that I don't want you to make another horrible mistake and burden yourself with a baby right now. It would ruin what we've got planned for you. I haven't mentioned this before, but we are thinking of opening a branch of our office in Montana. You would be the senior attorney there and live in the firm's million dollar condo."

The words seared into her brain. Senior attorney? Isn't that what she'd always wanted, to become someone with influence? She'd worked long and hard to make something of herself. Once she had thought she could be an outstanding horsewoman, but she'd lately discerned that wasn't realistic. But she was a good attorney, wasn't she?

"I can be the head attorney in Montana and still take care of a baby." She held up her chin, putting on her best defense attorney facade, and tried to maintain it under Charles's steady glare.

"And how fair would that be to the baby—raised by a sitter while you're at the office eighty hours a week? Wouldn't it be better to give it to a wonderful family with both a mother and father who would make it the center of their life?"

She slumped in her chair. "So you already have a family in mind?" Once again he'd taken matters into his own hands without consulting her.

"I might. Some people want a baby so much they try everything to get pregnant. Their whole life revolves around becoming parents. That's the first thing they think about when they wake up in the morning and the last thing at night. A child would be lucky to live in a family with such love and devotion. Contrast that with being raised by a nanny, or worse, taken to a babysitter day after day." His face was kind again, like that of a loving, trusted friend.

Maybe he was right. This baby did deserve to be the center of someone's universe. What could she give it? She couldn't even give it grandparents and cousins. But . . . a flicker of hope still glowed within her, and she ventured, "Well, since you just might have a family in mind, may I think about it a little longer?"

Charles stared at her for what seemed like a full minute. "Of course," he said finally. "I would never try to pressure you into anything. It has to be your decision." He forced a weak smile.

She saw a loophole and jumped through it. "I appreciate that, Charles." She stood to leave, his slight weakening offering some hope. "I'll be moving back to my own place as soon as possible."

A muscle flinched in his jaw and he blinked. Clearly he hadn't expected that reaction. "But you'll be going to Montana in the near future. Do you really want to move twice?"

She thought of Riskie fighting off the dogs. "Like I said, I'll be moving back to my own place right away."

Charles started to say something, but bit it back. Then through gritted teeth he said, "Suit yourself. I'll expect you at work tomorrow, though, and every other day following. You've been pretty lax lately."

Apparently new boundaries had been set. Stephanie hoped she'd done the right thing, yet she couldn't shake the eerie notion that she would live to regret what had just happened.

CHAPTER 18

Stephanie hung her clothes in the closet before plopping onto the bed, finally able to bask in the serenity of her own surroundings. Remembering the night she'd left in a panic and everything that had transpired since, the return home had proved difficult.

She'd teetered between tranquility and despair finally deciding she'd just choose to be happy for as long as possible. She piled both pillows beneath her head and pulled the comforter to her shoulders, rejoicing in the silence that encompassed her. Here she need not speak to anyone, be polite, make conversation, or talk about her baby. How she'd missed her solitude. She closed her eyes and for a moment heard nothing but the ticking of the clock on the wall.

Oh, no, was that the doorbell? Surely it wasn't Charles. She'd made her position quite clear today. She needed a few days by herself in her condo before she could give him a final answer. It had been a long time since she and Charles had last discussed the baby. She supposed he thought she'd come to her senses since she hadn't brought up her concerns again. In the office that afternoon, he'd mentioned finding a family for the baby. She realized then why she'd shied away from further discussions. Charles had been unable to hide his annoyance, or more likely anger, when she told him she still wasn't sure. Thank heavens she didn't have to stay at his house tonight.

The doorbell rang again, this time sounding more insistent. Reluctantly she forced herself off the bed and headed for the door. She'd peek out through the edge of the curtains and if it was Charles, or even Deirdre, she wouldn't answer.

Grinning at the unexpected sight, she swung open the door. There stood Josh Durrant, with a bouquet of red roses in one hand and a grocery sack threatening to overflow in the other.

"What are you doing here?" Stephanie asked, sure Charles had sent him to check on her, or worse still to try and influence her.

Josh shook his head. "No, no. Your line is 'Hello Josh, you handsome devil. How sweet of you. Are these for me?' And I'd say, 'Why yes, pretty lady. Their beauty is eclipsed only by yours'."

Stephanie laughed in spite of herself. Even if Charles had sent him here, Josh was charming.

"And no, Charles didn't send me," Josh continued. "I actually have a mind of my own, and I can even make my own decisions. Are you going to ask me in?"

"Do I have a choice?" Stephanie said, holding her ground.

Josh sighed. "Uh-uh. You're supposed to say 'Please come in. I'm so happy to see you'."

"I'm so happy to see you," Stephanie deadpanned. But strangely enough, she really was excited to see him.

"Great." He squeezed passed her.

She smelled his fresh spicy scent and admired the view as he sauntered in. His hair, though still long, was clean and brushed back off his face and his beard appeared freshly trimmed. He wore jeans, a white shirt, a beige bomber jacket and motorcycle-type boots. He looked rugged and strong, like a bodyguard for someone rich. Actually, she guessed according to Charles, Josh was her bodyguard, but of course, Josh had said Charles hadn't sent him.

"I decided all on my own that you'd need company your first night home," he said, emphasizing "all on my own."

As busy as Charles had kept Stephanie, it had actually taken nearly two months to make the move, but a water leak in her apartment had caused most of the delay. With Charles's continued appeal that she remain at his house, Stephanie had at first wondered if he'd had anything to do with the pipes in her condo breaking, but decided she was being melodramatic.

"So here I am all on my own," Josh said again, bringing Stephanie back from her thoughts.

Stephanie opened her mouth to object to Josh's presence.

"No. No need to thank me," he continued. "I've brought sandwiches, chips, ice cream, popcorn, M&M's, diet coke—all the major food groups, plus DVDs. I have quite a selection, even chick flicks. I know what you're thinking. And yes, I'm secure enough in my manhood to watch them."

The words, "There's nothing wrong with your manhood," slipped out before she could stop them. She brought her free hand up to cover her traitor mouth.

He grinned. "Okay then. We'll watch *Pretty Woman*."

"And eat junk food?" She took the sack from him and pretended to struggle under its weight. "Are you sure you brought enough?"

"I'm fairly certain." He exchanged the groceries she held for the flowers he held. While she found a vase, he unloaded the dinner items onto the kitchen counters.

She pulled placemats and plates from the cupboards and positioned the roses on the table as a centerpiece. She found fancy goblets for the diet coke and used cloth napkins instead of paper. Digging into the drawer again, Stephanie secured candles in brass candlesticks, setting them on either side of the roses. She lit the candles and stole a moment to admire her work.

"Thanks, Josh," Stephanie said when they were seated. "I guess I really did need company tonight. You're great."

He puffed out his chest and polished the tips of his nails on his shirt. "And this is only the beginning."

After dinner, where they mostly made small talk, they settled on the couch and ate popcorn and M&M's while they watched Julia Roberts and Richard Gere. Snuggling close like girlfriend and boyfriend, Josh put his arm around her and she rested her head on his solid shoulder.

Their companionship proved to be a little island of comfort in a sea of concern. For several hours Stephanie didn't think about her job, the baby, the health of the mare, Charles—nothing complicated, only Josh. It was the first time she'd felt completely safe and secure since Todd's death. No, on second thought, she hadn't felt this happy even with Todd.

Taking a deep breath, she realized how much Josh had burrowed his way into her affections. He had a way of making her feel good about herself, in addition to lightening the burdens of her life.

"Earth to Stephanie," he said after a prolonged silence. "Is everything okay?"

She blinked, wishing she could stay under his protective arm forever. "I'm sorry. Have I been ignoring you?"

"Yes. Should I be insulted?" he said, mocking anger.

"No. Were you saying something important?" Despite her newly acquired feelings, she wanted to maintain at least the appearance of indifference.

He pulled an indignant face. "Of course. Everything I say is important. I said that I hope we can do this again. It's been fun, hasn't it?" He raised his brows like he really wanted an answer.

"It really has." She smiled.

They stared at each other for a moment, before he leaned over and kissed her gently.

Her heart fluttered as warmth flowed through her body, like sunshine after a stormy day. She expected him to put his arms around her, and reveled in the thought, but suddenly he pulled away.

"I'm sorry," he said. "We share a nice evening. You act like you don't hate me anymore, and then I go and do something stupid and blow everything."

Stephanie moistened her lips. "Actually, I'm not sure that you blew it. Maybe we should try again, just to see."

His eyes brightened and a smile found its way through the heavy beard. "Good idea." He cradled her face in his hands and kissed her again. She kissed him back. They kissed with fervor several more times before they drew apart. She tried to maintain a degree of nonchalance as her pulse pounded. Then she giggled, brought a hand to her face and began to scratch. "I've always wondered how it would feel to kiss a man with a beard."

"And?" he asked.

"And . . . . " She scratched again. "Not too bad."

"Not too bad?" He held her close with one hand while he playfully tickled her in the ribs with the other. She squealed and giggled while half-heartedly trying to escape.

"You're supposed to say it was darn good," he laughed. "Now repeat after me, "It was darn good.'"

"It was darn good." Stephanie stared at him for a moment, then curled up next to his side. "Why does tonight have to end?"

He placed his cheek against the top of her head and stretched his arm across her middle. "Well, it doesn't. I can come back tomorrow. We have several more movies to watch."

When she didn't answer, he brought his head back to look at her. "What?" he asked.

"Your arm's around the baby. Did you feel it kick?"

Instead of pulling away as Stephanie surmised he might do, he snuggled her closer. "I didn't. I'm sorry, am I hurting the baby?"

"No. I'm sure it's fine." She lay her arm across his.

"You know, you hardly look pregnant," Josh said.

"Oh, come on." Stephanie laughed.

"I'm not kidding. How far along are you?"

"Seven and a half months."

Josh blew out a breath. "That's really hard to believe."

"I think Deirdre suspects."

"She just thinks you're getting fat." He chuckled.

Stephanie elbowed him. "Are you trying to make me feel better or worse?"

"Better," he said. "If people hadn't known you before when you were probably too thin, they wouldn't have any idea. Honestly, you're hiding it really well."

"Well, if what you're saying is true, I guess my shopping trips have paid off—larger, more roomy clothes." She straightened. "But I think my innards are all pushed out to my sides. I feel like a stuffed turkey on Thanksgiving."

Josh laughed. "So, am I coming back tomorrow?"

"You're sweet, and that would be . . . ." She didn't finish.

With his fingers under her chin, he directed her face to look at him. "What's wrong?"

"I just wish I could jump ahead a year or so and not have to face anything in between."

He nodded slowly. "Then everything would be over?"

Without warning tears flooded her eyes. "Could be, but I've been thinking more about maybe keeping the baby."

Clearing his throat, he blinked several times. "So is that what you've decided to do now?" He sounded concerned.

"I don't know," she said, her voice unsteady. When she'd told him earlier that she'd probably give it away, he'd sounded as if he felt she should keep it. Maybe if he thought they were getting together, he wouldn't want someone else's baby figuring into the relationship, or perhaps Charles had sent him here to persuade her to give the baby away.

"Didn't you sign a contract?"

His tone reminded her of the conversation she'd had with Charles when they'd discussed the baby. "I did, but then I told him I might have changed my mind and asked for time. We haven't discussed it for a month, or maybe it's been closer to two months. I assume he thought I was on board." She glanced at Josh out of the corner of her eye. "Until today."

Josh cocked a brow. "What happened today?"

"He told me he'd found a family for the baby, and I told him I still wasn't sure I wanted to give it up."

"I'll bet he didn't like that."

"No, he didn't."

Rubbing his beard, Josh seemed deep in thought. "See how long you can drag it out before you talk to him again."

Now he had her wondering. "I don't know if I can hold him off anymore. You know he's talking about my 'dream' job in Montana. He wants me to head up a new out-of-state office. I guess he plans on me hiding out there until after the baby is born, giving it away and then beginning work. I told him I can run the office and be a mom too. He thinks not. For some reason he doesn't want me to keep this baby. He acts like it would be the end of my career."

"It would definitely make it harder." It seemed as if Josh's mind were elsewhere. He stared at her with unseeing eyes.

Stephanie slid to the side of the couch so she was no longer close to him.

"Now what's wrong?" he asked.

"I thought you'd vote for me keeping the baby." She felt a little hurt, thinking she'd have an ally in Josh.

He shrugged. "Why would you think that?"

"I don't know. You just seemed like someone who'd want me to stick it to Charles and do what I wanted, regardless of the consequences." She sat cross-legged on the sofa facing Josh.

"Maybe," he said.

"So would you keep the baby?"

"I might, but it's not my decision." He tapped her on the knee.

"But what do you think?"

His brows rose. "What I think matters to you?"

"Sometimes."

A grin flitted across his face, then he grew serious. "Do you want to keep the baby?"

"I guess I do."

He rubbed his beard. "You really want my opinion?"

"Yes."

"Okay, instead of trying to postpone discussing the baby with Charles, you should let him believe you're giving it up and then . . . and then, we'll get you away from here."

"What? You mean go to Montana?"

"Or just someplace away from here, where you'll be safe." His face reddened as if the last word had slipped out.

"Where I'll be safe? I'm safe here."

He took hold of her shoulders. "I don't know if you are."

"What are you saying?" A shiver shot through her.

"I don't trust Charles." He flashed her a tentative glance.

No doubt her reaction surprised him. It did her. "You don't trust Charles?" He'd been wonderful to Josh, as he had to her. Now just because she'd shared a nice evening with Josh, even kissed him . . . . She really had kissed him, hadn't she? Was that all it took for her to change her loyalties? "Maybe he doesn't trust you. Maybe I don't trust you. Why would I trust you and not Charles? He's a little controlling, but he's been great to me. He's my boss. I just met you, in court no less . . . ."

His lip curled and he chuckled without mirth. "That crime thing again. I was found innocent. Doesn't that mean anything to you?"

"You were found not guilty because Charles helped you, and now you say you don't trust him. Is it because you know he stretched the law in order to get you off when you were really guilty?" Her head threatened to burst from uncertainty.

He reached for her hands. She pulled away. He reached for them again and held tight. "I know you have every reason not to trust me, and maybe I'm wrong. I just think we could buy ourselves some time if we got you away from Charles, so you won't have to see him every day, and he won't have so much influence over you."

"Or so he won't be able to protect me, maybe from you." Webs of doubt inched their way into her thoughts.

Josh shook his head and sighed. "Do you think you need protection from me, a guy who watches chick flicks? I thought we'd gotten past that. Do you kiss men you're afraid of?"

"I didn't say I was afraid of you. I'm just not sure I can trust you."

"Can you trust Charles?"

"He's been like a father to me for months." A pain shot across her forehead.

"Have you ever asked yourself why?" He squeezed her hands.

"Why he's been so nice to me? He said I reminded him of the daughter he lost." Again she tried to pull her hands away.

"Let's just get you away from here. Let's get you to . . . okay, to Montana, if that's where he wants you to go, and figure things out from there." He let her hands slip free.

"So you want me to tell Charles that I will probably give up the baby and that I'll go to Montana?" She chewed her lip. That might work, at least she wouldn't have to confront Charles for a while, but then when she did, how bad would it be?

"Yes. Then we may or may not have you move into his condo."

"Where else would I go?" Charles would want her at the condo.

"I might have an idea."

Stephanie didn't like the sound of that. She had concerns about living where only Josh knew her location. "I'd better stay where Charles says, or he'll get suspicious."

"Let's see what happens."

"So you're saying I have to trust you?" Her question was more to witness his reaction than to get an affirmative answer. No matter what he said, she doubted she fully could.

He slid closer to her on the sofa and touched her arm. "I know I'm asking a lot, but I give you my word that you can." His green eyes did not waver as he stared directly into hers.

Her breath caught. How she wanted him by her side through all that was to follow. She guessed she had little choice but to trust him, at least she'd let him think she did—for now. "I'll talk to Charles on Monday," she said.

Their attention shifted from each other to the television. The movie menu cast its glow on the screen while refrains of the *Pretty Woman* theme song played over and over.

Josh reached for the remote. "Are you ready to kick me out now?"

"Almost, but why don't you start the movie over so we can talk and eat while we watch, at least the first part. Here, have a chip. You've either got to eat the rest of this food or take it home with you." She'd really enjoyed Josh's company, but didn't want him to know.

"You mean I can stay as long as I eat?"

"Depends. How hungry are you and how fast can you eat?" She handed him a package of candy.

They watched the movie for a time while he crunched on chips and popped M&M's.

Her eyelids drooped and she relaxed her head against the back of the couch. She'd just rest her eyes for a moment.

* * *

"Well, I guess you could say we've just spent our first night together, actually second—first if you don't count the barn," Josh touched her face.

Her head rested on his shoulder, which wasn't exactly how she remembered falling asleep. Sitting up, she rubbed her eyes and squinted to look at her watch. "It's three forty-five?"

"Afraid so." Pulling himself up from the couch, Josh straightened his shirt. "I better be on my way, so maybe you'll invite me back."

The movie menu on the TV—ignored for the second time that night—played on repeatedly. Josh grabbed the remote and put it out of its misery.

Stephanie stretched. "I thought you were coming again tomorrow night, or I guess it's tonight."

"You want me to?" Josh grinned. "Oh, I can't come tonight. How about Sunday?"

"Okay, Sunday night. You do have an impressive selection of chick flicks." She yawned.

"So it's my chick flicks and not my magnetic personality that draws you to me?" He took *Pretty Woman* out of the player and placed it in its case.

She peered at him from under her lashes. "When you're right, you're right."

He laid the hand still holding the DVD over his heart. "You sure know how to hurt a guy."

Taking his arm, she walked him to the door. "You'll survive."

"Don't be so sure." He leaned down and kissed her cheek. "Now, can I count on you to stay put for the rest of the night so I don't have to worry about you?"

"You worry about me?"

"It's my job." He winked.

"You sure know how to hurt a girl."

He took her hand from his arm and kissed it.

Still smiling, she watched as he descended the stairs outside her condo. Closing the door, she went straight to her bedroom. Not even changing into her pajamas, she plopped onto her bed and pulled the comforter up over her.

* * *

Was she dreaming or could she really hear voices of children playing outside her window? She opened her eyes and glanced at the wall clock. It read ten forty-five. Thank heavens it was Saturday. Charles would have had a fit if she was late for work again. He would have gone on and on saying that she wouldn't have been late had she still lived at his house. She yawned, hating the exhaustion she felt all the time. How she longed to get her body back. It wouldn't be too much longer now, and if she gave the baby away . . . . No. Hadn't she decided to keep it? She thought about Charles and vowed to convince him that she could be both a mother and a valuable associate.

Still hearing the voices, she glanced out her back window at the large play area beneath. A group of young boys kicked a soccer ball back and forth. For a fleeting moment she thought of the child she carried who might someday be laughing and playing like these children.

A tingle shot through her as she imagined this appealing picture. She sighed. Enough daydreaming. Turning from the window, she worked the next few hours straightening her condo, then decided she'd spend what was left of the day with the horses. If she were actually going to Montana, she'd need to make arrangements for Riskie and tell Kingston's owner that she'd have to find someone else to ride the big gelding. Stephanie smiled when she thought of Riskie. Of the two horses, she'd miss the mare more. Days of caring for her had cemented their attachment. It appeared the little horse would make a full recovery. Bless Dr. Lee's heart.

As she dressed, her thoughts shifted to Montana. She'd known all along that she'd have to hide out when she could no longer conceal her pregnancy, but now that the time grew near, she hated leaving. She wondered about Josh, and what he'd said about her needing to go somewhere safe. Who was she supposed to fear? Charles? If so, why would Charles's condo in Montana be safe? And if she went to Montana she would have to make a decision on whether or not to hide her pregnancy. No one would know her history there, and if she did keep the baby, she could tell anyone interested that her husband was dead, which wasn't entirely a lie.

Now in the stark light of day, she realized there were many questions that had needed answers the night before. Maybe if she hadn't fallen asleep, she and Josh could have delved into them.

She smiled, thinking about him. How wonderful it would be to have no doubts about his motives. In spite of herself, she couldn't wait for Sunday evening. She shivered as a dark cloud of doom settled over her. She wished she could shake the feeling that something bad was going to spoil those plans.

CHAPTER 19

Why hadn't Josh stopped? Stephanie thought she saw his white truck pass by when she rode Kingston out of the trees onto the cross-country field. Maybe it hadn't been him, but it surely looked like it. Oh well, she'd think about that later. Right now she took some pride in herself for accomplishing two tasks she'd been dreading. She only wished things had gone better.

Not knowing exactly when Charles would send her to Montana, she decided she'd better be prepared for any eventuality and make arrangements for Kingston and Riskie.

Kathleen had acted strange when Stephanie paid her three months board for Riskie and asked if the barn manager would care for the mare's needs while Stephanie was away. It appeared Riskie was doing well, the danger period having long passed. The game little horse barely limped. Even Dr. Lee was impressed on his last visit. Stephanie hadn't mentioned the possibility of her staying in Montana, but hoped she'd be able to send for Riskie if that ended up being a reality.

The stable manager had disappeared with a furrowed brow and kind words to the effect that she hoped Stephanie would return soon and that she would be sorely missed. Stephanie hated telling her friend half-truths and wondered if Kathleen had guessed the real reason for her departure. Even though Stephanie had tried to camouflage her condition with big shirts, sloppy sweatshirts and the excuse that she'd gained weight lately due to the necessity of eating fast foods, Stephanie feared Kathleen had been unconvinced. She wished she'd just told her the whole story. Kathleen would have understood.

Kingston's owner had been unhappy when Stephanie told her she couldn't keep riding the gelding. She asked if Stephanie were still interested in buying him and Stephanie hadn't known what to say. If she kept her baby she wouldn't be able to afford any horse and even doubted she'd be able to continue supporting Riskie. Charles would be happy that the possibility of a no-horse future would force Stephanie to give up the child. Once there would have been no contest. Tonight she wasn't sure what her choice would be.

As the sun set, Stephanie lingered at Riskie and her baby's stall. The filly had grown several inches and loved the attention Stephanie lavished on her. She rubbed the foal's neck and the little horse nuzzled Stephanie with a soft nose. Her whiskers tickled Stephanie's cheek and made her giggle. Always happy when around horses, Stephanie hoped this wouldn't be the last time she'd see the mare and her baby—or Kathleen. Maybe she should just go up to the house and tell her friend the truth. Perhaps she would give Stephanie more time to work out her horse finances if she decided to keep her own baby. But just as Stephanie started for the house, she saw Kathleen's car heading toward town and knew she'd missed her chance.

Disappointed, she switched off the overhead stable light and started for her car. She sighed and chewed her lip. She wished Josh would come over again tonight, but remembered he'd said he had something else to do. But why hadn't he stopped by earlier? The more Stephanie thought about the white truck, the more convinced she became that it had been his.

Gravel crunched somewhere behind her. Heat prickled the back of her neck and she glanced around. Normally sounds didn't bother her, even here at the barn by herself as darkness descended. She walked faster, then turned and grabbed a pitchfork propped against the side of the stable. Hopefully she'd be able to return it tomorrow or call Kathleen and tell her where to pick it up. Of course, then Stephanie would have to fess up to being scared.

The crunching sound met her ears again, this time closer. Stephanie tightened her grip on the pitchfork and lengthened her stride.

All at once a big dark form barreled straight for her. Her heart nearly stopped and she raised the pitchfork, ready to scream.

The scream turned into a gasp of relief as she recognized the white blaze face of Kingston. She dropped the pitchfork and strode over to him. "Here, boy," she said, holding out her hand.

What was he doing away from his stall? Had she forgotten to secure it when she'd left? No, she distinctly remembered winding the chain around the bars of the gate. There was no way he could get out by himself, unless he jumped, but he'd never leave his dinner.

Her heart pounded. Good sense told her to get out of there and leave Kingston to fend for himself until she could get back with help. No. She couldn't do that. He might get out on the road in the meantime and be killed.

"Here, boy," she said again. He snorted. He never behaved like that around her. She walked to him and put her hand on his shoulder. It was damp. She slipped out of her sweater and tied it around his neck. He snorted again.

Suddenly someone grabbed Stephanie from behind, someone much taller than herself. It flashed through her mind that if it was Josh playing a trick on her, she was going to kill him. The arm across her shoulders grew tighter and another hand came over her mouth. It couldn't be Josh. He was hurting her. She tried to bite his hand, but he kept it away from her teeth and bent her head around.

"This is what happens to little girls who try to break their promises," a voice said.

Promises? Her mind struggled to formulate what he meant. Was he talking about the baby and the contract she'd signed? Only Josh and Charles knew about the contract and she and Josh had decided that she'd tell Charles she would give up the baby, but her boss's last information was that she was keeping her child.

Finding herself strangely calm, she didn't think this guy would harm her since he'd hurt the baby. Anger built inside her. She wasn't about to put up with this nonsense any longer. Adrenaline kicked in and warmed her body.

With the quickness of a cat, she stomped her boot heel on the attacker's instep, whirled around, coupled her hands and slammed them under his chin. She took an abrupt step back and kicked him between the legs.

As if Kingston sensed he should protect Stephanie, he reared, pawing the air, his front hoofs nearly striking the man's head. Then, ears flat against his neck, he stood menacingly on all fours.

"Good boy," Stephanie said, as she grabbed Kingston's mane and swung on, big belly and all. With a cluck of her tongue, she urged the gelding forward. She didn't care where he took her, only that it be away from here, away from this man who stumbled, slumped over, toward the parking lot.

She recognized nothing about the dark-clad, ski-masked stranger, and as Kingston whirled around it occurred to her that she didn't even see a vehicle. The man had probably hidden it. How she hoped it wasn't a white truck. She scolded herself. After last night how could she think such a thing? Feeling in her pants pocket, she realized she'd left her cell phone at home. Wonderful. Just when she needed it most.

With skill honed by hours of training, Stephanie was able to guide the big gelding using her legs and a little help from the sweater still tied around Kingston's neck. She thought about heading for the house but reminded herself that Kathleen was gone. Well, so was the man—she hoped.

She didn't know if she dared put Kingston in his stall and make the long walk back to her car, but she didn't really have a choice. This time she'd leave the stable light on. Although Kathleen wouldn't be happy, her friend could turn it off when she came home. Stephanie thought of the quirt in her locker and the pitchfork she'd dropped part way to her car. She'd be okay if the stranger didn't have a gun, but then again he wouldn't want to harm the baby. Of course, there was always the possibility this little scene hadn't been about the baby, but she doubted it.

Stephanie guided Kingston back to his stall and slid off. She rubbed his neck as she removed her sweater from around it. How she hated to leave him. She laid her cheek against his shoulder, then reached up and gave him a huge hug, all the time listening for any alien sound.

Quirt in hand, Stephanie flipped on the overhead stable light, walked a few feet and picked up the pitchfork. Weapons ready, she headed for her car, unlocked the door and checked the backseat. She decided to leave the pitchfork by the gate, but she kept her quirt handy.

Inside the car, she locked the doors and sat staring into the night. It wasn't until then that she began to shake. Tears flooded her eyes and rolled down her cheeks. She'd just been attacked by some strange man. He could have hurt her, or . . . it hadn't occurred to her until now . . . kidnapped her. If it was the baby they wanted, maybe they planned on holding her hostage until the baby came and then disposing of her.

She wiped her face with her hands. No. She'd been watching too many movies. No one could get away with kidnapping her. Charles would track them down and . . . . Unless it was Charles. Oh yeah, sure. Didn't she trust anyone anymore? A few minutes ago she'd been accusing Josh. Now it was Charles. Her imagination had no bounds. But who was the man who'd grabbed her and how did he know about the contract?

Her hand shook as she struggled to place the key in the ignition. Finally accomplishing the feat, she turned out of the parking lot, but where should she go? Her condo? She almost wished she could go back to Charles's house where Janeen, his housekeeper, would keep her company. She was losing it. Of course she should return to her condo and call her friend, Officer Christopherson. Maybe if he were on duty he could drive by her place periodically during the night. If only Josh was available. She didn't even know how to contact him. His cell phone number was in his file at the office and she didn't want to go there alone tonight.

Wait a minute. She'd been so certain she'd seen Josh's white truck earlier. She forced her mind to focus on the man who had attacked her. He seemed about Josh's size, but so were a lot of men. Josh wouldn't harm her. She'd spent a wonderful evening with him the night before, but perhaps everything had been a ploy to make her trust him. Maybe he'd had further orders today. Could Charles have told him to scare her into honoring the contract? She shook her head. Charles wouldn't do such a thing.

Stephanie glanced out her window, then peered in the rearview mirror. Gulping in deep breaths, she willed her heart to slow. Thankfully her car moved alone on the road. She slowed to negotiate a curve. Her mind went back to Charles.

Why hadn't she thought all this through before? Just stupid, she guessed. Perhaps Charles had already found a home for her baby and the people were desperate to get it. She recalled how upset he'd been when she'd mentioned keeping the baby. At the time she'd determined his objection pertained only to her future. How dense and conceited could she be?

As she pulled into her condo parking lot, she searched the landscape. She probably wasn't out of danger yet. She rummaged through her purse. She'd call Officer Christopherson now and have him come over. Shoot. Once more she remembered she'd left her cell phone upstairs. She'd have to go in. Her mouth went dry. She should have gone straight to the police department, but she was here now. She carried the quirt with her as she climbed out of her car. She had her key ready and ran up the stairs. Breathless, she closed the door behind her and locked it, sliding the chain into place.

She flipped on the lights, and still holding the quirt, searched through her entire condo. Still no cell phone. She was shuffling through papers on the kitchen counter when someone began banging on her front door. She crept forward, peering out through the corner of the drapes. The porch lights had come on automatically as they did for all the condos, but she wished she hadn't turned on her lights. Oh, no! Standing like an enraged bull, Charles almost pawed the ground.

"I know you're here, Stephanie. You've got to let me in. Your life is in danger." With ruffled hair and red face, he looked deadly serious.

Stephanie nearly went to her knees. Of course she was in danger, but Charles had no way of knowing it, or hearing about her earlier experience, unless he initiated it.

"Go away, Charles. I've already been attacked once tonight. That's enough."

"What? Someone tried to hurt you? We have less time than I thought. Stephanie, let me in." With an open palm, he slapped the door. "I'll tell you everything, but first let's get you safe. I have a gun."

So there were things he'd been hiding. Perhaps he'd finally admit to the lies he'd been telling, or was it a trick? "How do I know you won't use the gun on me?" Her voice went hoarse. She cleared her throat.

"Stephanie, we don't have much time. If I'd have wanted to hurt you, there were plenty of other times." That fact was true. No question in her mind. Still she hesitated.

"I've got my car down here. Come on, let's go. I know someplace where you'll be safe." He pounded on the door again.

She hoped he wouldn't have a heart attack, at least she guessed she hoped he wouldn't. She searched for the right words to answer him, but nothing came.

"Okay, Stephanie, see this?"

Moving the curtains aside, she looked through the window again as he held up some papers. As he unfolded them, she realized it was the original contract she'd signed, giving her baby away. "Open the door and I'll tear it up."

If he were willing to do that, his concern for her might be genuine. "Tear it up first."

"Unlock the door."

With an unsteady hand, she undid the chain, letting it drop against the doorjamb, then stepped to the window again. Good to his word, Charles tore the document in half. "We're running out of time. Come on, Stephanie."

Knowing she might live to regret it, or not live at all, Stephanie opened the door a crack. "Tear it up all the way."

Charles tore the remainder of the document into tiny pieces, letting it scatter in the wind. Now he pushed his way in. "Grab a jacket and your purse. You won't be coming back."

"Now listen, Charles." She tried to step in front of him.

He grabbed her purse off the counter and pushed it against her. "Do as I say. It's your life we're talking about. Let's go."

"You're not even going to let me change out of my riding clothes?" Strength seemed to be leaking from her body.

"No time."

Charles nearly dragged Stephanie down the stairs. He shoved her into his car and slammed the door. A sharp pain hit her belly and she bent over.

"Are you okay?" Charles asked as he backed his Lexus out and sped down the road.

"Like you care."

He scowled at her.

"I'm fine," she said finally. She did feel a little better. "Where are we going?"

"Someplace safe." Charles had a slash in the sleeve of his expensive suit and his shirttail hung out.

"What's going on? You said you'd tell me?" She gritted her teeth as a new pain struck. She tried to remember how long until the baby was due, but her brain wouldn't work.

Charles's knuckles went white on the steering wheel. "I'm so sorry, Stephanie. I didn't mean for everything to get out of control. It was supposed to be a simple matter of acquiring a baby for a very rich man and his witch-of-a-wife. I didn't plan on anyone getting killed."

"Killed?" Her mind raced. Todd! "Do you mean Todd? Wait. Do you mean my baby? You planned on giving my baby away from the beginning? How did you know there'd even be a baby?"

A trickle of sweat ran down Charles's face. "Because I hired Todd to make sure there was. I set him up in the cabin, gave him money, everything—and he was expensive."

Stephanie's pulse pounded. "You hired him to force me?"

"I didn't think it would take that. He was a handsome man. I thought everything would come naturally. I didn't know about your standards." The mocking way he said "standards" made Stephanie boil.

"So sorry to disappoint you," she spat, trying to sound tough when she really wanted to cry. Todd had seemed so sincere. He'd told her many times that he loved her. "But Todd wanted the baby," she said in a final defense. She felt like she was going to throw up.

Shaking his head slowly, Charles snorted. "Todd actually did want the child, and he wanted you. If it makes you feel any better, Todd fell in love. That part wasn't a lie. He wanted to marry you. He wanted out of our agreement. He came to me. We quarreled." Although Charles stared straight ahead, he blinked several times and Stephanie thought he looked sad. He should have.

She shook her head—that day at the office and Todd's car parked in front. She should have made Todd come clean with her then. Maybe he'd still be alive. Tears stung her eyes. "You killed Todd because he wanted to marry me and keep the baby and ruin all your plans? You low down filthy pig!" Her hands doubled into fists.

"Hold on there. I didn't kill Todd, but I think I know who did, if his death really wasn't an accident." Charles glanced around and turned the car down a back road. "I was going to let Todd out of our agreement so he could marry you, but someone else didn't want to give up your baby. I'm guessing he might have had Todd killed."

"Who's this someone?" Her back began to ache, low down, but there was just a dull pain in her abdomen.

"The same person who is after us now." Charles sped up, taking turns faster than Stephanie felt safe.

"You won't tell me who?' She grabbed the armrest.

"If we get out of this tonight, it's safer for you not to know."

She wished she could wake up from this nightmare. "How much, Charles? How much did you sell my baby for?"

He sighed, then mumbled. "Five hundred thousand, but it wasn't only the money."

"Five hundred thousand dollars? Who in their right mind would pay that much for a child?"

Charles pulled around a car in front of them. "This guy's so rich he wouldn't even miss the money. He and his wife tried everything for years to have their own baby, and there was always some hold-up when they tried to adopt through legal channels. I think people are afraid of them." Charles's hand on the steering wheel shook. He gripped the wheel harder. "Even though the man is powerful in his own right, his wife is the source of most of his money. She's a real nut case, so he tries to keep her happy. She decided that it had to be your baby, yours and Todd's. Nothing else would do."

"Mine and Todd's? How did she even know us?" Stephanie felt her mouth fall open as realization hit. "It's Matthew Dawson and his snooty wife, Jessica, isn't it?"

"No."

"Liar." Now she knew why Matthew had been so attentive at the office, and then there was that weird visit from his wife, Jessica. She'd made Stephanie feel like a frog on a dissecting table.

"I'm sorry, Stephanie." He wiped his brow with the back of his hand.

If she could have done it without causing a wreck, Stephanie would have slapped Charles's face. "What am I? A broodmare?" She snickered—like Riskie. "Let's just call the police." She held her breath as another pain hit her. It was too early for her baby to come, and now was certainly not a good time.

"I can't, Stephanie. I'm in too deep. Matthew knows about things in my past and threatened to expose me if I didn't get him your baby. The money was only his first incentive to keep me happy so I'd continue to do his bidding. He only threatened me when I got out of control and wanted to allow you to keep your baby."

She swallowed hard. "What's he holding over you?"

The muscle in his jaw clenched. He took a deep breath and began, "Your baby isn't the first one I've sold. It wasn't even the first one that Todd fathered."

"What are you saying?" Stephanie hadn't expected the news to be so bad and that it would involve her directly. For a moment she forgot about the pain in her belly.

Clearing his throat, Charles went on. "There was another girl who decided to keep her baby after she'd agreed to let Matthew and Jessica adopt it. She died when her car crashed into a river. Luckily, or maybe it was planned, the week-old baby wasn't in the car at the time of the accident. After a long legal battle and, I'm sure, multiple payoffs, Matthew and Jessica ended up with the child, a little girl."

"They already have a baby. Why do they want mine?"

"Several reasons. Remember your baby is a half sibling to theirs. Plus, you and Jessica could pass as sisters, as did the first mother, from what I've discovered. In addition, Matthew was hoping for a boy this time so he would have a male heir to carry on the name."

Charles passed another car. Stephanie watched as lights coming from the opposite direction moved closer and closer. She gave a little squeal as Charles turned back in his lane just in time.

"Are you trying to kill us? Slow down," Stephanie yelled.

"I can't." He wiped a sweaty palm on his slacks.

"This is all insane."

"Speaking of insane. I think Jessica truly is. She gets what she wants, or everyone suffers, and then you add Matthew to the mix and there's real trouble. They had me by the throat."

"Did you kill her, the baby's mother, I mean, or have her killed?" She wrapped her arms around her middle against the pain.

Charles's eyes flashed. "Of course not. I don't kill people. I just sell babies, from here and abroad. Most of the time people cooperate. It's been profitable. You didn't think I could have all I own on an attorney's salary, did you?"

"Do you think Matthew killed her?" Beneath her roomy sweater, Stephanie unzipped the zipper on her new oversized breeches, allowing her belly more room.

"I don't know. There's no proof. I'm not even sure about Todd."

The mention of Todd in that context reminded Stephanie of the girl she'd seen at his graveside. "Remember when we were leaving the cemetery, did you see a girl standing by his grave?"

Charles took a quick glance at Stephanie before concentrating on the road again. "I think that was Jenny. She's the sister of the first baby's mother. She never believed the death was an accident. Living across the country from one another, Jenny and her sister were never close, but Jenny fought the adoption anyway. Matthew gave her a little something to make her life more comfortable, at least that was how he put it, and she dropped the lawsuit."

Thankfully, the traffic had thinned. Now theirs was the only car on the road.

"It all sounds suspicious to me and I'm not supposed to be as smart as you." The pain in her belly subsided a little. If only her heart would quit pounding in her temples.

"I confronted Mathew once and he told me that he had nothing to do with either death, but he would make it look like I was responsible if any more were said." Charles focused on something outside, as if he were making sure they were on the right road.

"Wow. What a sweetheart, and to think you wanted to hand my baby over to him and his lunatic wife," Stephanie said breathlessly, and realized she was panting.

"Can you see now why we're leaving?" Charles glanced in the rearview mirror again.

"I still think we should go to the police. Just drop me off there."

"I can't do that, Stephanie. I guarantee that Matthew would get to you sooner or later. Besides, there isn't time."

"What about Paul? Is he involved? He'd help me, wouldn't he?" She hoped there was one honest partner in the law firm she'd been representing.

"You wouldn't be safe with him either. He knows everything, but turns a blind eye. He likes the money the firm brings in."

Stephanie threw her hands in the air. Even though Charles was now trying to undo the damage he'd done to her, she couldn't forget that he was responsible for it all. "I've been so stupid. I'm surprised you didn't just let Matthew take me. After all, you've pretty much only been thinking of yourself." She felt her nostrils flare.

"I told you. You're like a daughter to me. I care about you."

"Oh, please. You don't expect me to believe that, you do?"

"I wish you would." He reached one hand out to her.

She leaned away. "You've ruined my life."

"No I haven't. I've got a suitcase full of money in the trunk and a huge bank account in Switzerland. We're headed to a place where neither Matthew nor the authorities will ever find us. We'll live in luxury. You can raise your baby. I'll take care of you both. I always wanted a grandchild."

Laughing, but without glee, Stephanie said, "Am I just supposed to forget everything that's happened? Forget that Todd was killed and let his murderer go unpunished? I loved Todd."

Then a thought jolted her like a dentist drill to a nerve. She dreaded asking and wondered why it hadn't occurred to her earlier. "What about Josh? Was he a set-up too?"

"Josh works for me. I really hired him to help me look out for you, among other things. And, I thought he might . . . oh, never mind."

Stephanie shivered. "Don't tell me. Was he to be your next stud? How can you live with yourself? Just let me out. I'll take my chances. I can't stand the sight of you." Stretching the sides around her belly, Stephanie re-zipped her breeches.

"But you like Josh. I know you do. When we get settled, we can send for him, if you want."

"Why, so we can make more babies for you to sell?" She glared at him.

His face actually showed pain. "I guess I deserve that."

"You deserve much more than that." Her voice shook with anger. "Now let me out."

He glanced in the rearview mirror and pressed his foot on the accelerator. "I can't. We're being followed.

CHAPTER 20

Stephanie planted her feet on the floorboard of Charles's Lexus, glad for every dollar spent on the car's enhanced performance. "So we're running because you're afraid of what Matthew might do?"

Charles glanced in the rearview mirror and sped up. "I don't know how they knew about this." He spoke more to himself than to her.

"I still can't believe we shouldn't go to the police and then fight everything in court. We're attorneys. We're trained to use the law to straighten things out." She shifted in her seat and adjusted the seatbelt, trying to make the tenderness in her back go away.

"You are such a naïve little girl," Charles said, his voice barely civil. "Haven't you been listening? The law means nothing to Matthew. He gets what he wants regardless, and he wants your baby. He's a powerful man and now that he knows you'll cause him trouble, you'd never make it to court. He'll hide you out somewhere until the baby comes and then you'll have an unfortunate accident. Remember Todd? Remember Jenny's sister? Besides, there's no time."

"So Matthew really did kill them both?" Stephanie shivered. Perhaps that was what he'd planned for her, but she really couldn't fathom Matthew being that evil. Now Jessica was a different matter. Perhaps Charles was right. She rubbed her arms.

If Matthew had killed Todd, she hoped he and his dreadful wife would die slow painful deaths someday soon.

"I'm almost certain he killed them." Charles slowed, but only slightly.

Stephanie pictured the car careening around the corner on two wheels. She clutched the armrest. "Why haven't you turned him in to the authorities?"

Charles gave her a quick how-stupid-can-you-be look. "The law again. I'm afraid you've been brainwashed. Now listen to me. No evidence and no witnesses. Everything and everybody have a way of disappearing. It would be my word against his, and Matthew would make sure my word was worthless."

"So he's known about your past for a while. Why hasn't he threatened you before? Oh, wait! It's me. He wouldn't be after you tonight, if not for me, right?"

Wiping sweat from his brow, Charles replied, "I wouldn't be running yet, if not for you. Otherwise I might have had years."

She stared at him, wondering if Charles really was giving up everything here for her safety. Her anger toward him began to dissipate, but she knew she couldn't let that happen. If it weren't for him, she wouldn't be in this mess. "Why are you protecting me now?"

"I told you. You're like a daughter to me," he said simply.

She wished she could read the truth in his eyes, but they stayed riveted on the road, which was probably a good thing. He still drove at a frightening speed. She turned to check out the headlights behind them. They were still following, and Stephanie experienced a tremor of fear.

"I guess I should thank you, but somehow I find that hard to do." She couldn't keep from scowling.

"I understand." He almost sounded defeated, which added to Stephanie's worry.

She glanced again at the relentless headlights behind them, then turned away. "What are we going to do? It doesn't look like they're gaining, but we'll never lose them."

Charles stole a glance at her. "If we can make it to my plane ahead of them, we'll be okay. Josh is there. He'll fly us to California where we'll catch a flight out of the country."

At the mention of Josh's name, Stephanie's heart raced, but she didn't have the luxury of dwelling on the feeling long. "Won't Matthew be able to find out where we're going?"

"We won't file a flight plan, and we'll pay cash for our tickets in California. Hopefully we'll have a little head start; and once we get to Denmark, we'll disappear."

"Denmark?" Her voice indicated her dismay. "I don't speak Danish, do you?" She didn't want to give up her country; and, petty though it was, she'd never be able to send for the horses if she lived in Denmark. Besides, although Charles said he considered her a daughter, she could never think of him as a father—far from it.

Intent on his driving, Charles made no further comment about their escape to Denmark. His stiff stance hinted that he'd like her to be quiet so he could drive without interruption.

She couldn't just sit there stewing when, according to Charles, her life depended on the distance between them and the pursuing headlights. Talking at least directed her thoughts away from their predicament and the reoccurring ache in her belly. "So we're heading to the airport?"

"No."

"But you said we're meeting Josh at your plane." Again her heart fluttered at the mention of his name.

"It's my private runway."

"You have your own airport?"

"It's just a hangar and a field. I don't like crowds."

"Oh, I see. Then you can do as you please without anyone noticing. Have you kidnapped people before?"

He frowned. "You're not being kidnapped, at least not by me. I can't say the same for Matthew, though."

"This is all so—cloak and dagger. I still have a hard time believing Matthew is that dangerous."

"Stephanie, you have no idea."

Charles was really starting to scare her. Apparently her earlier attack marked only the beginning. Goosebumps rose on her arms. "So you think Matthew sent the man who attacked me?"

"I don't think there's any question."

The lights behind them disappeared once; and, in spite of herself, Stephanie grew hopeful, but not for long. Soon headlights shone again through the moonlit night. Did she dare believe they were farther back, or that maybe a different, innocent car followed? She doubted it. She wrapped her arms around her belly.

"What the . . .," Charles exclaimed. "Why isn't the gate open? Hold on!"

Stephanie froze as the Lexus headed straight for a closed gate in a chain link fence.

The impact threw her forward against her seatbelt, but then the car sped on through. Apparently Charles was more concerned about those who followed them than what happened to his beautiful car, to say nothing of the possibility of injury to her and the baby. How much money did he have in the briefcase and in his overseas bank? A lot if it would replace what he had here.

A stronger pain stabbed her belly, but she could do nothing about it now. She pondered her plight and reminded herself that her baby shouldn't be arriving for six weeks yet.

Charles kept the car moving as fast as possible down a winding dirt road, bordered by trees and bushes. The pathway soon opened up into a huge field, mowed short. The headlights revealed a large white building at one end of the property amidst smaller buildings and sheds. An orange windsock flapped on its pole atop the big building, no doubt designating where Charles kept his plane.

As the car slid to a stop, Charles jumped out. A large door opened on the front of the hangar, the light inside illuminating a section of ground in front. Josh manipulated an airplane out of the enclosure with a tow bar.

Stephanie's pulse pounded at the sight of him, but he didn't acknowledge her.

"I thought you'd be ready!" Charles yelled at Josh.

"Sorry," Josh said without explanation.

Charles opened the trunk of the Lexus and hauled out his briefcase and two large bags.

"Hurry, Josh. They're on our heels."

Josh seized Stephanie's arm and hustled her into the backseat of the airplane. No time for discussion, her eyes locked onto his. She hoped for some reassurance, but he said nothing. She grimaced at the throbbing in her back.

Charles tossed the bags in next to Stephanie and dropped into the plane's passenger seat.

Josh climbed in and began flipping switches.

The plane moved forward to the head of the large field, and Josh revved up the engine.

Conflicting thoughts swirled through Stephanie's brain. She didn't want to go with Charles, but was afraid to stay. Maybe if Josh went with them, she'd be able to stand it. She felt as if she had no control, like she was slipping toward the mouth of a deep, cold well and couldn't stop herself from falling in.

Lights shone through the trees at the gate they'd crashed through only moments earlier. Their pursuers were getting close. Stephanie felt sure she'd be sick.

The plane moved forward.

A car rounded the bend and sped onto the field.

Stephanie tried to gauge the closing distance between the car and the plane racing toward each other. "We're not going to make it!" she screamed.

"Keep going." Charles yelled and secured his seatbelt.

Josh reached for the throttles. He pushed them forward slightly, then, jaw clenched, he pulled back, cutting the power completely.

"What are you doing?" Charles turned to face Josh.

"I don't want to kill us."

Charles grabbed Josh's shoulder with fingers that Stephanie thought looked like talons. "They will, you fool."

The car skidded around in front of them. Josh fought with the rudder pedals of the plane to avoid colliding with the mass of metal and paint that now blocked their escape.

Three men leaped out of the big, black car. Stephanie recognized Matthew Dawson in the headlights.

Josh fingered the latch on the cockpit door and opened it.

"Do you know what you've done?" Charles clawed at him. "Do you even care that you've put Stephanie in danger?"

Face hard and expressionless, Josh turned away. "Would you have preferred that we burned to death in a fiery crash? At least now she has a chance."

"That's just it," Charles muttered through clenched teeth. "Now she doesn't."

"And I'm sure your thoughts are only of her," Josh protested.

A man dressed in dark clothes appeared at the side of the plane, pointing a gun inside. "Everyone out."

Josh shifted in his seat to obey.

"Stay where you are," Charles ordered.

The gun went off, shattering the windshield in front of Charles.

"That was a warning shot," the man said. "Next time, the bullet will hit you."

In the dim light of the cockpit, Stephanie studied their assailant. He could have been the man who attacked her. She felt the corner of her lip raise into a sneer. She had bested him once. Maybe she could again. No one was taking her baby. She would fight to the death if need be.

Josh climbed out, followed by Charles, who turned and extended his hand to help Stephanie. She groaned as a sharp pain attached her belly and back.

"Are you okay?" Charles whispered.

"I'm fine." She clenched her jaw, willing it to be true.

"Well, well," Matthew said, walking toward them. "So we meet again, Miss Saunders. I believe you are carrying something that belongs to me; and, since it appears you are trying to steal it, I will have to detain you for a while."

Walking forward, Stephanie stopped in front of Matthew, stared him straight in the eyes, then drew back and slapped him across the face with such force that it snapped his head around. "Leave us alone," she hissed.

One of Matthew's men took a quick step toward Stephanie.

Matthew held up a hand, stopping his protector. Then he turned to Stephanie, "I'm afraid I can't leave you alone. You see, you've given me no choice." He took a deep breath. "We could have been friends, you and I, but you went back on our agreement."

"It was never our agreement. Charles tricked me." Stephanie turned to glare at her boss. What gave her the courage to stand up to these two men who had always intimidated her, she couldn't fathom. All she knew was that they were not taking her baby. If nothing else, she vowed she'd go down swinging.

"That's a cop-out and you know it." Matthew folded his arms. "If you really wanted this child, you would have never considered giving it away even for one second, no matter how it came into being. Isn't that right, Charles?"

For a moment Stephanie felt guilty. What Matthew said had merit. Still . . . . "What do you think you're going to do? I'm not leaving with you and if I turn up missing, people will start checking, and what about Charles and Josh?"

Matthew sighed as if she were boring him. "First of all, you've told everyone you're going to Montana for an undisclosed period of time, and Charles . . . . Well, Charles is running off to places unknown because he has troubles of his own, and Josh—"

"You're not taking her, Matthew." Charles walked closer. "You'll have to go through me, and I'm not moving." Hand shaking, he drew his gun.

Even though Charles had said what she wished Josh would have, Stephanie's heart warmed. Maybe Charles really did care for her. At least he was on her side. She wasn't alone in this, after all.

"Sorry to hear that." Matthew nodded to one of the men who flanked him. In an instant, the taller of the two leveled his gun and pulled the trigger.

Charles's weapon slipped unused from his grip. He grabbed his side and crumpled to the ground.

Josh started forward, but Matthew stepped in front of him.

"No!" Stephanie screamed and ran to Charles. Kneeling, she grasped his hand.

"I'm sorry, Stephanie. I'm so sorry for everything," Charles mumbled. "I thought I could protect you." His eyes widened, then closed. His head rolled to the side and his hand went limp.

"Help him," Stephanie cried. "We need to call an ambulance. Josh, do something."

He didn't move.

"Oh, I guess you didn't know." Matthew smirked. "Josh works for me. Good thinking, my boy, detaining the plane. You had me worried for a second."

What was Matthew saying? Stephanie blinked to clear her head. Josh was on Matthew's side? Swallowing hard, she stared up at the man she'd come to think of as a friend.

He looked away.

Anger surged through her, making her face go hot. Josh was even worse than she'd ever suspected he could be. It had been bad enough when she thought he worked for Charles, but working for Matthew meant that instead of her ally, he was a threat to her and her baby, as well as poor Charles, if he still lived.

Betrayal burned inside Stephanie giving her renewed strength. She rose from Charles's side and rushed at Josh, pummeling him with her fists. "Do you know how revolting you are? I've been such a fool."

"Now, now," Josh said in a tone that made her seethe. She could see how someone could commit murder. She struggled to get away, but he held her tight against him.

"He's good, isn't he?" Matthew's mouth formed a wicked grin. "He fooled Charles, too." He glanced down on the ground at Stephanie's unconscious boss and would-be protector. "Josh, why don't you go ahead and fly Charles to California. I'll send Butch along with you." He nodded at one of his henchmen. "Check and see if he's dead. If he isn't, take care of it. You two can dispose of the body and the plane and catch an airline back."

"No," Stephanie cried.

Matthew picked up Charles's bags. "Now bring her to me, Josh. We're law-abiding citizens. We don't want any more bloodshed."

A heavy weight bore down on Stephanie's bladder. She grabbed her belly and felt it tighten. "I think I'm having the baby."

"That's a good one, my dear." Matthew chuckled. "I don't think anyone's going to buy it, though."

"I'm not faking," she groaned.

"Bring her along, Josh."

She tried to pull away, but he kept her close.

Matthew turned to open the trunk of his car. One of his dark-clad enforcers climbed into the driver's seat. The other stood nearby.

"Let me go," Stephanie sobbed, trying to stomp on Josh's foot.

He pulled her so close his mouth touched her ear. "Trust me," he whispered.

She gritted her teeth against the distress in her abdomen. Trust him? How could she? How could she not? "Help me."

"Sh," he whispered.

"Josh, the baby—"

"I know."

"Just let me stand still for a minute."

Josh loosened his grip.

Stephanie placed her hands above her knees and allowed her head to hang as pain doubled her over.

After closing the trunk, Matthew walked across the grass to stand between Stephanie and Josh.

Suddenly lights flooded the area. "Police! Drop your weapons!" one of them yelled.

Both Matthew and Josh jumped for Stephanie. Closer, Matthew grabbed her arm and dragged her toward the plane.

"Give it up, Dawson. It's all over," a deep voice said.

"If you don't want this girl hurt, you better let me go. Get the plane ready, Josh." Matthew brandished the gun he held at Stephanie's neck.

Both of Matthew's men aimed guns from windows of his car.

"Josh, open the door," Matthew ordered.

Slowly Josh stepped forward.

Stephanie cried out as her water burst, drenching her riding pants and boots.

His attention momentarily diverted, Stephanie elbowed Matthew in the ribs. He grunted, but continued to hold her as a shield.

In terror she watched as Josh leaped at Matthew.

Gun pointed, Matthew fired two shots.

Catching the bullets in his chest, Josh tumbled onto the grass.

"Josh," Stephanie cried and kicked Matthew in the shin with everything she had. He cursed and for one moment his grip loosened. She struggled to pull free.

A shot rang out followed by a groan. Matthew's arms went limp.

Stumbling away, Stephanie tripped and fell, her head striking something metal. She touched her forehead. Blood pooled in her hand.

Bullets flew overhead like hailstones. She tried to crawl away, but the ache in her head and belly held her rigid. She glanced up.

Matthew jerked back against the plane. Blood spurted from several wounds in his head and torso.

Good. Stephanie hoped Matthew was gone forever. He'd ordered Charles shot, and he'd pulled the trigger himself to fire at

Josh. Josh! Where was he? He couldn't be dead. She rose on one elbow, searching.

Men in black uniforms and helmets rushed out of the shadows. Some held rifles with flashlights hooked to the underside of the barrels. "Throw down your weapons and get out of the car," one of them shouted. "On the ground," another yelled to Matthew's goons.

Three lawmen headed toward Matthew and Stephanie. As they approached, they kicked his gun aside. One officer pointed his rifle while the other checked the pulse at Matthew's neck. "He's dead."

At last Stephanie spotted Josh. He lay in a heap where he'd landed, not far from Matthew. She tried to crawl over to him, but an officer stopped her. "Take it easy. Your head's bleeding."

She wanted to say that she was okay, but another pain struck like a saber to her side. "I'm worried about my baby. It's not due yet." She cleared a lump in her throat as a tenderness she'd never known before sent tingles through her body.

The sound of approaching sirens pierced the air. Stephanie wondered how help could arrive so fast.

"What about Josh?" She could see now that two officers knelt beside him. One shook his head.

"Is he alive?" she cried.

"We don't know yet," the officer near her said.

Stephanie held her breath as a new jab of distress confronted her. "I think I need help in a hurry." She placed her hand over the hard contractions in her belly.

"Right here." The officer motioned to the ambulance.

Flashing lights made patterns on the ground.

"That was fast," Stephanie mumbled.

Two men jumped from the rear of the ambulance, pulled out a gurney and hurried toward her.

"We knew there might be trouble so these guys were waiting about a block away." The officer helped the paramedics lift Stephanie onto the gurney.

"You knew about this?" she asked.

"Yes."

"How?"

"We have our sources." He pulled a belt across her legs and secured it while a paramedic tightened others. The second paramedic hurriedly applied a thick bandage to her head.

"Is Josh your source?"

"Who?"

"You know who." She grabbed the officer's hand. "Is there an ambulance for him, and what about Charles?"

"Don't worry. We'll take care of them." He glanced at Josh and forced a smile. "You just look after that baby."

His reticent expression made Stephanie uneasy.

"When are you due?" one paramedic asked and glanced at her belly.

"Not for six weeks, but . . ." She grimaced. "I don't think he's going to wait." It was the first time she'd ever called it a he. Although she'd never thought to ask the doctor about the sex of the baby before, she wondered now if somehow she knew. "Can you shift this vehicle into 'go fast'?"

"You bet," the paramedic said. "I guess we should at least get your . . . uh . . . spurs off."

Stephanie tried to see out the back window as they passed by, but could make out nothing about Josh. She laid her hand lovingly across her belly, willing the child to stay safe. No matter what else happened, if her baby was okay, they would face it together.

With siren blasting and lights flashing, the ambulance lurched forward. Stephanie hoped they'd make it to the hospital in time, but the rhythmic pain in her abdomen told her she might be presuming too much.

CHAPTER 21

"At least you have a handsome little guy to show for it." Deirdre's dark-lined eyes were smudged with tears and leaked mascara. "I feel so bad about Charles. I can't believe he's really dead." She sat in the straight-backed chair near Stephanie's hospital bed.

Stephanie's son had been born within an hour of reaching the hospital. He was a tiny little boy, but so beautiful, and he had all his fingers and toes. Stephanie had counted them last night just to be sure.

Now as he rested in his own special place in the hospital nursery, Stephanie and Deirdre sat ready to discuss last night's losses.

Stephanie had never been particularly fond of Deirdre, but given the process of elimination the girl was fast becoming a tolerable confidant. Stephanie really did need someone to commiserate with. Charles had been a big part of her life and now he was gone, and she didn't even know how she felt about it. Sure, he'd plotted to steal her baby—a baby she hadn't thought she wanted, but in the end he'd tried to rescue her.

"I feel bad too." Moisture welled in Stephanie's eyes. She thought she'd already cried enough for Charles, but there seemed to be an endless supply of tears, and then there was Josh. She took a deep breath. "Have you heard anything about Josh?"

A little rivulet of diluted, black mascara trailed down Deirdre's face, spilled off her chin and plopped onto her lap. "I don't think he made it."

"You . . . you don't?" Stephanie whimpered. She couldn't help it. "What have you heard?"

"Nothing! Not one solitary thing." Deirdre pulled her chair closer to Stephanie's bed. Her tight black skirt shinnied up her skinny legs as she sat. "No one will tell me zilch about him. He's not here in this building either. I know. I asked."

Stephanie sucked in a deep breath. "Maybe he's okay then." Her pulse pounded in her ears. She hadn't realized how much she hoped that were true.

"Didn't you say Matthew shot him in the chest?" Deirdre grimaced.

"I guess I was hoping his injuries weren't fatal." Stephanie pulled a tissue from the box on the tray table that extended across her bed, then offered the container to Deirdre.

"You know what I think?" Deirdre said, and blew her nose loudly.

"What?"

"I think you were falling for Josh."

Sighing, Stephanie said, "Maybe I was. Ridiculous, isn't it?"

Deirdre shrugged and reached for another tissue. "Well, no. I can see how it could happen."

"Here he was working for Matthew, plotting to steal my baby. But to his credit, he did try to stop that creep from taking me." Chewing her bottom lip, Stephanie paused for a moment before continuing. "One man, maybe two, are dead because of me, actually three, but I don't count Matthew."

Deirdre patted Stephanie's hand. "This may sound strange coming from me, because you know I always liked Charles better than I liked you; and of course, I liked Josh better, too. But let's be honest, neither Charles nor Josh were innocent bystanders. Even though at first you acted like a colossal idiot and wanted to give your baby away, they took advantage of you; no question about it."

Not knowing exactly how to take Deirdre's comment, Stephanie found herself silently staring, but decided Deirdre meant what she said in the best possible way. The girl was right, though, particularly about the idiot part. "Thank you for saying that, Deirdre. Maybe . . ." she bit back a smile, "even though I always liked Charles better than you, maybe we can be friends now."

Deirdre clasped her hands together. "Let's do be friends. We could be like Perry Mason and Della Street."

Stephanie felt her eyes widen. She couldn't believe a person of Deirdre's age and inclination would watch old Perry Mason reruns. Maybe she really had found a friend. "You enjoy Perry Mason?"

"Yes, and Matlock. I truly love Matlock."

"Well, Della," Stephanie mimicked in a low voice. "Do we have a law practice to go back to?"

Deirdre smacked her red lips. "That's a good question. Paul's under investigation, too."

"Oh no. Charles told me that Paul knew about the adoptions and was happy about the money they brought in, but he wasn't directly involved. He's going to need a good attorney to get him out of trouble."

Deirdre's penciled brows rose and she stared straight at Stephanie.

"Don't even think about it." Stephanie held up her hands in protest. "He'll need a better one than me."

"You're good," Deirdre said.

Stephanie blinked in surprise. Coming from Deirdre, those two words were an unexpected compliment. The friend scenario seemed more plausible all the time.

"Did you know that Charles left a will?" Deirdre went on.

"I would imagine he did. He was an attorney." Stephanie still had a difficult time referring to him in the past tense.

"He left some money and his home to his housekeeper."

For a moment, Stephanie thought about Janeen. Why hadn't she come to see her? Did she blame her for Charles's death? Probably. No doubt Janeen didn't care if she ever saw her again.

"Earth to Stephanie," Deirdre said. "Charles left most everything else to you."

"What?" Stephanie wondered if she'd heard correctly. "I'm the main beneficiary? How do you know?"

"The will was sitting on Charles's desk with a note saying it should be opened if something happened to him." Deirdre shrugged. "He died so I opened it." She pointed her finger at Stephanie. "You're going to be one rich girl." Apparently it was getting easier for her to refer to Charles in the past tense. "See, I told you, I'm glad we're friends."

"You may want to reconsider our friendship." Stephanie sighed. "I'm sure all of his assets will be tied up for a long time, until it's determined what was ill gain and what wasn't. I'm assuming he acquired a majority of his wealth illegally."

"Well that's a bummer." Deirdre dragged her large purse onto her lap and searched through it, finally extracting a pack of gum. She offered some to Stephanie who shook her head.

Unwrapping two sticks, Deirdre shoved them into her mouth. "I saw your baby."

Stephanie had never quite gotten used to Deirdre's quick change of subjects, but this was definitely a good topic. "You did? He's beautiful, isn't he?" Stephanie felt the tingle of a mother's pride and grieved over the fact that she'd once considered giving him away.

"Yep. I guess Matthew figured the baby would be pretty and maybe look like that hateful wife of his so he was willing to pay—what did you tell me?— half a million bucks for him." She covered a smile with her hand. "Do you realize that would work out to be about one hundred twenty-five thousand dollars per pound?"

"Deirdre!" Stephanie scolded, but struggled to keep from laughing. "Remember he was six weeks early. I'm glad for every one of his four pounds two ounces, and I wouldn't part with him for ten times Matthew's half million." She felt Deirdre staring at her. "What?" she asked.

"You may want to cut bangs someday to cover the scar you're going to have on your forehead. You're way too pretty to have an ugly scar." Deirdre popped her gum.

From the moment Stephanie had met this girl, she had wondered why Charles had hired her. She'd learned, however, that Deirdre did possess certain talents, and once in a while she expressed a plausible opinion.

Stephanie's gash had required thirty stitches, which were now covered with steri-strips. Gingerly she brought her fingers up to touch the injury. "Well, thank you. I think. Maybe I will cut some bangs. I need a change. Maybe I'll cut all my hair so it will be easier with the baby."

"No. No. Just cut bangs. I could get you an appointment with my hair dresser." She grinned.

Stephanie stared at Deirdre's hair, standing at attention in some sections and hanging long and limp in others, the right side longer than the left. It made Stephanie wonder if Deirdre had been run over by a lawn mower. "Let's not get carried away."

"What are you going to name him?"

Still thinking about Deirdre's hair, Stephanie had to switch mind gears again. "Who?"

"Your baby. Don't tell me you've forgotten about him already."

Deirdre was pushing the questionable-friendship button. "I haven't decided on a name yet. I have a few ideas but nothing seems to fit."

Deirdre peered at a bouquet of carnations and daisies that sat on a nearby shelf. "It looks like you have another admirer . . . already."

Stephanie narrowed her eyes at Deirdre. "They're from Kathleen, the manager of the stable where I ride. In the card she enclosed a bill for board on a horse I'm responsible for."

Deirdre smacked her lips. "The woman's all heart."

"She's okay." Stephanie supposed Kathleen was upset about the lies she'd told. Stephanie had a lot to make up for.

Deirdre opened her large purse again. "I'm sorry about the fat jokes. I wish you would have told me you were pregnant."

"I might have considered it, but I wanted it to remain a secret."

Taking out a tube of lipstick, Deirdre applied another unneeded layer of red to her lips. "Point taken," she said.

Just then the door opened wider and Deirdre jumped, the lipstick in her fingers skipping from her lips to her cheek. "Shi . . ." she began, but finished with "ger" after looking at Stephanie.

The nurse smiled as she came in holding a tiny blanket-wrapped figure.

"Oh. You brought him to me. I thought he had to stay in the incubator." Stephanie held out her arms.

"He can't be here long, but he's doing so well, you'll be able to take him home before you know it." The nurse zeroed in on Deirdre. "You don't have anything catching, do you?"

"Do I look like I have something catching? Don't answer that." Deirdre stood, wiped her cheek with a tissue and stared down at the baby. "I'm perfectly healthy."

Stephanie hoped she wouldn't try to kiss him with all that red lipstick.

The nurse handed the precious bundle to Stephanie, and she had to tell herself to breathe. Never had she felt such immediate love.

"That's one cute kid." Deirdre reached out to touch his cheek.

Stephanie fought the desire to pull him away. She would have to learn not to be so protective. She frowned, reproaching herself for not showing more love for him earlier, perhaps saving Charles from that final confrontation, and maybe Josh . . . she couldn't even think about him right now.

Pulling off her baby's little stocking cap, she concentrated on him. He lay in her arms like an angel with his little turned up nose and a halo of dark hair like his father's. The thought flashed through her mind that had he been Josh's, he'd have been blond. Quickly she brushed that notion away. He was Todd's son. She wished Todd could have seen his child, but she also yearned for Josh to see him.

She had loved Todd and now admitted to herself that she'd been falling in love with Josh. Nothing could have come of that relationship, however. Attorneys just didn't marry their criminal defendants. Her mouth twisted. She'd become quite the snob, hadn't she? She'd always felt superior to Deirdre. Glancing at the girl, Stephanie smiled. One thing was indisputable. Stephanie did have the superior hairstyle.

The baby opened deep blue eyes, staring at Stephanie as if trying to memorize her face. Even though she knew babies that age didn't see very well, Stephanie felt sure he sensed she was his mother.

How different it would have been had she been forced to hand him over now to Matthew and his wife. Stephanie allowed a brief moment to feel sorry for Jessica Dawson, but wondered if she had been in on the plot to steal her baby. Like Paul, the new widow would probably need a good attorney. If she'd been working with Matthew, though, Stephanie hoped the woman had seen the last of spas and beauty shops. The practice of law owed Stephanie a lot. There would be court cases for years to come because of her.

"Can I hold him?" Deirdre asked.

The nurse shook her head. "Only the mother for right now."

Stephanie sighed with relief.

"We're watching him really close because he's so small," the nurse said.

Maybe someday Stephanie would feel like sharing, but for now she wanted her son all to herself.

"I guess I'd better go," Deirdre said. "I suppose someone needs to be at the office just to answer phones. Everyone's called. I don't know what to say, so I've put them off for now."

"Thank you so much for everything," Stephanie said and really meant it. "I'll be in soon to help. Do you think the two of us can run a law firm for a while? You'll be my personal assistant." She winked. "Like you said, we'll be Perry and Della."

Deirdre grinned. "Why, Perry. I thought you'd never ask."

After Deirdre left, Stephanie gazed down at her son and loosened his blanket so she could see him better. She touched his palm and his tiny fingers wrapped around one of hers. Her heart seemed to swell and fill her chest. She would never be the same again. "We're going to have such fun," she told him. "We'll do so many things. I'll even buy you a pony and teach you to ride. We'll have a great life together, you and I, little son. What shall I call you?"

She supposed she could name him after his father. There would be only one Todd now, but another name kept poking through her subconscious and even though she'd always liked the name, it probably wouldn't be appropriate to call him Joshua.

Drawing her son closer, she felt blessed to be here holding her baby when so many had died because of her. Had she been spared in order to be this child's mother? Stephanie vowed she'd be the best mom ever and make something out of her life so her son would be proud of her. She owed it to him, maybe even to Todd and Charles, and . . . what about Josh? How Stephanie wished she knew what had happened to him. Was it true what Deirdre had said, that he hadn't made it?

For some reason she felt she would know if Josh were dead, but that was just plain silly. She didn't have that kind of connection with him. Sadly, she felt they might have if they'd been given more time together. She pursed her lips. She'd settle for being this child's mother. Of course, she'd have to continue working in order to provide for the two of them. She'd find someone perfect to watch over him and she'd never work overtime. As she went through various options in her mind, the phone rang.

"Stephanie, this is Janeen."

"Oh, hi." Stephanie prepared herself for the woman's wrath. "How can I tell you how sorry I am about Charles?"

Janeen sniffed. "Well, you know, if you walk among snakes, you're gonna get bit. Charles and I talked about that often. He actually signed the house over to me months ago. He knew it was just a matter of time before he'd have to leave. He just waited too long. We said our good-byes that night." She was quiet for several moments and Stephanie guessed she was crying. Moisture clouded Stephanie's eyes.

Finally breaking the silence, Janeen continued, "I want you to know, Stephanie, that things got out of control. Charles never meant you any harm. He actually became very fond of you, as I have."

Weeping now, Stephanie couldn't speak.

"I want you to come live with me," Janeen went on, "and I'll help you take care of your baby. I heard it's a boy. Charles would have been so happy."

"Thank you," Stephanie sobbed. She couldn't stop. It was as if the floodgates of her emotions had opened, letting out all of her pent-up grief. "It means so much that you want me to come, but can I let you know later?" Her voice broke.

"Of course, dear. Call me when you feel better."

"Thank you. I will," Stephanie forced out.

Hanging up, she glanced down at her son. He stared up at her and his little mouth formed an 'O'.

Stephanie burst out laughing and hugged him, then she cried again, laughed, then cried and laughed some more. She cradled him close to her body and for the first time ever began to sing. "Hush little baby, don't you cry . . . ." It was the only lullaby she knew.

He was asleep when the nurse came to get him.

Although Janeen's call had made Stephanie cry, it also cheered her. Somehow she knew things would work out. She was a mother to a beautiful son, and that was all that mattered, at least that was what she'd decided to tell herself.

CHAPTER 22

If Stephanie had learned one thing during the past year, it was that nothing is ever as it seems. She was about to be reminded of that fact to the power of ten.

Had she been able to clone herself, life would have been easier, but who needed easy? She knew now she would have to survive on less sleep, or none at all, more likely, especially after the responsibility of the baby was hers as well. After being released from the hospital, she'd spent several days at the office, forwarding clients who could not postpone their cases of action to other attorneys, and rescheduling cases that would not be jeopardized by a delay. Since Charles was gone and Paul's future uncertain, Stephanie knew she'd have to hire law clerks, paralegals, and maybe another attorney to help.

Deirdre proved invaluable. She was truly Stephanie's "Della" and seemed to thrive under the added pressure, often commenting, "Bring it on." Stephanie knew there would be months, maybe years of investigations of their firm before things were good again. She would cooperate fully. She owed it to Charles, Paul, Deirdre and their clients to do everything in her power to ensure that the firm survived. Besides, neither she nor Deirdre looked forward to seeking other employment. Fortunately, most of the clients had been sympathetic and promised to be as patient as possible.

Tomorrow her son would come home after two weeks in the hospital, and Stephanie was so apprehensive and excited, she could barely breathe. She knew, however, that if she were to spend any time with the horses it would have to be today. Sadly, she would ride Kingston for the last time. Kathleen had informed her that the horse had been sold. Stephanie would have appreciated it had the stable manager not sounded so giddy. Apparently Kathleen felt the sale of Stephanie's favorite mount was fair punishment for her deceit. At one time, losing Kingston would have deeply depressed Stephanie, but now she had a son and felt only mildly sad. She hoped the gelding would get a wonderful home, and was encouraged when Kathleen told her that the new owner had said she could have a final ride.

Now, as she urged Kingston into an easy canter, she tried not to think about how much she loved this horse. She wanted her ride to be memory-making and tried to memorize everything about it. Later she'd bring out this recollection when she began really missing him. Hopefully she'd be able to keep supporting Riskie, since Stephanie knew the mare's future would be uncertain if she didn't.

Riding in from the cross-country course, she decided to cool the horse out with a walk around the covered arena. Her eyes were drawn to the spot where Todd always stood to watch her ride and where Josh had waited for her several times. Of course, no one occupied that special place today, and her heart sank with the losses. She considered leaving the arena before Kingston was completely cooled out. She could feel herself descending into the depression she'd been trying to avoid and fought to redirect her thoughts to the next day when she'd truly become a mother to her son. She couldn't help but smile as she pictured his sweet little face and again wondered what to call him. Tonight she'd make that top priority, since they'd be asking for his name at the hospital tomorrow.

She circled the arena again. This third time around, her eyes caught and stared. Two men in dark suits stood in the spot reserved for Todd and Josh. Surely they weren't here to see her, were they? She couldn't look away. She thought of the night Matthew's man had grabbed her and was glad she sat astride a fast horse. Upon further deliberation, she decided if they were out to accost her, they would have dressed differently. Actually, they looked like attorneys in dark glasses, and she was immediately on guard. If they were here about the law firm, so be it, but if their visit had anything to do with her baby, they had better prepare for battle. Her hands on the reins tightened.

Deciding that a friendly gesture couldn't hurt, she nodded to them.

The shorter of the two men motioned to her. Maybe he was the one who had bought Kingston. He'd come here wearing a suit? Well, he might be the one. Luckily she hadn't ignored him. Perhaps he'd keep her informed about the horse.

"Hi, I'm Stephanie. Are you the new owner?" she asked as she approached. "Kingston is a wonderful horse."

"New owner?" the first man asked. "Afraid not."

"Oh," she said, a little embarrassed.

"Miss Saunders," the first man said. "I'm Keith Whittaker and this is—"

"If this is about the law firm, I'd appreciate it if you'd make an appointment with my secretary," Stephanie interrupted.

"It's not about the firm."

"I hope it doesn't have anything to do with my baby because he is my baby. Oh, I do hope you're not the Press. I've about had it with them." She knew she was babbling but couldn't stop herself.

Neither man spoke. It was as if each were expecting the other to continue the conversation.

"Miss Saunders," the first man began again. "I just wanted to meet you and introduce you to Detective Colton Taggert of the Salt Lake City Police Department, and apologize for . . . well, he'll tell you."

Apologize for what? She directed her attention to the taller man, who up to now had said nothing.

Surprised that she hadn't noticed him before, Stephanie treated herself to the view. Aside from how wonderfully he filled out the dark suit he wore, he had the most beautiful thick blond mane she'd ever seen on a human. Longer on top, it feathered back over his ears, surrounding his head like a golden halo. His strong jaw tapered into a slight cleft and his straight nose and perfect mouth completed his movie-star good looks. She wished she could have seen his eyes behind the dark glasses.

"I'll let you two talk," Mr. Wittaker said.

"Okay, but I've told the police here everything I know about what happened." Stephanie dismounted, flipping the reins over Kingston's head to lead him.

"Nice to have met you, Miss Saunders," Mr. Whittaker said and headed for his car. She guessed he had "met" her, but that was about all.

Stephanie walked past the officer. "Well, Officer Taggart, was it? If you'll come with me to put this horse away, I'll answer any questions you have." She led Kingston out of the gate and back toward his stall. The officer followed behind, still saying nothing. How strange was that? She hoped he could talk, or would. She quelled a tiny spark of fear that threatened to flare. This man wouldn't hurt her, would he? He was a police officer, wasn't he?

She haltered the gelding and cross-tied him in the saddling area. Glancing at the pitchfork leaning nearby, Stephanie turned to the officer. "I'd like to see some identification. A badge would be good."

Officer Taggert reached up to remove his dark glasses.

Stephanie gasped as she recognized his hands, Josh's hands. She peered upward into Josh Durrant's deep green eyes. "Josh?" she whispered.

He held out his arms and she melted into him, resting her head against his chest, dampening his white shirt with her tears. Her mind did flip-flops as she tried to make sense out of this man who looked so different, but was really much the same. How she had mourned his loss, but apparently he hadn't cared. Why had he let her suffer?

Her hands formed fists and she began beating on him. "I saw Matthew shoot you. You let me think you were dead. Where have you been? Why didn't you call? You've been gone two weeks. Didn't you think I'd notice?" She sniffed. "You . . . you tricked me for . . . for months. You said I could trust you and you lied to me just like Charles, Matthew and Todd."

"No, not like them." Like once before, he wrapped his arms around her so tightly there was no longer room for her to hit him. He held her close while she cried out her anger, grief and relief.

When she was done she looked up at him again, her eyes stinging. "Who are you? He said your name is Colton. Is that true, or another lie?"

He released her so she could stand on her own. "My name is Colton, Colton Taggert, and I really am a police officer. I've been working undercover with the local police, the U.S. Marshals and the F.B.I. for about a year now. I'm sorry I couldn't tell you. There were endless people involved and so much at stake."

Emotions still raw, she turned away from him, toward Kingston. "So it was okay to lie to me because you had an excuse? Was everything a lie? Were we a lie?"

Colton placed his hands on her shoulders. "Of course we weren't a lie." He touched his chin to the back of her hair. "Shall I help you put him in his stall so we can go somewhere private and talk? There's a lot I can tell you now since we've made our arrests."

"Arrests?" This wasn't just about the two of them, Stephanie reminded herself. Todd, Charles and Matthew had died, after all. Comforted by Colton's closeness, she let herself lean back against him. "I'd love to hear what you have to say, but . . ." She couldn't resist this new gibe. "Will there be anything resembling the truth somewhere in your story?"

He squeezed her shoulders. "You bet. It will be the truth, the whole truth and nothing but the truth." Giving her a final squeeze, he walked to Kingston. "Shall we?" Colton began loosening the girth.

"You'll spoil your suit." Stephanie wiggled in beside him and finished the unsaddling task. Her hand trembled as it brushed Colton's.

"I don't care," he said, and playfully nudged her.

Grinning, she placed the saddle on the rack in her locker and turned to him with a little nod. "By the way, you clean up pretty good."

"Really?" He smiled.

"Yeah."

He took off his jacket, hung it over a stall rail and rolled up his sleeves. Rubbing his hands together, he said, "So where do I start on this guy?"

Lightheartedly, she wagged a finger at him. "You're not using one of your delaying tactics, are you? I'm trying quite hard not to be mad at you. Remember, you've got a lot of explaining to do."

"Do you think?"

"I know."

"Would it do any good if I told you that I bought this horse for you as a peace offering?" He folded his arms.

"No you didn't." Surely he was back to his old tricks.

"Actually, I did."

"You're the new owner?"

"Yep."

"You bought Kingston for me?"

He nodded.

"Really?"

"Scouts honor."

"You were never a scout."

"Actually, I was."

She left the locker, walked a few steps, sniffled a little, and . . . and threw her arms around the horse's neck, hugging him soundly.

"Hey. You're supposed to hug me." Colton's hands went to his hips.

"Well, I guess my first impulse was to hug the one who hasn't been lying to me." She peeked out from under her lashes. "Are you sure you bought him?"

"Why did I know you wouldn't believe me?" He walked to where his jacket hung across the rail and withdrew several folded papers from his inside pocket. He held them out to her.

With an unsteady hand, she took the papers and slowly unfolded them. Tears filled her eyes as she read. The Bill of Sale was made out to her and attached to Kingston's registration papers. "You did buy him for me!" She blinked several times. "But I can't accept him, can I?"

"You better." He sounded serious. "I'm not really in the market for a horse right now."

"Josh …" This time she started for Kingston, but turned in midstep and came into Colton's waiting arms.

"It's Colton," he whispered into her hair.

She brushed at the tears that welled in her eyes. She couldn't believe Kingston was finally hers. "Thank you. Thank you. Thank you."

Colton lifted her chin with the tips of his fingers. "Tears? I thought you'd be happy."

"I am happy." She covered the hand on her cheek with her own. "Some day I'll figure out a way to thank you properly, but right now, let's put my new horse away and go someplace where we can talk. You're not off the hook yet, remember. I still have a ton of questions."

Colton's mouth twisted. "You mean the horse didn't do it?"

"Afraid not."

"Darn. I really was hoping."

She crooked her finger at him to follow as she led Kingston toward his stall.

"At least you said that someday you'd figure out a way to thank me." He jogged to catch up and turned to walk backwards so he could face her. "By that I'm assuming this isn't the end of our relationship."

"Do we have a relationship? The man I was falling for went by the name of Josh." After all the months of him lying to her, she wasn't going to let him think she would forgive him easily, although she probably had already. She walked into Kingston's stall.

"You were falling for me?" Colton stood at the gate.

"No. I was falling for Josh." She took off Kingston's halter, and glancing at Colton to make sure he was watching, hugged the horse again.

Colton made a sound of disapproval deep in his throat and stepped into the stall. "Let me hear you say my name."

"Josh?" She batted her eyes.

Closing the gate behind him, Colton walked over to take Stephanie by the hand. With an arm on either side of her, he pinned her against the side of the rails. "Call me Colton."

"Josh," she said and tightened her jaw.

"Colton." He brought his face closer.

"Josh," she whispered.

"Colton," he said and kissed her, then drew back to look at her.

Stephanie's tingling lips formed the word "Josh."

He kissed her again.

She sighed and said, "If this is the reaction I get when I call you Josh, then Josh it will always be."

"Let me hear you say my name." His face was about an inch away from hers.

"I've always liked the name Colton." Standing on tiptoes, she raised her lips to his.

His arms came around her and they stood there together for several minutes until Kingston plodded over, sniffed at them and licked Colton's face with a huge wet tongue. "Oooh, thanks, big guy. I didn't say I wanted you to kiss me."

Stephanie laughed so hard she had to hold her stomach. "He's just thanking you for buying him for me. I guess if he likes you, you can't be all bad."

Colton winked at her. "That's for you to find out."

She bent to pick up Kingston's halter, then took Colton's hand and led him from the stall. "I have an idea where we can go to talk." She emphasized the last word.

"So I still have to come clean?"

"It's not going to do any good for you to delay."

"Really?" He pulled on her hand and drew her into his arms again.

Giggling, she backed away. She gestured toward Kingston's halter and lead. "Do I have to hog-tie you?"

He took the halter and dropped it in front of Kingston's stall. He stared into her eyes. "Let's talk. I've been dying to tell you everything, but you keep delaying."

"Me?"

"Yes, you. I think you like to kiss. Funny thing, you seem to like to kiss me more now than you used to."

"Well, maybe I like kissing a clean-shaven cop more than I do a bearded criminal."

He leaned in for another kiss.

She stooped to grab the lead rope. "That does it. I am going to hog-tie you."

Holding up his hands, Colton laughed and said, "I give up. I'm not going to let you delay any longer. Where do you want to have this talk?"

"Come on." She pulled him away from the stable area, out onto the dirt road behind.

At the far end of the covered arena lay an outdoor ring. At the back of the ring three huge cottonwood trees spread their branches over two rows of white plastic chairs—popular seats for onlookers during training sessions and horse shows.

"See those big trees over there?" Stephanie pointed.

"Pretty, aren't they?"

"They're not only pretty, but there's a rumor going around that people sit under them and confess deep, dark secrets."

"Is that so?"

She nodded and pulled him into a run. "I'll race you."

"There goes my spit shine."

"Too bad. I'm in practically new boots and spurs myself." She took off in a dead run with him close behind, then in front, then way in front.

They were out of breath when they arrived at the trees. Laughing, they collapsed on the same chair, Stephanie landing on Colton's lap. She squirmed off onto her own chair, still giggling.

Trying to gain control of her breathing and laughter, Stephanie panted. "You're fast. Well, I already knew that. I mean you run fast."

He smiled with his perfect teeth and brought both arms up to flex his muscles. "They make us work out."

She felt one arm and nodded her approval. "Not bad," she said. "But I also know police officers write reports, so start reporting."

Colton leaned back in the chair and crossed his arms over his chest like this was going to be a long session. "Where do you want me to begin?" he sighed.

"At the beginning." Stephanie leaned forward, studying him. She'd waited a long time for this.

"Well, okay, I was born in nineteen hundred and—"

Stephanie let her head roll back on her shoulders to show her distain. "Not that far at the beginning, wait—how old are you, anyway?"

"Twenty-eight."

"Twenty-eight and not married? You're not married, are you?" She stared at him with narrowed eyes.

His lips hinted at a smile. "No, not even close. I've been waiting for . . ." He raised his brows.

She felt herself blush. She hadn't exactly waited for him, had she? But she was almost through feeling guilty about . . . about something over which she'd had no control, and now she had a beautiful son to love and he was worth everything she'd had to go through in order to get him. "I guess people sometimes wait for the right person, even though they don't know they're waiting. I think, contrary to common belief, I've been waiting too. I didn't feel the same about Todd as I feel about you."

"Is that good?"

"I hope you think it is." Her palm slipped easily into his.

He brought their joined hands up to hold against his chest. "I don't think you have any idea how deep my feelings are for you."

"I hope you can believe me when I say that my feelings for you are way stronger than they ever were for Todd."

He held on tightly to her hand and turned to face her squarely. "I'm glad because I have to tell you some things about him that I don't think you'll like."

"Okay." She knew she could bear anything with Colton by her side.

"His name wasn't really Todd," he began, and peered at her as if to gauge her reaction. He held up his free hand. "I know, I know, and my name wasn't really Josh. Sad, huh? I feel bad about how you've been treated. It about killed me when I had to make it look like I was working with Matthew."

Stephanie squeezed Colton's hand as if to say she forgave him, but then commented on the man she knew as Todd. "Was his name Chris?" She thought back to that day in the cabin when she'd discovered the picture.

"It was." Colton's brows drew together. "Christopher James Sumner. How did you know? I've been wondering about that ever since the day in your office when you put the name Christopher into the name search on your computer."

Still pondering her discovery and Colton's declaration, Stephanie spoke as if in a trance. "After he died, I found a picture of him when he was younger with wording on the back that made me wonder at the time about his name." She wanted to cry. She really hadn't known the name of her baby's father. Luckily she'd decided not to call her son Todd. "What's your connection to Todd, or I mean Chris, Colton—or shall I say Josh?"

Colton gave her a disapproving look. "Josh is gone. My name is Colton, Colton Taggert."

"Promise?" So now all of a sudden, the lies were over?

He nodded. "Promise. Someday soon I'll introduce you to a whole bunch of Taggerts. They'll vouch for me."

"That will be good." The breeze on her face felt wonderful. It was a beautiful October day. Soon fall would turn into winter. She hoped her life was about to change with the new season. For the first time in many months, she felt positive about it.

"That they'll vouch for me, or that you get to meet them?" Colton was asking.

She watched a girl ride by on a dark bay horse, its coat the color of her son's hair. She smiled. "I'd love to meet your family, Colton. I'm sure, like you, they are, uh . . . unique. After all, children are products of their families. I often wondered what Todd's family would have been like." She frowned. "I guess I should call him Chris now. Somehow he doesn't seem like a Chris. Todd fit him better."

"That's what Marshal Whittaker thought too. He helped him pick out the name Todd."

"Marshal Whittaker? Marshal?"

"Yes. He's a U.S. Marshal."

"Really. What did U.S. Marshal Whittaker have to do with Chris?"

"Do you know what U.S. Marshals do?" Colton asked.

"Don't they have something to do with the Witness Protection Program?" Stephanie took in a quick breath of air. "Was Chris in the Witness Protection Program?"

"He was."

"You're kidding, right?" She chewed her lip. "Well, that certainly explains a few things, although I don't know exactly what they are. What? Where? How?" She stood and began to pace.

Colton pulled her back into her chair, moved his chair around to face her and took both her hands in his. "He went into the program about four years ago after he witnessed a mob murder in Chicago. He testified and was almost killed. That's when the U.S. Marshals took over. Marshal Whittaker was his contact, the agent who set Chris up in his new life. Marshal Whittaker felt really bad about Chris—his death and what happened before. That's why he wanted to meet you today."

Chris had a keeper? Stephanie felt even more betrayed. "But he . . . Did they know what Chris was up to? Don't they keep track of their people? What was Chris doing with Charles? Did Charles really set Chris up to father my baby?" She stood again and tried to pull from Colton's grasp.

"It's over, Stephanie. Do you want to hear the rest of this, or not?"

CHAPTER 23

The autumn breeze scattered leaves across the surface of the outdoor arena, adding specks of yellow to the grayish brown ground.

Colton coaxed Stephanie back into her chair beneath the cottonwoods. Had she really forgiven him for his part in her betrayal?

"Well, what do you think?" she grumbled, trying to calm her breathing. She most certainly wanted to hear the rest of Colton's story, especially if it included how Todd—now Chris—had been set up to father her child and the U.S. Marshals had done nothing to stop him. Folding her arms, she sat stiffly in her chair.

Colton rested his hand on her knee, as if to calm her, and went on telling her what he'd earlier been forced to keep secret. "After people are set up in the program, the government backs off and lets them get on with their new lives. There aren't enough U.S. Marshals to babysit everyone in the program all the time. Chris had been in real estate and was good at it, making a lot of money—more than enough to support a gambling habit." Apparently satisfied that Stephanie was now ready to listen, Colton took his hand from her knee and settled back in his chair. He turned to observe several white geese waddle down the nearby dirt road.

Bending at the waist, Stephanie craned her neck around to obstruct his line of vision and motioned with her hand for Colton to continue.

He obliged. "After Chris was relocated, he was not allowed to go back to his prior employment for obvious reasons. Chris was excellent with computers and had played the stock market, so the government set him up as a computer programmer and paid him a wage for about six months. After a while, Chris started his own stock consulting business. I think that's how he got acquainted with Charles. Each time Marshal Whittaker checked in with Chris, he was told all was well, but it seems that was not the case. Chris got into gambling trouble again and rather than admitting his problem to Agent Whittaker, he went to Charles to see if there was any way Charles, as an attorney, could help.

"I guess Charles thought Chris was a pretty good-looking guy." Colton grinned at Stephanie.

For a moment, she watched the girl and the bay horse, the color of her son's hair, disappear into the stable area while she let Colton ponder what her response might be. Then she said, "Actually, he was one of the best looking men I've ever seen." Even now, she was not above giving Colton a little something to wonder about.

"Hey. You don't have to sound so enthusiastic." He lowered a brow.

It was precisely the reaction Stephanie had hoped for. She tried to contain a smile. "Go on."

"Apparently Charles thought Chris had good enough genes to pass on and Charles was in the genes-passing-on business. He investigated Chris's background, and since the government had changed everything, Charles thought Chris had no family ties." Colton hesitated before going on. "Before you, Charles had used—yes 'used' is a good word—had used Chris to father another baby." He glanced tentatively at Stephanie.

"I already know that," she cried, the wound to her heart still fresh. "Charles, the rat, told me."

"Oh, did he?" Colton said, his expression indicating that he disliked telling her such hurtful things. "Actually the deal was that he and the girl produce two babies, one after another, so the siblings would be close in age and bring in optimum money. Everything was going along fine until the girl fell in love with Chris and decided to keep the first baby."

Annoyed at herself, Stephanie blew out a quick burst of air. "That seems to be going around."

Colton appeared surprised at Stephanie's reaction, then must have realized how his statement had sounded to her. "I guess Chris could be charming."

"Yep," Stephanie said, her eyes studying the ground.

"Remember Stephanie, Chris loved you." Colton touched her cheek.

"I guess I have to believe that or I'll go crazy." She leaned her face into his hand.

He pursed his lips. "I'd say there's absolutely no doubt about that."

Mentally scolding herself for her need to be reminded of Chris's love, Stephanie pushed on. "Charles told me that the first baby's mother ended up dead."

Probably surprised that Stephanie was so well informed, or that she would speak of death so lightly, Colton regarded her for a moment, before going on, "She did. Apparently the brakes on her car failed while she was driving down a winding, mountainous road and the car careened off a cliff into a river."

An unexplained accident, just like with Chris's car. Stephanie cleared her throat loudly. "How convenient, especially since the

baby wasn't with her. Didn't the police think that sounded
suspicious?"

"Not at the time." Colton took her hand. "Accidents happen.
Remember, we have all this background now to guide us."

"So Charles told me the first baby's mother—"

"Victoria."

"What?"

"Her name was Victoria." He squeezed Stephanie's hand.

"Okay, so Charles told me that Victoria had a sister. Was she
really the girl I saw in the cemetery? I wondered at the time. I
thought she may have been the sister of Chris's friend who put
drugs in our drinks that fateful night . . . Wait—"

"There was no friend," Colton and Stephanie said in unison.

Stephanie fought back tears and tried to swallow the lump
that had formed in her throat. She remembered now how
Charles had told her that although she had been drugged that
night, Chris had not.

A horse whinnied in the distance, and Stephanie allowed her
mind to escape from harsh truths for a moment. Although the
sound could have come from the bay horse, she wondered if it
had been her horse, Kingston. A little thrill traveled through her.
Her horse, her son and Colton—she'd be okay. She could face
whatever Colton had to tell her.

She shook her head. "Boy, do I ever get the Award for Stupid.
Did Chris fall in love with Victoria, too?" How bizarre was it that
she was now referring to Todd as Chris?

Colton stared at her with unwavering eyes. "No, Stephanie, he
didn't. Chris was all for producing the second baby, taking the
considerable money and being on his way." His mouth twitched.
"I'm sorry to make him sound so heartless."

"Do you think Chris felt the same way about me and my
baby?" Wow. She sounded pitiful, even to herself.

Closing his eyes as if gathering strength, Colton said, "Absolutely not. If he hadn't loved you, he wouldn't have been in trouble with Charles."

"You mean, he wouldn't have been killed."

Colton released her hand and put his arm around her shoulder, drawing her close. "We don't know for sure if that's what got him killed, but even so, it wasn't your fault."

Stephanie's head began to throb, but she continued her line of questioning about the sister. "So Charles was right when he said the girl at the cemetery was Victoria's sister?"

Colton nodded.

"Okay, so let's review." Stephanie took a deep breath. "Chris and Victoria were to produce two babies. I'm assuming that Charles put the deal together for Matthew and Jessica. Victoria decided to keep the first baby and ended up dead. Then Chris . . . ." Her voice broke, but anger replaced her grief and she continued with force. "Then Chris ended up dead, but not before he got me pregnant with, oh, let me guess, the second of the two babies. Charles told me that Matthew and Jessica were able to adopt the first baby after court battles and more or less buying the child from Victoria's sister."

"Well, like I said, Jessica had her mind set on two babies, and what Jessica wants, Jessica gets. She didn't feel it was right," he shook his head, "to raise an only child. She was one and knew how much she missed having a brother or a sister."

Stephanie's anger flared. "Well, I'm an only child and I don't think it's right to kill people for their offspring."

"We have no proof at the present time that Jessica was directly involved, even though she's a demanding, spoiled witch—rich enough and pretty enough to get people to do her bidding." Colton's hand went from her shoulder to the side of her neck.

"We aren't sure if she knew what Matthew was doing, but we're going to find out. My guess is that she was the ringleader."

Kathleen, the stable manager, drove by on a tractor, hauling hay on the fork for the pasture horses. She waved at Stephanie and Colton and they waved back.

"She was in on your surprise, wasn't she?" Stephanie elbowed Colton in the ribs.

"Well—" His answer was interrupted when Kathleen's new Doberman dog, Duke, scattered the geese in his path, except for one hissing, disagreeable fellow who turned on the Doberman. Duke yiped and backed up, then whirled around, and bolted for Stephanie and Colton.

With no time to retreat, Stephanie had a lap full of dog. He cleaned her face with his tongue, then crawled onto Colton and tried the same.

Kathleen whistled and Duke bounded off Colton and headed for his master. "Sorry!" she yelled.

Colton brushed dirt of his pants and stared at Stephanie for a moment before saying, "Well that was unexpected."

Arms around her middle, Stephanie laughed until she couldn't catch her breath. Her emotions so close to the surface, they shifted from sadness to glee without restraint.

She sobered now as a silly, self-indulgent question popped into her mind. Although she reproached herself, her question would not remain unasked. "Charles and Deirdre thought Jessica looked like me. Charles said that was one of the reasons she wanted my baby? Do you think she looks like me?" Although Jessica truly was a beautiful woman, Stephanie didn't appreciate the comparison.

"She does if you only consider the outside appearance. Your goodness from the inside and her complete lack of anything honorable seeps through until the two of you look nothing alike." He caressed the side of her neck. "The strange thing is that Victoria looked a lot like Jessica too, and yes, a lot like you."

Even though his answer sounded rehearsed, it couldn't have been more perfect. Warmth flowed through Stephanie's body. Then she had another thought. "What will happen to the child if Jessica was involved in all this?"

"I'm not sure. That's definitely something the courts will have to decide."

"Charles said the baby was a girl."

"Uh-huh. She'd be over a year old now," Colton said.

"She'd be my baby's half sister, wouldn't she?"

"That's right."

"And Jessica's her mother." Stephanie's lip curled. "How unfortunate." Although she said nothing more on the subject, her mind continued to contemplate, but she had more questions to ask on further matters. "So how did you get involved in all this?"

"That's a long story." Colton sighed, folding his arms. "What Matthew and Jessica didn't know when they made the agreement with Chris and Victoria was that Victoria had a younger sister. They thought that both Todd and Victoria were alone in the world and no one would care about them or any offspring they produced. For some reason that I think involved money, Victoria and her sister, Jenny, had barely spoken since the death of their parents. Then something about settling the estate brought Jenny back from New York where she'd been living for a couple of years. Victoria was pregnant with the first baby and, although she left out all the names, she apparently told Jenny about the contract and the money she was going to make."

Elbows on knees, Stephanie turned her head to peer at Colton. "And you know this how?"

"Jenny came into the police department last January and asked to speak to one of our detectives," Colton said. "Her sister's case had been classified as an accident and the file closed, but Jenny never accepted their findings. While going through Victoria's belongings several months after her death, Jenny found a diary and a receipt showing that the car had been inspected and new brake pads installed just two days prior to the accident. That added fuel to Jenny's conspiracy theory."

Stephanie sat up straight, palms slapping her knees. "Where's Jenny now? She's alive, isn't she? Please tell me Matthew didn't dispose of her too."

Colton patted her hand. "We've had her in protective custody. She took a chance that day coming to the cemetery, and we let her know it. She was even more convinced, though, that her sister had been murdered when she saw how much you and Jessica looked like Victoria."

Stephanie heard the motor of the tractor and turned to see Kathleen returning from the pastures, Duke running ahead. Again the geese scattered, even the bold one from before. Apparently not satisfied with tormenting the geese, the dog started to run toward Stephanie and Colton. They drew in synchronized deep breaths, but a whistle from Kathleen brought the big dog back in line.

Colton and Stephanie watched silently as Kathleen and the Doberman disappeared around the corner of the barn.

"Whew," Colton said. "That was a close one."

Giggling, Stephanie slipped her arm through Colton's, still intent on their conversation. "So how did you meet Jenny?"

"Oh, yeah. Our close call almost made me lose my train of thought." Grinning, Colton wiped his brow. "Well, I'd been undercover for about a year on a drug deal and I still had the beard, the false identity, everything from my former covert life—everything but my fake tattoo, we had to reapply that."

"So it's not real?" Stephanie felt her eyes widen.

"You don't like my tattoo?"

"I didn't say that. I just prefer it on someone else." She grinned.

"Fair enough."

She squeezed his arm. "Go on. You were telling me how you met Jenny."

"Oh, okay. Well, since her sister's case was closed, the department had no manpower to investigate further, especially in view of the insubstantial new evidence. The detective who had spoken to Jenny briefed me on what had been said and asked for my take on it. The story sounded pretty shaky, but I had some vacation time coming and nothing special planned, so I decided to see what I could turn up just for the adventure of it." He paused for a moment, glancing around.

"Looking for big black dogs?

Colton smiled. "Actually, I was."

"Don't worry, I'll protect you." Stephanie said and nudged him.

"What a relief."

"Go on."

"Okaay. You're relentless, you know," Colton said.

Stephanie crossed her eyes and pulled a face. "Go on," she repeated.

Shaking his head, Colton continued. "Since there were no names in the diary, and Victoria had never mentioned anyone specific to Jenny, I didn't have much to go on. But tucked behind the cover of Victoria's diary, was a business card displaying Charles Connelly's name. That was my only lead at first. I told my chief what I had planned. He said he had no control over what I did in my free time, but to not get the department into trouble. He told me that if anything concrete turned up to let him know and then maybe he could justify more investigation into the case. Neither of us had any idea what I'd be uncovering or that it would take as much time as it did; but, when one thing led to another, everything Jenny told me about what she'd learned from Victoria began to make sense. When my chief finally became suspicious, he put me on the case and gave me backup whenever I needed it. Then I met you, Charles and Matthew, and when you told me you were pregnant, major alarms went off in my head."

It was a moment before Stephanie could settle her thoughts enough to speak. "I just keep wondering why Charles would involve me in all this," she said finally. "Sure, I look like Jessica—at least that's what people say, but didn't it occur to him that I might object and go to the authorities?"

Colton scratched his chin. "Yes and no. I think it was kind of like when a lion gets the taste of blood and he just can't stop until he's full. And then he was under pressure from Matthew to have Chris produce another child. I don't think he planned on using you at first, but when Chris became interested, it seemed like a done deal. You see, Charles had been involved in a very successful baby selling business for years. Here you were in his office every day—no family, career oriented, under his complete control, and you didn't like babies."

"I like babies. I love mine." She sat up straight.

Colton raised a brow. "But you didn't used to."

"I guess not." Stephanie folded her arms. "One day a client of Charles's came in with her baby and Charles asked if I'd watch it during the appointment. I backed away like it was a snake or something. I told Charles I couldn't because I was due in court. The kid was already fussy. I remember Charles looked at me strangely. Just then, though, Deirdre showed up and she took the baby. But I'll be a good mother to my son. I'd do anything for him, and I have Deirdre and maybe Janeen to help."

"I know you'll be a good mother. You've already proved that you'll do anything for him." He gave her a warm smile. "Anyway, all Charles needed was a few months of your life. Maybe he thought you'd go along with him after a while. When Chris told Charles about his night with you, Charles gave in to Matthew's pressure and used you as bait to satisfy him. Matthew took one look at you and the deal was set in concrete. All Charles had to do then was to make sure Chris got you pregnant, if you weren't already, and see that you gave up the child. He was going to make it worth your time, wasn't he?"

"Yeah, I guess. He promised me all sorts of things job wise—promotions, even a partnership." She studied the grass at her feet, recollecting that day at work when Matthew had charged into the office, brought Charles out of depositions, disappeared with Charles into his room, and came out a happier man with a creepy interest in her.

A sly smile crossed Colton's face. "You did give Chris and Charles a little trouble with the getting pregnant part, but they worked around it."

Her temperature rose to boiling. "Hey, I don't sleep around. I just don't believe in it. Worked around it—I'll say they did. I'd strangle them both if they weren't already dead. Maybe I don't even feel bad about that anymore." Realizing what she'd said, she slapped both hands over her mouth. "I'm sorry. I didn't mean that."

"It's okay. I don't sleep around either, and when I think about what they did to you, I could strangle them too, but that's behind us. It's over now and you have a beautiful son."

"I know. I can't wait to hold him." Her whole body ached to be close to her baby again.

Stephanie heard a tractor start up in the distance once more. Kathleen was probably feeding the horses in the barn. She and Colton glanced at each other and grinned.

"I wonder where jaws is."

"I think we're safe for now." She played along with their private joke. The time drew near when she'd bring her son home, but right now she hoped these remaining hours wouldn't pass too quickly. There were so many questions that still needed answering, and then, of course, she loved having Colton near. She cleared her throat. "I can't believe what Charles was doing right under my nose."

The girl on the bay horse entered the outdoor arena again. She nodded to them as she rode by.

"Hi," Stephanie said. "Beautiful horse."

"Thanks," the girl said and clucked to the gelding, but not before smiling at Colton.

He smiled back and Stephanie felt blood race to her face.

Colton seemed to sense her discomfort and shrugged, apparently checking out her jealousy gauge. That accomplished he continued.

"Well, you see, Charles had a lot of people working with and for him. He tried to keep as much of it out of the office as possible. You were new so you didn't have a chance to notice. Paul was aware of what was going on, even though he didn't participate. Did you know that years ago, in places like Romania, a child could be purchased for a very minimal amount? Actually the Romanian people were glad to have their children adopted in order to give them a better life. I think Charles started out small, bringing in children that he'd purchased and finding them American parents who couldn't qualify for a normal adoption.

These potential parents were so desperate they'd pay anything." Colton slapped at a horsefly that had landed on his arm. He hit his mark with precision and flicked the fly onto the ground.

Stephanie gave him a thumbs up.

"I think at first Charles thought he was performing a service," Colton went on, polishing the tips of his fingers on his shirt in answer to Stephanie's gesture. "When the Romanian government learned they could obtain money for their children too and made American adoptions more difficult and expensive, children began disappearing off the streets. Since children from foreign countries were becoming harder to acquire, Charles began a breeding program here at home—babies he could sell for really big bucks. I believe that was when he became involved with Matthew, and since Jessica wanted to pick suitable parents for her babies, the foreign born children simply would not do. Because Charles had been successful, Matthew wanted a piece of the action and began working with Charles and I think eventually tried to phase him out. The baby selling racket that they'd become involved in turned out to be huge. It reached all across the U.S. and into foreign countries. That's why we didn't arrest Charles and Matthew immediately. We wanted to find out who their superiors were. For months we've been working with the F.B.I., C.I.A., U.S. Marshals, and local law enforcement across the country. I couldn't say anything about it until we made our arrests. That's where I've been for the last few weeks."

Suddenly, filled with anger and embarrassment for allowing herself to be a pawn, Stephanie shot from her chair, tipping it over. "All this intrigue's been going on around me and you said nothing? And to think I was really sad when I thought you might be dead." She was only half kidding.

Colton favored her with a forlorn puppy look. "The vest only stopped the bullets Matthew fired at me, but you should see my bruises."

The girl on the pretty bay horse rode by again. She stared at Stephanie and smiled. Stephanie smiled back and righted her chair, determined to stay calm. She watched to see if the girl smiled at Colton. She did, but Colton didn't respond and Stephanie felt vindicated. Then she mentally kicked herself. It was only a smile. Just because Chris had proved to be untrustworthy, it didn't mean she couldn't rely on Colton. Was she so insecure that he couldn't even smile at another girl? Stephanie grit her teeth. No way. She wouldn't let herself be insecure.

"I'm sorry, Colton. Does it still hurt a lot?" She gently touched his chest.

He grabbed her hand. "I couldn't say anything, Stephanie. You don't know how many times I wanted to tell you. We figured the less you knew, the safer you'd be. It was my job to protect you. As I said before, I felt horrible when I had to pretend I was working with Matthew."

"So you were following me all those months. There was no friend. Hey, what about that man at the hospital who was supposed to be your friend."

"It was a setup. It's amazing what people will do when you show them a badge. I was at your condo that night, but only to make sure you got home okay."

"In your white truck?" She was afraid she already knew Colton's answer.

"Yes." His jaw flinched.

She chewed her lip.

"I'd be lying if I said I never felt guilty about what happened." He looked away. "At first I thought if Chris hadn't taken off after me, he'd still be alive. I was way out in front of him that night, thinking he'd soon give up the chase. All of a sudden his car seemed to go out of control and he hit that truck." Colton swallowed a couple of times before continuing. "I called 911 and hung around, out of sight, until the police arrived. I contacted my chief and he told me that I'd better keep my cover until a full investigation could be made. Then when the ambulance came, I followed it to the hospital."

Stephanie squeezed Colton's hand. This whole ordeal hadn't been easy for him either. "I'm glad you told me what happened. You couldn't have known it would end so tragically for Chris." She sighed. "I guess you're a pretty good guy even if you were following me for months and months." She accentuated the last "months" with a dip of her head.

Two horseflies buzzed around Colton. He peered at them with narrowed eyes, then picked up the conversation. "Once I started working for Charles I followed you under his orders." He slapped at the flies, but missed. "Ironic, isn't it? Charles didn't want anything happening to his investment. He was paying me to keep tabs on you, and my department eventually decided to pay me to watch him. I almost felt guilty taking his money. That's why I spent most of it on your horse."

"See, Colton. You shouldn't have bought Kingston." She noted that no horseflies bothered her.

He frowned, as if her comment really hurt.

"But I'm glad you did," she said quickly. " I'll pay you back as soon as I can."

He smiled. "You don't have to. He was my gift to you. The money should have been yours anyway. You were the most directly affected by Charles and Matthew. Hey, what's the deal? These flies don't bother you and they won't leave me alone."

"Maybe they're like bees and, since you're so sweet, they're searching for honey." She laid her head against his shoulder. "Thank you for Kingston."

His face turned red, but only for a second. "Like I said, you were the one most affected."

She shook her head as unbidden anger bubbled up inside her again. "I guess I was nothing but a brood mare." Again she pictured Riskie.

"I guess you could say Matthew liked the looks of the mare." He winked at her. "Although you look a lot like Jessica, you are far prettier and Chris was much better looking than Matthew. I guess you could say Matthew had high hopes for the foal because you're such a beautiful mare."

Smiling in spite of herself, Stephanie said, "You're not too bad yourself."

"Well, I don't want to brag." He puffed out his chest. "But I think Charles had plans for me down the line."

Stephanie burst out laughing.

Hand over heart, Colton feigned hurt. "Hey, Charles thought I was handsome, even under all the hair."

"You are handsome. See, even the flies like you." She giggled and reminded herself to speak more quietly. The girl on the horse rode by again. "Charles should see you now. You're more than handsome. You're a hot hunk and one of the kindest people I know—the light to Chris's dark, and I don't mean just looks."

"A kind, hot hunk." He grinned. A lock of golden hair fell across his forehead, stark contrast to his tanned skin. "I doubt Matthew and Charles would agree. I believe they thought that you and Chris had the most impressive gene pool. Charles probably talked himself into thinking that he was doing you a favor, finding a good home for your baby."

"A baby I was tricked into having." Stephanie watched as two more flies lit on Colton.

"I know. I know. Everything was going as Charles had planned until Chris fell in love with you, wanted to get married and keep the baby. That threw matters into overload. I don't believe this!" He slapped at the flies.

Stephanie shrugged.

"When Chris was killed," Colton waved his hand in an effort to knock the flies out of the air, "we ran the name Todd Saxton through the F.B.I. computers and found out he'd been given a new identity. We contacted the U.S. Marshals and everyone at first thought the mob had located him. Then it looked like it could have been an accident. After we discovered that his car actually had been tampered with, the mob became suspect again. Upon further investigation, however, we now believe it was Matthew's men who rigged the car." Colton shuddered. "If Chris hadn't died that night, you may have been riding with him later in his unsafe car and both of you might have been killed, actually the baby too."

Stephanie blinked back sudden tears at the thought of never seeing her baby, and she couldn't help feeling a new sadness about Chris. She really had loved him once. He had a lot of good in him, along with the bad. "There was a time I thought you might have killed Chris. I mean other than just leading the chase that night."

"What? Me?" Colton crinkled his brow, betraying his dismay. "Am I that good of an actor?"

"Well—yes, and you're a monumental liar." Stephanie grimaced and put a hand over her mouth.

"Sorry about that. It comes with the job. Even so, how could you think me capable of killing Chris?" Although he tried to cover it by looking away, his expression showed that her opinion of him really mattered.

She stood, moved behind his chair and wrapped her arms around him. "I'm so sorry, Colton. But you'll have to admit you were acting strange."

"Well, now maybe you can see I had my reasons. Did you ever wonder why your cop friend never got back with you about Chris's car? If I'd have had something to do with the murder, he would have reported the tampering to you." Colton still sounded hurt.

"Actually I did wonder about that, but with everything else going on, I guess I let it slip." She kissed him on the cheek, and to show her support swatted at a couple of horseflies buzzing around him.

"Officer Christopherson was going to tell you, but we asked him not to say anything. He was working with us, as was Judge Anderson." Taking her hand, he pulled her around onto his lap. A fly buzzed around them both.

The girl on the horse grinned widely as she passed by. Clearly, Colton and Stephanie were providing the afternoon entertainment.

"Judge Anderson? Do you mean to tell me that the whole battery thing was a setup too?" Stephanie stood to sit in her own chair. The fly lit on Colton.

"It was our way to get me into your firm. I hated lying to you." He took her hand. It seemed he needed that contact to continue his confession. "What must you have thought of me? That was one of the hardest things about this job." He made a kill with his free hand.

"I think it's your cologne." Stephanie sniffed his neck.

"You don't like my cologne?"

"I love it, but I think the flies do, too. It smells yummy, sort of like sugar cookies."

"Sugar cookies? So what you're telling me is that it's not something Josh Durrant would wear?"

She shook her head. "He wouldn't be caught dead . . . Uh, sorry. Where is Josh Durrant?"

"He's deceased, and he was such a scoundrel he didn't even have a funeral."

"Oh. How sad. I'd have given him one." She took another whiff of Colton's cologne. "Remember I was falling in love with him."

"Stephanie!"

"Okaaay."

"You and probably Deirdre are the only civilians who will know that I was Josh. I think she can be trusted, though, can't she?" He encircled Stephanie in his arms.

"Oh yeah. Deirdre's fine. We've grown close these past weeks."

"You and Deirdre? You?" He chuckled. "You're kidding me, right?"

"That's enough out of you." She wiggled in his embrace. "Yes, Deirdre and I are friends and yes, you can trust her."

"Okay. Good. As far as everyone else knows, except for a select few, I've been—that is Colton Taggert has been—undercover on a drug deal for months."

"So you've picked up all the bad guys? Is everyone safe now?"

"We think so. The big guns will keep an eye on us for a while and, of course, I'll probably have to stick pretty close by you just to make sure."

She giggled. "Oh, the trials."

He smiled.

More serious now, Stephanie peered into Colton's vivid green eyes, realizing the compassion that had always been there. How could she ever have thought he was capable of murder? "So you're going to be around for a while?" She was afraid to hope.

"I'm not going anywhere. I might even apply for a position with the police department here." He traced the line of her jaw with his finger.

She snuggled closer against him. "That would be totally awesome." She thought for a moment, trying to decide if all her questions had been answered. Her mind settled on something really huge that she was almost afraid to ask. "If my son has a half sister, does he have grandparents?" There it was out. She hurried on. "I was just thinking that if Chris's identity was false, maybe his parents weren't really dead."

Colton nodded slowly. "Your son does have grandparents and an aunt."

Stephanie bolted out of her chair again. She didn't even care what the girl on the horse thought. "Really." The fact made her happy, then sad. "They probably hate me because I got Chris killed."

"Don't talk like that." Now Colton stood. "You were a victim, too, and Chris loved you in the end. He knew the risks of the life he chose. He was willing to change in order to have you and his baby."

Choking back a sob, Stephanie asked, "So where are Chris's parent now?"

"They're in town from Chicago." Colton placed his hands on her shoulders. "I know you've been through a lot lately and I told them not to come, but they're still grieving. They've lost a son, and your baby is their grandson. They'd really like to see him."

Without so much as a single thought, Stephanie said, "Of course."

"You're okay with it?"

"Sure, as long as they know he's my child and he stays with me." She felt Colton's arms tighten on her shoulders.

"They know that."

"Maybe they could come to the hospital when I take him home. They are his grandparents after all. I don't remember mine. He should know his."

Colton pulled her into a hug. "That's very generous of you."

"No. It's just right."

Suddenly, a black and brown streak of dog appeared, coming from around the corner of the barn.

"Oh-oh. We're under attack. Better circle the wagons." Colton playfully pushed Stephanie behind him.

She portrayed the fearful heroine and cowered there.

Duke bounded over to them and leaped up to put both muddy front paws on Colton's white shirt. With a sloppy wet tongue, he cleaned Colton's face. Then he snapped at two circling flies, catching one in his mouth.

"That a boy," Colton said. "But I think I'd rather have the horseflies." Colton wiped his neck and jaw with the back of his hand and brushed at his clothes.

Stephanie laughed so hard she doubled over.

The geese honked, drawing Duke's attention. Then he was off after them, landing in the middle of the flock. Soon sounds of barking, hissing and honking filled the afternoon air, along with Colton and Stephanie's laughter.

"My hero." Stephanie giggled, hugging to Colton's side.

"I guess that means, I'd take a bullet for you."

Stephanie patted his chest. "I guess that means you already did."

"Oh, yeah, well kinda, but this time I didn't have the vest."

"You really are my super hero," Stephanie said.

"Oh shucks, Mam, it wern't nothin'." Colton spoke in a cowboy voice. "Oh, by the way, what are you going to name him?"

"His name's Duke."

"Your baby?"

"Oh no! I thought you meant the dog." She was going to have to quit doing that. Deirdre hadn't been impressed either. Embarrassed, Stephanie grimaced. "Actually, I haven't decided yet. Maybe it's a good thing. Both of the men I would have named him after don't seem to have their original names."

"Both men?"

"I love the name Joshua. Colton's not bad either. I'm just not used to it yet. I've thought of Joshua Todd, but I guess I can't name him that, can I?"

"You'd name your baby after me?"

"Do you mind?"

"I'd be honored. Maybe someday after all this is sorted out . . ." He squeezed her arm. "Well, you know."

"I guess if Charles hadn't been killed and he'd have had his way, down the road a bit . . . ." Stephanie didn't finish.

"Maybe we would have had a baby together?" Colton continued for her. "I can't judge Chris too harshly. I don't know what I'd have done in similar circumstances. I'd like to think I'd not gotten myself into a position where I'd have needed help, but it's hard to judge, isn't it?"

"It is."

"Look." Colton glanced around. "No flies."

"Pardon?"

"The flies are gone."

They stared at each other.

"Duke?" Stephanie asked.

"I think so." Colton smiled like he had a secret.

"What?"

"You know there's a moral to this story here somewhere."

"The Duke story?" Stephanie scratched her head.

"Yep." Nodding, Colton narrowed his eyes. "It could be something like, bad things can turn out to be good."

'You mean like Duke chased the flies away, or licked off all your cookie-smelling cologne so you like him now?"

Colton held up one finger. "Not exactly. More like, things you think are bad can turn out to be good, or at least better than you thought."

"Like I thought you were bad, but you turned out to be good."

"Exactly." He lifted his chin.

"But I also thought Charles and Chris were good and they turned out to be . . ." She paused as tears blurred her vision. "Actually they both died because of me."

Colton drew her into his arms. "I'm sorry, Stephanie. Me and my, there's a moral to this story."

"You know there really is a moral to the story." She blinked to clear her eyes. "I guess we could say, there's always a teeny bit of good in even the most deplorable creatures."

"Except for horseflies." Colton grinned.

"Except for Matthew and Jessica," Stephanie added.

Hands up, they high-fived each other.

The girl circled the outside arena again. Stephanie guessed if they were going to sit where people worked their horses, they'd have to put up with people working their horses. Stephanie smiled at her again.

Suddenly the horse shied as a pigeon flew up in front of him.

"O'Ryan," she yelled. "Stop it."

Colton and Stephanie stared at each other.

"O'Ryan? Ryan?" After all, both her son and the horse had the same color of hair.

"Not bad." Colton tilted his head.

"Ryan Joshua Saunders, Ryan Todd Saunders, Ryan Chris Saunders?" Stephanie recited in a teasing tone.

"How about Ryan Colton Saunders?" Colton asked, "for now," he added under his breath.

"What was that?"

"Nothing." Colton said.

"You know, I think the name Ryan Colton Saunders has a nice ring to it." She raised a finger. "I guess Kingston Colton Saunders is totally out of the question."

"Totally." And then Colton kissed Stephanie, right in front of the girl, the horse, the bird, the dog, the geese—everyone.

CHAPTER 24

The next morning Stephanie sat cross-legged on her bed and stared at the crib in the corner of the room. Her new realization that nothing she'd ever done in her life could compare with what she was about to undertake, chilled the blood in her veins. Was she nervous? You bet. Could she do it? She hoped. Was she ready to try? No question. And she'd thought jumping horses over four foot obstacles in the show ring unnerving.

Dropping her legs over the side of the bed, Stephanie stood. She had surprised her doctor and even herself with how quickly she'd recovered from childbirth, but she'd always been healthy and, of course, her baby had been small.

On the dresser lay the tiny blue sleeper outfit she'd chosen for her son's journey home. Luckily Deirdre's sister had four children and Deirdre, spiked hair and all, had been invaluable on their full-day shopping spree to purchase baby goods. Stephanie hoped her savings would hold out and her job keep producing. With her son and her new horse, she had two more mouths to feed. Of course, now with Charles gone and Paul indisposed for a while, she guessed she was the senior partner. At least that's what Paul had said when she'd visited him the day before.

She supposed she could save money if she did what Janeen suggested. Charles's former housekeeper continually begged Stephanie to move back into Charles's home—now Janeen's, so the older woman could help care for the baby. Stephanie felt she might consider such a thing later, but she wanted these first few days to be just for her and the baby—a bonding experience, like imprinting a foal—well, maybe Colton could join them part of the time, if he so chose.

Glancing at the clock, Stephanie reminded herself to hurry. Colton would arrive in less than an hour to escort her to the hospital. She had planned on going herself, but his offer to drive had been intriguing, especially when he'd shown her how to secure the baby seat in the car with such ease. Of course, Deirdre would have taken her, but somebody had to mind the office.

Dressed in slacks and a sweater, she brushed her long hair and pulled it into a ponytail. While in front of the mirror, she studied the injury to her forehead. It still looked red and a little swollen, but had begun to heal. Maybe she would cut some bangs as Deirdre had suggested, but there was no time now.

Grabbing the baby's outfit, diapers and other provisions, she stuffed them into a bag, pulling the strap over her shoulder. She dashed into the front room and tripped over a stuffed bear that had fallen from atop the television. Smiling, she wondered how one little human could require so much stuff. It seemed not a single horizontal surface of her normally uncluttered condo had escaped the intrusion. What was that box leaning against the wall? Oh yeah, a baby swing. Deirdre had insisted it was a must.

The bell rang and Stephanie bolted for the door, flinging it wide. Colton leaned against the railing, arms folded, grinning widely. He wore jeans and a caramel-colored jacket and with his blond hair back-lighted against the sun, he looked like a golden boy—no not boy, he was every inch man. "So are you ready to fetch Ryan Colton?"

"I am." A thrill raced through Stephanie, her skin tingling.

Outside, they walked down the stairs together. Colton wrapped her fingers around his forearm. "Your car or mine?" he asked.

"Where is yours anyway?" Stephanie glanced around the parking lot.

He pointed at a flashy, red Mustang, spotlessly clean. "Right there."

"What happened to your white truck?"

"It wasn't mine. Government issue, you know."

"Of course. Let's take mine. Remember it's got the car seat in it already. By the way, how is it that you know all about baby car seats? Cop training?"

They headed toward her car.

"I'm an uncle. My brother Tyler and his wife, Heather, have two-year-old twin daughters, Kaylee and Kylee. Try keeping those names straight, especially when our sister's name is Katie. It's a good thing you didn't name your son Kyle, or some other 'K' name. I have a lot of those to remember."

"So is Colton spelled with a 'K'?"

"No, thank heavens," he said, a little shiver in his voice. "Do you want to drive, or should I?"

"You drive."

He followed her to the other side of the car and she clicked it open.

"Yes and there's also Kingston," she said.

Chuckling, Colton opened her door. "I almost forgot about him." Colton walked to the driver's side and climbed in.

"I still can't believe you bought him. That was one of the nicest things anyone's ever done for me," Stephanie said when they were both buckled in the car. "I'd really feel better if you'd let me pay you back—someday. My finances are a bit tight right now what with the baby, the firm's loss of Charles and all."

"Keys?" Colton smiled and held out his hand, palm up.

Stephanie dug in her pocket and handed them over. The keys always seemed to find their way in there when she unlocked the car.

"And now you're wondering how you're going to support both Kingston and Riskie." Colton fit the key into the ignition.

"How did you know?" The words slipped out before she could stop them. She didn't like admitting that his gift had caused her concern.

"Mind Reading 101. We take it in cop school."

"Mind Reading what?"

"I'm kidding." He winked.

"Oh." She playfully punched him in the arm. "Funny."

Still smiling, he went on, "I have an idea that might help. My brother and his wife are big into horses, I mean big. They show them, give lessons, raise and sell colts—well, just about everything 'horse.' My folks have a place on Flathead Lake in Montana."

"Montana?" She felt her eyes go wide. "I wonder if it's near Charles's condo, which I suppose will be confiscated because of all the legal trouble."

"I don't know. Charles never got around to telling me where it was."

"I interrupted," Stephanie said. "You were talking about your brother and his wife and everything 'horse.' How could I interrupt that?"

"I was wondering." He cocked a brow. "Anyway, Ty just finished vet school. They actually took a horse with them while they were away, but now they'll be moving back and Dad wants them to manage the lake property so he and Mom can get a smaller place. I talked to Ty and Heather last night, and they will retire Riskie up there if you want."

He'd backed the car out of the parking place and started down the road before Stephanie answered.

"I couldn't do that, could I?" It really did sound tempting. "You've already done so much for me and I'm afraid I'd wor—"

Colton laughed. "That you'd worry too much," he said before she had a chance. "When I die I want to come back as one of their horses."

"You read my mind again." She wagged a finger at him.

"Just one of my talents."

"Is there anything you can't do?"

"I'm afraid I don't ride very well. Ty and Heather have laughed a great deal at my expense."

Stephanie giggled. "They sound fun. I bet I'd like them."

"Oh, you will."

"You mean I get to meet them even if I don't decide to take Riskie up there?" She glanced out the window at the sunny day. How fortunate she didn't have to take her baby out in bad weather.

"Of course, but you'll feel better about taking Riskie once you talk to Heather. We'll call her tonight."

"Tonight?"

"If you're not too busy. Actually you might be, huh?"

"Uh-huh." They had just gone by the high school, about halfway to the hospital. Stephanie became more nervous with each passing block, or was she excited? Actually she'd never been more excited in her life.

"You should have seen Ty and Heather's wedding," Colton went on as if to further convince Stephanie. "They rode their horses down to the edge of the lake where one of Dad's judge friends married them. Heather, wearing her white wedding dress, rode her grey, almost white horse, Possum, and Ty rode her black horse, Image. Ty was all decked out in a black tux, so it was black

on black and white on white. They switched horses for some of
the pictures, and then it was white on black and black on white.
Mom and Katie had flowers everywhere. Even I had to admit it
was gorgeous. All the neighbors from around the lake showed up
and said it was the event of the season. The horses, of course,
were in the middle of everything. I think Possum even had a
couple bites of wedding cake."

"How perfect. I can imagine how beautiful it was." Actually
what she was visualizing was how wonderful Kingston would be
as a mount for a bride.

"I've always wanted to have a wedding at the lake too, if only I
could find a girl who would agree." He reached across the seat
and took her hand.

"You have, have you? Of course you'd have to learn to ride a
horse better." She grinned at him.

He pulled a face. "Oh, I hadn't thought about the horse part."

"The horse part is a must." She loved kidding him.

"Is that so?"

"No question." She squeezed his hand, then released it so he
could drive.

"Well, I guess I'll have to give that careful consideration," he
said. "So you would like to meet my family?"

"I would love to meet them."

"When can you leave?"

She guessed he really was ready to see his family again after
being undercover so long. "Probably not as soon as you. I want to
settle in with Ryan and, of course, the office is in a mess. Thank
heavens for Deirdre."

Colton laughed. "Somehow I never thought I'd hear you say
that."

"I know. I've learned a lot in the last year."

"I may have another suggestion."

"Another one?" She peeked at him through lowered lashes. "Aren't you just full of them?"

"It's just a thought. You can do whatever you want, as I know you will."

She sighed. "After what happened last year I feel I should make all my own decisions."

"After last year I'm sure you will, but that doesn't mean you shouldn't allow people you trust to help you." He stopped the car at a red light. "You trust me, don't you?"

Reaching over and touching his arm, she said, "I do trust you. It's just that I feel I need to take charge of my life for a while."

He nodded slowly. "I wouldn't have it any other way."

"So what's your suggestion?" She chewed her bottom lip.

He tapped the steering wheel with both hands. "I thought you'd never ask. My sister, Katie, has a friend named David. Actually Heather was engaged to him before she married Ty, and Katie and David dated for a while before they each went off to school, but that's a long story. Anyway, Katie and David have started dating again, now that he's out of law school and she's just beginning. She acted on stage for a while and says that her acting might come in handy in law school."

Stephanie shrugged. "It might."

The traffic moved forward.

"Anyway, I think you could charm him away from his present law firm, first because you can charm anyone, and second, because Katie tells me he's not happy there," Colton signaled for a turn. "But you have to promise you won't fall for him. He's pretty hot, or so Katie says. I guess Heather thought so too, once, but Ty won out, as Taggerts usually do."

"Oh, no conceit in your family," she kidded. "Since I fell for Todd, or Chris, and was starting to like Josh, you're just concerned about my history of falling for men?" She grinned at him, seeking a reaction.

"But what about that Colton fellow?" He favored her with an innocent little boy look. "Were you starting to fall for him?"

"No."

He looked horror stricken. "No?"

"No starting about it. I'd already fallen for him."

His face relaxed. "And don't you forget it."

"I won't." She smiled. "You like kids, don't you?"

"I love kids. It's horses I'm not sure about."

"What?" Now it was Stephanie who was horror stricken.

"Just kidding. I couldn't be a Taggert and not like horses. Ty and Heather would kick me out of the family."

"As well they should."

"No lie." Colton said, as he stopped for a red light. "If you ever need a babysitter and I'm available, you have only to ask."

"How about Monday through Friday, eight to five?" She batted her lashes.

"Funny girl. I was hoping we could spend some time with him together."

"Nothing would please me more." Stephanie studied Colton's strong hands on the steering wheel. She knew those hands would be gentle both with her and the baby.

"Good. I'm going to hold you to it." He fisted one hand and held it up in triumph.

"David, huh?"

"What?" Colton asked.

"Your friend's name is David?"

"Well, actually he's Katie's friend, but his name is David—David Cane. I think you'll like him. Everyone does. Just as long as you don't like him too much."

Stephanie shook her head. "Not a chance."

Her response seemed to please him. Colton nodded and focused on the road again. "Oh, by the way, since ownership is up in the air, I moved out of Chris's old place."

"You did? That's probably good. Where are you living now?"

"With an old friend of yours."

She didn't have any old friends that she knew of. "Who?"

"Joseph Jacobsen from across the road."

Stephanie smiled at the thought of the old gentleman. "Mr. Jacobsen. What a dear person. I bet he keeps you entertained."

"You can say that again. I now play Chinese checkers like a pro." Colton gestured with an open palm. "He wanted to come see you and the baby today, but he and his friend, Clyde, have a killer Chinese checker competition going on and Mr. Jacobsen—actually, he told me to call him Joe—said he felt this was his lucky day. Clyde is going down. I'm supposed to bring you by to see him, though, as soon as I can."

She rubbed her hands together. "I can hardly wait."

For someone who had been so alone before, Stephanie realized that her son had brought her more blessings than she ever could have imagined. She still felt bad about Chris and even Charles, but she knew that time would heal her sadness. Both of them had been sucked into a whirlwind of evil to the point where they'd been unable to pull themselves away. She'd have to remember to never let herself get into that kind of a predicament.

Today was the first day of her new life and she felt strong. Her child had given her a reason to be a better person. She'd be a good mother and a better attorney, too, helping others wherever she could. If anyone sought her services for an adoption, she'd make sure each and every case was performed with the utmost skill and propriety. Maybe she would contact David. Even with Deirdre, she desperately needed help.

And Riskie. Perhaps she would send the little mare to Montana after she checked it out. Then she could concentrate on taking Kingston to his full potential. Horses were a big part of who she was. Colton understood that and she loved him for it. He knew she had to be herself and maintain her own identity. If their relationship deepened, as she hoped it would, they would be a team; each pulling one's own load like matched coach horses now with a little foal trotting along beside them, clinging to their sides for safety and guidance. She smiled.

"What?" Colton asked, again reaching for her hand with his free one.

"I'm happy," she said. "I've been worried, wondering what I was going to do about most everything in my life, but now, thanks to you, I realize that things will work out, if I don't give up."

He smacked his lips. "Just one day at a time."

"Thanks for the suggestion about Riskie. Maybe I will take her there."

He nodded. "Heather and Ty said they would treat her like one of their own."

"And David. If you'll get me his number, I'll call him."

Colton glanced in his rearview mirror, then side to side as he changed lanes. "I'll check with Katie. She'll have it. Those two could actually get together. They met when she was just sixteen."

"Really? Just sixteen?"

"Yep." He let her hand slip from his.

"Well, we've solved two problems." Stephanie pulled down the sun visor to peek at herself in the little mirror attached. "Now, what shall we do about inflation and the war in the Middle East?" She flipped the visor back up, deciding it was too late to do anything more about her appearance.

"Maybe we could work on those tomorrow." He grinned.

"Good idea."

As they pulled into the hospital parking lot and searched for a spot, all Stephanie's courage evaporated. She sat with her hand frozen on the armrest.

"Ready?" Colton asked.

"I thought I was."

"Wanna take a minute?"

"Do you think they'll be there?"

"Chris's parents?"

"I'm sure they will be. Is that okay? They're pretty excited to meet their grandson . . . and you."

Stephanie imagined they were. If only she could see them first without them seeing her. "It will be okay." She gripped his arm. "You're going with me, right?"

"I was hoping you'd ask." He put his hand over hers. "I'm kinda excited to reacquaint myself with the little guy as well."

"Me too."

He patted her knee before climbing out of the car to open her door. He offered his hand to help her out and kept hold of it as they walked to the hospital and into the elevator. She watched the lights on the control panel go on and off, indicating each floor as they went up.

She drew a deep breath. "Here we go," she said as they stepped out. After this moment, Stephanie knew that her life would never be the same. She squeezed Colton's hand and he smiled at her. They slowed when they neared the nursery.

Chris's parents were so intent on staring through the glass window at their grandson, they didn't even notice that Colton and Stephanie had arrived, so Stephanie got her wish.

Chris's mother looked trim and elegant in a tailored, charcoal suit and heels. With her perfectly styled dark hair and a strand of pearls at her neck, she reminded Stephanie of pictures she'd seen of Jacqueline Kennedy. His father, tall and stately in a dark suit with his thick, graying-at-the-temples hair could have been president of any nation. Mrs. Sumner dabbed at her eyes with a lace hanky, taken from a black leather bag that matched her shoes.

Stephanie wondered, with parents like this, how Chris could have fallen into Charles's trap, but maybe growing up with this apparently rich lifestyle had been part of the problem. He wanted what they had. But she wouldn't think of that now. She vowed to remember Chris in his last days when he was the Chris of these parents, the Chris she would always remember with fondness, the father of her son. Even now the negative things about Chris had begun to fade. She supposed she would always have a tender spot in her heart for him.

Dropping hands, she and Colton apparently sensed it would be unkind for Chris's parents to think that he had been replaced so soon.

As they drew closer, Mrs. Sumner's head whirled around. Stephanie felt like a rodeo clown facing down a bull. She had no idea what to expect. The women stared at each other for a moment until Mrs. Sumner opened her arms and, sobbing, ran to Stephanie.

Tears stung Stephanie's eyes as she hugged Chris's mom. Soon Mr. Sumner joined them, placing his arms around both women.

"I'm so sorry," Stephanie said.

Unable to keep her tears in check, Mrs. Sumner continued crying.

"Can you ever forgive me for getting Chris killed?" Stephanie asked. There it was. No matter what anyone else had said, she still felt guilty. Only his mother could grant her absolution. What would she say? Right now, though, she couldn't say anything. Her voice was racked with sobs.

With Mr. Sumner patting her shoulder, Mrs. Sumner finally managed to speak. "It is we who should be asking forgiveness of you for Chris getting you involved in all of this. He was such a good boy until he started running with that gambling crowd. He'd head for Las Vegas, or wherever, whenever he got the chance, and then he witnessed that murder. For years, we didn't know where he was. It's been a nightmare."

Stephanie flicked away tears with the tips of her fingers. "I can only imagine how horrible that was, but I have to tell you that Chris was changing all that. I wish you could have seen your son toward the end. You'd have been proud of the man he'd become." Stephanie realized that she herself actually believed what she was saying.

"Thank you for telling me that, dear. You are charming. I can see why Chris fell in love with you." Mrs. Sumner stepped back. "Oh, but look at your poor forehead. I'm so sorry you were hurt."

"I'll be okay. Don't worry." Stephanie touched her wound, deciding that she'd cut some bangs without delay.

Mr. Sumner joined Colton and they began a conversation. Maybe Colton would share with her later what they'd discussed.

"Your young man told us everything," Mrs. Sumner said. "I hope you don't mind."

He'd told them everything including that he was her "young man." She was glad he had—both that he had told them about what had happened and that he was her "young man." That was surely how she thought of him now. "I loved Chris very much. I really did. I guess you know we were going to be married."

"Colton mentioned it. Too bad things couldn't have been different. I would have loved having you as a daughter-in-law. Would you mind very much if we kept in touch?"

"I'd like that. You are my son's grandparents, after all."

Mrs. Sumner looked back toward the baby lying in his clear bassinette. "Isn't he beautiful? He looks just like Chris did when he was first born."

"Does he really?"

"I hope you don't mind me saying that."

"Of course I don't," Stephanie said, even though she thought her son looked more like her. "Chris was his father. I'll tell my son about Chris when he's older."

"You will?" Tears flooded Mrs. Sumner's eyes again. She dabbed at them with her now crumpled handkerchief. "Thank you so much for that. What are you going to name him, by the way?"

"Ryan," Stephanie said simply. She hesitated discussing the "Colton" and the "Saunders" part. She really didn't want Mrs. Sumner to suggest that he take his father's last name.

"Oh my, oh my." Mrs. Sumner cried some more and blew her nose delicately. "You're naming him after his grandfather, Chris's dad? How did you know James's middle name is Ryan? It was his mother's maiden name."

"His mother's maiden name is Ryan? I didn't know that. I actually named him after . . . ." Stephanie's voice trailed off. She decided she wouldn't spoil the moment. "I guess it was meant to be."

A nurse stepped to the door of the nursery. "There's a young man in here who is ready to go home. His mother and father can come in and get him ready."

Mrs. Sumner and Stephanie stared at each other for a quick moment. "I'm so sorry," Stephanie said again.

Straightening her shoulders, Mrs. Sumner replied, "Colton should go in with you, because unless I miss my guess, he will be Ryan's new father."

Stephanie glanced over at Colton and smiled. He left Mr. Sumners's side and joined her.

"Will you go in with me?" she asked.

Moisture formed in Colton's eyes. He glanced at Mr. and Mrs. Sumner. They both nodded.

Although Colton said nothing, his face revealed overwhelming emotions. He pulled Stephanie to him as they walked to the nursery door.

Stephanie thought of how many people loved her baby. She'd had no one growing up. Her son would never experience that disadvantage. He had grandparents and an aunt. He had a half sister who Stephanie had every intention of them meeting someday soon and maybe more than just meeting—time and her determination would tell. And Stephanie felt certain her son would also have Colton and his family to guide him. How fun it would be to meet Tyler, Heather, Katie, and Colton's parents. Stephanie smiled to herself. Someday she'd introduce Ryan to horses and take him riding on Kingston, and when he was older she'd buy him a pony to love.

She snuggled against Colton. His green eyes shone with love and promise.

"Do you mind if we wait for you to come out with Baby Ryan?" Mrs. Sumner asked.

"You better," Stephanie said. "We're all family now."

"Or will be," Colton added, with a raised, questioning brow.

"We're all family now," Stephanie repeated, smiling up at him.

They walked through the door to ready their new son for his journey home.